UNSPOKEN

A DJINN WARS NOVEL

CHRISTINE POPE

DARK VALENTINE PRESS

UNSPOKEN

ISBN: 978-1-946435-24-8

Copyright © 2019 by Christine Pope

Published by Dark Valentine Press

Cover design by Lou Harper

Book formatting by Indie Author Services

ONE

Note: This novel takes place slightly after the events in *Awoken,* two years since the Dying changed the human world forever.

Amber McCoy sat back on her heels and inspected the results from the day's foraging expedition. A couple of cans of baked beans, a box filled with unopened packets of chicken broth, an oversized can of cooked chicken, some granola bars that were probably so hard by now that she'd have to soak them in water to make them edible. It wasn't much, but better than nothing. Enough to keep her alive.

Which, she thought sourly, seemed to be an increasingly unwelcome prospect these days. Honestly, she didn't even know why she kept going anymore, except that something inside her wouldn't quite allow her to give up, no matter how bad things got.

Early on, not long after the world ended, she'd found a calendar while searching for food and brought it back with her to her hidey-hole, and had carefully marked off each day that passed. Doing so had helped her to keep track of the weeks and months that went by, although half the time, she didn't really pay attention to the date, only that another endless day was over.

Today hadn't been anything particularly memorable, only another thick black stripe from her Sharpie, crossing off another date, although she realized it was now ten days into October. Two weeks ago—that had been the really important day.

That was the two-year anniversary of the world ending.

Of course, at the time, Amber hadn't realized the world was ending. It had been a Friday—September twenty-sixth. She'd been over at her friend Kelly's house, listening to Kelly wail on and on about how she'd found a bunch of titty pics on her boyfriend Cade's phone...and how she knew those tits were definitely weren't hers.

"You sent Cade photos of your boobs?" Amber had asked her, trying not to roll her eyes. Seriously, when would people learn?

Kelly admitted that she had sent Cade photos, but Amber had done her best not to give her friend too much crap, just because they'd all been there, one way or another. All right, she'd never been dumb enough to send nude photos to any of the guys she'd dated, but that didn't mean that some of them still hadn't managed to mess with her head in a variety of new and creative ways. In fact, male misdeeds were the whole reason she was back in San Marino at all. Her boyfriend had turned out to be just as much of a cheat as Cade, except that Tyler had been smarter about his sneaking around.

Anyway, Amber had gone home to the big chateau-style house she'd grown up in while she tried to put her life back together. Luckily, her mother, who had never liked Tyler to begin with, took her in without question. Maybe she'd gotten tired of rattling around the place by herself, although Amber wasn't entirely sure about that particular reason for the welcome home; Judith McCoy had always been eerily self-sufficient. Or rather, she kept herself busy with charity luncheons and volunteering at various local nonprofits and museums, all while making sure that Amber's father, a thousand-dollar-an-hour attorney, paid the spousal and child support on time, even though she had plenty of money of her own and didn't need the support to survive. Judith had never dated after her marriage fell apart, never showed any interest in having any kind of a romantic relationship with anyone. And while Amber couldn't entirely understand writing men off completely, she had to admit that her mother had one of the best bullshit detectors she'd ever encountered. Too bad she hadn't paid enough attention to Judith's antipathy toward Tyler Brooks, a sports agent who made great money for a twenty-six-year-old and talked a good game, but apparently was just as much of a dog as Amber's father had ever been.

The TV had been on in the background at Kelly's house, and a newscaster broke into the show to talk about a strange fever that had begun to sweep through Los Angeles and other major cities around the world. Amber hadn't paid the story much attention, because it seemed like there was always some disaster or another taking up airtime, and she had better things to expend her energy on. Anyway, here in San Marino, one of the country's richest suburbs, she felt insulated from that sort of thing. Possibly it was the walls and gates that hid so many of the houses, or simply the impression that her family's money was more than enough to protect her from the world's nastiness.

Eventually, she'd gotten Kelly calmed down—with a little help from Xanax—then drove home in her Mercedes SLK convertible. It had been a warm, windy day, so Amber had the top down, letting the sun shine on her bare shoulders and the breeze play with her long blonde hair. While she'd been concerned for her friend, otherwise, she'd felt calm. Sure, her own relationship had fallen apart and she'd had to move back home, but it was just a temporary situation. One of her mother's friends would offer her a job, probably as an assistant in an art gallery or a consultant in a high-end boutique, and she'd find a house or maybe a condo in Pasadena, and start over again. She was only twenty-three, after all. Plenty of time to figure out what she was going to do with the rest of her life.

Only there wasn't plenty of time. That warm, sunny Friday, the clock had already started ticking down on humanity, and she'd just been too stupid and preoccupied with all the meaningless minutiae of her life to realize the glory days were almost gone.

Her mother had never come home—she'd been at a charity lunch in downtown Los Angeles...at the Biltmore, Amber remembered clearly. Night had fallen, and the reports on the TV got worse. She tried to call her mother and couldn't get through, only got a fast busy signal that told her there was something wrong with her cell service. The land line in the house hadn't worked, either.

And when she'd gone to check on Kelly the next morning, since no one was answering the phone over there, Amber had found her friend's house unlocked and empty, nothing there at all except a weird gray dust on the couch where the two of them had been sitting the day before.

At the time, she hadn't known what to make of that. Later on, she came to the realization that the little pile of gray dust was all that remained of Kelly Mattis. And almost as soon as Amber began to realize that everyone around her was dead, that she seemed to be the only person left alive in San Marino—or maybe all of Southern California, for all she knew—she saw the first of *them*.

She still didn't know what to call them. Angels? Devils? They looked like people, although she'd never seen a person who could take to the air like these strange beings were apparently able to. But she'd been walking back to her house after raiding the stale baked goods at the Starbucks down on Huntington Drive, and one of them had swooped down on her like some brilliant oversized tropical bird, green silk robes fluttering in the sun. More startled than terrified, she'd stared up at the man—or whatever he was —wondering if she'd somehow lost her mind, that the solitude of the past couple of days and the lack of any news were already preying on her. But then she saw the murderous glint in the strange flying man's dark eyes, and she realized that he meant to kill her.

Of course, she'd run, even as she knew there was no way she could get away from an airborne creature while she was only on foot. Terror had given her feet their own wings, and she ran as fast as she could, the bags of stale food she'd gathered falling from her arms as she fled.

Out of nowhere, another shadow appeared, blotting out the sun. Amber had risked a glance over her shoulder, saw that a second of these beings was bearing down on the one pursuing her. His robes were night-black, and his dark hair fluttered in the wind.

To her astonishment, he came to a stop in midair, blocking the progress of the other flying man, the one in the parrot-green robes. For just a second, the dark, sooty-lashed eyes of the newcomer met hers. Then he spoke a single word.

"Run."

And she had fled, not looking back, not trying to figure out how in the world those men could be flying through the air without wings or any other visible mean of holding them up. She'd pounded her way back to her mother's house, losing her flip-flops in the process, and had run inside and shut the door, then locked it. After that, she'd closed every blind, double-checked the locks on the back door, gone back to the front door and checked that lock as well.

The whole time, though, she'd wondered if any of it would be enough. After all, if those men, or whatever they were, could fly, then maybe they had other powers she'd never heard of. At this point, it seemed as though all bets were off.

That was why, after another day of cowering in the empty house, Amber knew she couldn't stay there. Maybe it would all be fine, and they wouldn't come back.

But maybe they would. Maybe now that they knew she was in the area, they'd start searching from house to house. It would only be a matter of time before they discovered her.

If they were so hell-bent on killing her, though, then why had the one flying man told her to run?

Her brain couldn't quite wrap itself around that conundrum, just as it couldn't quite absorb her terrible new reality, that everyone she knew—everyone, period—seemed to be gone.

She needed to go to ground...and she knew exactly where.

Her mother had been a massive donor to the Huntington Library and Gardens, which was located basically just beyond the backyard of Amber's own house. Yes, high walls separated the two, but since the security guards at the Huntington were probably dead along with everyone else, that wasn't much of a deterrent. And because her mother had been such a high-level donor, Amber had gotten to see parts of the facility that weren't open to the public, including the levels below the visitor's center near the entrance. Down there were stored rare art not currently on display, more books, and other valuable artifacts that were part of the library's collection.

Not a lot of people knew there were multiple floors below those offices. She'd have to hope those flying men didn't include X-ray vision along with their other strange powers, or else they'd be able to figure out almost immediately where she'd gone.

Apparently, they didn't, because she'd now spent two years down there, in what used to be the photography department head's office and was now her makeshift home. The first few weeks, she'd been so scared that she hardly ventured out of the cramped space, had lived off items from the vending machine in the break room down the hall. After that, she'd gone a bit farther afield, to the pantries of what had once been the museum's restaurants and tea room. Eventually, driven by desperation more than anything else, she'd ventured past the grounds of the Huntington to forage from the abandoned homes of San Marino.

In all that time, she saw no one else, not a single human being, not even the men who could somehow take to the air. At last, made bolder by her fears of what it might be like to be alone in the basement of the Huntington with winter approaching, she'd made the long hike to the REI store in neighboring Arcadia, had filled backpacks with freeze-dried food and sturdy clothing, had lugged a camp stove back to her lair so she might have some warm food for once.

Since no one tried to attack her, she assumed it was safe, and made the same journey multiple times, bringing back anything to make her solitary existence a little more comfortable.

Now, though...now she had to wonder why she'd even bothered. In all those forays, all those expeditions, she'd never seen anyone else. At REI, she'd found a solar-powered shortwave radio, had used it to search the bands over and over, listening for some signal that there was someone else out there, even if they were on the other side of the world. In two years, she'd heard absolutely nothing.

Which meant she had to be the last person left on earth. By this point, so many months past the last time she'd seen even the flying men, she was starting to wonder whether she'd hallucinated the entire incident. Maybe she'd been so distraught at the realization she was all alone, her brain had manufactured a vision of men flying through the air. Why that particular hallucination, and not, say, Chris Hemsworth walking toward her, telling her that he was here to take care of all her needs, Amber had no idea, but it made more sense than anything else that had happened.

You should go, she thought for the hundredth time, ripping open a packet of chicken broth so she could dump its contents into the pan of water that sat on her camp stove. *Pack what you can and get the hell out of here. You've walked ten miles round-trip to go to REI, so it's not like you can't handle it.*

That was probably true. After two years of roughing it here in this basement office and walking everywhere on the Huntington's grounds and beyond, Amber knew she was a lot tougher than she used to be. But still...to walk out into the unknown, to venture forth into that empty land-scape with absolutely no hope of finding anyone else...she wasn't sure if she was strong enough to do that. Not with absolutely no destination in mind. True, she realized her only hope of finding anyone else was to leave this place, since she already knew there was no one left in San Marino and the southern parts of Arcadia, but still....

Well, the world wasn't going anywhere. She'd crack open that can of chicken to add to her broth —and hope it was still okay—and have some crackers from her stash, and possibly a teeny piece of the dark chocolate she'd been hoarding.

And maybe, just maybe, she'd somehow figure out a way not to feel so tired, so empty.

So alone.

———

Istar tilted her head at Idris and asked, "You're sure of this?"

"Yes," he replied. Although he was an elder, on an equal footing with her, Idris could never quite shake the notion that both she and her partner, Ibram, somehow looked on him as their junior. Perhaps he was; his origins, and theirs, were lost so far back in the mists of time that none of them could exactly remember when they had come into being. They had always existed...and yet, he thought that possibly the two others had existed for a few seconds or moments before he had.

"It is wise, actually," Ibram put in. He was tall and dark-haired, like Idris himself, and yet, unlike most of the djinn, his raven locks showed a bit of white at the temples. Otherwise, as with all the other djinn, he bore no outward evidence of the many centuries he had lived. "With you and I settled here, Istar, it makes sense for Idris to make his home on the other side of the world. That way, the three of us can keep a better eye on things."

"What 'things' are there to keep an eye on?" Istar inquired, looking amused. She rose from the heavy carved chair where she had been sitting and went to the window. The curtains had been pulled back, showing a fine early October day, with only the poplar trees that bordered the garden beginning to turn, making them into pillars of molten gold. Fifty yards or so past the fine, smooth green lawn that surrounded the chateau, the glinting waters of the Loire River could just barely be seen through the trees that bordered the river. The warm sunlight seemed to turn her long copper hair almost molten and lit amber gleams in her green eyes.

Idris had to admit to himself that Istar had a point. Now, two years after the Heat had swept through the human population of this world, all seemed to be in order. The communities of djinn who had selected human partners thrived without incident, and those who had been immune to the deadly fever but not Chosen had been surgically removed by the djinn who enjoyed such sport. This world, which had been so close to utter devastation, had now returned to its natural rhythms, the weather calming, its original balance restored.

And the only thing such order had required was the removal of nearly all its human population.

"Things are calm, true," Idris said. "But Ibram is also wise in thinking we should not let our guard down. With you here in France, and me in North America, we can make sure we keep watch over the globe."

"Perhaps," Istar replied, her tone almost dismissive. "I see no reason to think there will be much else that requires our attention. The work continues, of course, but otherwise, this world is now far more peaceful than it has been for millennia."

"The work" referred to the monumental task which faced the djinn now that humanity was no longer a problem. While most of that warlike, troublesome species was now eradicated, there remained the issue of removing most of their works from the face of the earth. Certain noteworthy structures—such as this chateau, which Ibram and Istar had taken as their new home— would be allowed to remain, but all the factories and warehouses, the skyscrapers and the strip malls and the miles and miles of tract homes…all those needed to be removed so this world could grow green and lush again, restored to its former beauty.

"True enough," Idris allowed. "I suppose I will be more occupied in tending my garden than worrying about the nearby communities of djinn and Chosen, all of whom seem to be doing well enough. There have been no complications of late, nothing that requires my attention. And while I have enjoyed the hospitality you have offered me here in your home, it is time for me to strike out on my own."

"And you're sure of this place you have selected?" Ibram asked then. He had remained seated, but his gaze tracked to the window where Istar still stood, the afternoon sunlight glinting on the sapphire-blue silk jacket she wore, cut close to follow the curves of her slender form.

Not for the first time, Idris experienced a small stab of jealousy. No, he had never truly desired Istar, for he knew that she and Ibram were promised to one another with a bond so deep, most djinn could not truly comprehend its strength. What he envied was their connection, the way they seemed to know one another's thoughts, to instinctively understand when their partner was troubled or in need of comfort. He had had his affairs with women of his kind from time to time, but they had never lasted for very long. Those relationships had always been doomed from the beginning, mainly because his partners had looked on him with awe, or perhaps a certain calculation, trying to determine the maximum benefit they could wring from an association with someone who occupied such an exalted position. None of them had seemed to see him for who he was, rather than what he was.

He cast those thoughts away, and replied to Ibram's question, "Yes, I think it an excellent choice. The climate in Southern California is quite accommodating, and the gardens are magnificent, even in their current neglected state. I will have plenty to occupy myself, even though the house itself will require some work to restore it to its original function. No one has lived there for many years."

Istar stepped away from the window, lovely features alight with curiosity. "And what was this place called again?"

Offering her a smile, Idris said, "The Huntington Library, in San Marino, California."

TWO

THE CANNED CHICKEN HADN'T SAT SO WELL — OR
maybe it was the rainwater she'd collected in a
carefully concealed barrel, even though she'd
been careful to boil it—but she'd gotten past the
stomach rumblings and managed to sleep as well
as she ever could. Not for the first time, Amber
wondered whether she should dare to try cultivating a small vegetable patch in a hidden corner
of the gardens somewhere, if for no other reason
than to give herself some fresh food to eat. She'd
supplemented her bad diet with vitamins she'd
scrounged from the local Walgreens, but lately,
she'd been feeling weak and tired and rundown,
as if her body had finally begun to rebel against
the ongoing lack of decent nutrition.

And if she felt this crappy now, was she really
in any shape to be contemplating some kind of

cross-country trek to search for humanity's survivors?

Well, she could figure out all that later. For now, it was enough to eat a protein bar and some dried cranberries, to do one of her utterly unsatisfactory spritzes with the rainwater she used for drinking and for washing her face and body as best she could. There was still plenty of standing water here on the grounds of the Huntington, in the ponds in the Chinese and Japanese gardens, but Amber doubted it was suitable for bathing. She knew she should be glad that the past two winters had been singularly wet for Southern California, as if the drought that had plagued the area for years had somehow disappeared the same time as all the people. But, pretty as the ponds were—and as well-stocked with frogs, which she could hear burbling away during the quiet evenings here—they wouldn't help much with getting her clean.

After she was done with her sponge bath, she pulled her hair back into a ponytail and got dressed in some jeans and a T-shirt and hiking boots. The clothes were practical, but God, she hated them. She hated this not-so-brave new world, really; more than anything, she wished she could snap her fingers and return herself to a time when she could walk into a party on her four-inch Christian Louboutin stilettos, Prada bag slung over her arm, a slim-fitting Versace showing off the sleek curves of her figure. True, she'd looked every inch the shallow SoCal rich bitch most people thought she was, but she'd also known she looked *hot*.

And now...now she thought she'd seriously murder someone for a shower. Even a lukewarm one.

Amber rolled up her sleeping bag, put the empty water bottle in the big trash can she emptied once a week into a pile out back behind the building, and then began her customary careful ascent up the stairs to the main level of the visitors' center. As usual, she had a hand-cranked flashlight to illuminate the pitch-black stairwell, even though by this point, she probably could have navigated the steps blindfolded.

When she emerged into the hallway, she looked from side to side, just as she always did, one hand resting on the hunting knife she'd taken to wearing on her belt. Whether or not she'd be able to use that knife in any effective way was up for debate, but it made her feel a little safer, a little braver. Back when all this had started, she'd thought about getting a gun and then quickly discarded the notion, mostly because she'd never shot a gun in her life and was worried she might accidentally hurt herself with the damn thing.

Just as on every other day since she'd taken up residence here, the hallway was clear, as was the main reception area toward the front of the building. Outside, the day was already bright and sunny, a faint breeze stirring the day lilies in the garden beds in the courtyard. Once upon a time, that courtyard had been full of people eager to walk the garden paths or view the priceless works of art in the main gallery, but now it was just as empty as the rest of the world. The little kiosk where she'd once bought chai tea and watched people go by while her mother was occupied with a meeting with the other Huntington Fellows still remained, but she'd long since looted it of anything useful.

In addition to that shower, Amber thought she'd kill for one of those chai teas, foamy with milk, spicy with cinnamon. Who cared about the calories? She'd always been slender, but now she was downright skinny. In another year, she probably wouldn't have any boobs left.

If she lived that long, of course.

After giving a cautious glance from side to side, she emerged from the building, walked across the courtyard, and went down the steps, heading toward the Japanese garden. She couldn't really articulate why, but she found herself drawn there the most often, liked to sit on one of the stone benches outside the Japanese house that had apparently been brought here all the way from Kyoto. Even though she'd known doing so might attract attention, she'd been careful to close the screens that protected the interior of the house, since she didn't want any of the sparsely elegant furnishings inside to get ruined by the rain or by wild animals. Squirrels and rabbits were plentiful here, and there had been times when she'd heard coyotes howling at the moon, so she knew there was plenty of wildlife around. Whatever had killed off the people, it didn't seem to have done anything to the animals. In fact, she'd spotted roving bands of dogs from time to time, but they'd always kept a safe distance from her. They'd looked healthy and happy, though, so clearly they'd found plenty to eat in the ruins of the world.

She sat on a bench and let the sun touch her face, warm her all through her body. Yes, it felt good to be outside like this, to not feel like the scared creature she knew herself to be, too afraid to even leave this place and go somewhere that might be an improvement, that could have people still living there.

Because as good as this felt, Amber knew it would be a whole lot better if she could have someone sitting here next to her.

Idris emerged in the main gallery at the Huntington Library, then stood there for a long moment, arms crossed, surveying the portraits displayed there. They were all uniformly large in scale, his own height or even more, in grand gilt frames that appeared to shimmer against the dark green walls. The subjects of those portraits, in dress from days long gone by, seemed to stare down at him with narrowed eyes, as if they knew all too well the role his people had played in ensuring that this world would be free of their kind.

Strangely, he found himself wanting to speak, to tell them that, while the elders had not prevented the majority of djinn from carrying out their bloodthirsty plans, neither he nor Istar nor Ibram had had any active part in that genocide. Their duty was to intercede when personal feuds among djinn threatened to become deadly, or when one of their kind went against the few laws that bound them. But most of the djinn had agreed that humanity had become far too dangerous, and that it was time to end their reign on this world they'd treated so shabbily. The elders could do little except allow the conscientious objectors, the One Thousand, to save a human each, and to be able to live apart from the rest of their people in new communities of Chosen and djinn.

But there was no point in making such protests to these painted portraits of people long dead, and so Idris made himself narrow his eyes and look at the room in an objective fashion. Honestly, he did not see much to change here, although he would remove the tables from the center of the chamber, and provide more comfortable seating so that he might sit here if he wished and look at the paintings. Gone, too, would be the modern track lighting installed on the ceiling; perhaps he would open up the ceiling with a skylight and allow natural light to enter. All in all, though, those changes would be minor, something he could accomplish in very little time.

He left the gallery and went out into the main hallway, surveying the high ceilings and elegant columns and cool marble floor. Here, he saw nothing at all he would change, so he ascended the graceful curving staircase, one hand trailing along the metal of the railing as he went. While djinn were not the most social of beings, preferring to stay alone in the palaces they had constructed, or at best with a partner, Idris thought this would be an excellent setting for a gathering of some sort. He could imagine others of his kind coming and going on the steps, the brilliant silks of their finery glowing against the white marble.

And if not the djinn who'd cleansed the world —for they had never seemed to be a very sociable group—then perhaps some from a nearby community of djinn and Chosen. There was one not so very far away, only fifty or so miles to the west in the place that was once Bel-Air.

Satisfied with that plan, Idris continued his inspection, walking from room to room on the second floor, glad to see that so many of the original furnishings remained in place. Really, all he would have to do would be to remove the stanchions protecting the antique furniture, along with the nameplates and other badging that called out items of particular note. The library he admired particularly, with its floor-to-ceiling built-in bookcases and enormous Aubusson rug on the wooden floor. A series of windows looked out onto the gardens, and he went there almost by instinct, laying his fingers on one of the handles so he might step out onto the balcony beyond.

A gentle breeze played with his hair, and he lifted his head to draw in a deep breath, smelling flowers and warm grass. From what he had been able to tell, the roses had survived quite well, although they were all in need of a good pruning. The grass, too, looked green and lush and wild. For a place that had just suffered two years of neglect, his new home appeared to be in far better repair than it had any right to. For now, it seemed as if he would not have to put in as much effort to make the place livable as he had thought.

He shifted, looking toward the Japanese garden and the enormous curved bridge that spanned the pond there. For just the barest instant, he thought he saw a flash of something pale near the house beyond, and he frowned. Surely someone else couldn't be here?

But as he stared for a moment longer, he realized his eyes must have been playing tricks on him, or possibly what he had seen was merely the white tail of a deer. That made much more sense, for the local wildlife had begun to take over, ranging into suburban neighborhoods that had formerly been hostile to them. For all he knew, the main reason why the grass here looked so neatly cropped was because the deer and rabbits had been keeping it shorn.

Even so, he gazed toward the Japanese garden for another long moment, then let his eyes scan the grounds between here and there, looking for something that might indicate he wasn't alone. Idris knew he was probably being foolish; there were no humans left, except those living with their djinn partners in their carefully protected communities. The last one living in the wild, so to speak, had been the young woman who'd stumbled onto Hasan al-Abyad's property. Hasan was probably the last djinn Idris had ever thought would lose his heart to a human, but he'd proved to be more vulnerable than anyone had imagined, and now lived with his woman Jordan in Santa Fe.

At any rate, as far as anyone knew, Jordan was the last. Before she emerged, no other humans had been seen for many, many months, and while Idris supposed there might be one or two living in hiding here and there, he thought the odds of anyone lurking on the grounds of the

Huntington Library were so low as to be laughable.

But then he recalled the young woman—barely more than a girl, really—whom he'd saved just as the Heat had begun to wind down, its deadly work done. He had come to this area to inspect the Huntington as a possible future dwelling place, since he and Ibram and Istar had already begun to consider where they would finally settle, even though they knew that day would be some time off. Already he'd rejected the Vanderbilt mansion on the East Coast of the United States as being too cold and too large, and he'd done the same with Hearst Castle in the northern part of California, while at the same time filing away the design of the indoor pool there for future reference. It had been quite grand, with its cobalt blue and rich gold tile, and something he thought he might enjoy adding to his home.

The Huntington Library, however, seemed to offer everything he wanted—a fine, large house, grounds of exquisite beauty and variety, enough books and priceless art to keep even a djinn occupied for some time. Add to that the comfortable Southern California climate, and he thought he'd found the perfect place to make his earthly home.

So it was while making a tour of the surrounding area—and determining how many of the homes in the immediate vicinity would need to be knocked down—that he encountered the terrified young woman who'd been fleeing Mahmoud al-Saqir, one of the djinn who had appointed himself to be judge, jury, and executioner for any hapless humans unfortunate enough to be immune to the Heat. Although Idris had told himself he should stay out of such confrontations, he found his resolve vanishing when he looked into the terrified face of the woman who was about to meet a terrible fate. Something made him intervene, to block Mahmoud from dealing the killing blow. There had been perhaps the merest flash of gratitude in the human female's big blue eyes, and then she'd turned and run as fast as the ridiculous thong-style sandals she'd been wearing would allow her to.

Luckily, as far as Idris could tell, Mahmoud had never complained to Istar and Ibram about their fellow elder's interference, although it would have been within Mahmoud's rights to do so. The elders had agreed that they would stay out of the affair, since a majority of the djinn had decided it was their wish to seek humanity's destruction. While Idris harbored his own reservations about this decision, he had not spoken out, had not done anything to stop the genocide… which made his own impulsive action in saving the young woman that much stranger.

From time to time since then, he'd wondered what had happened to her. In his mind, he'd concocted the pleasant fantasy that she'd somehow learned of the human settlement in northern New Mexico and had made her way there, although he had to admit to himself that such an outcome did not seem terribly likely. Los Alamos was a very long way from San Marino, and the woman in question had not appeared to be the sort of hardy type who could survive such a long trek on foot, across thousands of miles of hostile territory where she might be attacked by a djinn at any time. She had been very slender, with delicate features and a fall of pale blonde hair— the sort of hair almost calculated to attract attention.

Because of those factors, he knew the chances of her survival were very small. About all he could do was hope that, whatever end she had met, it had been a quick one. She had been too fragile to survive this harsh new world, but he did not want to think of her suffering.

That notion made him frown, and he looked out toward the Japanese garden again, not really sure what he expected to see. Now all seemed still, except for a pair of crows who had settled on the peak of the roof and were inspecting their surroundings from their new, lordly position. Idris doubted they would have been quite so forward if there had been a human in the vicinity. At any rate, he should have sensed such a thing, although he knew that his inborn djinn ability to know when he was in the presence of a mortal only extended so far. The garden in question was a good ways off, far outside the limit of his senses.

Besides, he knew it really didn't matter. Even if he transported himself from where he stood on the balcony of the main house over to the steps outside the Japanese garden, he wouldn't feel anything. No one had been there. All he had seen was a trick of the light and nothing more, no matter how much he might hope for something else.

An odd sort of melancholy came over him then, and he turned and went back inside the house, closing the French doors behind him as he went. These were foolish fancies, and no more. He was home now, and knew he needed to attend to the changes he wished to make.

At the same time, he couldn't help but wonder at the futility of such an endeavor, to attempt to make such a haven for himself when he would have no one to share it with.

———

Amber flattened herself against one of the columns that held up the grapevine-covered pergola, hardly daring to breathe. There was someone here on the grounds. Who, she didn't know for sure, because all she'd gotten was the faintest glimpse of a balcony door shutting on the second floor of the main house, but even that sighting was enough to get her heart pounding, to make her cower here, afraid that if she took a single step, whoever was up there would discover where she was hiding.

Her own damn fault, really. So much time had now passed that she knew she'd gotten careless. She'd gone back and forth from her hiding place beneath the visitor's center to the Japanese garden —or the Chinese garden, or the desert garden, depending on her mood—so often that she'd begun to believe it was perfectly safe, that there was no one left in this part of the world to take any note of her comings and goings.

Well, obviously, she'd been wrong.

Amber shifted a fraction of an inch and stared up at the impressive mansion with its rows of Doric columns and the columnar box hedges—not so neatly trimmed now after two years of neglect —that flanked its wide loggia. As far as she could tell, all was quiet there; the windows were shut, and she couldn't detect the faintest sign of any movement inside.

Even so, she knew what she'd seen. However, she also knew that she couldn't stand here forever, skulking beneath a grape arbor. Sooner or later, she'd have to go back to her basement hide-out, if only to collect her things so she could get the hell out of here.

She closed her eyes, pulled in a breath, then

expelled it and opened her eyes again. Time to go. She'd have to make it fast.

The past two years had taught her how to be quick and quiet. The hiking boots she wore probably weren't the world's best running shoes, but they were still worlds better than stilettos or flip-flops. She took off from the place where she'd been hiding as though a starter had fired a gun, running as though her life depended on it.

Maybe it did.

She had a heart-pounding moment or two when she had no choice but to come into the open, since the pathways that stretched between the main exhibition hall and the visitors' center cut through wide lawns with very few trees, but she made it to the doorway without incident, then hurried inside and ran downstairs as fast as she could. Or rather, she moved much more quickly than she normally would during a return home, although not so fast that she risked tripping on the steps and falling and hurting herself. So far, she'd managed to survive without much more than some bruises and a strained ankle she picked up when she'd been roaming around the desert garden and stepped on a rock that slid under her careless foot, making her lose her balance and twist her right ankle. However, she knew that one untreated cut, one broken bone might be enough to finish her. It wasn't as though she had anyone around to help her if she injured herself.

Once she was back inside her hideout and had closed the door, then pushed the office chair she'd been using for the past two years as an additional security measure under the door handle, Amber sat down on her inflatable mattress and drew in a sharp breath. Now that she was someplace relatively safe, she began to wonder whether she'd invented that flash of movement she thought she saw.

"It could have been a shadow from a bird," she said, speaking aloud. Over the past few years, she'd picked up the habit, mostly because it felt better to talk to herself than to live her entire life in complete silence. Of course, she was quiet when she was outside, but here, two floors underground, she really didn't see the harm. "There were those crows hanging around in the Japanese garden."

She'd spotted the pair while she was sitting outside on the bench, soaking up the sun. Neither of the oversized black birds had seemed especially happy to see her there, but they also seemed to know that she meant them no harm, and had flapped lazily away after spending a few minutes on the roof of the house. They might have headed over to the main exhibit hall, could have been sitting in the sun on one of the balconies. In fact, the more she thought about it, the more that particular scenario made sense. It was kind of silly to imagine that someone might have been wandering around in what had once been Henry Huntington's mansion, especially after so much time had passed.

The entire facility had once possessed a state-of-the-art security system and a crew of very well-trained security guards, but the guards had passed into dust along with the rest of the world's population, so the museum had been wide open ever since she'd come here. And without electricity, all the high-tech cameras and sensors in the world couldn't function, so she'd always had an easy time coming and going in the main exhibition hall or any of the smaller galleries located on the grounds. Actually, she had never spent much time in the main house, mostly because it was unnerving enough to be all alone in the world without wandering through a place where she felt as though the portraits' painted eyes were always fixed on her, watching. She made sure all the doors were secure so wandering wild animals and rain or damp couldn't get into any of the buildings, and mostly left it at that.

No, she must have seen the crows, or maybe some other kind of bird. Lord knows the grounds were busy with all kinds of winged wildlife, from a family of ducks that had taken up residence in the pond in the Chinese garden, to a variety of sparrows and blue jays and the adorable black phoebes with their chipper little pointed heads.

She'd given herself a scare, but that's all it was.

In a way, Amber couldn't be too angry with herself. At least she'd just proven she could make it back to her hideout in record time. That had to count for something.

Thus satisfied—or at least not quite as on edge —she reached for the book she'd been reading, a rare first edition of *Sense and Sensibility*. The library was full of books like that, volumes that probably should have been kept locked up in an antique bookstore but which had been on the overflow shelves down here like they weren't any more special than a bunch of old Dan Brown paperbacks or something.

Back in high school, she hadn't had much use for Jane Austen, but now Amber found something curiously comforting in the dry wit so evident in the author's words, her pithy commentary on the upper class and minor nobles who populated the pages of her books. Besides, Austen's books all had happy endings, even if it took some work to get there.

It was good to know such things still existed, if only in fiction. Amber kind of doubted she'd ever experience a happy ending of her own.

THREE

HE'D SLEPT IN THE BED IN THE ENORMOUS MASTER bedroom—or rather, he'd procured a new mattress to fit in the exquisitely carved bedstead, and slept on that—and awoke refreshed, feeling a cool breeze on his face from the window on the opposite wall. The day was sunny and promised to be comfortably warm and not hot, a blessing on this early October morning. In other parts of the world, the leaves would be turning, but here in San Marino, autumn's display wouldn't arrive for more than a month.

After he rose from the bed and went to the window, however, Idris found his gaze drawn once more to the Japanese garden, even though he had no real reason to be looking in that spot. Certainly, he hadn't detected any strange movements, nothing that would make him think he wasn't alone here in his little demesne.

Well, after he had bathed and eaten, he would walk the grounds and see what he could see.

The bathrooms in the house had been closed off to the public and never upgraded, but that was no real impediment. A wave of the hand was all that the situation required, and in the blink of an eye, all the fixtures had been updated, the paint refreshed, the old tile replaced. There hadn't been water or electricity here for two years, but again, that was no hindrance for a djinn. Soon enough, he stood under a flow of hot water, washing his hair and body, breathing in the warm scent of the shampoo and soap he had conjured for his use.

Breakfast was similarly simple to execute. He took a seat at the head of the enormous table in the dining room, and immediately coffee in a fine china cup appeared in his hand, while a plate with buttered croissants—which he'd developed a weakness for some time back—flashed into existence before him, a plate that also held fresh fruit and bacon and a hardboiled egg.

After he'd consumed this repast, the cup and the plate and fork and napkin all disappeared whence they had come, and Idris thought it was time to go exploring. He exited through one of the French doors that opened onto the loggia and stood outside for a moment, breathing in the fresh morning air and allowing himself to enjoy the blue, blue sky overhead, in which the smallest puffs of white clouds floated lazily by.

Yes, he had definitely come to the right place.

A path wound away from the steps to one side of the loggia, and he went there, walking slowly, allowing himself to take a brief detour into the Shakespeare garden, which had been constructed to mimic the carefully patterned outdoor spaces of this world's English Renaissance. All the beds were woefully overgrown, but their wildness didn't bother Idris. Rather, he looked on them as a project he would undertake in the near future. The same with the herb garden opposite the little complex that housed the facility's various eating establishments; it would need some care to bring it back to its former glory, but really, what else did he have to do with his time?

From there, he walked over to the Japanese garden, noting as he went the enormous wisteria vine that covered a nearby pergola. It must be quite a sight in the spring, and he found himself wishing he might skip past the coming winter so he could witness the gardens in all their glory. Unfortunately, speeding up time was a power that not even the djinn possessed.

For now, he allowed himself to drink in the beauty of his surroundings, the sparkle of the sun on the pond's surface, the way the weeping willow's branches trailed along the water, the faint, happy croaking of the frogs on their lily pads. Up and over the moon bridge, and on to the elegant little Japanese house on its small hill. To his surprise, many of the bonsai trees in its enclosed courtyard appeared to have survived, although they, like everything else here, were in dire need of a good pruning.

The sliding panels that protected the interior of the house from the elements had all been shut, and Idris stared at them for a moment, frowning. He supposed that someone working on the grounds might have had the presence of mind to close them all before succumbing to the Heat, but it seemed a strange thing for a mortal to be preoccupied with such a detail while dying from a raging fever. If the disease had swept through the population during the week, he might have speculated that the gardens hadn't been open to the public. However, he knew very well that the fever had begun to spread on a Friday, and therefore this place should have been full of tourists.

Shaking his head, he came around to the front of the house, to the small covered doorway. There, he saw something that made him pause once again.

On the wooden boards that covered the ground was a small but definite footprint, as if someone had walked in the dusty gravel on the other side of the structure before coming here. Idris carefully put his own booted foot next to it for comparison's sake, noting that his was much larger. The print had to have been made by someone smaller than he, probably a woman or a child.

The print could have been here all along, he thought, but he almost immediately rejected that notion. Even in a covered spot such as this, how could a footprint have remained intact through more than two years of wind and rain? He knelt down and touched it with his forefinger, then looked down at his fingertip. It was definitely dusty, which seemed to indicate the fine, silty dirt had been left here recently. Otherwise, it should have been blown away by the warm, dry winds that had swept over the area only a few days earlier.

Idris straightened and looked around, hand shielding his eyes against the glare from the sun overhead. There was absolutely nothing in the landscape to show anyone had been here in the recent past, but he knew that didn't mean much. Once again, he thought of the pale flash he'd glimpsed here the day before.

The girl he'd saved two years ago had possessed extremely light hair, almost flax-pale.

She couldn't be alive, though. That was impossible.

Or…was it?

He'd already resolved to walk the grounds, but now he had a new purpose. Leaving the Japanese garden, he made a careful circuit of the entire property, through the Australian garden, around the lily ponds, past the desert plot with its strange, scrubby cacti specimens, and on through the palms before stopping on the walkway by the visitors' center. During this entire span of time, which took him more than an hour, he'd continued to reach out with his djinn senses, trying in vain to catch even the faintest hint that anyone other than he might be present on the museum's grounds.

And…nothing.

Frowning again, he moved toward the visitors' center, wondering if the person he sought might be hidden somewhere within the large building. If that were the case, it might take some time to locate her, since presumably she must know the warren-like structure much better than he.

Still, he had nothing to lose by trying, except a little time. Time, which he had an abundance of.

Now resolute, Idris went up the steps to the visitor center's front door. It was unlocked, which didn't surprise him; the Heat had struck too quickly for anyone to secure the facility. However, while one would have expected the space to be filled with the small piles of gray dust that humans left behind after the fever was done consuming them, they appeared to be conspicuously absent. Oh, the place was dusty enough, as it should be after two years of neglect, but only the ordinary sort of dust lay on the tables and the enormous desk in the reception area.

Otherwise, nothing appeared to be disturbed. He moved behind the desk and picked up one of the brochures there, hoping it might tell him something of the layout of the building, but it only provided a map of the grounds overall and highlights from the various collections, nothing that would help him here. And while the windows in the front of the building and the enormous domed skylight overhead provided natural light for the public spaces, he guessed he would need a little assistance if he delved into the lower levels of the structure.

A large flashlight appeared in one hand and he moved forward, searching for a stairwell. He passed an elevator, but he would have been forced to use his own energy to operate it, and he thought it wise to save his powers for better things.

A faint twinge somewhere behind his eyes informed him of the human's presence a split-second before a door opened a few paces in front of him. For a shocked moment, wide blue eyes that he remembered all too well met his own startled gaze. She stood there in the doorway, hand still resting on the knob, her entire form practically vibrating with fear.

Yes, it was the girl he'd saved, but so very changed, he wasn't sure whether he would have recognized her if it hadn't been for her eyes. Before, she had been slender, but now she was thin, the bones of her porcelain-pretty face sharp, bluish shadows under her enormous eyes. Her pale hair was straggling and dirty, pulled back into a messy ponytail. And instead of the short skirt and form-fitting top she'd worn as she ran away from him on that warm afternoon two years ago, she had on a baggy pair of the blue pants mortals called jeans, along with a shapeless shirt and workmanlike boots on her feet.

Her hand lifted from the doorknob, went to her throat. "What…?" The word came out in a rusty whisper, and she shook her head and started over, voice a little stronger this time. "You're real?"

"Yes," Idris replied, a pang of unexpected pity moving through him. "What is your name?"

"Am-amber." She stumbled over the syllables, as if it had been a long time since she'd had to say her name aloud.

And of course it had been. A whole two years, merely an eye blink for a djinn, but probably an eternity for a woman alone.

"You have been here all this time?" he asked, making sure he kept his tone gentle.

"Yes," she replied. "Ever since that time you rescued me." Her head lifted, and he thought he saw color flare in her pale, thin cheeks. "It was you, wasn't it?"

"It was," he said simply.

"Why are you here?"

A good question. He could give her an answer, but that would only lead to more questions. And yet, as he had just told himself, he had plenty of time to answer those questions, as long as they were not too uncomfortable. "This is my home now."

Her eyes widened, and she glanced down the hallway past him to the open, skylit main room of the visitors' center. "Here?"

He couldn't help smiling a little. "Well, not here exactly. The main house."

"You're living in an art gallery?"

"It was a home once, and is a home again now. Let me show you."

She had to be dreaming. Or maybe she really had fallen down the stairs and hit her head, and was now lying on the landing with a concussion, hallucinating that probably the most gorgeous man she'd ever seen was leading her out of the visitors' center and on to the main exhibition hall.

But the sun felt warm on her face, and the wind that touched her messy hair seemed real as well. That thought made her remember what an utter disaster she must look right now. When she was by herself, it hadn't seemed to matter too much. Now, though….

The stranger was telling her his name was

Idris. *Like Idris Elba,* she thought, although this man, despite being equally gorgeous, definitely wasn't black. Maybe Middle Eastern; he had dark hair and eyes and olive skin, and he had a slight accent, one that reminded her of a Saudi guy she'd once known at USC.

Well, Saudi prince, to be more accurate. A very minor prince, but still rich enough that he had a bodyguard who went with him to classes. Anyway, Reza had had that same kind of accent, mostly very posh British boarding school, but with a faint singsong intonation that hearkened back to his Saudi roots.

"Are you immune, too?" Amber asked, wondering if that sounded rude. But then, Idris had to be immune, just like her, or he would be a pile of dust along with approximately seven billion other piles. "I thought I was the only one."

The smile he gave her then was hesitant, but also somehow sad. But that wasn't so strange, was it? After all, the deaths of billions of people were a big enough reason to be extremely sad.

"In a way," he said, then stopped. "I will try to explain everything to you later. For now, though, wouldn't it be better for you to get clean, then eat something?"

The offer seemed awfully presumptuous of him. Then again, she had eyes and a nose; she knew she looked terrible and didn't smell much better. His words sank in, and she stared at him in shock.

"You have hot water? Seriously?"

"Seriously," he repeated, one corner of his mouth quirking a bit. "All the hot water you could want, and then a real meal afterward. Does that sound good?"

Sound good? She didn't know who the hell he was—or what he was, more to the point—but right then, she could have thrown her arms around him and kissed him. Well, if she hadn't been a raging stinky mess, of course.

"That sounds great," she replied. "I didn't even know there was a shower in the house. I thought they closed all that off when they turned it into a museum."

"They did," Idris said. "I've made a few improvements."

That remark made Amber raise her eyebrows, although she told herself that anyone who cared about the Huntington Library had died two years earlier. If Idris wanted to put in hot showers—hell, if he wanted to put in a nightclub—that was kind of his prerogative, wasn't it?

She followed him across the loggia and up the steps to what had been the main gallery. When he opened the French doors for her, she saw that the interior didn't look too altered—all those enormous old portraits still occupied their same positions, and the walls were the same muted dark green. The track lighting was gone, replaced by a series of skylights overhead, and the wood parquet floor was now covered by the largest Persian rug she'd ever seen.

"This way," he said.

They went up the sweeping staircase and on to the second floor. Again, many items and pictures seemed to have stayed in their same places; Idris had simply removed the stanchions and the badging for the various pieces of art.

"I've only redone the one bathroom," he told her as they went into the master bedroom. "You are welcome to use it for now."

What he meant by that vaguely ominous "for now," Amber wasn't sure, but she decided to take his remark at face value. The lure of a hot shower was simply too strong.

"And here you are," he went on, opening the door to the bathroom. "Take as long as you like—there's no danger of the hot water running out. I'll wait for you in the dining room."

"Thank you," she said. All right, it was simply too weird for this guy to have appeared out of nowhere after two years and then offer her a shower, but she pushed the weirdness aside as best she could. She absolutely needed to get clean. Everything else was secondary.

He nodded and closed the door, and she turned to take in her surroundings. The walls and floor of the bathroom were white marble, and a set of the fluffiest white towels she'd ever seen—even better than the imported long-staple Egyptian cotton ones her mother used to mail order—hung from a brushed-nickel rack. Matching fluffy bath rugs lay on the floor. The shower itself was an enormous enclosure with a wall of glass on one side, and enough fixtures built into the marble to probably wash three people at once.

Where had all this come from? The fixtures looked new, barely used at all. Amber supposed Idris could have installed everything himself, but how in the world had he managed to pull off such a construction project without her noticing at least something of what was going on?

Like so many other things in her world, she'd have to file that away for future examination. For now, the most important thing was to peel off her filthy clothing and toss it on the floor, then step into the shower and tentatively turn the handle to get the water going. At once, it came flowing out of those multiple heads, blessedly warm on her naked flesh.

And oh, God, the sensation of the water pouring down on her was almost orgasmic, especially after she took the bottle of shampoo that had been sitting on one of the built-in shelves and kneaded it into her hair, once, twice, three, four times. At last, it felt squeaky-clean enough that she could move on to conditioner and let that soak into the battered strands while she soaped every inch of her body over and over again.

She could have sworn she hadn't seen the razor when she reached for the soap, but she told herself she'd been so preoccupied with cleaning herself off that she'd simply overlooked it. It was heaven to get the hair off her legs and underarms, to finally begin to feel like her old self again.

When she stepped out of the shower, there was a pristine white robe hanging from the hook on the back of the door. Again, she didn't remember it being there earlier, but did it really matter? At least this way she wouldn't have to put her dirty clothes back on top of her shining clean skin.

This was like being in a suite at a five-star hotel…never mind that five-star hotels were probably a thing of the past, just like the rest of the luxurious world she'd once known. In a drawer, Amber found a wide-tooth wooden comb and ran it through her hair, which still had a few knots in it despite the conditioner, which she'd allowed to stay on for at least five minutes. But the knots came out quickly enough, and once she was done with that task, she located body lotion and leave-in hair serum under the sink. Both the body lotion and the serum were brands she had once used, and she frowned even as she spread the lotion on her arms and legs, worked the serum into her hair. Out of all the brands of beauty products in the world, how the hell had Idris managed to have the ones she preferred?

Another mystery. Amber shook her head, then poked around some more, looking for a blow dryer. There didn't appear to be one, and she shrugged. Back in her old life, she'd blow-dried her hair and then wound it into careful loose curls, but her hair texture was wavy on its own. She'd just have to let it dry naturally; the serum would help with that.

Moisturizer and tinted lip balm and mascara waited for her inside the mirrored medicine cabinet, and once again, she found herself shaking her head. Most of the time, she'd worn far more makeup than that, but after she'd smoothed the moisturizer into her skin and applied the lip balm and mascara, she had to admit that she felt more like herself than she had since…since whatever it was had happened.

When she went out into the bedroom, she found a pair of jeans and a lacy white blouse with angel sleeves lying on the bed, along with a white lace bra and matching panties. Everything still had tags attached—from Macy's—making Amber wonder if all these things had come from the store only a mile or so away, over on Lake Avenue in Pasadena. That seemed to be the most plausible explanation, but how had they come to be here in the first place? Even if Idris had sized her up, then jumped in his car and driven over to the department store to get her some new clothes, he couldn't have gotten there and back here that quickly. Besides, she'd had the shower going, but she still thought she would have heard him coming and going in the bedroom.

Despite the implausibilities involved, she figured that was the most reasonable explanation. And all right, it was a little creepy that he'd been able to figure out her sizes just by looking at her, but she wasn't going to complain, not when she was clean for the first time in longer than she wanted to count, not when she was wearing new, pretty clothes. Maybe the top was a little bohemian for her taste, but when she looked in the mirror, she realized it suited her, as did the simple silver sandals that had been left for her along with all the other clothes.

But damn, she was thin. And pale...way too pale, despite the time she'd spent in the sun the other day. The pink-tinted lip balm helped a little, but she still looked drawn and tired.

Frowning, she pinched her cheeks to bring some color into them, then smoothed her blouse. Her nails were clean at least, although she hated how short they were. She'd stolen clippers and emery boards from the local Walgreens on one of her scavenging expeditions, and had tried to keep them as neat as she could, but she would've killed for a mani/pedi right then.

However, she still had the diamond hoop

earrings she'd been wearing the day the world ended, and the diamond and pink sapphire band ring Tyler had given her for Christmas. Amber honestly didn't even know why she'd been wearing the ring that day, except that it gave her a sort of grim satisfaction to know he'd probably spent way more on it than he could afford. Served him right, the jackass.

Anyway, thanks to the earrings and the ring, she looked somewhat put together. Her hair was drying into pretty, ripply waves, too. Mermaid hair, her friend Kelly had used to call it. Which sounded fun, but it hadn't been the style, and so Amber had never worn her hair natural. Right then, though, she didn't have much of a choice.

She turned toward the door, hesitating a little now that she didn't have anything else to delay her in going downstairs. It was one thing to stand here and primp and fuss with her hair and clothes like she was going on a date or something, but this was no date. Idris was waiting for her, presumably to tell her something of what had happened to the world during the time she'd been hiding in the visitor center's basement. However, she didn't know whether she really wanted to hear his explanations or not...just as she wasn't sure if she wanted to know the truth about him. He'd been acting friendly enough, but even though two years had passed, she hadn't forgotten how he'd hovered in the air just like that other flying man. She didn't know who or what he was, and yet she guessed he had to be something more than a regular garden-variety human being. No one she'd ever known could float on the air like that, no harness, no jetpack, no nothing.

Which meant there was probably something else going on, something she probably would find upsetting. Over the past two years, she'd spent a considerable amount of mental energy picking at the problem before deciding it wasn't worth driving herself crazy over. Clearly, he hadn't been able to track her down, so he wasn't all-powerful, all-seeing or -knowing.

Then again, he'd obviously found her today.

She had a feeling she was about to learn why...whether she liked it or not.

FOUR

AT THE SOUND OF AMBER'S STEPS IN THE HALLWAY outside, Idris rose from where he'd been waiting at the dining room table and watched as she entered the room. Her head was up, and she offered him a friendly smile as she approached the table, but he still sensed something wary about her, something that made him believe she would bolt if given the opportunity.

Well, she could try, but she wouldn't get very far.

For the moment, he was simply glad to observe how improved she looked, although she was still far too thin, too pale. Now that the dirt was gone, he could see once again the delicacy of her features, the curve of her pretty mouth, far more lush than he'd remembered. The clothes he'd acquired for her fit her very well, and she seemed comfortable in them. At first, he'd thought to get her a dress but then realized that might seem presumptuous, as most mortal women appeared to have lived in blue jeans rather than far more flattering dresses and skirts.

"Feeling better now?" he asked.

She nodded, but he noted the way she fingered the lace-edged hem of her shirt as a slight frown pulled at her graceful brows. "I am," she replied before adding, her tone almost challenging, "Where did you get the clothes?"

"From a nearby store," he said, which was true enough.

That reply made her nod to herself, as if he'd just confirmed something she'd guessed at. "How did you get them so quickly? I know the store you're talking about, and that would've been almost twenty minutes roundtrip even without having to go through the store to find the things you were looking for."

Twenty minutes by car, certainly, Idris thought. *The way we djinn travel…not nearly so much.*

"Why don't you sit down?" he responded, ignoring her comment.

Her mouth pursed, but she gave a lift of her shoulders that seemed almost too practiced before she came over to the table and pulled out one of the chairs. Belatedly, he realized he should have gotten it out for her, but it was hard to remember all the customs humans had once practiced.

"Expecting company?" she asked wryly, her gaze traveling the length of the enormous table.

True, this dining room and the furniture in it had been constructed on a grand scale to accommodate a great many diners. Amber looked quite small, sitting there in the high-backed chair while a dozen more chairs marched their way down the table.

"No," he said, then sat down as well. "I suppose it does seem like quite a lot for the two of us."

Her eyes met his and didn't waver. "Is there anyone else left in the world to sit at a table like this, or is it really just...'the two of us'?"

Once again, he was struck by the realization that she knew nothing of what had happened in the intervening two years, had hidden herself away so expertly that she could have no real idea of how changed the world truly was.

"I assume you are hungry," he said, evading the question for now.

Amber folded her hands in her lap and gazed at him, delicate features almost expressionless. He had the impression that she was taking his measure somehow, trying to determine exactly what he intended by having her here.

Well, that was something he didn't quite know himself yet.

"Starving," she said frankly.

He could imagine. She looked as though she

hadn't had anything decent to eat in a very long time. And while he'd sampled a good many of the foods this world had once offered, he didn't want to provide anything that would be too heavy, too difficult for her to digest after such a prolonged period of eating barely enough to keep herself alive.

A wave of his hand, and before her appeared a plate of bread and cheese and fruit. Her eyes widened, and the stare she gave him was one of fear and awe.

Voice hardly above a whisper, she asked, "How did you do that?"

"I will tell you, but first, have some fruit and a little bread. It will not be such a shock to your system."

She hesitated for a second, then picked up the fork that had appeared next to the plate and speared a piece of sliced strawberry with it. Her eyes shut as she chewed, as if she needed all her focus to concentrate on the flavor that had filled her mouth. There was something strangely satisfying about watching the delicate muscles of her throat move as she swallowed, and after a moment, Idris made himself glance away. He knew he should not be quite so entranced by her, by the graceful way she set the fork down and broke off a piece of bread, then consumed it as well. Surely someone as hungry as she had to be would have torn into the food, tried to eat as much as she could, as quickly as she could. But she sat there and ate as delicately and genteelly as if she were at an elegant restaurant.

After another moment passed, and she'd eaten more bread and cheese and fruit, she reached for the glass of water he'd also made appear by her plate. Several swallows of water, and then she said, "What are you, Idris?"

"Why would you ask that?"

She set down the glass and folded her hands in her lap. Most of the food he'd summoned for her remained untouched, but she ignored it, her gaze still fixed on him. "I know it's been two years, but I still remember how I saw you floating in the air. I watched you stop that other man— whoever he was—from attacking me. And now, the food—and these clothes—and unending hot water in a bathroom that shouldn't even exist. When someone dressed like a cast member from *The King and I* shows up and starts conjuring things out of thin air, it kind of makes a girl wonder."

Although he had no idea what "the King and I" was, Amber's half-bemused, half-wary tone seemed clear enough. This world belonged to his people now, so Idris saw no reason to hide the truth from her. "I am a djinn," he said simply.

For a second, she didn't say anything, only sat there and stared at him. When she spoke, it was with a half-ironic lift to her voice, as if she couldn't quite allow herself to believe what he'd just told her. "You mean like a genie? With a magic lamp?"

Sometimes, Idris wished that legend had never come into being. Holding back a sigh, he said, "'Genie' is one way of saying it, I suppose, but there was never any magic lamp."

"Too bad," she remarked. "I always liked that story." She picked up her fork again and selected another strawberry slice. "You look human."

"Yes, we do."

That comment made her tilt her head to one side. Her hair was really quite extraordinary, so silky and pale, falling in delicate ripples around her thin shoulders. "'We'?" she repeated. "How many of you are there?"

"A number," he replied cautiously. "Enough."

"That's not a real answer."

No, it wasn't. He laced his fingers together and wished that he had summoned some wine. But no, taking refuge in drink would not make this conversation any easier. "Some twenty thousand, give or take."

"Why haven't I seen you or any other djinn, then? I mean, except for that first time."

"Because I had other matters that kept me from settling in my chosen home until now," Idris said. "And apparently I made it clear to the others that they should stay away."

For that did seem to be what had happened.

He certainly had not delivered any formal edicts that the area around the Huntington Library and anyone in it were to be left alone, but his intervention while protecting Amber must have reached the ears of the reaver djinn, for none of them had come back here, had gone on to seek their sport in other places.

Amber stared at him, wide-eyed. "This whole time," she whispered. She'd already been pale, but now she looked so white-faced, he wondered if she was about to faint.

"I don't understand," he said.

Her fingers gripped the fork she held. Voice stronger, she told him, "I've been hiding in that goddamn visitor center for two years. Two years, because I thought for sure one of you...whatever you were...was going to come back and kill me. I hid in the dark for two years, for absolutely no reason." Hand shaking, she set down the fork. "I need some air."

She pushed her chair back and stood, and Idris rose as well, not sure exactly what he should do. This was the most intimate interaction he'd ever had with a human being, and he hadn't expected his and Amber's discussion to disturb him on a level he couldn't quite understand. The raw pain in her voice made him want to reach out to her, to offer some sort of comfort, and yet he guessed that such a gesture would not meet a very warm reception.

"Don't follow me," she said, then walked out of the dining room. A moment later, one of the French doors in the gallery slammed shut.

Idris knew he should probably let her go—as he already knew…and she had just realized…that this place was perfectly safe, even for a human—but he found himself following her outside, even as he hoped she hadn't decided to run, to flee and leave him behind.

But no, there she was, standing on the loggia, arms clasped around herself as though she had taken a chill, even though it was quite pleasant and warm outside. As he approached, she said, in low, fierce tones, "Tell me what happened. *Exactly* what happened. Don't sugarcoat it, either."

That was the last thing he wanted to do…but he knew she deserved the real story. After two years of darkness, she needed to step into the light of the truth.

So he took a breath and then, as she stood there and gazed out over the gardens, over a lawn that a day before had been thick with dandelions and desperately in need of cutting and was now as manicured as it been back in the days when an army of gardeners had tended this place, he told her what had transpired. Voice as neutral and dispassionate as he could make it, he spoke of the disease the djinn had let loose on the planet, the one that burned its victims into dust so there would be no fear of pestilence from all those human bodies left behind. He spoke of how the djinn had claimed this world for their own, how each of them now had his or her own piece of land that was theirs for eternity. And then, after the briefest of hesitations, he told her of the djinn reavers, those who had made it their duty to make sure the world was cleansed of every single living human being who had managed to survive the Heat, as those few survivors had come to name the djinn-created pestilence.

When he was done, Amber remained where she was, arms still gripping herself tightly. He could see the way her short nails dug into the flesh of her upper arms, see how a shudder went through her slender form.

"So…I'm the only human being left?" She sounded resigned rather than sad, but perhaps that was only because she had most likely spent the past two years thinking exactly that very thing.

It would be so very easy to lie to her. The nearest settlement of human and djinn was more than fifty miles away, and there was very little chance she would ever learn of their existence.

But he had sworn to tell the truth here, and so he would.

"No," he said, and now she turned toward him, forget-me-not eyes full of confusion. Before she could speak, he went on, "There were among the djinn those we call the One Thousand. They did not agree with the destruction of humanity. But because they were such a minority, their voices were not strong enough to prevent their fellow djinn from releasing the disease that killed most of your kind. However, we agreed that they should be able to select partners from those who were immune. Those djinn and their human partners—who are granted unending life and youth—now live in their own communities, away from the rest of us."

Amber didn't speak immediately, but only stood there with the gentle breeze playing with the glory of her hair as it spread over her shoulders. When she spoke, it was to pose a question he hadn't been expecting. "You said 'we' agreed. Who are 'we'?"

"Myself, and the two other elders, Istar and Ibram."

For the first time, he saw a glint of amusement in her wide blue eyes. "You don't look like an elder."

"Age is of little importance among djinn."

"Must be nice." She pushed a strand of hair away from her face, tucking it behind one ear. "So that's why the other djinn didn't try to come after me? Because he saw you were protecting me and didn't want to get in trouble with an elder?"

"More or less."

"Ah." Another silence, and then she asked, "You said the djinn saved some humans who were their partners. Is that like...*partners, partners?*"

Idris wasn't sure why he should be so discomfited by such a question. Perhaps it was only that there was something far more intimate than he'd expected about standing here with her, no other souls within miles. There really wasn't anything terribly strange about djinn fraternizing with humans, since those sorts of liaisons had been occurring for millennia, although they had never been formally recognized before now. But still, admitting such a thing to this human with her porcelain doll prettiness felt awkward beyond belief.

"Yes," he said stiffly.

"Wow," was her only reply. She moved away from him, but only a step or two. Possibly, she had also been made uncomfortable by their proximity. Her head went up, and she appeared to be gazing in the direction of the rose garden, but he had a feeling her thoughts were much farther away than that. Still not looking at him, she asked, "You said these djinn of the One Thousand chose their human partners from the people who were immune?"

"Yes," he said again, now feeling wary, as though he couldn't be quite sure which direction her questioning might take next.

Voice challenging, she said, "You knew who was going to be immune?"

Again, he could only reply in the affirmative. "Yes." And now of course she would ask why no one had chosen her. After all, she was young and beautiful, the sort of woman who certainly should have attracted a djinn's attention.

That, he knew, was a question he couldn't answer. It was not the business of the elders to ask why a member of the One Thousand made a particular selection over another, and he and Istar and Ibram had done their best to stay firmly out of such affairs. Only when these matters resulted in open conflict—such as Jasreel and his half-brother Aldair battling it out over a human woman among the Santa Fe survivors—did the elders step in.

However, Amber surprised him, because she asked no such question. Instead, expression thoughtful, she said, "So...what now? I'm kind of the odd man out, aren't I? All your djinn are paired up, and all the rest of the humans are dead, so where does that put me? Back in hiding?"

"No," Idris said immediately. Such a thing was unthinkable. To have all her bright beauty hidden once again in the dark?

He realized then that there was one more truth he needed to tell her. The prospect was not very appealing, because it only pointed out how the djinn weren't quite as invincible as they liked to believe, but she needed to understand the choices available to her.

She stood there, arms crossed, expression expectant, as if she knew there was still more.

He said, "There is…a community of human survivors in a place called Los Alamos. One of their scientists has devised a system of devices that shield the place against the djinn. If we pass that barrier, we lose our powers."

"Which means you have to fight humans on their own level."

"Something like that." Idris did not see the need to explain that the devices did far more than merely strip a djinn's power, that they actually drained life and energy to the point where one of his people was rendered far less powerful than even a human being. "At any rate, it is a place where someone like you would be safe."

Amber went quiet again, fingers once more playing with the lace that edged her delicate blouse. "I don't think I could even find Los Alamos on a map." She lifted her chin and looked up into his face, although her own expression was unreadable. "Do I have to decide now?"

"No," he replied, wondering why her question had made sudden relief course through him. "I know that all this has been a shock for you."

"Okay." She smiled then, but he could tell right away it was an expression she'd put on to hide some of her inner turmoil, rather than anything that might show what she was truly feeling. "I think I'd like to go inside and have a little more to eat."

The food Idris had provided was good, but Amber knew it wouldn't be enough to hold her for very long. It was almost as if her stomach had just woken up from its long sleep and turned ravenous, needing far more than just cheese and bread and fruit to satisfy the gnawing ache inside her.

A steak, she thought. *No, too much work. A double-double from In 'N' Out and a chocolate shake.*

Back in the day, she would never have allowed such hideously calorific food to pass her lips...or at least, not very often. Now, though, she could only think of how good such a meal would taste. Anyway, she'd lost so much weight that she figured she could probably eat whatever she wanted for the next few months.

Or nachos. Nachos piled high with gooey melted cheddar cheese and tomatoes and olives and jalapeños. Chocolate cake. Bacon. Piles of bacon.

She had a feeling she was obsessing about food because it was easier than trying to process everything Idris had just told her. The disease that had swept everyone away had no natural cause at all, but was something created by the djinn. Did they have some kind of secret lab where they cooked up that kind of stuff? She had no idea, because, despite the revelations she was now trying to absorb, she still knew very little about the djinn themselves.

Except that they looked human, and they took humans as partners...humans who apparently never had to worry about growing old and dying.

Only no one had Chosen her.

Amber wasn't sure she wanted to examine that particular galling detail very closely. She'd been the girl everyone loved to hate back in high school, and she'd attracted that same kind of negative attention in college, but was she maybe not *quite* as pretty as everyone had told her? Were there enough gorgeous women survivors that the djinn hadn't seen any need to bother with someone they saw as less than?

Maybe they'd thought she was too high-maintenance, not really suited for this post-apocalyptic world. Amber had known she gave that impression and didn't do anything to dispel it, mostly because she figured it was better for a guy to know up front that she wasn't a jeans and T-shirt, camping under the stars kind of girl. Once upon a time, the very word "camp" had been enough to induce shudders.

Joke's on them, she thought, *considering I just spent the last two years basically camping under the Huntington Library's visitor center.*

Idris was watching her with some concern.

Damn, that meant she probably wasn't doing as good a job at hiding her tumultuous thoughts from him as she'd hoped. She picked up a piece of bread and set a smaller piece of smoked cheddar on top of it, and consumed the morsel as if it was the most important thing in her world. Her actions didn't seem to faze him, though; he continued to sit there at the table and gaze at her, brow furrowed and fingers steepled under his chin.

And why did he have to be so good-looking, anyway? Were all djinn that attractive? She tried to recall the features of the djinn in the parrot-green robes, the one who'd been hell-bent on murdering her, but she couldn't remember much of his face except that he'd been dark, too, his hair even longer than Idris' raven-hued shoulder-length locks.

Anyway, it was distracting to have someone she would have been flirting with in a heartbeat—if he'd been human—sitting there and just watching her, not speaking.

Then there was that whole Los Alamos thing. While Amber would admit to herself that it was something of a relief to know there were other people out there, that she really wasn't the last human being on the entire goddamn planet, she still wasn't sure she really wanted to go and live there. She'd told Idris she didn't even know where exactly Los Alamos was located, and that was partly true. That is, she knew it was in New Mexico because she'd seen the signs on the highway when they went to Santa Fe to go to the opera, but that was about it. Her mother had been very big on the Santa Fe Opera. Amber had hated those trips because she didn't like opera and thought Santa Fe was boring as hell, but it was a pilgrimage the women in her mother's circle liked to take each summer, something that proved how cultured they all were.

Anyway, nothing about New Mexico was very appealing to Amber. She was a Southern California girl born and bred, and it didn't seem fair that she'd have to relocate just because the end of the world had happened.

"Why the Huntington?" she asked abruptly, and Idris sat up a little straighter in his chair and gave her a curious look.

"What do you mean?"

"I mean, why did you choose here particularly? There are lots of other places in Southern California that would have made a good place for an elder djinn to settle." Amber wasn't quite sure why she'd asked the question, except that maybe in the back of her mind she'd thought she might be able to convince Idris to move on and leave the Huntington to her, now that she knew she was hands-off and didn't have to worry about any other djinn hunting her down.

Now his mouth quirked in that way she'd

noticed before, as if he'd meant to smile and then decided maybe it wasn't a good idea. She sort of liked the expression, even as she realized that staring at his mouth probably wasn't helping the situation any.

"I liked the house, and I liked the gardens," he said simply.

"It gets really hot here in the summer," she responded, although she knew that particular statement wasn't exactly true. Not anymore, anyway. She didn't really understand quite what was going on, but the past two summers had definitely been cooler than what she was used to, almost as if the climate had begun to shift back toward where it was supposed to be now that there weren't many people around to affect its normal cycles.

"This building has a more than adequate cooling system," Idris said, and she stared at him for a moment, nonplussed.

"But there's no electricity," Amber said, then realized that was a really stupid remark. All right, they were sitting here with the French doors open to let in the breeze and no lights on because it was barely past noon, but still, obviously the lights in the bathroom had worked. She'd flicked them on without barely even noticing, an automatic gesture.

"I don't need electricity. My powers are sufficient to power the climate-control system."

Well, of course they were. She supposed if he could snap his fingers or wave a hand and make food appear in front of her, then he could also power the lights and the air conditioning and anything else he wanted. No wonder the djinn had no use for human beings; these magical creatures could make their world run just fine without electricity and cars and all the other modern conveniences the human race had been so damn proud of. Maybe she should be offended on humanity's behalf, but she had to admit that the djinn way was a lot more elegant.

"Still," Amber went on, knowing she sounded desperate but determined to give this a try, since she'd already basically dug a hole for herself, "there are other mansions that would work just as well. The Doheny mansion in L.A.—and if you like living in museums, there's always the old Getty building in Malibu. It's made to look like a Roman villa…a djinn should like that, right?"

Now he did smile, a sort of slow, lazy lift of his mouth that made a strange little thrill go through her. She was used to having that kind of reaction to good-looking men, but this was different.

Because he's not really *a man,* she thought. The problem was, she knew that intellectually, but her eyes kept telling her he sure as hell looked like a man.

"The Getty in Malibu is a very fine building," Idris agreed. "As is the Doheny mansion, and

Hearst Castle, and other locations I've already considered. But this one suited me best."

Of course, it did. Amber picked up a blueberry and put it in her mouth, mostly because she was feeling flummoxed and needed some time to rethink her approach. It had been so long since she'd had any interactions with anyone at all that she knew she was second-guessing herself. Now, confronted by an apparently all-powerful and immortal being who should have been her enemy but somehow, strangely, wasn't, she really didn't know what to do.

"There is no need for you to worry," he said. "You and I have already agreed that you can stay here a while longer. Perhaps you would like to choose which room to use as your own?"

When she was a little girl, she'd dreamed of living here, of having one of those high, canopied beds as her own. She would have felt like a princess, even though she knew her own bedroom at home was very nice by pretty much anyone else's standards. Now, however, with Idris making such an offer, Amber wasn't sure whether that was such a good idea after all. It would feel very strange to sleep under the same roof as a djinn, even though she was fairly certain he had no designs on her. He was just trying to be hospitable.

"I was thinking maybe the Japanese house,"

she blurted, and he looked at her with raised eyebrows.

"Does it have a bed?" he asked, and she shook her head.

"No, but you could put one in there, right? And a bathroom and anything else I might need?"

"I suppose so," he replied, the flicker of amusement back in his dark eyes. "Although I am not sure the space will accommodate everything you might need. It is fairly compact."

Well, that was true. But, considering she'd been living out of a sleeping bag in an underground office for the past couple of years, she thought she could get by with a single bed and a modest bathroom, maybe a small closet for her clothes.

"I don't need much," she said.

For a moment, he didn't reply, only sat there with that small lift to his lips, the one that made her want to keep staring at his mouth. Then he said, "Very well. The Japanese house it is."

FIVE

As he watched Amber walk away toward her new quarters, Idris wondered if he had made a very great mistake. Not by allowing her the Japanese house; he could understand why she might not feel comfortable sleeping in the same place he did, even though the Huntington house was very large and they certainly would both have adequate space to avoid one another, if that was her goal.

No, he thought possibly he had been too lenient, and that it would have made a great deal more sense for him to tell her there was no place for her kind here, that her only possible refuge would be with the other human survivors in Los Alamos. Why he hadn't done such a thing, and taken her there immediately, he really couldn't say. Her reluctance to relocate to the New Mexico town had been obvious enough...as were her attempts to get him to consider another home for himself. Even if he had been willing to do such a thing—which he most certainly was not—she wouldn't have been allowed to stay here at the Huntington on her own. The djinn reavers might have continued to leave her alone, but Istar and Ibram would have wanted to know why he had changed his mind about his earthly domicile, and then they would have found out about Amber.

They were going to discover her presence here sooner or later anyway. While the elders could not see into one another's lives in quite the same way they did with the djinn who were their subjects, so to speak, Ibram and Istar would probably want to visit him at the Huntington at some point. Idris hoped that day was far enough in the future that there would be little chance of their running into his human guest.

Well, he would deal with that problem when the time came…if it came at all. For now, it was enough to imagine a compact but well-appointed new bathroom in a corner of the Japanese house, a futon with a comfortable mattress so she might sleep easily, a small closet off the bathroom, one filled with more clothing like the items he had already fetched for her. At least he had been correct in guessing at the sizes she required, so it was easy enough to acquire more of the same. He would have to leave it there for now, and, perhaps, hope she would be pleased by the alterations he'd made in order to ensure her stay in the little wood-framed structure was a comfortable one.

And if he thought it odd that she should accept him so easily, well, he could readily believe that she was happy to reach out to anyone after such a prolonged period of utter solitude.

Even a djinn.

For himself, he had been happy to see renewed color in her cheeks as she ate, a sign that the simple food he'd given her for her midday meal was doing some good. Tonight, they should have something a bit more substantial, but still fish or fowl, no red meat, which might be difficult for her to digest after so many months of eating substandard rations. Pheasant, possibly. Chicken seemed far too prosaic a meal for such a setting.

He wanted to smile then. So many plans, so many considerations, all for the benefit of a single human female. Should he really allow her that much space in his thoughts?

Then again, what else did he have to occupy himself?

A sad truth, but one he needed to face. While there had been numerous growing pains as the djinn slowly settled into their new lives here on Earth, by this point, everyone had established themselves in their roles, the communities of humans and djinn flourishing, children being born, land being plowed and made fertile again.

The same, too, for those of his people who'd wanted nothing to do with the humans. Those djinn had made their homes in the lands allotted to them, were taking on the difficult work of clearing away human-made structures and roads so the world might flourish and be green and bountiful again. He supposed those djinn would also have their own pairings, their own offspring, but he and his fellow elders had very little to do with that, either. After all the upheaval, this world was calm and peaceful once more. Although privately he'd wondered if this current state of affairs could continue indefinitely, so far there had been no signs that it wouldn't.

Whether Amber felt happy to have an unexpected companion in her solitude, Idris couldn't begin to guess. She'd seemed remarkably self-possessed for someone who had undergone such an ordeal, but he was starting to get the sense that she'd been someone who'd had most of her life made easy for her...until the Dying, of course. Even so, being raised to expect things to go a certain way might have given her something of the self-assurance he'd witnessed, despite the strangeness of the world she now found herself in.

He could imagine her now, moving around the small wooden house in the heart of the Japanese garden, inspecting the new bathroom and the bed and the clothing he'd put there for her. While he had no idea how long this arrangement might last, he was glad she would be comfortable during the time she was here.

Her presence made the place seem less lonely.

―――――――

Amber knew the bathroom and the futon and the closet full of clothes must have just appeared, mostly because she'd visited this spot only the day before, and none of these things had been here then. Once again, she wondered at the powers Idris seemed to command. Was anything beyond him? What was it like to be so, well…magical?

She didn't know. What she did know was that she could live like a civilized person again, with a real bathroom and clean, pretty clothes and a soft place to sleep. The futon had surprised her a little, but when she opened it up and lay down on it, she was delighted by how comfortable it seemed to be. Tonight, she thought, she might actually be able to sleep…*really* sleep, without fluttering awake two or three times during the night because she thought she heard something that shouldn't be there.

The rest of the little house was just as it had always been, with the flat woven bamboo mats on the floor and the low tables and the sliding screens, but everything seemed somehow newer and cleaner. More of Idris's magic, she assumed, although a more subtle kind than the powers that had apparently performed the remodel in the time it had taken her to walk down here from the main house.

It was very quiet, except for the birds singing in the trees and the rustle of leaves in the light wind. Amber supposed it had always been this quiet, although she knew that when she'd come here before, she'd always been nervous, looking over her shoulder for an attack that never came. She really hadn't had the luxury to pause and simply be in the space.

Something tight and tense in her chest seemed to ease itself now. She breathed in and breathed out, reminding herself once again that she was safe, that the horrible death she'd feared every day for the past few years had been nothing at all. Idris had protected her then, just as he was continuing to protect her now. It felt odd to think of a djinn as a protector, when it was the djinn who'd made sure humanity was a thing of the past, but she still had to be grateful to him, grateful for what he'd done to make sure she didn't meet the same fate as everyone else.

The same fate....

For so long, she'd done her best not to think about what she'd lost. Surviving from day to day had been hard enough—hard and nasty and dirty, full of unpleasant details she'd done her best to grit her teeth and ignore. Now that she no longer had to worry about any of that nastiness, she found her thoughts going to the people who had once been integral to her life—her mother, of course, but also Kelly and Tiffany and Marisa and all the other girls in her circle, her mostly absent father, her grandparents and cousins and….

No, she couldn't. Amber gulped in a breath, even as the serene landscape around her blurred with tears. It was just too big to think of them as all gone, disappeared into dust, both literally and figuratively. Her mother had been a formidable woman, Amber's grandmother Eileen even more so. Both those women had seemed as if they could have survived anything…and yet, they hadn't.

Why had she lived when so many others had died? What was it about her that made her worthy of the strange immunity she'd been granted? She didn't understand it, not at all. If there were any justice in the world, shouldn't someone important have survived, someone like a doctor or a scientist or a college professor, a person who had something to offer the world, rather than a girl whose particular talents included being able to rattle off all the names of OPI's seasonal nail polish colors going back the past three years?

She put her hands up to her face, felt the tears on her cheeks. As she wiped them away, she heard his voice.

"Amber, are you all right? Is there something that displeases you about the house?"

All she could do was shake her head. Right then, her throat was too tight with tears for her to manage any kind of a reply.

Black robes fluttering in the breeze, Idris came up the low steps at the front of the house. He seemed to hesitate for a moment, but then he came over to her. Even as she wiped at her tears again, his arms went around her, and he pulled her close.

Oh, dear God. It had been so long since she'd had any contact at all with another living being, and now the most gorgeous man she'd ever seen was holding her against him, murmuring soothing words in his deep voice as he stroked her hair. Need pulsed through her, a sort of cramping heat, even as she told herself he was only trying to offer what comfort he could. Funny how a djinn could sense her pain, was doing pretty much what a human might have done in the same situation. Were the two races really that different after all?

"Sorry," she said in a choked whisper, and he went still, one hand resting on her hair.

"What do you have to be sorry for?" he asked, voice very gentle.

"For getting all hysterical," she replied, and he shook his head.

"You do not seem hysterical to me. Upset, yes. Is it something about the house?"

He was obviously worried that he'd done something to make her break down like this. Amber shook her head, then made herself step away from his embrace. As much as she'd enjoyed being held by him, she thought it better to put a little distance between them.

"No, the house is great. It's just…." The words trembled into the air between them, then faded away. She wasn't sure how she could ever tell him why she was so upset. While any rational person should be able to understand the reasons behind her grief, her sudden breakdown, she thought if she tried to explain what was going on, he would only take it as a criticism of him and his kind.

Which he should, she supposed. After all, it was the djinns' fault that the world was the way it was. And although he'd made it sound as if he had nothing to do with any of that, could she really believe him? How could one of the people who was supposed to be in charge have stood by and allowed the rest of the djinn to commit such heinous acts?

"'It's just…'?" Idris repeated, tone questioning now. He didn't look particularly upset with her for moving away, but she'd be the first to admit that she didn't know him well enough to be able to interpret his every expression, his every movement.

"I guess it all just hit me at once," Amber said. "I haven't had much time to stop and think about everything that's happened. That's all."

"All," he said, voice musing. "Yes, I suppose the situation could be somewhat overwhelming, especially now that you know you are safe, don't have to always be looking over your shoulder."

For a djinn, he was just a bit too perceptive. Or could his people read minds, along with all their other talents? Idris hadn't said anything about that, but then, she could see why he wouldn't. Being able to see someone else's thoughts could be a real advantage, one it might be better not to share.

"That's it," she said. Crossing her arms, she looked up at him. His face had gone impassive again, revealing very little. "So why did you come down here?"

The words sounded accusatory almost as soon as they left her mouth, and Amber had to keep herself from wincing. However, Idris didn't seem offended, but only said, "I came here to see if the changes I made in the house would work for you, and also to see if you would come up and share dinner with me. The food you had at lunch seemed to help, so I thought perhaps something a little more substantial for the evening meal would be in order."

He wanted to have dinner with her. Then again, she supposed it would have seemed strange for the two of them to be sharing this enormous property and yet avoid each other as much as possible. Besides, he was the one with the power to conjure whatever meal he liked. He probably wanted to make sure she continued to eat well so she could regain all her strength. Why exactly, she didn't know. So she'd be in tiptop shape whenever he shipped her off to Los Alamos?

"That sounds good," she said. "But no Brussels sprouts."

Her request made him chuckle. "Of course. Any other dietary restrictions I need to know about?"

Amber thought of all the fads she'd subjected herself to—the kale smoothies, the wheatgrass shakes, the apple cider vinegar cleanses—and then said firmly, "No, not really. I usually didn't eat a lot of red meat, but after being deprived of it for two years, I think I can handle some from time to time."

"Duly noted," he said. A brief pause as he seemed to study her expression for a moment, and then he added, "You are sure you're all right?"

"I'm fine. Really." Because she wasn't really sure she was fine, and would prefer to have him gone in case she had another breakdown, she said, "What time do you want me to come up for dinner?"

"Time isn't as important now as it once was," he replied with an enigmatic smile. "Just after dusk, I think. I'll make sure you'll be able to find your way."

"Okay." She hoped he was right, because it could get dark out here after the sun went down. Then again, she supposed a djinn could manage a little landscape lighting. "I'll come up then."

"I look forward to it."

Without saying another word, he turned and went back the way he had come, sunlight glinting off the rippling silk of the loose robe he wore. He looked very tall and proud, and Amber almost wondered whether she'd imagined the way he'd held her as she wept.

No, her body remembered. She could still feel his arms around her. It had been a gesture of comfort, nothing more, and yet she shivered slightly, recalling the flush of need that had gone through her.

It's not that strange, she told herself as she went inside and sat down on the futon. *You might have managed to go without for two years, but you're just horny. That's all.*

Stating the fact so crassly actually made her feel a little better. If she boiled everything down to a simple biological reaction, then she didn't have to be angry with herself for the weird attraction she'd experienced at his touch. Because it was weird. Even when she'd met guys she thought were hot, she made them pursue her. She wasn't the type to throw herself at someone.

Especially not someone who wasn't even human.

Right then, she was very glad that she wouldn't be sleeping under his roof tonight.

The afternoon passed. Idris halfway wondered if Amber would even appear for dinner that evening, since she'd seemed so diffident when he took his leave of her earlier in the day, but no, there she was, walking up the lighted pathway to the loggia, which also gleamed with the light of numerous candle lanterns he'd set out there earlier that day. In their warm glow, she looked incandescent, pallor banished from her cheeks, her hair painted a soft gold.

"Are you having a party?" she asked, a teasing note in her voice. Whatever melancholy had possessed her a few hours ago, it seemed to have gone now.

"No," he replied, his expression serious. Obviously, he'd taken her question at face value. "It is no real effort for me to have these things, and they make the surroundings even more beautiful."

"True."

Idris gestured for her to come inside and she did, gaze moving over the candlelit dining room, pausing on the centerpiece of chrysanthemums and twining ivy, the gleaming china and crystal that sat on top of a snowy tablecloth.

Hands on her hips, she said, "If this is *not* throwing a party, I kind of hate to think what it must look like when you actually are entertaining."

"We djinn like our gatherings," he replied, although that was not precisely true. His people did congregate for feasts, and certainly were quite elaborate in their decorating, but those parties were not the sort of thing the elders ever attended. They were supposed to hold themselves aloof so they could not be accused of showing favoritism when called upon to adjudicate a dispute.

In fact, this was the first time in all his long, long life that he'd ever been called upon to decorate in such a way. Perhaps, in his enthusiasm, he had gone a bit overboard.

"Some wine?" he asked, hoping she would not see his sudden unease.

"God, yes," she replied, in tones that seemed to indicate she hadn't consumed any alcohol for a very long time. Strange, because she could have looted bottles of wine while gathering the other supplies that had kept her alive all the time she'd been hiding underground. Possibly she feared she would put herself at a disadvantage by consuming alcohol, and so had decided to remain sober.

He didn't comment, however, but went over to the sideboard and poured two glasses of the burgundy he'd decanted earlier. From the way her gaze went to the decanter and back to the glasses, he guessed that perhaps she was a bit discomfited by not seeing a bottle, that she worried he intended to drug her or some such nonsense. Which was ridiculous, of course; a djinn did not have to resort to such crude methods if he wished to subdue a mortal.

But she only murmured, "Thank you," as she took the glass from him. Not standing on ceremony, she sipped at it, then nodded. "That's good. Did you break into Henry Huntington's wine cellars, too?"

"As you know, there was no need to break into anything here," Idris replied, his tone perhaps a bit more severe than he'd intended. "Since everything was left open and unlocked when the Heat struck. However, you probably also know that the cellar of the man who built this house was removed long ago. This is a Burgundy that I drank several years back. I thought it would go well with our meal."

"And you brought it here just like that." Amber snapped her fingers, adding, "Because you could."

"Well, yes," he said. "That is how our powers

work. But please, sit down. I hope you are hungry."

"Always," she responded. "Well, what you fed me at lunch helped. But I'm ready for something a little more substantial."

As he'd guessed. While she seated herself, he waved a hand, and the roast pheasant and wild rice pilaf and grilled asparagus he'd planned all appeared on the table, along with a silver basket of bread and a plate of butter. He could see how Amber's eyes widened, but she didn't say anything, only placed her napkin in her lap and then waited for him to sit down as well.

"Who knew there could still be five-star dining after the apocalypse?" she quipped.

Idris, however, could feel himself frown. "Is that how you view what happened? I thought an apocalypse involved the end of the world, and, as you can see, the world is still very much here."

"Not my world," she said, then swallowed some more of her Burgundy.

Yes, he supposed she was correct enough in that statement. This building might still stand, and the sun still shone and the tide came in every day, but everything she'd known, every person she'd ever cared about, was now nothing more than dust. He remembered how he had reached out to her to offer comfort, how frail and delicate and small she had felt in his arms. For all that, he'd also sensed a spine of steel in her, which made sense. How else could she have survived on her own for all that time?

"Point taken," he said, making sure he kept his voice neutral. "But let me dish you some food."

He loaded her plate, and saw her eyes widen at the amount of food he'd given her. Perhaps he'd overestimated how much she could eat. Well, she could consume as much as she wanted and leave the rest. There wouldn't be any real waste, not when he could dispatch the leftovers back to the component atoms they had come from.

Her first few bites were tentative, as if she hadn't been completely sure of the food he'd provided for her, despite the bread and fruit she'd had at lunch. But then she ate with more relish, only slowing down when she paused to retrieve a roll from the basket and break it in half, then butter the smaller of the two halves.

"A couple of years ago, I wouldn't have let myself eat this roll," she remarked, just before she took a bite.

Idris stared at her, puzzled. "Why not? Did you have some kind of allergy to bread or wheat?"

"No, but bread is just loaded with carbs, right?"

"Carbohydrates."

"Exactly." She shot him a sideways glance, mouth pursed in tight little smile. "You know what they say—'a moment on the lips, forever on the hips.'"

No, he hadn't known that "they" ever said something like this, because he hadn't paid all that much attention to the doings of mortals. However, one look at Amber's slender form was enough to tell him she certainly did not need to worry about such ridiculous strictures. "I do not think that is a problem for you. You are very thin."

Her smile widened. "Back in the day, I would have been thrilled to hear someone tell me that. But I can't really argue. The apocalypse diet probably dropped me to a size zero."

Which was true, as that was the size of the jeans she was wearing now, that, and an extra-small shirt. He hoped she would start to fill out a bit once she'd been eating regular meals for a while. The women who'd caught his eye in the past had always been the well-curved ones.

And that thought made him want to shake his head at himself. Certainly, he should not be thinking about Amber in terms of what he found attractive in females. She was a mortal, and he was a djinn elder. Her physical beauty—or lack thereof—should mean nothing to him.

"I have never understood the human obsession with weight," he remarked as he fetched a roll of his own.

Head tilted to one side, she asked, "Do djinn even have to worry about that sort of thing?"

No, they really didn't. Of course, there were djinn who were bulkier in build and those who were more slender, but they were never judged on the basis of such minor variations in their shape. At any rate, there was no such thing as a fat djinn.

He shook his head, and she said, "Must be nice. Well, it wasn't as easy for us humans."

Since he wasn't quite sure of the best way to respond to her comment, Idris decided to eat his roll in silence, alternating bites of bread with sips of wine. Amber returned to her roast pheasant and wild rice, and was quiet as well, although he got the impression that her thoughts were churning with unanswered questions.

"How long have there been djinn?" she asked abruptly, setting down her fork.

He hadn't been expecting that line of inquiry, but he supposed it was harmless enough. "Since before man," he replied.

"So there were djinn while we were still running around looking like apes?"

When she put it that way…. "In a sense, yes."

Now Amber frowned. Her fingers were wrapped around the stem of her wine glass, but she hadn't yet lifted it to take a drink. Gaze fixed on him, she said, "What do you mean, 'in a sense'?"

He held back a sigh—it was a question that required a complex answer, and he was not sure even he could correctly articulate what had occurred so long ago. Still, he thought he should make the attempt and replied, "You evolved from those creatures, but you were not yet what anyone could call 'mankind.' Your spirit, your consciousness, was not truly human. It was in the time just before modern man and those you call Neanderthals existed side by side that the djinn first came into being." Idris hoped this explanation, although grossly simplified, would be enough to satisfy her. It seemed he was mistaken, however, because she asked another question.

"You evolved side by side with us?"

"No."

At last, she lifted the wine glass to her lips and took a large swallow. "I don't understand."

"We djinn were first spirit and flame. God brought us forth from the dust of stars and gave us our powers. This world was meant to be ours." Idris stopped himself there, wondering if he had already said too much.

Apparently so, because a sudden fierce light shone in Amber's eyes as she said, "That's why you did this to us humans? To take back what you thought was supposed to be yours?"

Those words were almost exactly the very ones that the djinn who'd first proposed eradicating mankind had used. To attempt to deny this particular truth would be disingenuous, and so he said simply, "Yes."

"I guess I can understand that," she replied, startling him with the frankness of her tone. "I mean, obviously, I can't agree with what you did, but no one can deny that we humans were royally screwing up the place."

Somehow, he managed to say, "Still, the measures we djinn took were…a bit extreme."

Amber didn't say anything for a moment, but only sat there with her fingers still wrapped around the stem of her wine glasses, the liquid inside rippling as she slowly swirled it around and around. When she spoke, again she surprised him. "I don't think we need to talk about that anymore. Done is done, right?"

"You don't hate us for what happened?" It had been difficult to ask the question, but he wanted to know. He had never been one to shy away from hard truths. Perhaps his was the sort of perspective that came with so many millennia of existence.

"Some of you, sure." Amber drank a bit of her wine, then set the glass down and spread her hands against the white tablecloth as if she was using her inspection of them to avoid looking at him. Her nails were short, the cuticles a bit ragged, and yet he still thought her fingers were pretty, long and delicate. She looked up suddenly and said, "But *you* didn't order them to do any of that, right? From what you've told me, it doesn't even sound as though you really could have stopped them once their minds were made up. So no, I'm not going to hate you for something those other djinn did. That wouldn't be very logical, would it?"

No, it wouldn't be logical. Or at least, he had never seen the point in assigning blanket blame to a group simply because one or a few of their number had done something wrong. While he agreed with her, he also thought it a bit surprising to realize her thoughts aligned so closely with his.

"I suppose not," he said. "And since we both feel this way, I suppose you are right in thinking there is no reason to discuss the matter further."

She nodded, and appeared relieved that he showed no desire to press the subject. Now wearing a slight smile, she said, "But I would really like to know how you can just make all this food appear out of nowhere."

Glad for the change of subject, Idris did his best to explain how all djinn could gather what they needed to them as long as the components for the item in question were available some-where in the world. It was all about energy in the end, whether using that energy to bring the food to him...or utilizing it to create a new bathroom in the time it took to visualize what he wanted.

Amber seemed intrigued by his explana-tions...and willing to leave other, touchier subjects aside. Perhaps, like him, she wanted this first meal they shared to be a harmonious one. Which it was, and when they were done eating, she thanked him for the food and said she was tired and wanted to go to sleep. He offered to walk her back to her house, but she only shook her head.

"It's safe here, after all," she said. "I'll be fine. Have a good evening, Idris."

And she got up from the table and let herself out, her blouse and her long blonde hair pale glimmers in the reflected glow from the lights that lined the pathway. He watched her go until she was little more than a dim blur disappearing into the darkness, and then at last he turned toward the table with its remains of the meal they had shared. A lift of his hand, and all the dirty plates and bowls and glasses disappeared. There was now no trace of the dinner he had set out for her, and yet he thought it would remain in his mind for some time, because it was during their meal that he'd realized there would be no acrimony between them. She seemed willing to look ahead to the future and not dwell on the past, and he was more than glad to do so as well.

What exactly that future might be, he couldn't begin to guess.

SIX

Bright, diffuse light filtered through the screens that protected the interior of the little Japanese house. Amber opened her eyes and stared at those screens for a long moment, recalling where she was, how she had gotten here. Idris had found her and given her a safe place to stay.

Idris. How crazy was it that she'd sat down and shared a meal with him—a meal that wouldn't have been out of place at some of the fancier restaurants she'd patronized back when the world had moved blindly onward, oblivious to the fate hanging over it. Never in a million years had she thought that a djinn could be so courteous…so, well, kind.

Then again, she hadn't even known djinn were an actual thing, so there was that, too.

It was strange to remind herself she didn't

have to cower underground anymore, didn't have to calculate every move she took like the way she had during the rare times she'd felt bold enough to emerge from her hidey-hole in the basement of the visitor center. That whole time she'd been safe, thanks to Idris. Maybe she should be angry about all the weary months she'd wasted being afraid for no reason, but she couldn't really blame him for that. He hadn't chased her underground. Besides, it was obvious that he'd only returned here very recently, and so had no idea that she was even still in the vicinity.

In a way, that realization made her feel a little better. He was a very powerful being, obviously, but he wasn't all-knowing, all-seeing. He wasn't a god. She recalled how he'd spoken of God so matter-of-factly the night before, as if Idris knew for a fact that the djinn had been created by Him, as well as everything on this earth. Amber wasn't quite ready to acknowledge that there really was a God—if He existed, why the hell hadn't He stopped the djinns' murderous plans?—but obviously there was a lot more going on here than she ever could have imagined.

Taking a shower here wasn't quite as luxurious as it had been in the huge bathroom Idris had constructed for himself in the main house, although still enormously satisfying. She was pretty sure she would never again take for granted hot running water, or shampoo or moisturizing body wash or any of the myriad items she'd utilized to make sure she looked flawless. Not that she pretended to be flawless now, skinny with no makeup and no curling iron or blow dryer, but she knew she was doing much better than she had been even a day ago.

If she asked for those things, would Idris provide them for her?

Probably, but Amber realized that pretty much everything she needed was close by, presumably still languishing in the drawers and cupboards at her house. After she'd run away before, she'd studiously avoided returning to the place, not wanting to see her former home as empty and dead as the ones she'd raided in her searches for supplies, but now she thought she could go in without being too traumatized by the experience. Knowing that she was safe and under Idris's protection made a world of difference.

Maybe she could get him to come with her. There probably wasn't any real need, not with all the other djinn avoiding the Huntington and its environs, but she thought she'd still like him to be there, possibly for no other reason than she wanted him to see where she'd come from, for him to be reminded of what the djinn had taken away from her. She'd been telling him the truth the night before when she said she didn't blame him for what had happened, and yet he still needed to know what his people had done to her, done to every other person on the planet. All those people had had lives, pasts, relationships, all things that had been stolen from them as soon as a group of angry elementals decided it was time for them to take this planet back.

Idris hadn't invited her for breakfast, but there didn't seem to be any food here in the little house he'd given her to use. As far as she could tell, he was fine with her sleeping and bathing here, but he wanted her to come up to the mansion for her meals. Clearly, he had no intention of starving her, not when he'd shown such concern over how thin she was…not when he'd fed her a meal last night that probably would have been enough for three or four people.

Standing out in the sun for ten minutes brought her damp hair up to nearly dry. Amber ran her fingers through it, then began to make her way along the path toward the main house. However, she hadn't gotten very far before she smelled something she thought she'd never smell again.

Bacon.

Almost at once, her mouth began to water. As she looked around her, then took another step or two forward, she realized the delectable aroma was coming from what had once been the museum's tea room.

Pace quickening, she walked over to the tea room, whose front door stood open. Now the bacon smell was almost overwhelming…or maybe it just seemed that way because it had been so long since she'd had any.

Inside the tea room, Idris was just setting a vase filled with cheerful daisies and mums down on the center of one of the tables. All the rest were empty, although their surfaces had been covered with white cloths. At her approach, he straightened and looked over at her, a smile touching his lips.

"I was just about to come fetch you," he said.

"No need," Amber replied, feeling her own mouth lift in response to that smile. He looked cheerful and rested this morning, despite those somber black robes he always seemed to wear. "The smell of bacon works pretty well as a way to get my attention."

His dark eyes glinted. "I took a gamble. I know you told me yesterday that you didn't eat very much red meat, but—"

"But bacon is in a class by itself," she finished with a grin. She looked past him to the buffet table against the wall. It was crowded with plates and bowls—a platter piled high with bacon done to just the perfect level of crispiness, a bowl of sliced fruit, one of those multi-tiered serving plates crowded with various breakfast pastries, a gleaming golden circle of what she guessed was quiche lorraine.

Well, if Idris was trying to fatten her up, he'd

definitely figured out the most effective way to do it.

"Coffee?" he asked politely. "Or do you prefer tea?"

"Tea, please." Some of her friends had teased her for being a freak, but she could never get into coffee. She drank English breakfast in the morning and sipped plain black iced tea almost all day long, and that was it. On the upside, she'd never had to worry about all the calories a Frappuccino might contain.

Out of nowhere, a pretty little teapot hand-painted with roses appeared, taking a place of honor on the table he'd set for them. Along with it came a matching teacup, a container filled with various packaged teas, and a creamer and sugar set.

Since she knew she needed to get used to the way Idris could make food appear out of thin air, Amber decided not to comment, but only went over and selected a bag of English breakfast, then placed it in the teacup and poured hot water over it. While she was busy with that, he summoned a big mug of coffee for himself and took a sip.

"Djinn drink coffee?" she asked, amused for some reason.

"This djinn does," he replied, unruffled. The liquid inside the mug was almost the same near-black as his hair; clearly, he didn't believe in cream and sugar. "Others prefer tea, or no morning drink at all."

Just like regular people. She supposed they must all have their own personalities, their own quirks and eccentricities, the same as mortals. It had been easier to think of them as a monolithic block of strange creatures with murderous intent, but meeting Idris had changed all that. He might not be like anyone else she'd ever known, but in a way, that was a good thing. Some of the people in her circle hadn't been exactly paragons, even though she would never have admitted such a thing back in the day.

"I guess we'd better get some food before everything gets cold," she suggested, and his dark eyes twinkled at her.

"Oh, it will not get cold."

"Djinn magic?"

"Something like that."

About all she could do was shake her head, then get a plate and fill it up with a reckless amount of food. Maybe at some point in the future she'd have to watch what she ate, but right now she had a hell of a lot of ground to make up.

Idris also piled his plate high, thus reinforcing what he'd told her the night before, that djinn really didn't need to worry about their weight. No, he seemed to be all muscle; those open robes he wore were definitely distracting, although Amber was more interested in his face, in the lift of his dark brows, the finely sculpted lines of his mouth, those deep brown eyes, just heavy-lidded enough to be positively sexy. Of course she liked guys with good bodies, but she'd known enough gym-obsessed men to realize they tended to make lousy romantic partners.

And then again she wanted to laugh at herself, because Idris wasn't her partner, not even a prospective one. They were…friends? Maybe not friends yet. Friendly, though, and that was enough for her right now, and much better than thinking he was actively trying to kill her.

They sat and ate quietly for a while, only punctuating their conversation with the occasional innocuous comment about the weather. Amber got the feeling he was trying to keep things light after their somewhat intense interactions at dinner the night before, which was fine by her. While she was refilling her teacup, however, she ventured, "I thought I might like to go by my house later this morning."

Idris raised an eyebrow at her. "Why?"

"Just to get a few things."

"I can get you whatever you need."

Which she assumed was simple fact and not boasting, but still. "Is there a problem with me leaving the grounds here?"

"No," he said immediately. "There are no other djinn anywhere nearby. It is safe."

"Well, then." Since he still looked nonplussed,

she continued, "I just want to get a few personal things. You can come with me."

This suggestion made him appear to relax a little. Why, Amber wasn't entirely sure. Had he thought she would try to run away? There was no way in the world she would do anything that stupid, but maybe he wasn't entirely certain of her yet.

"Of course," he said. "If you wish it."

Without hesitating, she told him, "I'd like it."

He nodded and ate half a piece of bacon, which seemed to indicate his agreement with the plan. She'd already consumed two pieces of bacon, but she figured two years of deprivation entitled her to another. Mirroring Idris's actions, she broke a slice in half and ate part of it, inwardly reveling in the salty, smoky, savory flavor. This was like a little piece of heaven.

Well, almost. Amber couldn't help noticing all the empty tables around them, tables that should have been crowded with people coming here for brunch, or an early tea. She remembered how her mother had brought her here at least once or twice every month, starting when Amber was only six years old. Those outings had been so exciting to her back then—the chance to wear a frilly dress and new shoes, to have all those adults exclaiming over her and saying what a beautiful child she was. And also to sit at the table like a grown-up and eat little sandwiches with the crusts cut off, to have her mother show her exactly the proper way to crook her pinky finger as she lifted her tea to drink it. Back in those more innocent days, she'd been eager to please, as if she'd already begun to sense the undercurrents of resentment and anger between her parents and was trying to be extra good so they'd have no reason to be mad at her…or at each other.

"You look troubled," Idris said quietly, and Amber startled a little and sent him a quick smile.

"I'm not," she replied, then set down the half-piece of bacon she still held. "I was just thinking about the times I'd come here when I was a little girl. It's just…different now."

"I know." He looked around at the empty restaurant, then continued, his voice quiet, almost sad. "I can do many things, but I cannot bring back the people who once gathered here. This is the world we live in now."

Her throat was tight. She pulled in a breath and reached for her tea, and somehow, the warm liquid helped to relax the tense muscles of her neck, made her feel a little better about life. All those scenes in the books she'd read about people having a cup of tea to calm them down seemed to make more sense right now. There really was something magical about tea.

"It's all right," she said. Whether or not that statement was actually true was up for debate, but she reminded herself that she was in a much better place now than she'd been just the day before. The world would never be the same, but she was warm and clean and dressed nicely, was just about to take a bite of the best quiche lorraine she'd ever eaten. Things could be a lot worse, considering. "Let's finish breakfast, and then we can go over to my house."

He nodded in reply, but something in his expression was still abstracted, as if he worried that she was making sure to hide her emotions from him. In a way, she supposed she was, and yet, what else was she supposed to do? If she let him see everything she was feeling, then he'd know she continued to wrestle with the reality of this new world the djinn had made. No, she really didn't blame him for what had happened, but not assigning blame wasn't the same thing as putting aside her sadness, her mourning for what was gone.

She honestly didn't know if she would ever be able to do that.

It actually came as something of a shock to Idris to realize how close Amber's family home was located to the Huntington's grounds. Rather than lead him out one of the facility's two entrances, she took him down to the bottom of the gardens, where a tall vine-covered wall marked the border of the property.

"It's just on the other side," she said. "I climbed over when I decided that it was safer to hide in one of the museum buildings."

Resourceful of her—coming in that way would have been far less conspicuous than taking the much longer route that would bring her to the closest entrance—but Idris had no intention of doing anything as undignified as climbing over a wall. "That is not a problem," he said. "I will carry you."

"You'll what...?" she began, but didn't get much farther than that, as he came over to her and wrapped one arm around her waist.

He could have argued that he did so only because holding her as he took to the air was the simplest way for the two of them to get past the wall. However, he knew he would be lying to himself if he didn't admit that he enjoyed the sensation of holding her against him, of feeling how slim that waist was, of breathing in the sweet scent of her newly washed hair.

Within the span of a few seconds, they were on the other side of the wall, standing on a patchy, overgrown lawn that surrounded an enormous swimming pool. Because there had been more rain than usual this past season, it was not empty, but it still presented something of a forlorn sight, thanks to the dead leaves floating on its surface and the unmistakable scrim of algae that marred its concrete walls.

However, Amber gave it only a brief glance and said, "This way."

She led him to a set of French doors that opened on a large patio. Here was an island of herringbone brick with a barbecue enclosed within it, and also rusting wrought-iron lawn furniture whose cushions had long since been torn open and the stuffing taken away by birds or other animals. Once upon a time, it had probably been a very pleasant place to sit and enjoy the sun, or lounge outside on a warm summer night, but those days were no more.

Inside, the house looked much more orderly, but that must be because Amber had clearly been careful about closing the door behind her as she left. No animals had ventured in here, and while a thick layer of dust lay over everything, he could still see the grand scale of the living room where they now stood, the high coffered ceilings, the enormous crystal chandelier that hung in the middle of the space.

"This was your home?" he asked, somewhat shocked by its grandeur. No wonder she had been so at home in the Huntington, seemingly unfazed by the rare and priceless art and furniture and books it contained. This house had been built on a smaller scale, true, and yet he still understood that only people who possessed very great wealth could have lived here.

"Yes," she said carelessly. "My parents bought it when my mother got pregnant with me. I lived here my whole life." Before he could say anything else, she added, "And yeah, we were rich. Like, *really* rich. The funny thing is, a lot of people thought the money came from my father, because he was this lawyer who charged a thousand dollars an hour. But the real money was from my mother's family. My great-grandfather bought a bunch of land in Southern California back in the 1920s and '30s when it was cheap, then sold bits and pieces of it here and there when the time was right."

Personal wealth was something the djinn had no great concept of, mostly because they all had the ability to build their own palaces in the other-world as they liked. There were no rich djinn or poor djinn, for they neither lacked for anything nor saw the need to hoard their belongings. Money did not exist.

But Idris could see how someone might be able to amass a large personal fortune by acquiring land and selling it at judicious times, for property in desirable areas could command a great deal of money. Perhaps a mortal might have found the question rude, but curiosity prompted him to ask, "What do you mean by 'real money'?"

Amber didn't appear offended. In fact, she

grinned at him, sky-blue eyes dancing with amusement. "I'm not totally sure. I didn't keep track of that stuff. But I think it was around a half billion, maybe a little more."

A very great amount, indeed. No wonder she had grown up in such a house, in such a wealthy area. Her family could have gotten her anything she wanted.

She went on, smile fading, "In the end, it didn't matter much, though, did it? All the money in the world couldn't save my family from the disease you djinn created."

No, it couldn't. The only thing that had protected Amber—and other immune mortals like her—was a certain genetic mutation which kept the disease from taking hold in her fragile human flesh. That mutation was not hereditary, but only a trick of birth, which was why the Heat's survivors were left orphaned, had no family to help guide them through such a terribly altered world.

"I am sorry," he murmured, and she shook her head.

"We've been over this, Idris," she said, her tone just slightly too brittle. "Anyway, I need to go upstairs."

She took him away from the living room and through a grand foyer two stories high, with marble floors and another crystal chandelier dangling from the ceiling. Then up the gracefully curved staircase with its intricate wrought metal balustrade, and down a hallway lined with art, both landscapes and abstracts, the mix of styles and colors and patterns somehow managing to work gracefully together.

At length, they came to an oversized, airy bedroom with its walls painted a soft peach, and a large bed covered in white placed up against one wall. Here, too, was a layer of dust over everything, but Idris could still see how this would have been a comfortable, soothing place to rest or simply relax, whether on the cushioned seat next to the bay window that overlooked the yard, or on one of the armchairs placed in front of the pretty little fireplace with its delicate plaster mantel.

Amber did not seem to pay much attention to her surroundings, except possibly to let out a faint, disgusted huff of breath at the dust she saw. Instead, she went over to a door on the other side of the room and opened it, revealing a large walk-in closet. Her hand reached for the light switch—probably by instinct—and he immediately channeled some of his power into the house's wiring.

The miniature chandelier mounted to the closet's ceiling came on, and she chuckled. "You did that, didn't you?"

"Yes," he replied. "I guessed it would not be easy for you to find what you were looking for if it remained dark in there."

"True."

He heard her rummaging around inside the closet and came over to stand by the doorway so he could see what she was doing. She'd pulled down a large bag of some heavy brown vinyl-like material with gold stampings all over—some kind of initials, he thought, something that resembled an elaborate "LV." Into that bag she was placing various items of clothing, her fingers tracing their way along the crowded racks until they would pause on something that caught her eye. Then it would be taken off its hanger, folded carefully, and put into the bag.

The number of items she was choosing, in fact, was vaguely alarming. Idris found himself compelled to say, "The closet I gave you is not very large."

"I know," she replied. "But you can make it bigger if these don't fit, right?"

"Yes," he said, even though he had to wonder why she thought so many items of clothing would be necessary. After all, what he had provided for her would do for nearly a week's worth of wear.

But now he had seen the house where Amber had grown to adulthood, he could guess that she was capable of being quite particular in her wardrobe. Having been deprived of these things for two years, she probably was reaching out for the pieces that gave her the most joy. And really, she was right—he could expand her closet as much as she liked, or provide furniture to store those items that didn't need to be hung up.

In fact, she was now pulling lacy bits of nothing out of a cabinet on the far side of the closet, and Idris found himself looking away, strangely embarrassed at the sight of something so personal, so intimate. He had only caught a glimpse of those pieces, and yet he thought they must have been what humans had called lingerie, far fancier than the utilitarian undergarments he'd provided for her.

Why she was packing those as well, he didn't know for sure. Perhaps wearing them brought her some kind of happiness.

Surely…surely she couldn't be expecting *him* to see her in them.

This time, a flush touched his cheeks, and he made himself step away from the door and go over to the window so he might look down at the backyard below them. Now he saw that the grounds were more extensive than he'd thought, and included a tennis court on the other side of the ivy-covered colonnade that surrounded the pool. The clay surface of the court was partially obscured by dead leaves, the lines painted there almost washed away by two years' worth of rain.

He found he did not like gazing at such things. Yes, this house was the work of man, and the djinn were doing their best to methodically remove such places except for the ones they had taken as their own homes…and yet he couldn't quite hold back the melancholy that moved through him as he gazed upon the slow destruction of what had once been a grand and beautiful house, a place where people had lived and laughed and made love, watched their daughter grow to become a beautiful young woman. While it wasn't possible to change what had happened to the world, he wanted to make sure that the new one the djinn were building was a worthy successor to what it had once been.

"I think that's it," Amber said from behind him, and he turned to see her holding the now-bulging bag with both hands, as if it was too heavy to be entrusted to the grip of one set of slender fingers. "Will you be able to fly with me holding this thing?"

Of course, he could, but he had a more efficient means of travel in mind. "Yes," he said, then went over to her and took the bag from her hand. "I will need you to put your arms around my waist."

Now it was her turn to flush somewhat, but she didn't argue, only moved closer and circled his midsection with her arms. This way, she was pressed up against him, her breasts pushing into the bare flesh his robe left exposed.

The wave of desire that passed over him was almost shocking in its intensity. He forced in a breath and made himself think of their destination and not about Amber's delicious proximity, or of the long waves of her hair brushing against his hands, his chest.

An eye blink lasted longer than the amount of time required to bring them to her temporary home. They stood in the center of the living area, and at once she stepped away from him and took the heavy bag from his fingers.

"Well, that was...interesting," she said, not quite looking him in the eye. "I'll just go put this down by the closet."

Idris didn't try to prevent her from heading off to the sleeping quarters. Indeed, he was glad that she had gone, glad he had a chance to catch his breath. He had not expected to react to her in such a way and needed time to recapture his equilibrium. Perhaps it was only that quite some time had passed since his last liaison, and his body was trying to tell him it had certain needs that should be met.

Or maybe, he thought as Amber reemerged from her bedroom, tucking a long lock of wavy flaxen hair back behind her ear with nervous fingers, *maybe it was more that I recognized something I would rather ignore.*

And, if the way she was rather studiously avoiding his gaze was any indication, it seemed she had felt something as well.

Because he knew he needed to defuse the situation, he said quickly, "I'll leave you to put your things away. If it turns out that you require more space, come up to the house and let me know."

"I will," Amber replied, looking subdued. "Thanks, Idris."

"It is nothing," he said, then gave her a nod and made himself walk away.

The problem was, he knew it wasn't nothing.

Whatever had begun to grow between them, it was very much something.

SEVEN

THERE HADN'T BEEN THIS MANY HANGERS IN THE closet when Amber got out the clothes she wore today, but that was all right. Idris must have quietly magicked them into existence for her, or whatever it was that djinn did to manipulate time and space and matter to bend the universe to their whims. By the time she was done hanging up everything she'd brought back from her house, the little closet here was hopelessly crammed, but everything managed to fit…sort of. She really did need to ask him to expand the space to accommodate her wardrobe, and yet she found herself reluctant to go up to the big house and ask him for that particular favor.

It had felt good to put her arms around him, to have her cheek pressed into the warm bare skin of his chest. Way too good. Once again, she'd felt her body flush with heat, with need. And that was just stupid, because he was a djinn. Or rather, while she knew some djinn had no problem being with humans, she doubted Idris fell into that category. He was an elder, someone who could probably have his pick of any djinn woman he wanted. Why would he want her?

Once upon a time, such a thought would never have even entered her head. Maybe she couldn't have exactly snapped her fingers and gotten whatever man she wanted, but she'd definitely never lacked for guys sniffing around, even when she was obviously attached. Neither had she been the sentimental sort, the kind of girl who thought relationships were all unicorns and rainbows and pastel-hued sunset walks on the beach. One guy—Cassidy?—had been so besotted with her, he announced he'd kill himself if he couldn't have her, to which ultimatum she'd replied acidly that he was probably suicidal over the thought of not having access to her money, rather than because he thought she was so wonderful. He'd stormed off in a huff, and that had been the last of that particular melodrama, but still, Amber knew she was not the type to get all swoony and light-headed over a man no matter how handsome he was.

Or kind, or intelligent, or strangely gentle despite all the insane powers he appeared to wield.

"Well, crap," she said aloud. There really

wasn't any point to enumerating all of Idris's many sterling qualities, since this was only a temporary arrangement. He was humoring her because he thought she'd suffered a shock and needed time to come to grips with this strange new world she'd found herself in, but sooner or later, he would have to pack her off to Los Alamos so he could get on with his peaceful eternity here without having a pesky mortal underfoot.

Maybe it would be better if she just went to him now and told him he might as well send her to Los Alamos today. That notion didn't appeal to her at all, but it might be a better solution to her current conundrum than loitering here until he told her to get out.

Or until he figures out you're getting all moony over him, she thought as she went into the bathroom to finger-comb her hair and apply a fresh coat of pale pink lip gloss. *Because that would be super-awkward.*

Yes, it would. Because this was Idris she was dealing with, Amber guessed he wouldn't make fun of her or show his distaste for the very idea that a mortal might want to drag him to bed and do all sorts of deliciously unspeakable things to him, but even so, she didn't want to be rejected… or, worse, pitied.

But God, Los Alamos. She had the vaguest idea that back during World War II they'd built the atomic bomb there or something, but that was the limit of her knowledge when it came to that particular New Mexican town. Obviously, there couldn't be much to recommend it, or she and her mother might have made a day trip to visit there, like the one they had taken up to Taos one of the times they'd come to Santa Fe for the opera. Taos had been even smaller and pokier and duller than Santa Fe, and an afternoon of exploring its museums and the dinky little plaza had been more than enough for her.

But clearly, Los Alamos had to be completely unremarkable. The thought of spending the rest of her days there was unappetizing, to say the least, but Amber knew she didn't have a lot of options. Where else could she go? No djinn had chosen her —which she still found vaguely insulting—and so that meant there was only one place she could logically end up.

Well, she really did need to ask Idris to expand her closet, even if she wasn't going to be hanging around here for very long. Deep down, she knew she didn't have the guts to ask him to take her to Los Alamos, at least not today.

Although she'd held it together around him, that visit to her former home had shaken her more than she'd realized at first. Sure, she'd known it was going to look dusty and neglected, but what freaked her out more than that was actually how unchanged it had been. No one had tried to break in during all that time; no animals had made it their home. It was as if the place had been frozen in time, quietly gathering dust, for the past two years, just as all the other houses around it had been untouched as well. Seeing its current condition, realizing no one else had set foot in her home since the day she'd fled it two years earlier, made her understand just how empty the world really was. Maybe somewhere in the back of her mind, she'd thought there had to be other people around—and her house would have made a tempting crash pad for anyone who didn't realize there was danger living in the open—but now she knew for sure that there really were very few people left.

Idris hadn't said how many djinn and their human companions lived here in Southern California, but Amber guessed it couldn't be that many, not when there were only a thousand of those "conscientious objector" djinn altogether scattered across the world. Even when you factored in the other nineteen thousand djinn, that wasn't so many more than had lived in her little town of San Marino. Except those people weren't confined to an area of less than four square miles, but were apparently spread across the globe.

She went outside, glad that at least it was a sunny day. Right then, she didn't think she could handle gloomy, overcast skies or chilly temperatures. That was one of the nice things about Southern California—October tended to be a warm, pleasant month, as long as you didn't have any of the hot, dry Santa Ana winds to contend with. But they didn't seem as prevalent as they once were, as if the climate conditions that had once caused them had shifted somehow...or maybe because the djinn liked to fiddle with the weather to keep it as comfortable as possible.

There was no need for her to go all the way to the house in search of Idris, because she spotted him as she made her way along the path. He stood in the rose garden, arms crossed as he surveyed his surroundings with a faint frown tugging at his brows.

"What's the matter?" she asked as she approached, hoping that whatever troubled him, it was something fairly minor.

"These roses are very overgrown," he replied, his tone so disapproving, it was as though he thought their current condition was the roses' fault.

Amber smiled. "Well, that's what happens when they don't get tended for two years."

"We should prune them."

"We"? she thought, but only said, "Can't you just wave your hand and make them look the way you want them to? I mean, that's what you did to the lawn up by the house, right?"

He nodded, but his expression still appeared distractedly disapproving. "Yes, but roses seem as if they require more individual care than that."

Which was probably true. Amber hadn't paid that much heed to exactly what the gardeners did to make her mother's roses look so flawless, but she had a feeling it took a lot of work. There was something to be said for giving each rosebush particular attention, although she didn't really know what form that attention should take.

But she did know one thing. "You can't prune them right now, anyway," she pointed out.

"Why not? No one's touched them for two years."

Obviously, while Idris seemed to know far more than he should have about this world and the people and animals and plants in it, he wasn't infallible. "Wrong time of year," she said. "Our gardeners would always prune the roses in late January or early February. You want to do it while they're still semi-dormant…or at least, that's what I always heard."

"You know this much about gardening?" he asked, surprise clear in his face.

"I don't know a lot," Amber replied quickly. She didn't want him to think she was some sort of expert, because that was definitely not true. "I just remember that was when our rosebushes always got cut back. I asked my mother once about it when I was in junior high, because I always hated how stubby the plants would look until they started to sprout again. She told me that you should prune when they're not growing much, because otherwise it confuses them. So to speak."

Idris nodded, and some of the tension that had knotted itself at the back of Amber's neck ever since she'd realized what an effect he was having on her started to dissipate. Maybe he was doing his best to make sure they had something completely innocuous to discuss, but she wasn't about to look a gift horse in the mouth. For all she knew, he'd picked up on some of her vibes and had decided he needed to do something to defuse the situation.

"The same with a lot of the trees, I think," she went on, glad of the excuse to gaze around the grounds, as if trying to identify all the possible projects he had in mind. "You want to cut them back before the sap starts running."

"Thank you for the advice," he replied as he also gave their surroundings a quick look-over, apparently cataloguing all the work that needed to be done. If he really planned to do it all himself, then he would have enough to keep him busy for a very long time, djinn powers or not. When he looked back down at her, he appeared noticeably more relaxed. "Was there something you needed?"

"Oh, just that extra closet space we talked about earlier," Amber said. Even as she spoke, she tensed a little, wondering if he would take her to task for retrieving so many items she really didn't need. To tell the truth, she wasn't even sure whether some of them would fit. It was more that she'd wanted something familiar around her; the same motivation had prompted her to take the photo of herself and her mother and her grandmother that had been sitting on top of her dresser and stow it in her bag. Honestly, she didn't know whether Idris had even noticed, since he'd been gazing out the window at the time.

"That is no problem," he said. "Consider it done."

And it probably already was done. She still didn't understand how his powers worked, but she knew he didn't need to be physically present to make something as simple as her closet expansion happen. "Thanks," she said, then turned, planning to head back to the house.

His voice stopped her, however. "Dinner tonight in the tea room? It is a little more casual in there, I think."

"Sure," she replied, glad she sounded so steady, so casual. So he wasn't going to tell her to eat alone in the Japanese house, or try to think of some other way to keep a careful distance between them. She didn't know exactly what that meant, but a quiet sort of relief spread through her. This attraction she'd been experiencing was worrisome, true, but she'd rather deal with trying to hide it than have to eat alone. She'd already done that hundreds more times than she'd ever wanted to. "A little after dusk?"

"I will see you then."

She waved at him and headed back to her modest little house, probably happier than she should be. Whatever else happened, at least he wasn't trying to avoid her.

———

Dinner passed without incident, and Idris was glad of that. Possibly, it was the less formal surroundings of the tea room, or the inspiration he'd had to conjure a meal of Chinese food, which didn't require a wine accompaniment, but either way, Amber seemed to understand that the conversation should be casual. She didn't speak of her family or the visit to her house, but only thanked him for adding some extra space to her closet, then spoke more of what they might do to the gardens, which plants could be cultivated during Southern California's mild winter and which ones should be cut back. Actually, he was rather surprised by her knowledge, for all her demurral that she really didn't know very much. He supposed he could have learned these things from books or from personal observation as time passed in the gardens, but her insights would save him both time and effort.

"Was the climate so different where you came

from?" she asked as she carefully dunked a wonton into a dish of sweet and sour sauce.

"I don't know that you could really call it a 'climate,'" Idris told her. "Where we lived…it was not like this world. In fact, we called it the 'other-world,' for it was so very different from the place we had been promised."

"That was where you had to go after you couldn't live here anymore?"

He nodded.

Her delicate brows drew together, and her expression was thoughtful as she ate the wonton she'd just dipped in its sauce. "What did you djinn do to get banished from here in the first place?"

Good question, and one that his people had been wrestling with for millennia. Because they had been disobedient was the most facile answer. God had given His favor to man, once he had evolved to a point where he was capable of rational thought, and He had wanted the djinn, who had been here first, to be men's servants. Unlike the angels, who followed God's will in everything, the djinn rebelled and had been exiled to the otherworld.

Idris shrugged, breaking an egg roll in two. "We were disobedient. God wished man to be foremost, even though we djinn were here first. We would not be men's servants."

This answer had seemed simple enough to

him, but Amber's frown only deepened. "You keep talking about God. Do you really mean, like...*God*, God?"

Sometimes Idris had been surprised by humanity's unwillingness to recognize the force that had made their world—indeed, this entire universe—possible in the first place. But then, he had been alive long enough to see this world be shaped into its current form, to see humankind evolve from simple hunter-gatherers to the technologically evolved beings who had come so close to destroying the planet that was their only home. He had seen God's hand at work, but for all those who had been alive when the Heat came along, their deity by then had retreated to a distant entity at best, a being held on to through sheer belief and not any personal experience.

"Yes, I do," Idris said. "I know that must surprise you, but although He has been absent from this world for a very long time, He existed then and must still exist now. It was His decree that your race would have sovereignty over this world."

"And you were sent to the otherworld."

Idris could feel his expression cloud, but he tried to sound neutral as he replied, "Yes. It is... outside this world entirely."

Amber's fingers tapped against the side of her water glass. "Like another planet?"

"Not precisely. More like...another dimension,

one that exists beside this one, but of a different vibration. It was a place where humans could never travel, for djinn magic is required to get there. In fact, humans cannot live there for very long, since the air is different. We did not enjoy it much, but at least we were able to survive in that place."

"I'm sorry," she said, and she actually did look genuinely sorry for him and for his kind, for what they had suffered. In fact, in that moment she looked so lovely, clear blue eyes wide and wondering, pretty mouth pursed slightly, that he found himself wishing he could reach out and touch her hand, wrap his fingers around hers.

Pull her close and kiss her, and taste sweet and sour sauce on those lovely lips.

He straightened, and made himself reach for his own water glass so he could take a sip. The liquid trickled down his throat, cool and refreshing. It helped to clear his head a bit. "There is no need for you to be sorry," he said. "It is a hardship we endured, but certainly it was none of your doing. And besides, I am sure that those of your kind who have survived would say it was nothing more than we deserved, considering what we did to your people."

Her back stiffened, and she looked away from him and fussed with the napkin in her lap. "Maybe," she allowed. "Although if there are a bunch of humans living with djinn now, obviously they've learned to forgive and forget."

"Some of them," Idris said. "Others...." And he let the word trail off, because he realized he was about to say things to her that perhaps would be better left unspoken.

He should have known she would not let it go. On the surface, Amber might look as fragile and beautiful as a piece of spun glass, but she was far, far stronger than she appeared. Voice sharpening a little, she said, "Others...what?"

Ah, well. He supposed there was no real reason for her not to know the truth, not when—sooner or later—she would leave this place and go to live among her own kind in Los Alamos. There, she would probably get an earful, for the survivors in New Mexico had suffered perhaps more than any others at the hands of the reaver djinn. Terrible things had been done, cruel acts that had been hidden from him and the other elders.

"We djinn have a power over mortals," Idris said carefully. "A power beyond our control of our particular elements, whether fire or air, earth or water. We can slip into mortals' minds, create a haze where a person's will is not quite their own. We call this the glamour."

For a second or two, Amber only stared back at him without speaking. Was she wondering whether he had used the glamour on her to make her more docile? For of course he hadn't, but neither did she have any true frame of reference for comparison.

After a moment, though, the tightness of her mouth seemed to relax, as if she'd quickly recalled their interactions and realized she couldn't pinpoint any particular instances where he might have done such a thing to her. "So...the djinn used the glamour on their chosen humans if they had to? Like, if the person they chose wasn't quite as happy to be their partners as they should have been?"

Once again, he found himself startled by the quickness of her mind. Very little seemed to escape her. "Yes," he replied. "Not necessarily for nefarious purposes, you understand. Being Chosen was those mortals' only way to survive, and if they had fought back against their protectors, had resisted in any way, then they would have put themselves in danger. It was sometimes better to use the glamour to ease them into their new lives so they would feel comfortable with their protectors."

Although this all seemed sensible enough to him—if not entirely desirable—obviously, Amber didn't see the situation in the same light. Her pretty mouth took on a wry twist, and she tilted her head slightly as she said, "Sort of like the djinn equivalent of a roofie."

"A what?" While he thought himself familiar

with English, certain idioms and slang terms had never entered his vocabulary.

"A drug," she said. "Rohypnol. It was supposed to be some kind of sleep aid or something, but stories used to circulate about how guys would put it in a girl's drink to make it so she wouldn't know or remember what she was doing. That was why you always had to be careful at a bar not to leave your drink unattended, since you ran the risk of some guy trying to roofie you and have sex with you when you didn't want to."

A horrifying story, uttered in an almost too-casual tone, as if Amber was so used to all the machinations men used to go to in order to bend women to their will that she had become hardened to such predations. However, much as he disliked the comparison, Idris could see why she had said the djinn glamour was not terribly unlike this Rohypnol drug.

"Perhaps there are some similarities," he said carefully. "But you must realize that these djinn only used the glamour to protect their Chosen, not to hurt them."

"That sounds like a pretty self-serving argument to me," she retorted. "Maybe those mortals didn't want to be Chosen. Maybe they lost someone to the Heat and didn't want to be forced into another relationship with one of the very people responsible for it."

"The One Thousand were not responsible for that illness," Idris felt compelled to point out.

Her shoulders lifted a fraction. "Right. Okay, even so, being compelled to be with a djinn just because he or she decided you were hot doesn't seem all that fair."

When she put it that way…. He gathered a breath and said, "The djinn were careful in making their selections. All of the Chosen were under the age of twenty-five, and, in almost every case, were not in any significant relationships when the Heat came along. We understood that it would not be fair to expect a mortal to replace a loved one so quickly."

Again, Amber was quiet, her expression now thoughtful. She touched her fork but seemed disinclined to pick it up. When she spoke, she sounded tired. "I suppose you tried to think of everything, didn't you?"

"We did our best," he said. There had still been a trace of condemnation in her tone, but he attempted to ignore it. Yes, there were elements of the djinn/Chosen relationship that would always be problematic, and he couldn't do much to change that, only try to have this new world run as smoothly as it possibly could. Already he'd begun to wonder if he could do more, however, could think of a way to manage the tensions that still bubbled beneath the surface. It would not do to have those tensions erupt.

"I'm sure you did." Now she looked sad, and Idris wondered if she was thinking about how no one had selected her. He still couldn't quite understand such an omission, because he knew if he had taken a mortal as his Chosen—not that he had ever considered such an option—then she was just the sort of woman he would have been drawn to.

But then again, perhaps not. He thought these past few years of privation might have changed her, quite possibly could have taken the privileged, protected girl she had once been and turned her into the person she was now. Perhaps the djinn of the One Thousand had considered her, attracted by her beauty, then decided she was not for them, that they did not want a spoiled young woman as their partner for eternity. It was really impossible to say, and he supposed at this point, it didn't matter so much. She was here now, alone, and while he knew what the only possible outcome of this odd little interlude could be, he found he didn't want to dwell on it.

For now, he would be with her and be her friend. Anything else...anything else was dangerous.

EIGHT

DESPITE THE ODD TENSIONS THAT CROPPED UP between her and Idris from time to time, Amber thought she'd never before had a period in her life that had been so oddly tranquil, so full of quiet moments which made her happy without her really understanding why. Back in the time before, she'd lived her life at a frenetic pace, buoyed up by her family's money, going from party to party, gallery opening to gallery opening, movie premiere to movie premiere...whatever sounded interesting and fun, whatever would catch her interest for a few hours before the next shiny thing beckoned. She shopped and went to yoga and Pilates and had lunch with friends and dinner with whichever man she was seeing at the time, but none of it had really seemed to touch her.

Now...now everything was different.

The days drifted by, one after the other. She

realized one morning with something of a start that she had been living in the little Japanese house with its lovely gardens for almost two weeks now. Honestly, she hadn't paid much attention to time passing, mostly because she was occupied with the novelty of her life here at the Huntington, of having a companion who never asked anything of her except that she share some of her time with him. And indulging him was not really much of an effort, because the two of them always seemed to find something to occupy themselves, whether that was walking through the gardens and making note of which plants to trim and which plants to cull altogether—easy enough to do, since Idris could basically wave a hand and make a dying lily plant disappear into thin air, only to be replaced by a new, healthy specimen—or wandering the galleries and looking at the art, with Amber doing her best to parrot some of the factoids she'd heard the tour guides or her mother say about the various pieces in the collection.

And then there had been the day when he surprised her by showing up on her doorstep with a couple of easels and paintboxes and suggesting that they try *plein air* painting. She'd seen people painting those impromptu landscapes at the Huntington in the past, but she'd certainly never been tempted to try. Why make the attempt, only to prove how bad you were at something?

"I don't have an artistic bone in my body,

Idris," she protested, whereupon he'd only given her one of his wry, yet gentle smiles and told her it was worth trying.

"For neither am I an artist," he said, "but it seems like the sort of diversion that might serve to while away a few hours. And the light is very fine today."

Which it was. A warm offshore wind had been blowing through the museum's grounds, not strong enough to be called a Santa Ana, but definitely not the moist sea breeze that brought ocean fog and clouds and cooler temperatures to the area. The whole place felt as if it had been traced with the faintest layer of burnished gold, and it hadn't required much coaxing for her to follow Idris to a nice level spot on the lawn in the Japanese garden and do her best to re-create the gracefully drooping willow that grew next to the pond there, or the exaggerated arch of the moon bridge that spanned its waters.

"You have a very good eye," he told her as he got up from where he'd been sitting on a stool he'd conjured, then walked over to inspect her painting. "I think you must not have been telling me the complete truth about your artistic ability."

"Seriously, I've never done anything like this before," she protested, even though she was inwardly pleased at his praise—possibly a little too pleased.

He stood a few feet behind her, arms crossed

as he examined her work. "Well, I wouldn't have known that if you hadn't told me."

"I want to see yours," she said with a grin as she set down her brush on the easel's tray.

Idris shook his head, looking resigned. "I fear it is not nearly as good as yours."

When she went over to look at his work, she realized he'd only been telling the truth. He might have been able to command all sorts of supernatural powers, but he couldn't seem to get paint on canvas in a way that didn't look like something a second-grader might have done, the colors muddy, the planes and angles not quite right.

She looked up at him, not quite sure what she should say, and he shrugged.

"Djinn have never been known for their artistic ability."

"Why is that?" she asked, a little startled by this confession. "You'd think you would have plenty of time to practice."

"True," he responded. He didn't look particularly upset by this obvious shortcoming, but instead almost resigned, as though he'd wrestled with this particular conundrum before. "However, there is more to art than mere practice. Some have said that artistic striving in humankind is due to their need to reach out to the ineffable, to make something that will last long after they are gone. We djinn do not have that compulsion, for we know we will always be here. We know what it is to look on God."

What was she supposed to say to that? Never before in her life had she had felt any need to pause and reflect on what it was that made people express themselves through art and music and dance, but in a way, she thought she understood what Idris was telling her. Still, it seemed odd and a little sad to contemplate living such long lives without any art or music to serve as a distraction. She said as much to him, and he shook his head.

"We have music—the sort of thing that might be played in the background while we consume our meals, or tunes that can be danced to. But there is nothing like a symphony or a quartet, music that was only meant to be listened to and appreciated on its own merits." His gaze moved from his clumsy painting to the scene he'd been attempting to portray on the canvas. "The same for art, I suppose. We can build fine palaces to live in because we all need shelter, but we most often collect items made by human hands to decorate the interior of those palaces."

Well, at least the djinn could appreciate art, even if they seemed to be lacking a certain essence of creativity necessary for making those pieces in the first place. Amber found she didn't like using the word "lack" to describe someone like Idris, because as far as she was concerned, he was just about perfect. So what if he couldn't paint his way out of a paper bag? She doubted whether any of the guys she'd dated could have managed such a feat, either, but they also hadn't been what you could call kind or thoughtful or even all that smart, to be perfectly honest. They'd all been good-looking and charming on the surface, and most of them had come from the "right" families, or at least had careers that put them in the same orbit as someone like her.

Actually, now that she thought about it, she realized those men had mostly been a prize collection of assholes. Tyler was probably the worst, just because he'd turned out to be so bad at covering up what a cheating jerk he was, but none of them had been anyone she could imagine herself spending the rest of her life with. Which had been fine at the time; she hadn't even been twenty-three when the world changed forever, and back then she'd thought she had plenty of time.

Funny how it had taken the apocalypse to finally meet a decent guy. The irony of him being a djinn wasn't lost on her, either, although probably the saddest thing about her current situation was his complete obliviousness to the attraction she was finding harder and harder to ignore. There hadn't been any reason for him to transport her djinn-style, so the last time they'd had any physical contact was the day he'd taken her to her former home to get some of her things. You'd think that lack of contact might have made things easier, but she found herself craving his touch, mentally going over the memory of his arms around her waist, of the way it had felt to press up against him. Time and time again, she tried to tell herself that she needed to let it go, that it was obvious he wasn't interested in her. Otherwise, why wouldn't he have tried to make some kind of a move? They were alone here together, so it wasn't as if they had to worry about any of the other djinn snooping on what they were doing, or making their disapproval of such a relationship obvious.

Because she was pretty sure none of them would approve of one of their fellow elders shacking up with a mortal. Idris hadn't ever said anything like that out loud to her, but that was probably because the notion of something happening between the two of them had never even entered his head. Why would it?

He was looking at her now, obviously expecting her to make some kind of reply to his last statement. She managed to smile and say, "Well, you've definitely picked the right place to live if what you djinn like is surrounding your-selves with art made by mortals. There's enough here to keep you occupied for centuries."

"True." However, she noticed he wasn't looking toward the mansion that housed such a priceless collection, or even the former carriage house that had been turned into a gallery and contained works by nineteenth- and twentieth-century artists such as Mary Cassatt and John Singer Sargent. No, Idris was staring at the painting she'd done, very loose and impressionist in style, but still with a recognizable weeping willow and moon bridge.

A sudden impulse struck her, and she said, "Do you want it? My painting, I mean. There really isn't any place for me to put it in the Japanese house anyway."

At once, his expression lightened. "I would like that very much."

She went over to the easel and picked up the canvas, carefully holding it by the edges because she knew the paint must still be, if not wet, then at least tacky and not all the way set up yet. "Here you go," she said, offering it to him.

He took the small rectangle and gazed down at it for a moment. Then he looked up, his dark eyes catching hers. "Thank you, Amber."

What was it about the sound of her name in his warm, deep voice that made delicious shivers want to work their way down her spine? She knew it was stupid to react to him like this, but for the first time in her life, she realized she wasn't entirely in control of her emotions, that she couldn't simply tell herself how to feel about a person.

And of course she had to be feeling that way

about someone who could never return those feelings.

You should really go, she told herself then, as Idris stood there and looked down at the simple little painting she'd given him. *Let him know that you're ready to go to Los Alamos, then get the hell out of here before you make a complete fool of yourself.*

That seemed like a very practical plan. Too bad she didn't want to go to Los Alamos, didn't want to leave Idris. How in the world would she ever find another person like him?

The obvious answer to that question appeared to be that she wouldn't. Oh, maybe she'd meet a halfway decent guy in New Mexico…although she had her doubts…but he wouldn't be Idris. He wouldn't be insanely handsome and he wouldn't be so quietly, wonderfully charming. He probably wouldn't want to take long walks with her and be fine with remaining quiet just so he could absorb the beauty of a sunset, and she knew he sure as hell wouldn't be able to summon a perfect Cordon Bleu meal with just a snap of his fingers.

In short, he wouldn't be Idris, a djinn elder. There was no way some bumpkin from Los Alamos could ever begin to compete with the only man she'd ever actually fallen in love with.

That thought made her cold, even though the day was warm, one of those lovely, mild October afternoons in Southern California that made you think winter would never come, that you would always get to enjoy these perfect jewels of days for the foreseeable future. She knew better, though, remembered all too well how cold she'd been when the rains of January and February lashed the building where she'd hidden. True, she'd had sleeping bags to huddle in, and extra blankets she'd pilfered from empty houses in the area, but she still had never felt warm.

"Are you all right?" Idris asked then, clearly noticing the length of time that had passed without Amber responding. "If you want to keep the picture—"

"No," she cut in. "I really do want you to have it."

Something to remember me by, she thought. *You can hang it next to one of the Gainsboroughs and have a good laugh every time you look at it.*

"Very well." His dark eyes scanned her face, and she did her best to look open and guileless, as if nothing more important was going on in her head than possibly worry over whether he would want to continue with their painting session. "Would you like to go inside for a while? Perhaps the sun is getting too warm—you look flushed."

Great. So much for hiding what she'd been thinking. Amber managed to keep her hands at her sides, even though she had an impulse to lift them in an attempt to conceal the blood that rushed to her cheeks. Her blush had absolutely nothing to do with the sun, even though it was very bright. But better Idris think that than begin to realize what actually had been going through her head.

A wave of his hand, and the easels and paint-boxes were gone—along with his own failed attempt at a landscape, although he still held the canvas she'd given him. By unspoken agreement, they both headed toward the house. When they weren't walking the grounds, they often ended up there, reading and lounging in the library, or sharing a meal in the dining room if they didn't want to eat in the cozier confines of the tea room.

Now it was the middle of the afternoon, past lunch but far too early for dinner. Sometimes they had a snack that could be called tea, for lack of a better term, but usually only on the days when they'd spent a lot of time walking around the gardens and working on the plants and garden beds. Painting a landscape really didn't seem strenuous enough to call for another meal, so Amber doubted Idris had anything like that planned.

Idris set the painting down on a side table, then made a couple of glasses of water appear from thin air and handed one to her. Since she was thirsty, she took it gratefully, once again a little surprised by how easily he was able to antic-ipate her needs.

"Some reading this afternoon?" he asked, and she nodded.

"Sure. It would probably be a good idea to sit down for a while." Also, if they were both reading, then she wouldn't have to stumble along in conversation with him, trying to ignore the urge to reach out and take him by the hands, pull him closer to her. Besides, reading books filled with other people's problems could only help her avoid dealing with her own issues. Sooner or later, she would have to work up the courage to ask him to send her to Los Alamos, but she wanted to put off that evil day for now, despite what had been going through her mind just a few minutes earlier. Right then, she just felt tired, with no good reason for why she should be experiencing such weariness.

Except, of course, that it was exhausting having to hide her feelings from him. In that moment, she could only be glad that the djinn, for all their powers, didn't appear to be mind readers, weren't always accurate when it came to deciphering human emotions and reactions. Idris seemed to have sensed something was going on with her, but so far he didn't seem to have any idea what it was.

She needed to get out of here before he figured it out.

In silence, they walked down the hall to the library, just as they had many times before. When they entered the room, however, Amber stopped dead, barely holding in a gasp, even as Idris went still and wary beside her.

Standing by the fireplace were a man and a woman—a djinn man and woman, Amber realized almost at once. The man was tall and handsome in an angular way, and had black hair with streaks of silver at his temples, and the woman was movie-star gorgeous, with coppery red hair that fell in shining waves all the way to her waist. Their gazes fixed on Amber for a moment, cool and appraising, and then shifted to Idris, who still hadn't moved, who might have been one of the marble statues that dotted the Huntington's grounds.

The strange djinn man stepped forward. Black eyes fixed on Idris, he said, "It looks as though we have a few things we need to discuss."

NINE

IDRIS HAD KNOWN THIS DAY MIGHT COME, AND YET the shock of seeing his fellow elders standing there in the library was so great that for a moment, he hardly dared to breathe. Next to him, Amber stood unmoving, although he could immediately detect the tension in her slender form, a wariness that reminded him of a doe about to take flight the second something startled her.

And, judging by the faintest flicker of a frown that crossed Ibram's face before he spoke, Idris guessed that the other djinn was not pleased to see the kind of company he had been keeping.

Despite that subtle warning, Idris said, his voice steady, "Well met, Ibram, and to you as well, Istar."

She stepped forward to stand next to her partner, expression pleasant enough—which was often her way. Istar always had been very good at only letting a person see what she wanted them to see. "And who is your guest, Idris?"

There was no point in dissembling, and so he replied, "This is Amber McCoy. She has spent the past few years here."

"In hiding?" Ibram asked.

To Idris's surprise, Amber spoke up then. Possibly she hadn't liked the way the djinn elders had spoken as if she was not even there, because she said, "Yes, I was hiding all that time. It was the only way for me to survive."

"Very resourceful," Ibram said, in tones that seemed to indicate he was not particularly impressed by her resourcefulness. Gaze moving back to Idris, the elder went on, "We would have a word with you, Idris. In private," he added, just so there was no way Amber could possibly misconstrue the request.

Before Idris could say anything, she replied, "No problem. I'll go down to my house." She glanced up at him, eyes bright and curious beneath her thick lashes. "Come by when you can."

And then she left, bright hair swinging as she turned to make her way back down the corridor.

"Shut the door," Ibram said.

Idris did not like being ordered about at the

best of times, and now there was a condemnation in the other elder's voice that told him the conversation which was about to ensue would not be a pleasant one. An edge to his tone, he said, "You needn't worry about Amber trying to listen to us. She is too honorable a person to act in such a manner. You can trust that she is already well on her way back to the place where she has been staying."

"I am sure she is admirable in all ways," Ibram responded, his tone so bland, it became its own condemnation. "And yet, it is better not to take the risk."

Annoyed, Idris lifted a hand and made the door close—with far more of a bang than was strictly necessary.

"You are angry with us," Istar said. She did not seem particularly troubled by this notion, although in general, she tended to act as the peacemaker whenever a dispute arose between her fellow elders.

"'Angry' is too harsh a word," Idris told her, although it wasn't that far off from the truth. Angry...and worried. "Anyway, to what do I owe this visit of yours?"

Her green eyes widened. "Why, only to see how you have been faring. It has been several weeks since you left us to make your home here, and since we hadn't heard anything, we thought it best to come by and see if you were doing well."

"And now we know exactly why you had no wish to speak with us," Ibram said, crossing his arms. His mouth still looked set and angry, making it clear that he was less than happy at what he had discovered here at the Huntington, no matter how conciliatory his partner might have sounded. "You were hiding this mortal, hoping you would not be caught."

This pronouncement was close enough to the truth that Idris knew he could not credibly dispute it. Instead, he spread his hands wide and lifted his shoulders. "I would not call it 'hiding,' precisely, since we often walked these grounds in plain sight of anyone who might have observed us."

Now Istar laughed, even as she raised an eyebrow at him. "Oh, do not be disingenuous, Idris. Who would have come here to observe you? The other djinn know better than to intrude on the home of one of their elders unless the matter is grave, and all is at peace now. They would have no reason to come anywhere near here."

Well, that was true enough. While the djinn did call on their elders to mediate disputes and the like, they would probably approach Ibram and Istar first, since they had made sure to let those who looked to them for guidance know where they had taken up their permanent residence here on this world. He, on the other hand, had come here to San Marino much more recently, and it was probable that many of the djinn had no clear idea exactly where he had settled.

"You have a point," he said, "but still I will say that I did nothing to conceal Amber's presence here."

"That is as may be," Ibram countered, now sounding quite testy, "but the point remains that she should not have been here at all. As soon as you discovered her presence, you should have sent her to Los Alamos to live with the other human survivors."

"It is a prospect we have discussed," Idris replied. "And I have no doubt that is where she will end up eventually. However, she spent so many months in hiding that I thought it kinder to allow her some time to remain here and recover from her ordeal. She grew up very close to the Huntington, and so she has had less of a shock adjusting to this changed world because at least she is in familiar surroundings."

"That is kind of you," Istar said. Her tone was so neutral, however, that he wasn't quite sure whether she was being sarcastic or not.

Deciding to take her comment at face value, Idris said, "And she will go to Los Alamos. We have already discussed this. We simply had not yet decided when such a transition would occur."

Arms still crossed, Ibram tapped his fingers

against one elbow. "How long has she been living here with you?"

"She is not 'living with' me," Idris countered. "She has never spent a night under this roof. She is staying in a small house on the grounds some distance from this mansion."

Ibram and Istar shared a glance, although neither of them spoke. By this point in his existence, Idris knew he should have become somewhat accustomed to the way they seemed able to share nonverbal communication, but the sight only increased his annoyance. Whatever they had to say, they could say it aloud to his face.

"That is something," Ibram said after a pause, although the grudging note in his voice was impossible to ignore. "But surely you can see how this situation cannot be allowed to continue indefinitely."

Idris knew that all too well. More and more, he'd been looking forward to his first sight of Amber's face each morning, anticipating hearing the sound of her voice, her laugh. Because he'd made sure he would have no reason to touch her or even get particularly close, he had avoided a repeat of that sudden flare of desire he'd experienced for her, but he knew the need still lurked somewhere deep inside him. He wanted her, wanted to touch her soft skin, kiss her deliciously full mouth.

Wanted her in his bed, in his life.

But it was one thing for a djinn to reach out and select a human as his Chosen. An elder most certainly could not do such a thing. Why, even the liaisons he'd had with djinn women had troubled him on some level, for he had perceived that they could never be his equals in power the way regular djinn males and females were with one another. With a mortal, that power imbalance would be even more severe.

Not for the first time, he wondered at the capriciousness of a God who would create three elders, thus dooming one of them to be eternally alone. There had never been any question as to whom Istar would bond with, and so Idris knew he would always be the odd man out. Yes, he supposed that having an odd number of elders ensured that there would never be a tied decision on something that truly mattered, but he still bridled at the unfairness of the situation.

However, he could say none of this to Istar and Ibram. Their little coalition had lasted for countless millennia because they all knew one another's boundaries. It would serve nothing for him to remark upon their relationship and how it had relegated him to outsider status within their small group. And he also must keep his feelings about Amber to himself, for he was sure that Ibram and Istar would both be horrified that he could harbor such feelings for a mortal.

And, he thought with a grim inward chuckle, *I*

fear that would only make Istar determined to find some djinn woman to take my mind off such an inappropriate match, and the outcome of that kind of awkward arrangement could not be good at all.

"The situation will not continue indefinitely," he said, knowing he sounded tired and irritated, and not much caring one way or another. That in itself surprised him somewhat, since in the past, he had done his best to keep his personal feelings out of any interactions with his fellow elders. "I have already told you this. I will speak with Amber, and we will determine the best time to send her to Los Alamos."

"Best not wait too long," Istar told him, and though her tone was light enough, he could tell from the faint frown which touched her brow that she expected him to heed her words. "For we all know that the weather in northern New Mexico is much harsher than it is here in Southern California, and I think it would be better for her to have at least a little of autumn there before she is forced to deal with winter."

Idris hadn't even considered that aspect of the situation, but he knew Istar was correct. Although he had not spent a great deal of time in that part of the world, he had been there to experience the raw winds of winter, the rough, windy spring that was often nearly as bitter. "I already said I would speak with her. She has known all along that she could not stay here forever."

For the first time during this conversation, Ibram looked almost approving. He came to stand next to his partner, although at least he did Idris the courtesy of not reaching out to touch her. "It is for the best. And while you are working out those details with her, I think Istar and I should investigate this matter more closely. This Amber McCoy is a lovely young woman, and of the right age to have been Chosen. I find it strange that she was not selected by anyone."

Idris had thought much the same thing. However, he knew he couldn't volunteer too much information, for he knew that his fellow elders would not appreciate hearing how he had interfered two years ago to protect Amber from the djinn who had been prepared to kill her. "I am not sure you will find much of anything, but I suppose any anomaly bears looking into."

"Yes, it is strange," Istar agreed. "If we discover any pertinent information, of course we will let you know."

"Thank you," Idris said, although he felt far from grateful right then. "I will be most interested to hear about your findings."

"Until then," Ibram responded, and he and Istar abruptly disappeared—on their way back, no doubt, to their lavish chateau in the Loire Valley.

Idris remained where he was for a moment, then released a breath. He did not much look forward to the coming interview with Amber, but at least once they had determined when she was to go to Los Alamos, they would have a difficult task out of the way.

And perhaps, after she was gone, he would also be free of the inner torment she had caused him.

———

Amber glanced up from her book when a shadow fell across the room. On a warm, bright autumn day like this one, she had left the screens to the house wide open, and so there was nothing to keep her from seeing Idris just as soon as he arrived.

His expression was grim, and her stomach sank. Oh, she'd known what was probably going to happen as soon as she saw those two other djinn standing in the library and realized what their presence meant, but it was one thing to have those possibilities dancing around in your head and quite another thing entirely to see the face of the man you loved, and read in his eyes that he was about to send you away.

She set down the book and looked up at him from the futon where she was sitting. "So, what's the bad news?"

"Why do you assume the news I am here to deliver is bad?"

"Because I can see your face."

He almost smiled then. Or at least, the corners of his mouth lifted slightly, but there was no answering light in his eyes. "We both knew this day would come."

Which was a really oblique way of saying he was going to kick her out. Her heart started to pound, and she blinked away the sudden sting of tears. No, she was not going to let him see her cry. In the past, she'd used tears as a weapon if she thought bringing them to bear might change a situation, but there was nothing fake about the sudden thickness in her throat or the way she had to clench her jaw to push back the gathering moisture in her eyes. Another breath, and she said, "When?"

"That's what I came here to talk to you about." He looked away from her, at the bright afternoon outside. "Perhaps we could take a walk."

Sure, she thought, *take me around and show me everything I'll never get to see again. That'll make this so much better.*

But because the cramped interior of the little wooden house suddenly felt almost as constricting as the pressure in her throat, she nodded. Maybe it would be good to get out. "Okay."

She got up from the futon and went to meet him out on the little platform that served as a front porch. "Which way?"

"The Chinese garden?" he suggested. "We haven't been there for a few days."

"Sure."

They walked in silence for a few minutes. The sun felt good, although it didn't seem to do much to penetrate through to the icy core in the pit of her stomach. As they went, Amber tried to tell herself that she shouldn't be this upset. She'd only known Idris for a few weeks. They'd never even kissed or held hands. He was a friend, nothing more. Yes, it was sad to have to say goodbye to a friend, but she shouldn't be acting as though the love of her life was being torn away from her.

Except he was. She knew she loved him...had fallen in love with him...and it didn't matter one single bit. Because he didn't know she cared, and there was no way she was going to tell him, no way she was going to say a single damn word. The last thing she wanted was for him to feel sorry for her, to shake his head at the stupid little mortal who'd been dumb enough to let herself fall for a djinn elder.

The camellias were still blooming, showing white and pink and red-streaked flowers on the trees. She and Idris had gone through here at the end of the previous week, clearing away the dead blossoms and the fallen branches, tidying up the garden to return it to its original splendor. They'd brought back some of the blossoms, and he'd set them drifting in wide bowls of water with floating candles around them during one of their dinners, making it seem as if they were eating in some kind of enchanted grotto. For someone who claimed not to have any artistic talent, he definitely had an eye for making things beautiful.

They went to the little summer house with its whimsical curved roof and took their seats there. Here in the shade it was cooler, although that could also have been due to the fresh breeze passing over the water that surrounded them on three sides. A pair of mourning doves cooed from a nearby tree, and really, it was an entirely idyllic scene...or at least, it would have been if Amber hadn't known their real reason for being here.

"I don't suppose there's any place like this in Los Alamos," she remarked, and Idris turned sad, dark eyes on her.

"I haven't been there, so I cannot say for certain," he replied. His head lifted into the breeze, as if he was trying to see so many hundreds of miles away and tell her what waited for her at her destination. "But I would suppose not. It was a town built around a research laboratory, and now its residents are very much focused on surviving and thriving in a changed world, which I doubt leaves them much time for frivolities like pretty gardens. I believe they have expanded beyond the town's limits down into the valley below and are doing a good deal of farming."

Farming. Great. She might know a little something about making a garden pretty, but she knew less than nothing about raising crops or animal husbandry. A nightmarish image of being forced to help birth a calf or a lamb or a goat ran through her mind, and she barely held back a shudder.

"How many of them are there?" she asked. "In the Los Alamos community, I mean."

"More than a thousand, I think. Survivors from the northern part of New Mexico have gathered there, and their numbers are growing because of the children."

The children. Right. Normal, ordinary human beings meeting up after the apocalypse and deciding to see if they could continue their race for a few more generations. As far as she could tell, the elders seemed resigned to the situation, which meant the Los Alamos community of survivors should be safe enough.

So she should be safe, too.

Not that she could find much energy within herself to care. At some point, she assumed the shock would wear off and she'd do her best to fit in with the group of survivors. Maybe a day would come that she might even try to have a relationship with one of them...assuming there was anyone even remotely compatible for her. After all, the people in Los Alamos had had two years to get to know one another, create their own connections. It wasn't outside the bounds of possibility that any guys close to her age had long since paired off with any available women, and she'd be left to stay on the fringes forever.

Damn it, those tears were burning her eyes again. Amber swallowed and stared down at her feet. "It won't take me too long to pack my things. I can go tomorrow, if you like."

Since she was studiously staring downward, she couldn't see Idris's face. However, there was a flick of anger in his voice as he said, "I don't 'like' it at all. But this situation was not sustainable, so here we are."

Should she be glad that he sounded upset? Maybe that meant he did care for her, or at least had gotten used to having her around and wasn't looking forward to having to spend his days alone once she was gone. Then again, he was an elder, and absolutely gorgeous into the bargain; she supposed he could basically reach out and get any unattached djinn woman he liked. Unlike her, he probably wouldn't be alone for very long.

"Then it's probably better if I go as soon as I can," she replied, hoping she sounded noble and brave, and not as though her heart was being twisted into knots. "Are you going to tell the people in Los Alamos that I'm coming, or are you just going to drop me on their doorstep?"

"Amber." His tone was gently reproachful, as if she'd offended him by making such a statement. When she didn't respond directly, he said, "Please look at me."

Since she had her tears under control again, she thought it was safe to raise her head so she could meet his gaze. *Just hold it together for now,* she told herself. *Just until we're done with this horrible conversation. Then....*

Then, she would probably cry her eyes out. But silently. She didn't want Idris to know how upset she was.

Apparently, she was doing a good enough job of hiding her emotions that he didn't seem overly troubled as he looked into her face. "We djinn cannot go to Los Alamos directly because of the shields they have in place. However, I thought I would pass on a message to the community of djinn and Chosen in Santa Fe, since they have frequent contact with their neighbors. They would make sure that the people in Los Alamos knew to expect you."

How civilized. In a way, though, it was slightly encouraging to learn that the two communities appeared to work together. Maybe then Los Alamos wouldn't feel so isolated.

"Thanks," she said. "That sounds like a good idea."

He nodded, then went on, his tone a little too cheerful, "Well, now that we have that settled, what would you like for your dinner this evening? I would like it to be special, since it will be the last one we will share."

Right then, the thought of eating anything made her feel vaguely ill, but Amber knew she'd have to do her best to soldier through it as though nothing was wrong, as though she was looking forward to this new phase of her life. "Oh, I don't know. You can surprise me."

"Truly?" he asked, looking confused, as though he'd expected her to be more decisive about their dinner together. "There is nothing you've wanted, nothing we haven't eaten yet?"

"Lasagna," she said, since obviously he wanted an answer of some kind. Besides, lasagna —and most Italian food—had been something she tried to avoid back in the day, even though she loved it. All those carbs were ruinous, however, and so it had been a very long time since she'd had any. And although she'd noticed that she'd begun to fill out over the past few weeks, thanks to all the good food Idris had been feeding her— enough that she'd stopped wearing the size-zero jeans he'd acquired for her and gone back to her regular size-twos—she doubted one big Italian meal was going to make that much of a difference. "And Caesar salad and garlic bread."

Might as well go for broke.

Now he looked relieved, obviously glad that she'd given him something concrete to focus on.

"That sounds like an excellent idea. Come up at the usual time."

Which was a little past six-thirty, earlier than she used to eat dinner back in the days before… not that it mattered now. At that hour, there was still enough light to easily make her way up to the mansion, and although it was dark by the time they finished eating, she had all the landscape lights—powered by djinn energy—to guide her back.

Would he keep the landscape lighting going after she was gone?

She pushed that thought aside and said, forcing a smile, "I'll be there."

He lifted a hand in a gesture of farewell, then turned to make his way along the path that led toward his home. Amber had noticed that he almost always walked everywhere, very rarely using his djinn powers to blink himself from place to place. Well, when you lived in a spot as beautiful as this one, it made sense to spend as much time in it as possible.

Her smile faded, and she knotted her hands together in her lap, staring down at her fingers. The nails had grown out these past few weeks, and her skin was in better shape, too, thanks to the lotion she'd been faithfully using every morning and evening.

Not that Idris had noticed. Not that it mattered.

Her head drooped then, and she finally let herself cry. Not stormily, not in sobs, but quietly, tears running down her cheeks as she felt her heart break.

She had a feeling she'd never be able to put it back together again.

TEN

Although the Huntington Library had contained a great many books, some of them even devoted to cuisine of various sorts, Idris did not find the information he needed on the grounds. However, the little town of San Marino also possessed a fine public library, and it was there that he located a book on Italian cuisine. Lasagna sounded like quite an intricate dish, but he thought he should be able to manage it without too much difficulty. Actually, he was glad that Amber had set such a complicated task before him, because that way he was able to focus on the dinner he was preparing for her...and not on their imminent separation.

She had tried so hard to conceal her sadness at knowing their time here was about to come to an end, but over the past few weeks, he'd learned something of her moods and expressions, and she could not completely hide what she was feeling. More than anything, he'd wished he could reach out to her, lay a comforting hand on her shoulder, but he had worried that even such an innocuous touch might be more than she wanted or needed in that moment. Better to let it go. Soon she would be gone, and he….

To be honest, he didn't quite know what he would do.

He'd just finished reading a recipe for Caesar salad dressing when Ibram popped into existence a few feet away from him, frowning mightily. His precipitous appearance startled Idris, partly because he had not expected to see his fellow elder again so soon, and partly because it was odd to see Ibram go anywhere without Istar. Very seldom were they out of one another's company.

Feeling irritated—for he believed Ibram must have come here to hasten Amber's departure—Idris said, "I have spoken with Amber. I will take her away to Los Alamos tomorrow morning. Surely that must be sufficient haste for you, Ibram?"

"I am afraid it is not that simple," the other elder replied. Still frowning, he glanced around the kitchen, gaze pausing for a moment on the pile of cookbooks that rested on the marble countertop. "Let us go sit down and talk."

Not that simple? For a moment, hope leapt into Idris's heart, a hope that Ibram had come here to tell him that Amber need not be sent away after all, but somehow he knew that his old friend's visit was not motivated by anything quite so welcome.

"Of course," Idris said. "We can go into the drawing room."

He led Ibram out of the kitchen and down the hall to that formal space, a room he did not use very often. Most of the time, it seemed that he and Amber preferred the library, or to sit outdoors when the weather was fine. In a way—if Ibram had come here bearing bad news—it felt more fitting to receive it in a place that had far fewer memories of her overlaying it.

They sat down, Idris in a rose-upholstered Louis Quinze chair, Ibram on the matching divan that faced it. He looked rather distrustful of the fragile piece of furniture, but it appeared he preferred not to dwell on that, but to attend to the matter at hand.

"I have discovered something," he announced, and Idris lifted an eyebrow.

"What have you discovered?"

The other elder leaned back against the divan, arms crossed. "Well, as I told you I would, I went to do some investigating. The first place I looked was the rolls of the immune."

Yes, the three elders had long possessed a list of those mortals who would be immune to the Heat. It was the very list that those among the

One Thousand had used to select who would be their Chosen, a list that had been annotated with each human/djinn pairing so it would be easy enough to keep track of them if such a thing turned out to be necessary.

"And...?"

Ibram uncrossed his arms and leaned forward slightly, his expression one of some satisfaction, as if he was pleased with himself for discovering a truth he had already suspected. "It seems that Amber McCoy was Chosen. Specifically, a djinn named Bariq al-Dawud laid claim to her."

For a moment, Idris could only stare at the other elder. Yes, he had thought it strange that Amber had not been Chosen, for her beauty and youth surely should have attracted someone's attention. But...but this did not make sense. He knew that she had gone into hiding here at the Huntington several days after the Heat had wiped out the world's population, which meant Bariq al-Dawud should have had plenty of time to come to her and take her away to the nearest djinn/human community—in this case, Bel-Air, most likely. But he hadn't come. She'd been left on her own, and had done the only thing she could think of to ensure her survival.

Indeed, if al-Dawud had arrived in a timely fashion to take her to her new life, then she would not have been out wandering the streets of San Marino, a tempting target for the reaver djinn who had just begun their systematic eradication of any immune humans who had not been lucky enough to be selected as an elemental's partner. Anger stirred in Idris, although he tried to keep his voice calm when he spoke next.

"Have you spoken to Bariq? Has he given any explanation for why he did not come to claim Amber at the appointed time?"

"Not yet," Ibram replied. "I have summoned him to meet with all three of us at the chateau. I felt it better for us to speak there, rather than here. That way, there will be no chance of him encountering Amber."

That seemed like a good enough plan, although Idris did not quite like the idea of leaving her here alone. Some of his apprehension must have showed in his expression, for Ibram shook his head.

"You know she will be safe. Who would come here to bother her? For that matter, who would even know she was here?"

True. No djinn would come to visit an elder's property unless expressly invited, and so there was not much fear of trespassing. Besides, Idris doubted he would be gone all that long. Just enough time to speak with this Bariq al-Dawud, and for them all to determine what they should do next. From the satisfied expression Ibram already wore, it seemed clear enough that he thought the matter already settled. They would ask al-Dawud if he still wished to take Amber for his Chosen. If he did, then he would take her away to his home. If not, then she would be sent to Los Alamos, as they had already decided. Either way, she was an inconvenient loose end that would be handily tied up.

Unfortunately, Idris could not quite view the situation so dispassionately. It was one thing to think of her going to live in Los Alamos with others of her kind. Even though he would miss her, and might be inwardly dismayed at the thought of her eventually giving her heart to a mortal man one day, that was not the same thing as knowing she was with a djinn. His traitorous mind might feel tempted to ask a question he knew he should not contemplate.

If she can be with him…then why not with me?

He deliberately pushed that thought far, far back in his head. Facing Ibram directly, he said, "You are quite right. Let us go and speak with Bariq al-Dawud and see what he has to say for himself."

Amber knew she should begin to pack her things, and yet, as she stood in front of the closet Idris had built for her and stared listlessly at its contents, she couldn't quite find the energy for that necessary task. Maybe it was partly that she knew everything wouldn't fit in the Louis Vuitton overnight bag she'd used to bring her clothes here in the first place, but she thought a large part of her reluctance was simply that doing such a thing felt so…final. Once she had packed, then the separation looming over her would be real. If her wardrobe and her one treasured family photo went in that bag, she would be gone the next day. Simple as that.

Instead, she walked out of the bedroom and through the living area, then out of the house altogether so she could go visit the Zen garden a few yards away. Leaning against the wall there was a rake, and she picked it up and used it to trace patterns in the sandy soil, taking care to keep the lines even and flowing. This was harder than it looked, but she'd begun the practice a few days ago, remembering how this spot had looked back when the Huntington had an army of gardeners to manage such tasks. Besides, right then she was hoping that focusing on the simple but difficult work would help to free her from her thoughts, might help her to relax somehow.

Might, in other words, let her be a little more Zen about the whole situation.

It was very quiet. Even the birds she could usually hear singing in the trees seemed to have gone still for now, or maybe they'd just decided to go hang out in another section of the grounds for a while. Right now, the only sound was the *scritch-scritch* of the rake as she dragged it along the ground, but in a way, that was soothing. She could almost hear herself breathing, her heart beating.

Her heart breaking.

No. She'd already been through that, already cried herself out. This was about being calm, about doing her best to be relaxed and ready to say her goodbyes to Idris. It was going to be hard, so horribly hard, to go have dinner with him tonight and act as though she was eager to be around other people again, but she would do it if it killed her. She didn't want him to know how much it hurt. All he would see was an Amber who smiled and praised his dinner and then thanked him for giving her shelter these past few weeks. That was it. Neither of them owed anything to the other, except friendship.

Wow, aren't you noble? she sneered at herself, then resolutely pushed the thought away. No, the old Amber probably wouldn't have acted like this. She would have told Idris how she felt, fully expecting those feelings to be reciprocated. But that had been someone who'd never fully felt the sting of rejection—even Tyler's cheating on her hadn't been all that unexpected, and because she hadn't loved him, not really, it hadn't hurt too much—who'd never experienced a single day of hunger or want in her entire privileged life. This Amber...she'd lost everything. Maybe for the briefest space, she'd thought she might have something in her life again, something real, but that had only been a fantasy.

Even though she was hurting, she didn't want to hurt Idris by making him feel guilty about sending her away. From the very beginning, they'd both known that could be the only possible outcome here.

So she tried to convince herself that all this was inevitable while the rake scraped away at the dirt, creating patterns and lines and an order she was pretty sure she'd never be able to experience in her own life.

And if a few tears fell down into the bare and sandy soil, so what?

They only added to the pattern.

Idris had to fight the urge to dislike Bariq al-Dawud on sight. It was not the other djinn's fault that Idris had fallen in love with the woman al-Dawud wanted.

Bariq was tall, although not as tall as either of the male elders, and his hair was lighter, too, a tawny, lion-ish mane that fell over his shoulders and contrasted with the coppery silk of the robe he wore. As he stood in the drawing room of Ibram and Istar's chateau, he looked ill at ease, not certain as to why he had been called here.

Idris supposed he could not blame him for that, since one was rarely summoned to the elders' presence for a mere social call.

However, Istar did her best to assuage the man's unease, and offered him a seat on the divan, then asked if he would have water or wine or coffee.

"Water would be very good, elder," Bariq replied to her question, looking a little less awkward as he sat down on the embossed velvet cushion.

At once, a pitcher of water and a glass appeared on the table in front of him. Istar filled the glass with her own hands—a gesture of respect among their kind, for of course she could have used her powers to perform such a simple task—and then gave al-Dawud the water. As he sipped, Ibram spoke.

"You may be wondering why we have asked you here," he said.

Bariq al-Dawud nodded, his expression one of cautious relief that the elders had broached the subject, and therefore he didn't have to ask the question which must have been plaguing him. "I am sure you will tell me why," he responded.

"Yes, we will," Idris said, his tone sharper than he would have liked. Doing his best to control his irritation, he went on, "We have discovered that you claimed a Chosen, and yet it seems you have been living alone these two years since the Dying. What happened?"

The tawny-haired djinn suddenly seemed very interested in the contents of his water glass. "I am not sure."

Istar raised a delicately arched eyebrow. "What do you mean, you are not sure?"

"I am sorry if I was vague, elder." Bariq drank some of the water she had given him, then went on, "Yes, I chose a young woman to be mine. But when I went to claim her, to take her to live in the new community in Bel-Air, she was nowhere to be found."

Of course she wasn't...she'd already gone to ground by then. However, Idris held his tongue, knowing it was probably better to keep this knowledge to himself. He could not count himself entirely blameless in this situation, not when he had interfered, had told her to run.

"When was this?" Ibram inquired.

Bariq set down his water glass. A casual gesture, or a way for him to avoid the watching elders' gaze? "A few days after the Heat began."

"You waited that long?" Now Ibram's tone was sharper, and he scowled as he stared down at the other djinn, arms crossed. Truly, he could look quite fearsome when he did that, and apparently al-Dawud thought the same thing, because he seemed to shrink back into the divan's velvet cushions.

"My apologies, elder. Yes, I fear I did hesitate."

"Why?" Istar asked. She, too, appeared quite disapproving, and Idris wished he could thank her for asking the question he knew he did not have the right to ask. "Did we not make it quite clear that you all should claim your Chosen as soon as was feasible, so they would not be left alone and afraid as their loved ones died around them?"

Bariq moistened his lips. He sipped his water again, looking as though he wished he had asked for wine instead. "Yes, elder. I knew what I was supposed to do. But…."

"But?" Idris asked. He wanted to sound neutral, but he knew a lash of anger had crept into that single word. Ibram sent him a single questioning glance, but said nothing.

"But…I had begun to have doubts," al-Dawud confessed.

"'Doubts'?" Istar repeated, her tone sharpening. "You did not think the woman you had Chosen was worthy of the honor?"

"No, not that," the djinn said hastily. "She was a beautiful young woman with eyes the color of the sky and hair like spun silk. The doubt was all on my part. I questioned whether I truly had the temperament to be with one woman—and a human woman at that—for the rest of my days."

"If you did not think you were suited for such an arrangement, then perhaps you should have thought of that before you decided to have her as your Chosen," Ibram observed dryly, and Idris could only be glad that his fellow elder had been the one to speak those words, for he had been thinking much the same thing.

Bariq's throat moved as he swallowed. Truly, he looked so dreadfully uncomfortable that Idris might have felt some pity for him—if it were not that his cowardice had put Amber at risk. She deserved better than that.

"I know," he said. "And I realized soon enough that she was the choice of my heart. Someone so beautiful should not be left to the mercy of the reavers. And so I hurried to find her, but the house where she lived was empty, and so were all the other houses in the neighborhood. I searched and searched, but I could not find her. For a time, I lived among the mortals and djinn in Bel-Air, for they were kind enough to welcome me into their community while I looked for the woman who should have been mine. But it seemed she was gone forever, and so I gave it up at last. For more than a year, I have been living on the land that would have been mine if I had remained alone...down in a place called Costa Rica."

Istar and Ibram looked at one another. Idris could guess at what they were thinking—that they should have remembered that Bariq al-Dawud was to have had a Chosen, and should not have been granted those lands at all. However, there had been far more chaos in the months following the Dying than any of them had planned for, and they most likely had forgotten that al-Dawud had any designs on a mortal woman, and had gone ahead and given him land to call his own.

And, now that he was mulling over the situation, Idris could guess why the djinn he had driven away from Amber had never gone to the other two elders to inform them of his interference. That djinn had probably guessed she was Chosen, and thought that Idris had stepped in to save her because those special few mortals were sacrosanct, untouchable. To attack one of them was to risk being sent to the outer circles as punishment. The reaver djinn would have kept his silence, thankful that Idris had apparently not mentioned his transgression to anyone.

"Well, you are in luck," Ibram observed then. "Because, as it turns out, she has been in hiding this entire time, and only recently made her presence known to us. Idris has been keeping watch on her at his estate until we could decide what to do with her. In fact, we were about to send her to live with the other immune humans in Los Alamos, but then I discovered that you had laid claim to her back before the Dying. If it is still your wish to have her, then she is yours."

Such a casual tone to use when discussing the

disposition of another living person. Idris wanted to protest, to tell the other elder that the woman in question deserved so much more. But of course, Ibram did not know Amber, knew nothing of her strength and drive, of the incandescent light of her smiles. She was only a problem that needed to be solved, and, now that they had discovered Bariq al-Dawud had once wanted her, giving her to him seemed to be the simplest solution to their problem.

It appeared al-Dawud was of a like mind, for as soon as Ibram made this revelation, the other djinn's green-gold eyes widened, and he set down his glass and got to his feet. "She is truly alive?"

"Yes," Idris said. "And well, now that she has had some time to adjust to living in the world after spending so much time in hiding."

"May I—may I see her?"

Well, he seemed eager enough. Idris supposed he should be glad that Bariq appeared so enthusiastic, and yet he had to fight to keep himself from frowning. How much of this was true eagerness to see the woman he had once wanted, and how much a show he was putting on to make the elders think he was all too willing to go along with their plan?

Unfortunately, he could not read minds, and so Idris doubted he would ever know the real truth. What he did know was that he hated the thought of handing Amber over to this man, of forcing her to go with a complete stranger. Yes, that was how it would have worked out in the very beginning if al-Dawud had not been so weak, had gone to her immediately as soon as her family was dead. But now many months had passed...and, Idris thought, someone who had vacillated so much did not deserve her.

He was not sure whether he deserved her, either, but he knew he would be a much better partner for her than Bariq al-Dawud, if only because Idris knew he loved her.

Not that it mattered. She could never be his... especially now that he knew someone else had a prior claim.

"Soon," Istar said gently, once she seemed to realize that Ibram was not going to reply to Bariq's question. "I think she needs to be told of the situation, and then we will determine the best way to manage the transition."

"I will tell her," Idris said, although his gut clenched with apprehension at the very thought of what that conversation would be like. "Over our evening meal, I think, since that is already planned. And actually, tomorrow might be feasible, since she believes she will be going to Los Alamos at that time. Instead, she will have a much brighter future. She will be Chosen."

He hated to even utter those words, but they appeared to have the desired effect, for both Istar and Ibram looked at him approvingly, and al-

Dawud seemed pleased that he would not have to suffer much more of a delay.

"And after that I can take her to live with me in Costa Rica?" he asked.

"Only temporarily," Istar replied, eyes narrowing slightly. Even though it had been two years since Bariq had searched in vain for his Chosen, he still should have remembered that he could not stay in the place where he'd been living for much of that time. "For once Amber is living with you as your Chosen, then of course you must go to dwell with the other djinn and their Chosen in one of the local communities in Southern California. There is Bel-Air, and also Laguna Beach, but the two of you can discuss which would be better for you after you have had a little time to become accustomed to one another."

"Of course," Bariq said. "Bel-Air was quite lovely, and the djinn and the Chosen there very agreeable, but if Amber prefers Laguna, I assume that would work as well."

How very accommodating he was. Then again, he had every reason to feel magnanimous, for he was about to have a wonderful woman given to him on a silver platter.

The thought made Idris's blood want to boil. However, he assumed what he hoped was a pleasant expression and said, "It sounds as if we are all in agreement, then. I will return to my home and inform Amber of what is to come next, and then, Bariq al-Dawud, you may come tomorrow at noon and take her away with you."

"That sounds like an excellent plan," the other djinn said. "I look forward to it."

He rose from the divan and bowed to them all, then disappeared. For a long moment, none of the elders said anything. Istar still wore a speculative expression on her face as she gazed at Idris, as though she was doing her best to divine what he might be thinking. Luckily, she did not have the ability to read his thoughts, and he had to hope that she could make out little from his visage.

"I will go," he said abruptly. "I must speak to Amber, and she must make her preparations for departure."

"You don't seem terribly pleased by this outcome," Ibram observed, making Idris wonder whether the other two elders had been communicating with one another via thought.

Still, he made himself lift his shoulders, as if he cared very little about the situation one way or another, and said, "On the contrary—I am most pleased that this can all be taken care of so conveniently. It was time to move on, for I was beginning to find that having Amber living on the grounds interfered somewhat with my plans for my home."

This, of course, was a bald-faced lie, since she had done a great deal to assist him in restoring the Huntington's gardens. However, neither Ibram nor Istar had visited during that time, and so they could have no real idea of what had or hadn't been happening at the estate.

"Excellent," Ibram responded. "Then we will let you go. Just think—by this time tomorrow, this whole affair will be satisfactorily concluded."

Idris didn't quite trust himself to reply to that statement in a way that wouldn't invite suspicion. Indeed, the very thought of handing Amber over to Bariq made it feel as though someone had buried a dagger in his heart. He nodded, first to Ibram, then to Istar, and said, "I will be back tomorrow to let you know everything went as planned."

Then he blinked himself away...although he had no more stomach for the conversation he was about to have with Amber than the one which had just concluded.

ELEVEN

AMBER APPROACHED THE MANSION SLOWLY, LETTING herself take in the details highlighted by the last light of the setting sun—the rows of columns, the elegant balustrades on the upstairs balcony, the slender shapes of the Italian cypress in pots that flanked the main entrance off the loggia. Maybe she was torturing herself by trying to commit all this to memory, rather than push it aside as an interlude that never had any chance of lasting, but she wanted to keep this house and the man who lived in it in a secret place in her heart, like the hidden compartment in the jewelry box her parents had given her as a Christmas present when she was a little girl. That way, when no one was looking, she could open the little drawer and pull out the treasures inside, only they wouldn't be rings or pendants, but memories of her time here—Idris smiling at her as a breeze played with his long hair, sunlight reflecting on the koi pond in the Japanese garden...Idris holding her as she stood in the doorway of her little house and suddenly realized the depth of the world's loss. All these things, so precious...so soon to be gone.

She'd put on her favorite white dress, mostly because she wanted Idris's last experience of her to be her looking her best. It was probably silly to wear something like that in the middle of October, but the weather had stayed warm, and she would have to put it away soon enough. Probably she'd never have a chance to wear it again; from what she'd been able to tell, Los Alamos didn't exactly sound like the kind of place that would encourage wearing frilly, short white dresses.

As always, the French doors that opened onto the loggia were unlocked, so she went ahead and let herself in. The dining room table had been covered with a fine white cloth, and a large silver bowl filled with roses from the gardens—red and yellow and white and pink—adorned the center of that table. More roses sat in a pair of matching silver vases on the mantel as well, and candles flickered from almost every flat surface. In a previous time, she would have looked at the scene and thought it a complete setup for a seduction, but she knew Idris didn't have anything like that in mind for tonight. No, he probably just wanted to give her something lovely for her last night here, especially since she'd praised his other decorating attempts, and so he knew she enjoyed and appreciated this sort of thing.

He came into the dining room then, carrying a large glass casserole in its own pierced-silver carrier. The lasagna inside the casserole smelled amazing, but she still didn't have much appetite.

"Amber," he said, and though he smiled at her, she thought she could see the strain in his expression. Maybe this was going to be hard for him as well.

She pushed that thought from her mind. More likely, she was only manufacturing what she wanted to see, hoping against hope that he would reconsider their plan to send her to Los Alamos.

"Hi, Idris," she replied, trying to sound casual. "The dining room looks gorgeous."

"Thank you," he said. "I wanted to make our last dinner together something you could remember for a long while."

Somehow, she managed to smile. Why was it so hard now, when in the past she'd always found it easy to fake happiness or enthusiasm as necessary? "Then you've succeeded."

"Please, go ahead and sit down. I only need to bring out a few more things."

Amber nodded, although she was a little puzzled by his request. Why couldn't he just wave a hand and make the rest of the food appear on the table? Was he trying to stall for some reason, doing his best to prolong their last evening together?

She didn't know. About all she could do was sit down in her usual spot, in the chair to the right of Idris' place at the head of the table, then take the fine white napkin and spread it over her lap. It occurred to her that she couldn't really tell where the napkin ended and her skirt began. She'd have to be careful when she wiped her fingers.

Then again, what did it really matter? Was she ever going to wear this dress again?

Before melancholy could begin to creep over her, however, Idris reappeared with a large glass bowl of salad in one hand and a silver basket containing a folded white napkin in the other. Judging by the savory aroma that arose from inside the basket, it had to be filled with garlic bread.

"There," he said, setting down his burdens so he could sit in his chair at the head of the table. "What would you like to drink with this? Chianti, or perhaps something a little off the beaten path... Montepulciano, or Aglianico?"

"Whichever you think is best," she told him. At some point, she probably would have tried to educate herself on wine, but back in the day, her crowd had mostly drunk cocktails or high-end spirits. She'd begun to learn a little...obviously not enough, though, since she'd never even heard of the last two varieties Idris had mentioned.

He looked thoughtful for a moment, then waved a hand. A decanter full of a rich dark wine appeared on the table in between them, but because there was no bottle with a label to read, she still had no idea what they would be drinking.

"I've always been fond of Montepulciano," he said, clearing up the mystery. He lifted the decanter and poured an inch and a half into her wine glass, then did the same thing for himself. "Let me know what you think."

Right then, she felt so jittery and ill at ease, about all she could hope was that the wine wouldn't taste like vinegar to her. She raised her glass, then made herself say, "Should we toast to something?"

The smile he'd been wearing slipped a little. "I suppose we should. To new beginnings?"

That was the last thing she wanted to celebrate. She wanted to stay here, in a place she knew with the man she loved. However, she couldn't possibly tell him that, so she clinked her glass against his. "To new beginnings."

They both drank. To Amber's relief, the wine wasn't vinegary at all, but smooth and rich and dark, oddly comforting. Maybe that was why he'd chosen it to go with their Italian comfort food meal of lasagna and garlic bread.

He reached for the basket and handed it to her. "Some bread?"

"Thank you." She pushed back the napkin and

selected a modestly sized piece, although right then, she felt like stress-eating the entire basket. When she was done, she gave it back to him, and he took a piece for himself. After that, he dished salad and lasagna for both of them.

The food smelled incredible, and she thought she had made a good choice. As nervous as she was, she didn't think she could have managed the task of carving meat off a tiny quail, or trying to cut her way through a steak.

For a few moments, they ate without speaking. Amber could tell Idris was not entirely at ease, either, because he didn't seem to want to look at her, and appeared far too preoccupied with eating what was, after all, a pretty simple meal.

At last, though, he set down his fork and said, "About tomorrow…."

Her stomach clenched, but she managed to reply calmly enough, "I already have most of my things packed, but I need you to get another bag for me. I don't have enough room in the one I brought from my house."

"That is not a problem," he said, although he didn't look particularly relieved. "However, there is something I need to speak with you about."

The knot in her midsection seemed to wind itself a little tighter. Amber reached for her glass of wine and took a large swallow, then said, "Oh?"

Maybe he really had had a change of heart.

Maybe he'd realized he didn't want to send her away. For all she knew, he'd gone to speak with the other elders about the situation, to ask them if they could maybe bend the rules in this case.

When he replied, though, her hopes were immediately dashed. "You will leave tomorrow, but not to go to Los Alamos. Ibram thought your situation merited further query, and so he looked into it further and discovered that you actually had been Chosen back in the time of the Heat. The djinn who selected you could not locate you, and has spent the last two years fearing you were dead. He was overjoyed to hear that you lived, and it is to him you will be going tomorrow."

The food she'd just eaten felt as though it had turned to stone in her stomach. This couldn't be happening. In fact, Idris's revelations shook Amber so deeply that all she could do was sit there and stare at him, wine glass still clutched in her fingers, which also felt like they'd been turned into stone, they were so cold and unmoving. What the hell was he talking about? There couldn't have been someone else, or he would have come for her all those months ago, just as Idris had explained it was supposed to happen.

"I don't understand," she said at last, the syllables coming slowly, as if she had to consciously recall how to pronounce each word before it left her mouth.

"I know this must be something of a shock to

you," he replied. His gaze moved away from her, and he also reached for his wine and allowed himself a swallow. "But we all wondered why you had not been Chosen, when it seemed as though you should have been a perfect candidate. Bariq did want you—it was only that you were gone when he came to claim you."

"'Bariq'?" Amber echoed. "Is that his name?"

"Yes. Bariq al-Dawud. He has been living at his home in Costa Rica these past two years, and I believe he plans to take you there first. Permanently, of course, you will need to settle in one of the human/djinn communities here in California, but the two of you can discuss that arrangement as you get to know one another."

Idris was speaking so reasonably, so calmly, as if all this made perfect sense and there was absolutely nothing for her to be worried about. Amber, on the other hand, felt as though she was about to scream. How could he just hand her off to a perfect stranger without batting an eye? All right, she knew the original setup had been for these djinn to come along and take the mortals they'd decided to save, but that ship had sailed. Two years had passed, and she hadn't seen hide nor hair of this Bariq al-whatever. Obviously, he hadn't been that broken up about not finding her, or he probably would have tried a little harder to discover her fate.

"So you're just going to give me to some

random djinn and wash your hands of the whole thing," she said, her tone acid.

Idris's brows drew together, and his mouth tightened slightly. "He is not 'random,' Amber," he replied. "He is the man who Chose you."

"Well, he's random to me," she retorted. "Don't I get a say in all this?"

"You would not have had a say if he'd claimed you at the beginning, as was planned."

"Yeah, and how medieval is that?" Before Idris could reply, she went on, "Or maybe it's more caveman. You know, dragging the woman off by her hair and all that."

"He would not have dragged you anywhere," Idris said, and although he still sounded calm enough, she thought she could detect an edge to his voice, as if he was beginning to grow angry with her for not rationally accepting the situation.

Well, she sure as hell wasn't going to accept it. This might be the djinns' world now, but if Idris or the other elders—or Bariq al-whatsis—thought she was just going to roll over and do whatever they asked, they had another thing coming.

"What if I don't want to go with him?" she asked.

"Then I suppose you would go to Los Alamos as we originally planned," Idris said. He set down his wine glass. When he spoke again, his voice sounded pleading rather than angry. "You know those are your only two choices, Amber, but I must ask of you that you at least give Bariq al-Dawud a chance. Come with me tomorrow to meet him. Let him speak with you, tell you his side of the story. If, after that point, you still are not convinced, then yes, I can take you to Los Alamos."

She still didn't like the sound of any of it—it was like being asked to choose between a shit sandwich and a turd pie—but she could tell Idris was doing his best. Probably Ibram had sprung all this on him out of the blue, and now about all Idris could do was try to make the situation seem just a little less awful than it really was.

"All right," she said at last, knowing how sulky she sounded and not really caring. "I'll meet him. I'm not promising anything, but I'll meet him."

"That's all I can ask," Idris replied, relief clear in his voice. "And I will make sure to let Ibram know to communicate your wishes to Bariq, so he knows in the end, it will be your choice."

Her choice. There was a joke. She really didn't have much of a say in any of this, because otherwise, she'd tell all of them that she was staying here with Idris, end of discussion. But that option was clearly off the table, no matter what else happened.

"Sure," was about all she could say. They continued the rest of their meal in silence, although neither of them seemed inclined to eat very much.

When she left the house soon afterward, that was the first time she'd ever actually been glad to get away from him.

Because of her white dress, it was easy for Idris to mark Amber's progress as she walked down the path to her house, just as she had done so many times before. Tonight was different, though. This would be the last time he would stand here at the door and watch her go. After this evening, she would either belong to Bariq al-Dawud, or she would have thrown in her lot with the mortals in Los Alamos. Either way, she would be lost to him forever.

His heart was heavy, and he poured himself another glass of wine, although all the other evidence of their shortened meal was already gone from the table. The lasagna and garlic bread had been quite good, but now it seemed they might as well have been made from sawdust.

Part of him wanted to set down the wine glass, to go down the path and find her in her house… and what? Kiss her, make love to her? Of course he wanted those things, but he knew he could not indulge himself in this. He'd seen baffled anger and naked worry in her face this evening, and yet he thought that must have been more because he'd sprung the news about al-Dawud so unexpectedly on her than because she had any particular interest in him. She was a forthright young woman, and surely she would have otherwise said something.

Actually, it was good that she had not. Otherwise, the situation would have been even more difficult than it already was.

He drained the rest of his wine and went upstairs to his bedroom. Not for the first time, he wondered what it would have been like to have Amber in that enormous silk-hung bed, how blissful it would have been to wake up with her at his side after a night of lovemaking.

Now you are only torturing yourself, he thought as he removed his silk robe and hung it in the closet, then went into the bathroom to clean his face and teeth. *You know that could never have been. It is a pleasant fantasy and nothing more.*

Only a fantasy…one he couldn't seem to get out of his mind.

But no, he would not have her, and Bariq al-Dawud instead would be the one to have her in his bed. If she chose him at all. There was always the chance—and possibly a strong one—that she would instead go to Los Alamos and a far less certain future. At least in that particular future, she would have an equal say in who would be her partner, rather than having him selected for her.

And perhaps that would be best. Idris did not like to think of her growing old and dying, her bright beauty fading as she bore some mortal's children and spent all her life working to support the Los Alamos community, but perhaps that would still be better than knowing she would always be young and eternally lovely…and eternally out of reach, partner to a djinn other than he.

No, he did not like either of those scenarios. Unfortunately, the one he wanted was no longer an option for him. Perhaps, before Bariq al-Dawud had surfaced—before he realized another man had a prior claim to Amber—Idris might have found the courage to argue his case with Ibram and Istar, to tell them there had been no explicit injunction against an elder choosing a mortal as his partner. But of course there wasn't, mostly because none of them had ever imagined such a stricture should be put in place. Even a month ago, Idris knew he would have laughed at the thought of losing his heart to a human, especially when he had never done so with a djinn woman.

Well, now it seemed as if the universe was laughing at him…and damned if he knew what to do about it.

TWELVE

THEY'D BOTH PRETENDED THIS WAS A NORMAL DAY, but they knew better. Just as she'd done for the past few weeks, Amber met Idris in the tea room and shared breakfast with him, and just as they'd done many times before, they went for a walk in the gardens afterward. She'd almost hoped the day would be gloomy and dark, a fitting echo of her inner state, but, just as it had been for the past week, the weather was sunny and breezy and warm, cheerful the way only a Southern California autumn could be.

Luckily, he didn't try to force their conversation, only walked quietly next to her—but not too close, not so close that it would have been easy to slip her hand into his.

As if she would have had the guts to do that.

A few times, he made a comment about the gardens, but that was it. She reminded him of the pruning schedule they'd discussed previously, and told him not to neglect the herb garden planted out back behind the tearoom. Although she still couldn't exactly figure out how he was able to produce food from thin air, she thought he probably could do something with the herbs, and so they should be looked after with the same care as the rest of the gardens.

And then he looked up at the position of the sun, and back down at her, and said quietly, "It's time."

No, it wasn't possible that the morning had passed so quickly. It had to be just ten, or maybe closer to eleven, but there was no way it could be noon...could it?

Heart pounding with dread, Amber glanced up at the sky as well, but the sun seemed to be pretty much directly overhead, despite her devout wish that it be much closer to the horizon. "Oh, I guess it is. We'll need to get my bags from the house."

"No need." Idris waved a hand, and two Louis Vuitton bags—because of course he'd provided one that matched hers—appeared sitting on the ground next to her.

So much for that. She bent to pick them up, but Idris was faster.

"You know it's easier if I hold them," he reminded her, and she gave him a resigned shrug.

"Right. I forgot."

Then came the moment she'd been both dreading and anticipating, when she had to put her arms around his waist so she could safely travel with him djinn-style. Even though she knew it was foolish, she couldn't quite prevent the thrill that went through her at the feel of his body pressed up against hers, the strength of the muscles at the small of his back.

But she didn't have too much time to dwell on his physical presence, because before she could even blink, he'd whisked them both away from the grounds of the Huntington. They reappeared in an enormous room with gray stone walls and elegant furniture that didn't quite manage to fill up the space. A fire danced in the oversized hearth, and she was glad of that, since it felt much colder here than it had been in the sunny gardens they'd just left.

Three people were waiting for them by that hearth—the two elders Amber had seen before, and a third djinn, a stranger. Like all his people, he was tall, although not as tall as either Idris or Ibram, the oldest of the elders. The stranger—who she guessed had to be Bariq—had dark blond hair that fell past his shoulders, and green-hazel eyes and golden-tanned skin. Amber had to admit to herself that if she didn't know who he was, had just seen him in a club or at a party or something, back in the day she would have thought he was pretty hot.

But because she knew she was already in love with Idris, she was already finding fault—his eyes were just a little too close together, and those same eyes didn't have the same thick, sooty lashes as Idris, the kind that were so heavy, they made it look as if he was wearing guy-liner or something. And though Bariq was just as muscular as Idris, because he was shorter, those muscles made him seem almost squat in comparison, which she realized was kind of a stupid thing to think about a guy who had to be six foot two or three.

"Idris...and Amber," said Istar, the one female elder. Maybe she'd noticed the way Amber was appraising the djinn who'd claimed her, maybe not. However, she seemed to understand how awkward the situation was, because she went on, "This is Bariq al-Dawud. He has been waiting anxiously to meet you."

"That I have," Bariq said, taking a step toward Amber. He was smiling, but she saw the way he looked her up and down and then gave the slightest nod, as if he was glad to see she hadn't managed to turn ugly over the past two years.

You should've seen the way I looked when Idris found me, she thought wryly. *You might not have been quite so impressed.*

But she realized she didn't want to think about that, because then she would have to remember how startled she had been to stare up at Idris and realize he was the one who had saved her so many months earlier. Her terror in that moment had quickly given way to something else…something she really didn't want to acknowledge.

"It's very nice to meet you, Bariq," she said, in the almost too-polite tone she would have used with someone her father had introduced her to at his country club. Then again, that analogy probably wasn't too far off the mark, since a lot of those old perverts had stared at her in much the same appraising way that Bariq looked at her now. It hadn't mattered that she was the daughter of one of their friends, and that they were definitely old enough to be her father. Those guys didn't care; they almost all were on the make for a newer model…the younger, the better.

"Perhaps the two of you would like to take a walk in the garden," Ibram suggested. "It is a fine day, and that will give you a chance to become acquainted."

There wasn't anything right then that would have appealed to her less, but since Amber had promised Idris she would give Bariq a chance, she knew she needed to go along with the elder's plan. "Sure," she said.

Although I doubt the gardens here will be any nicer than the gardens I just left….

She allowed Bariq to take her by the arm and lead her outside. As they left the drawing room, she caught a glimpse of Idris's strained face and wondered whether he was beginning to think this whole plan wasn't quite as neat and tidy as he'd originally believed. Maybe it had all been very well in the abstract, but as soon as he'd caught a glimpse of her and Bariq together....

Or maybe he'd been thinking of something else entirely. She was probably reading too much into his expression.

It was cool outside, almost chilly. The building they'd just left was a huge pile of gray stone, clearly a castle or enormous manor house of some sort. That meant they were probably in Europe somewhere, which would also explain the temperature difference. She'd put on a light cardigan over her sleeveless top, but she could tell it wasn't helping all that much.

Then again, it was possible that the shiver which passed over her had a lot more to do with her current company than the weather outside.

Apparently, Bariq noticed because he asked, "You are cold?"

"No," she said hastily. Even though she wasn't all that comfortable, better to do this here than inside with the two elders and Idris watching them. That would have been beyond awkward. "I mean, it's cooler here than it was in Southern California, but I'm all right if we stay in the sun."

Which, luckily, was out, shining down on the yellowed grass and making the row of poplars that outlined a lane somewhere off in the distance blaze like a line of fiery beacons. It was beautiful here, although very different from San Marino.

"If you like warmth, then you will like Costa Rica," Bariq said. "It is even warmer than where you come from."

She slanted a look up at him. They were walking slowly, a brisk breeze playing with the hem of his reddish-brown silk robe, but he didn't seem to mind the cool air very much. Then again, why would he? Djinn didn't seem to be affected by those sorts of things. "I thought we were supposed to settle somewhere in California."

"Well, yes, eventually," Bariq allowed. "But the elders have said we might go to Costa Rica for a time before we decide where we will live permanently. Have you ever been there?"

Actually, she had, on the same trip when she'd gone to Cozumel and Cabo San Lucas. She'd liked Costa Rica, liked the warm, shimmering waters off its coast, the surprisingly vibrant nightlife. And the tree sloths. They were adorable.

"Once," she said. "It was fun. I wouldn't mind going back there."

"Good," Bariq responded. His gaze met hers, and the corners of his mouth lifted slightly. It was a good enough mouth as mouths went, she supposed, and yet she couldn't imagine that mouth ever kissing her. How could she, when all she really wanted was Idris? But since he was off limits, she knew she needed to look for some kind of an alternative. Greenish-gold eyes warming, Bariq asked, "Then you are agreeable to going to Costa Rica with me?"

For a second, Amber wavered. In a way, she thought it would be more honest to go to Los Alamos and live a normal life there…or at least, as normal as a mere mortal's life could be in this post-Heat world. If she went with Bariq, she knew she would only be doing so because she liked the idea of being forever young, of never having to worry about death and disease. She didn't feel anything for the djinn who walked beside her now. How could she? They'd just met.

But maybe she'd come to feel something for him, would eventually forget Idris. It was too bad that she and Bariq couldn't stay in Costa Rica, because that way she'd be thousands of miles from San Marino, far, far away from the place where she'd walked in the rose garden with Idris, where she'd felt his arms go around her as she wept…where she'd realized that she'd never truly loved anyone until she loved him.

In the past, she'd been pretty good at skimming along the surface of a relationship, at not letting her heart get all that involved. If she'd been able to do it back then, she didn't see any reason why she couldn't do the same thing now.

And maybe…eventually…this all wouldn't hurt as much.

"I'd love to go to Costa Rica with you," she

said easily, hoping Bariq hadn't noticed her slight hesitation. "Ready when you are."

When Bariq and Amber returned to the drawing room, they were chatting and smiling, and looked as though they had shared a very good walk. Idris had to fight to keep a scowl off his face, for the sight of the two of them together, apparently so carefree, annoyed him, even as he told himself that it was better this way. He should be glad that they were getting along. Perhaps Bariq had realized there was something in their characters that would be compatible, rather than desiring Amber merely for her lovely face.

And that thought reminded him that al-Dawud truly did have the first claim on her. Idris might view the other djinn as an interloper now, but really, he was the interloper, not Bariq. He would have to remind himself of that fact as often as necessary, and maybe over time he would become resigned to the situation.

Now, though…now he only wanted to stride across the room and tell al-Dawud that he had no right to Amber, thanks to the way he'd abandoned her so many months ago. And maybe shock all of them by pulling her into his arms and kissing her the way he'd been dreaming of for the past few weeks.

However, his self-restraint was still intact enough that he did not do such thing, only remained standing by the hearth next to Ibram and Istar. She was the one who stepped forward first, a smile on the full lips that always seemed curved with a secret amusement.

"So?" she asked.

"It is resolved," Bariq replied. "Amber is all too happy to come with me. She understands that this is how it was always meant to be."

As those words left al-Dawud's lips, a small frown creased Amber's forehead, one she almost immediately erased as soon as she saw that Idris was staring in her direction. He had to wonder at her frown—was she second-guessing her decision, or thinking that perhaps he had put words in her mouth?

Difficult to say, and because she now looked serene and untroubled, gaze fixed on the other two elders rather than on him, he couldn't know.

"Meant to be," he grumbled inwardly. *If you cared that much, you would have gone to her when you were supposed to, rather than hesitating and wondering if pairing yourself with a mortal for all eternity was truly what you desired.*

Somehow he rather doubted Bariq had bothered to mention that particular detail to his Chosen. No, he probably would do his best to make it sound as if fate had intervened and that none of what had happened was his fault.

But that was none of Idris's concern. The very rules that he and Istar and Ibram had created for the Chosen stipulated that whoever selected a mortal first had the only true claim to that person. These matters could be disputed by physical combat, as had happened with Jasreel al-Ankara and his brother Aldair a few years earlier, but in most cases, these sorts of conflicts simply did not occur. Besides, Idris knew he could not challenge Bariq for Amber; it was one thing for two ordinary djinn to go up against one another in single combat, but as an elder, he far outmatched Bariq. These sorts of djinn battles involved the two elementals in contention using their individual powers—over earth or fire or air or water—against one another. Since Idris commanded all those powers at once, such a battle would not be anything close a fair fight.

"This is excellent news," Ibram said. Now the gaze he bestowed upon Amber was approving, whereas earlier Idris could tell that his fellow elder was not quite sure what to think of the young woman. "It is unfortunate that the two of you did not meet when you originally were meant to, but at least the situation has resolved itself."

"Thank you, elder," Bariq said. His hand now held Amber's and she smiled slightly, although Idris couldn't help but notice the way she still wouldn't look over at him. "I am gratified beyond measure that you took the time to find out what my Chosen's true fate was intended to be. Now we will go forth to fulfill that destiny."

Istar smiled. "Go, and enjoy yourselves. But do not linger in Costa Rica too long. Otherwise, we will have to go and remind you of your duty, and such things make me impatient. It seems as though we have already spent far too much of our time reminding our djinn of their obligations to the rules we have set down."

"That will not be a problem," Bariq told her. "Only a few days, or perhaps a week at the most, and then we will be back in California."

"Good," Ibram said sternly. "For if you are not, we will send Idris to check on you."

He managed not to startle, but again annoyance grew within him. Already he had had to remind several djinn to settle with their Chosen in the appropriate community, rather than wherever their whims took them. Doing so had not been an enjoyable task, and he feared it would be even worse when the Chosen in question was the woman he loved.

"As I said, it will not be an issue," Bariq said, his tone smooth. He glanced down at the woman who stood next to him. "Are you ready, Amber?"

"Yes," she said.

Her bags still sat on the floor where Idris had set them down when they first arrived. Now Bariq gathered them up, then returned to her side.

His arm went around her waist, and the two of them disappeared.

Perhaps she had mouthed *goodbye* at him. Idris couldn't know for sure, since their leave-taking had happened far too quickly. All he knew now was that she was gone, and the gnawing, empty ache inside him was one that would not be filled soon.

Or ever.

"Well, that went smoothly enough," Ibram said. He crossed the room to a small table that held a crystal decanter and several brandy glasses. "Would you like a drink to celebrate, Idris?"

"I think not," he replied. "I have much to attend to back at my estate—all those matters that were pushed aside while Amber was in my care."

"Of course," Ibram replied, not looking much put out by his fellow elder's demurral. Standing by him, Istar appeared more troubled, her green eyes fixed on Idris's face, but she did not say anything.

All the more reason to get out of here as quickly as he could. He did not want her to turn her keen gaze on him for too long, lest she see something he'd been doing his best to keep hidden.

Perhaps if he was alone with his grief long enough, he would be able to move past it, could tell himself that this was all for the best. He had no claim on Amber, absolutely none.

Maybe...just maybe...if he repeated that cold reality to himself enough times, he might finally come to believe it.

THIRTEEN

They emerged into warm, moist, tropical heat, the sun beating down overhead. The contrast with the chateau where she and Bariq had just been was so strong, Amber could only stand where she was for a moment, blinking as she did her best to acclimate.

Lush banana tree fronds waved in the breeze. Just ahead of her was an infinity pool that overlooked a shimmering white beach. As she began to take in her surroundings, she realized she was in a place that reminded her very much of a house where she'd attended an insane party on her last night in Costa Rica—the same sleek, modern architecture, with a vaguely Art Deco feel to it, like something you might see in Miami, only bigger and even more lavish.

In fact….

It was the same house. That is, she supposed

there could be two places like this, with the same curved infinity pool and astounding view of a half-moon beach with shimmering blue-green water just beyond it, two places with the same covered patio and "conversation group" of outdoor sofa, love seat, and chairs perched under the shelter it provided, but she kind of doubted it.

"You like it?" Bariq's voice came at her ear.

She looked up at him and arranged a practiced smile on her face. "It's gorgeous. And actually, I think I've been here before."

True surprise flitted across his features. "You what?"

"When I visited Costa Rica about four years ago, I went to a party at a house that looked just like this. I suppose there could be two houses here that are exactly the same, but I kind of doubt it."

The shocked expression he wore quickly transformed into an easy grin. "Well, then. It seems that we must be meant to be together, for that is too much of a coincidence to be overlooked."

Maybe. She still didn't know much about djinn, but even her limited experience seemed to indicate that they liked to latch on to the biggest, most extravagant houses they could find. It would make sense that Bariq had taken a place like this for his own, since she doubted there were too many mansions quite this lavish in Costa Rica. There had always been a lot of nice real estate there, sure...but if her memory served, she'd guessed that this particular party house had been worth at least ten million, probably more.

However, contradicting him didn't seem like a very good idea, so she kept smiling as she said, "It sure looks that way. You want to show me around?"

"Very much," he replied. "Only you must not get too attached to this house, for of course we can't stay here permanently."

"I know," she said. "This can be like...a vacation. A chance to get to know each other in a tropical getaway."

His gaze lingered on her mouth, and she could practically see the lust gleaming in his heavy-lidded eyes. "I think I like that idea."

Of course you do, she thought. *The real question is how long I have before you try to jump my bones.*

Somehow, she managed to hold back a shudder. Even though she'd tried to tell herself that Bariq was very good-looking, and that she could make herself accept this arrangement, now she was starting to have her doubts. The impulse to say yes to him had been born of a need to get away from Idris before she did something really stupid, but she'd begun to wonder whether all she'd done was shoot herself in the foot.

The really scary thing was how alone they were here. There was no one to help her, no one to come to her rescue if things went south. And if he tried to force the issue before she was ready, she knew she wouldn't be able to stop him. Even if he'd been an ordinary mortal, he was far larger and more muscular than she. And when you factored his djinn powers into the equation…there was no way she'd be able to fight off the supernatural equivalent of a roofie. Her only comfort was knowing she'd probably be so out of it, she wouldn't even realize what was happening to her.

However, his next words reassured her a little. "Let me show you your room. I thought you might prefer to have your own quarters here…at least at first."

Well, thank God for that. At least he wasn't expecting her to sleep in his bed right away.

"Sounds great," she said. "I can't wait to see it."

And she wasn't disappointed. The room was large, with its own balcony overlooking the beach and a private en suite bathroom all done in travertine and glass. In fact, the bathroom was so big, it was almost the same size as the Japanese house she'd been occupying at the Huntington. If Bariq had wanted to play petty games, he probably could have installed her in a smaller secondary bedroom without its own bathroom, just to see whether cramped quarters would make her more likely to move in with him that much more quickly. But he hadn't. She knew she should be grateful for that, but right then she just felt numb, as if she was making the right responses, saying the correct words, even as nothing seemed to really touch her.

"You approve?" he asked as he deposited her bags in the enormous walk-in closet. It was absolutely empty except for those two bags, which seemed to indicate he hadn't been sure of her coming here after all, since otherwise he probably would have provided some sort of a wardrobe, just as Idris had for her.

Don't think about him, she told herself. *Put him out of your mind. That ship has sailed.*

"It's amazing," she said. "That view!"

And she went to the door that opened onto the balcony and unlatched it, then stepped outside. The ocean breeze felt fresher up here, pulling at her loose hair. It had been far too long since she'd gone to the beach, and she shut her eyes and breathed in the wild, salt-scented air, glad of this if nothing else.

"It is quite beautiful," Bariq said as he came out onto the balcony. However, his gaze was fixed on her face, and not the shimmering beach below them. "As are you."

Amber looked away, feeling blood rush to her cheeks. A strange reaction, because once upon a time, she'd been all too used to receiving compliments, and either accepting or deflecting them as the situation warranted. Now, though, she couldn't quite figure out where to look, whether she should gaze up into his face or glance down at her feet, or simply keep watching the waves crash on the shore, nearly a hundred feet beneath where they stood. She decided it was probably safest to keep looking at the beach. At least that way, she wouldn't have to shift her position.

"Um…thank you," she replied, since she knew she needed to say something.

"You are not used to hearing men say such things to you?" he asked, as if sensing her awkwardness.

"It's been a while," she admitted.

He didn't respond at first, although she thought she saw a flicker of satisfaction in his expression. Was he relieved to know that Idris hadn't made any kind of advances toward her, hadn't even paid her a compliment?

"Well, you did spend far too long on your own."

She couldn't argue with that observation. And while she wished she could blame him for that, she knew what had happened wasn't really anyone's fault. Two ships passing in the night, and that sort of thing.

"I suppose I did." Now she forced herself to look up at him. Really, it wasn't his fault that he wasn't Idris. Even a few weeks ago, if she'd known that she'd be alone in a fabulous house in Costa Rica with a golden god of masculinity, she would have been thrilled.

And he really did seem to be trying.

"I will let you get settled in," he said, possibly picking up on her awkwardness. "You can meet me on the patio when you're done—the second patio, not the one where we first arrived."

"There are two?" she asked. She didn't remember that particular detail about the house, but then, she'd been drinking a lot of rum-based cocktails that night.

"Yes. This one is off the dining room, and has a bar."

"Drinks, then?" she asked.

"Absolutely," he replied with a smile.

Then he went back inside, and headed out into the hallway and down the stairs. Amber let out a sigh of relief and found her way into the closet, where she pulled the clothes she'd brought with her out of their bags and hung everything up. They didn't take very much space, but that was probably just as well. She and Bariq weren't going to stay here forever; there was no need for her to have a lot of clothes.

However, she left the picture of herself and her mother and her grandmother inside the bag where she'd put it. Somehow, she didn't want them looking at her, as if she worried she might be able to detect some kind of disapproval in their expressions, distaste for the situation she now found herself in.

Better not to think about that. For now, she just needed to find something that would work for sitting outside on the patio. Amber ditched the cardigan she'd been wearing and paused for a moment, wondering if her current sleeveless floral top and jeans and flats would be good enough. Probably. If she came downstairs in a dress, it would seem like too much. Better to save the big guns for later.

She went out into the wide upstairs hallway and allowed herself a moment to admire the fine abstract art on the pale walls, the lush potted palms tucked into unexpected corners. This really was a gorgeous house. Yes, the home where she'd grown up was extremely nice, but even one of San Marino's finest properties had a hard time competing with oceanfront luxury like this.

As advertised, the second patio had a large bar and a long table for sit-down eating. Bariq was behind the bar, just setting down a pair of heavy hand-blown margarita glasses with cobalt blue rims.

Margaritas. Oh, dear lord, when was the last time she'd had one of those?

If her new...companion? partner?...Amber wasn't sure how to think of him...had been expecting her to show up in a new outfit, he didn't show any sign of it. He pushed one of the drinks across the bar to her and said, "I hope you like these. I found the recipe in a book in the cupboard here."

"I love them," she replied. "Thank you."

He looked pleased. "I am glad to hear that. There were many interesting concoctions in the book, but this is the one I've gotten best at making."

Amber lifted the glass and took a sip. He hadn't been exaggerating—that was one good margarita, just the perfect balance of flavors without it tasting too strong. "It's really good." She glanced past him to the Vitamix blender sitting on the granite countertop. "You really make them from scratch? You don't just will them into existence?"

"I enjoy making them." He took his own glass and sipped from it. "Really, being alone down here, I had to think of ways to fill my time."

That was something she really hadn't thought about. Idris had always seemed so busy, working on the gardens or making small improvements to the house or making sure the Huntington's valuable books and other research materials were properly maintained, that she hadn't thought about what it might be like for someone whose home was basically turn-key and didn't require anything close to that amount of work.

"You've been here by yourself this whole time?" she asked, feeling pity stir in her...and not quite sure what she was supposed to do about it.

"Yes," Bariq replied. "When I couldn't find you, I was not quite sure what I should do with myself, so I came here to regroup and decide what to do next. I suppose the time passed more quickly than I realized."

Maybe that was an occupational hazard of being immortal. Amber had wondered what it must be like to have to fill up an unending existence, whether time didn't feel the same to the djinn as it did to human beings, whose lifespans rarely even reached the century mark. If a djinn didn't note each passing day as it flashed by, then maybe two years really wouldn't have felt like all that long.

"Besides," he went on, "we djinn tend to be solitary creatures. Did Idris not speak to you of any of this?"

"Not all that much," she admitted. Oh, he'd talked about the djinn a little bit, but he definitely hadn't spoken very much about the kind of relationships they had. At the time, she hadn't thought much about it, except to think that he was probably being reticent because she might find the subject matter awkward. Also, Idris's situation wasn't exactly the same as it would be for an ordinary djinn. He was an elder, and therefore somewhat apart from the rest of his people. It looked as though Istar and Ibram had paired off, but who had there been for Idris?

No one, she realized. *No one at all.* And even though she'd sworn to herself not to think about him, she couldn't help thinking he'd gotten a very raw deal.

"He probably decided there wasn't much point, since at the time he hadn't known you had been Chosen," Bariq said. "But our people do not bind themselves to one another for a lifetime. Our liaisons may span a few years or even decades, but we always retreat to our own homes, our own lands, when a relationship ends."

Amber sort of hated to ask the question, but his comments had left it hanging out there. "And…children?"

His green-gold eyes glinted at her over the bright cobalt rim of his margarita glass. "Are you asking whether we have them?"

She raised an eyebrow. "Well, no, I kind of figured you must, since you're all here, right? But if you don't stay together all that long, who's responsible for the kids?"

That was probably a naïve question. After all, she had far more friends with divorced parents than otherwise. Possibly she'd been hoping that the djinn had figured out how to make long-term relationships work.

"If we agree to have children, then the parents remain together until the child reaches his or her majority at two decades. Once they have reached that age, they go their own way, as do the parents. Our notion of family is probably a bit looser than yours."

Which had to make life a little less complicated. She could see how having parents who continued to interfere in your life after you were three or four hundred years old would truly suck.

"At any rate," Bariq continued, "I suppose at some point I would have sought out a djinn woman to share some time here with me, but luckily, Ibram reached out and let me know about you, and here we are."

"Here we are," she echoed, and raised her margarita glass so he could join her in the toast.

He touched his glass to hers, and they both drank. The tequila was starting to work on her a little, not enough to make her feel truly loose, but just enough that the tense knot at the back of her neck had begun to release a bit. That had to be good, right? She certainly wasn't at the point where she was ready to get drunk and fall into bed with Bariq—not while Idris still haunted her thoughts—but at least she could feel herself relaxing around him, had begun to think that she might be able to make this work after all.

It was a start.

No matter where he went, it seemed as though every spot in the gardens, every room in the house, was haunted by his memories of Amber. Idris tried to tell himself that was foolish, that she had only been here a scant two weeks, but after all, he had not lived at the Huntington on his own for very long before he found her. It was not as though he had years of experiences here that could outnumber the days they'd spent together.

He had been so pleased to take this place as his residence. Now, he rather thought he hated everything about it.

Even so, there was work to be done. He went around the grounds and dead-headed the flowers himself using clippers he'd found in the gardening department's storage area, worked up a sweat by manually raking leaves when really, all he had to do was wave a hand and make them disappear. Perhaps if he labored hard enough, he could begin to erase his memories of her, could blot out the nightmarish vision of her being held in Bariq's arms, of him kissing her, of him....

"No."

Idris realized he'd said the word aloud and straightened, one hand still clutching the rake. Right then, he'd been dangerously close to breaking the slim wooden handle right in two.

Not that it would have mattered if he had, only that such an action would have shown how dangerously unaware he was being. This couldn't go on.

It won't, he told himself grimly as he waved a hand and made the pile of leaves near his feet disappear into thin air. *She has only been gone a few days. Soon enough, the wound will be less raw, and you will be able to go on and forget her.*

Assuming, of course, that his path would not cross hers once she and Bariq came back to Southern California to settle. In reality, it was probably ingenuous of him to think he would not see her at some point, for although the djinn/mortal communities tended to move along without much interference from the elders, there would at some point be an occasion where he and Ibram and Istar might be called in to adjudicate.

And then he might see Amber. Would see her with Bariq.

What if they had a child?

Somehow, he managed to prevent himself from letting out a groan. This whole fiasco had taught him one thing—he had a heretofore undiscovered talent for torturing himself.

Idris went up to the house and allowed himself a long, hot shower to wash away the perspiration of the afternoon's labors. That helped a little…a very little.

Perhaps it would be better if he went away for a while. He'd thought he would love his new home, but now it only felt haunted by the ghost of Amber's presence, a nagging sensation that something vital was now missing from the place. Possibly, a change of scenery would do him some good. But where to go?

He knew that Ibram and Istar would always welcome his company for a few days—after all, they had shared a palace in the otherworld for uncounted centuries. Indeed, when he had first come to live here at the Huntington, Idris had wondered if he would find it strange to be on his own after so many years of living under the same roof with the other two elders, even though that "roof" had been a very large one, and there had been many days when he had remained in his wing of the palace and hadn't seen them at all.

But what if Ibram or Istar saw something of his unease and commented on it? That was always a possibility, although Ibram would probably be pleased enough with how the situation with Amber and Bariq had been managed that he might overlook his fellow elder's disquiet. Istar, though…her brilliant green eyes missed very little. If he went to visit them in France, Idris would have to be very careful. Perhaps this wasn't such a good idea after all.

Frowning, he got out of the shower and dried himself off, then scowled at his reflection in the mirror. Although he was flushed from the hot water, and probably his labors in the sun this afternoon, he still looked hollow-eyed to himself, haunted and desperate.

He would have to do something about that before he went to visit Istar and Ibram.

FOURTEEN

SHE'D ALMOST GOTTEN USED TO THE WAY BARIQ looked at her in her bikini. Back in the time before, she hadn't thought much about flaunting her body in front of other people, especially since her friends did exactly the same thing whenever they went to the beach or to a pool party. Now, though, it felt strange to expose so much skin, even though, if you weren't going to wear a bikini on the beach in Costa Rica, where would you wear one?

The house had a long, curved staircase that cut through the hillside and wound its way down to the shore. It wasn't precisely a private beach, because there were three other houses along this stretch of coastline, and she supposed they'd all had to share back in the day. In this new world, of course, there was no one else here to use this beach…or any of Costa Rica's beaches. As far as she could tell, she and Bariq were the only people in the entire country. It was sort of a strange feeling, to know that all these miles of coast would remain completely untouched, unused. Even this small piece would be empty once the two of them departed for Southern California.

Bariq watched her stride over to the chaise longue next to his, then lie down on the towel spread over its surface. She'd just swum in the warm water, marveling that the ocean could still be so comfortable when it was almost November, but now she wanted to rest.

"A good swim?" he asked.

"Yes," she replied, glad that she was lying down. She'd felt the most exposed when she was walking across the sand toward him, but now he'd have to obviously lean over to ogle her, so this felt a bit safer. Not for the first time, she told herself that she really needed to loosen up. This had been her decision. She could have said no to Bariq, could have gone to Los Alamos, where she would have had more freedom to be with whatever man she chose. Only…she had a feeling the situation probably wouldn't have been that easy. The pickings in that unique human settlement could have been extremely slim.

Which was partly why she was here in the first place.

Anyway, she needed to get used to Bariq looking at her. So far, he hadn't made any moves, had been almost too solicitous, and yet she had to wonder whether a lot of that was only pretense. Maybe he'd detected her unease and so was putting on the nice-guy act in order to lull her into a false sense of security. She was reminded of the time that her friend Jaclyn back in seventh grade kept trying to coax a wary stray cat into her house. The animal ran whenever Jaclyn got too close, but she kept on putting out little bowls of food for it, gradually moving them closer and closer to the back patio. Over time, the cat got to the point where it wouldn't bolt the second Jaclyn opened the sliding glass door, and then eventually, it would let her pet it. At last Jaclyn was able to get the cat to come inside, and that was the end of the story. She had her pet, and the cat had lost its freedom. No more roaming the neighborhood for you, little kitty.

Amber had a feeling she knew exactly what that cat had felt like...only the end result here would be a lot more personal than having to wear a collar and getting all her shots. Sooner or later, Bariq was going to lose his patience with her. The real question was, how long would that take?

"I thought we might take out one of the boats from the marina," he remarked, shielding his eyes as he looked out over the water. The day was utterly perfect, probably in the low eighties, with just a few puffy clouds floating here in a jewel-bright sky. "It looks as though the weather is right for it."

"That sounds like fun," she responded, although her inner alarm was already pinging. She'd always been wary whenever a guy tried to get her someplace alone.

But then, what was the difference between being out on the ocean with Bariq in a yacht or being here in his house? Either way, they were utterly isolated. There wasn't anything he could do on a boat that he couldn't do right here on dry land.

"Have you ever gone fishing?" he asked, and Amber wondered if she'd completely misread the situation. Fishing sounded like a pretty innocuous occupation.

"No," she replied. "That is, I went on what was supposed to be a fishing trip to Catalina once, but everyone seemed more interested in getting wasted."

"'Wasted'?" he repeated, looking puzzled.

"Drunk," she explained. Funny how the djinn seemed to have perfect mastery of English but didn't quite have a good grasp of human slang. Then again, there were a *lot* of euphemisms for getting drunk. One time, she and Kelly had tried to list them all after an afternoon of drinking margaritas at the country club, but they could never get past around twenty or so.

"Ah," Bariq said. His brows drew together,

and then he shook his head. "I do not see how fishing and drinking would go very well together. The movement of the vessel tends to upset the balance of quite a few mortals."

Amber suppressed a grimace, remembering how that fishing trip had turned out. As she recalled, she and her friend Lora, who'd gone with her, had nicknamed the cruise "the Puke Patrol." "It doesn't go well at all," she said. "But I never get seasick, and I assume it isn't an issue for djinn."

"No, not at all," he told her. "And besides, on a vessel of the size I'm contemplating, you will not feel the motion of the waves very much."

Because of course there had to be some pretty impressive yachts docked at the marina, probably owned by the same people who'd once lived in these houses...or rather, used them as their vacation homes. Usually, when you were dealing with this kind of real estate, the people who owned the houses involved probably had at least four or five or six of these places scattered around the globe. In fact, she sometimes wondered why her parents hadn't owned more houses. They certainly could have afforded them. But they'd had the San Marino house and a beach house down in San Diego for a while, and that was it. Her mother hadn't seemed inclined to travel much after the divorce, except for her annual visits to Santa Fe and New York and San Francisco.

"I can't wait to see it," Amber said, and Bariq gave her a pleased smile.

"Then let us go now."

Neither Istar nor Ibram seemed all that surprised to see him, but Idris thought that was merely because they'd extended an open invitation to him just before they came to claim their earthly residences.

"It might seem strange to be separated after all these years," Istar had said. "So please, know that you can join us at any time."

His stated purpose now was that he desired more time to explore the gardens at their chateau, since he was contemplating making a few changes to his own grounds. That, of course, was a flat-out lie, because he'd already come to love every inch of the varied offerings at the Huntington and had no desire to change a single flowerbed. Luckily, neither Ibram nor Istar could possibly guess at the real reason behind his visit.

In fact, she offered to give him a tour, although Ibram demurred, saying he wished to stay inside, where he was cataloguing the library of the great manor house. This was an activity that had never been required of Idris, for of course the contents of the Huntington had already been catalogued by its large team of volunteers and staff.

Istar wrapped a voluminous embroidered wool shawl around her shoulders, then led him outside to the rose garden. Here, most of the blooms had already died off, although there were a few of the hardier specimens that still remained.

They walked in silence for a few moments, Idris pretending to study the layout of the flowerbeds and the gravel paths that wound among them. Then Istar said, "You seem troubled, Idris."

"Do I?" he responded, hoping he sounded blithe and not troubled at all. "I am sorry. I suppose I was just concentrating."

She paused, and so he was forced to stop as well and look down at her. Although her mouth wore its usual faint curve of a smile, he could see worry in her clear green eyes. "We have known each other for far too many centuries for you to lie to me, my friend. What weighs on your heart?"

He wished he could tell her. It would be good to be able to unburden himself, to tell her of the pain he'd suffered in letting Amber go with Bariq al-Dawud. But, good friend that she was, he still feared how she might look at him when he confessed that he had given his heart to a mortal woman, someone whose brief lifespan was barely a finger snap to either of them. Worse, a mortal woman who had already been claimed by another.

"Is it Amber?" Istar asked, and he couldn't

quite prevent his eyes from flaring open in surprise.

"What makes you say that?" he replied, knowing that he had probably already given himself away.

She chuckled, then pulled her shawl a little more tightly around herself. This could have been an affectation, for although the air was chilly, the temperature should not have made much of a difference to her. Staring off into the distance, at the rows of poplar trees that outlined the lane leading to the chateau, she said, "I suppose I should not laugh. You were trying your very hardest to be calm and indifferent, every inch the elder. But even so, I could see the way you looked at her, the expression on your face when she left with Bariq. You did not want her to go, that much was clear."

And this was why he should have stayed away. At the same time, though, Idris felt a sense of relief. Oddly, it was good to know he would not have to hide this secret from Istar. "Does Ibram know?"

At once, she shook her head. "No. He sees the situation as a loose end that was neatly tied up, and not much more than that. It would never occur to him that you might lose your heart to a mortal."

"I suppose you think me very foolish."

"No." Istar stepped closer, laid a hand on his

arm. "Do you not think that I have grieved for you, seeing how alone you have been all this time? It is not our place to question the will of God, but more than once, I wondered why you should be left to yourself in such a way, especially when Ibram and I were so blessed in one another."

As Idris himself had thought on far too many occasions, although he had had the sense to keep such inner turmoil to himself. Now, though…now it was something of a relief to know that Istar's feelings on this subject were aligned with his. "I am glad you don't think I am a fool," he said. "And yet, I must find some way to forget her. She belongs to another."

"That is something of a conundrum," Istar agreed. She took her hand from his arm, but she still remained close, gazing up into his face with a speculative gleam in her eyes. "I must confess— now that it is just you and I speaking—that it seems to me we are missing some part of the story. Bariq's claim does seem to be a valid one, and yet, out of all the djinn who claimed their Chosen, he is the only one who did not approach his mortal during the allotted time."

"You know why," Idris, not bothering to hide the harsh rasp of his voice. Truly, it was a relief to be open with her like this, to not have to conceal his feelings. "Because Bariq al-Dawud was a coward and hesitated when he should have gone to her immediately."

"True, that is the story." Istar's eyes narrowed slightly, so sharp that he felt as though they might be able to bore directly into this soul. "But I do not think it is the whole story."

"What do you mean?"

"Come, let us sit."

She turned from him and walked toward a stone bench a few yards away, and he had no choice but to follow her. At least here they were in the sun, its warm rays settling into the black silk robe he wore, although he still bore an inner chill that even the sunlight could not dispel.

After they had taken their places on the bench, she played with one end of her shawl, her long, elegant fingers running over the tassels it bore. "Do you not think it strange that she should be able to survive for so long, all on her own? Amber is a beautiful young woman, and, it appears, resourceful enough, but no other human survivors were able to hold out as long as she."

"That girl who ended up with Hasan did," Idris pointed out, hoping that example would be enough to deflect Istar's questioning.

However, she was not deterred by his statement, saying, "True, but she was with a community of other survivors. They helped one another —were strong enough to defend themselves with guns—which it does not seem was the case with

Amber. I've spoken to some of the djinn who cleared that area, and they said they never saw a sign of a human survivor after the first few weeks."

She had been busy, it seemed. But that was Istar's way—hers was a curious, probing mind, always looking for inconsistencies, for things that did not seem to make sense.

One thing she had said sent a cold tendril of worry through him. "What else did they say?"

Now she smiled widely, as if pleased that he'd confirmed a suspicion of hers. "What do you think they said, Idris?"

Very well. He supposed it had only been a matter of time before the truth emerged. "I am guessing that one of them told you he had been driven off by me."

"Why, yes, Mahmoud did," she said. An eyebrow arched, and she went on, "He was rather reluctant, true, although I am not sure that was because he did not want to create dissension in his elders, or because he feared what might happen to him after I told him that the woman he'd tried to attack had been Chosen."

All Idris could do was shrug. He'd wondered the same thing as well, whether Amber's attacker had kept silent because he knew he had been in the wrong.

"I told him we believed it was a mistake and he left, since he had given me the information I wanted." Istar stared up at him, lovely face a study in puzzlement. "Why, Idris? Why would you do such a thing? Did you know she was Chosen?"

That would have been the easy way out, but of course, he hadn't known such a thing. By that point, several days after the Heat had cleansed the world, all the humans who were Chosen had been claimed by their djinn. All of them...except Amber. At any rate, he'd believed her a regular survivor, someone immune and nothing else.

"No," he said heavily. "It was...I saw the terror in her face, Istar. I could not let her be killed. So yes, I drove Mahmoud off, and she fled and took refuge in the basement of the Huntington's visitor center. Later, I realized that my interference is what continued to keep her alive, for clearly Mahmoud had told the other reavers that she was under my protection, even though I certainly had not said such a thing in any formal kind of way."

"And so when you found her a few weeks ago...." Istar prompted.

He shrugged. "I thought it must be luck...and some skill...that had kept her alive. But because I had saved her, I felt a responsibility to her as well. I allowed her to stay at the Huntington with me until she could become accustomed to this new world, to all the changes that had occurred while she was in hiding. I suppose I assumed that at some point, I would send her to Los Alamos to live with the other human survivors. Believe me, the last thing I ever imagined was that I might…."

He let the words trail off, because even though Istar knew the truth now, he was not sure he could summon the will to speak that terrible truth aloud.

However, Istar was made of stronger stuff. "You never imagined that you might fall in love with her."

"No," he said simply. "It was…a gradual thing. I never spoke of it to her."

"You do not think she felt the same way?"

"Of course not," he replied immediately. "If she did, why on earth would she go with Bariq?"

Now Istar laughed aloud, even as she rose to her feet, pulling her shawl around her. A breeze moved through the garden then, playing with the shawl's gilded tassels and the long, loose waves of her coppery hair. "Idris, for someone who has lived many thousands of years, you don't seem to know very much about women."

That was probably true. The women who had come in and out of his life had not spent enough time with him to allow him any real knowledge of their natures, of the secrets they held close to their hearts. "Tell me what I have missed, Istar, if I am as foolish as you say I am."

"You just told me that you never spoke of your feelings to Amber," Istar said. Her tone was fond, rather than condescending, and yet he had a sense that she was somewhat amused at his utter incomprehension. "I do not pretend to know her at all, but she is a beautiful young woman, someone who probably had her share of suitors back before the world changed. Such a woman would not confess what was in her heart unless she was sure of it being reciprocated. I know you, Idris. I know how you can close yourself off from others, make it difficult to know what might be passing through your mind. If you did the same thing to her, then why on earth would she have had any reason to open herself to you? She went with Bariq because she felt she had no reason to stay."

"She would not have been able to stay, even if she had refused him," Idris said, doing his best to focus on the particulars of the situation, rather than the terrible possibility that Amber had loved him all along and he had been too blind to see it. "At best, she would have had to go to Los Alamos."

"Why is that?" Istar asked, looking genuinely curious. "Have we ever agreed that an elder might not have a Chosen?"

"Well, no," he replied. His head was beginning to spin. Had she really just asked such a question? True, they had never come out and explicitly stated such a thing, but it had seemed obvious enough to him that it was out of the question for an elder to pair himself with a mortal. That would make it seem as though he was choosing sides, was throwing his lot in with the One Thousand, and not the other djinn who had decreed that humanity must perish. "But surely such a thing is out of the question."

She shook her head. "Oh, Idris, you do like to complicate matters for yourself. I see you standing there, thinking that an elder must be neutral, but the only way for you to be neutral would be to remain alone for the remainder of your days. If you chose a djinn woman, then you would be with someone who agreed that it was right to remove mankind from this world. If you chose a human, then you would be siding with the One Thousand. It seems that all of these possibilities have their own difficulties, so I must ask you, what is it you want...*truly* want?"

"I want Amber," he said, the words leaving his lips as if they had been spoken by someone else, someone with far more certainty than he. "But... she is Bariq's Chosen. I cannot simply take her away. Neither is it fair to challenge him for her, since he would never be able to win such a battle."

"True," Istar replied. She was silent for a moment, head tilted to one side as though considering all the complexities of the matter and weighing them carefully against one another. Then a smile touched her lips.

"What is it?" Idris asked. Could he dare to hope that she might have thought of a way out of this conundrum?

"Come with me," she said. "I think I have an idea."

FIFTEEN

THE YACHT WAS HUGE, THE KIND OF BOAT—SHIP? IT seemed kind of disrespectful to call something so massive a "boat"—that had its own baby submarine tucked into a sort of little underwater garage near the stern of the vessel. Amber thought that would be fun, to take the submarine and explore the crystal-clear waters near the coast and watch all the colorful marine life flit past the observation windows, but today it was all about catching those fish, not observing them.

She and Bariq had gone out about half a mile from shore, close enough that she could clearly see the expanse of white sand beach with its edging of multi-million-dollar homes, and then the lushness of the rainforest just a little way beyond the developed area, showing that nature was always close by, ready to reclaim the land people had taken for their own use. Actually,

Amber was sort of surprised that the trees hadn't begun to encroach on some of the houses; maybe Bariq had done some careful clearing to keep things looking civilized for a while longer.

He stood a few yards away from her, muscles in his arms bulging as he battled the enormous fish he'd hooked just a few minutes earlier. She didn't pretend to know much about fish, unless it was on her plate at a seafood restaurant, but she thought the thrashing creature on the other end of the fishing line was probably a marlin. At least, it looked like the big fish one of her friend's fathers had mounted on the wall of his study, and that one had been a marlin.

In a way, she felt almost sorry for the fish. There it had been, swimming along, probably thinking that life was pretty hunky-dory now that it didn't have to worry about sport fishermen showing up and throwing a monkey wrench in its day, and now, out of nowhere, some random person had appeared and decided to get himself a trophy.

However, Amber had no doubt that Bariq would emerge the victor here. He was letting out the line and pulling it back in as if he'd done this sort of thing hundreds of times before...and maybe he had. After all, he'd told her earlier that he liked to make margaritas from scratch. Maybe he also liked to go fishing and catch his supper, rather than just snapping his fingers for it the way most other djinn would. And no matter how powerful the fish, it couldn't possibly prevail against a djinn.

She had to admit that he did look kind of magnificent standing there, feet braced against the deck, dark gold hair glinting in the sun. For this expedition, he'd abandoned his usual robes and wore swim trunks, a pale blue T-shirt with the logo of a local fishing company on it, and tennis shoes. She hadn't bothered to ask where he'd gotten the clothes, since she already knew it was way too easy for a djinn to conjure just about anything he wanted. But as she gazed at him in his casual attire, she thought she could have easily mistaken him for a regular human...if she hadn't known better.

At least he was occupied for the moment and not paying any particular attention to her. She'd changed as well, trading her bikini for cargo shorts, a tank top, and a pair of tennis shoes. Not exactly the most glamorous outfit in the world, but she was fine with that. As it was, the tank top probably showed off a little more cleavage than she would have liked, but it was still worlds better than the swimsuit she'd had on earlier.

She picked up the water bottle sitting on the table next to her and took a sip. Bariq had asked her if she wanted to fish, and she'd immediately shaken her head and said that she'd rather just watch. Her reply didn't seem to have discouraged him at all, as if he was glad to stand there and show her what a he-man he was while she sat on a lounge chair and observed his battle with the marlin.

Was that unfair of her? Amber thought maybe her inner voice was being a little bitchy, especially since he hadn't done anything to arouse her suspicions, but she still couldn't shake the feeling that the hammer was about to fall. They'd been down here for five days now, and it had all been purely platonic fun, whether lying on the beach or swimming or taking a Jeep to explore the rainforest just beyond the villa where they were living. Dinners together, but no candlelight or wine, just local food prepared well—she'd give Bariq that much—and margaritas or mojitos. She'd been careful to only have one drink, or at most two, at a single time. That way, she didn't have to worry about losing control and doing something she'd regret in the morning.

Through all of this, the djinn hadn't done anything to make her nervous, except to look at her with puppy-dog eyes from time to time, as if puzzled as to why she was being so reticent, why she hadn't given the slightest hint that they should become intimate. In a way, she knew she must seem like a terrible tease, since at their first meeting, she'd made it seem that she was more than willing to be Bariq's partner. But even though she knew she should try to unbend, try to accept her new reality, some part of her remained stubborn, heels firmly dug in.

And of course, she knew why.

Even though she tried her best not to think about him, she still couldn't help hearing Idris's voice as she lay down to sleep at night, couldn't stop thinking about the fine, sharp outline of his profile, the strength in his arms as he held her. The delicious, clove-like scent that seemed to cling to his robes. Everything about him seemed damn near perfect, especially viewed from a distance, as she was doing now. How in the world could she willingly give herself over to Bariq when Idris was still occupying so much space in her head?

The answer seemed to be that she couldn't, which was why matters still stood where they were now…and she couldn't think of how to move past their current impasse.

A mighty tug, and Bariq hauled the marlin on deck, where it flopped around madly, spraying water everywhere. Amber didn't know how this would have gone down in normal circumstances with a human fisherman, but the djinn quickly knelt and placed his hand along the side of the fish's head and it went still, obviously dead.

She set down her bottle of water and brushed some stray droplets of seawater off her bare legs. The damp spots on her tank top and shorts would just have to dry in the sun. As she walked over to Bariq, he stood and gave her a ferocious grin.

"Did you see that? What an animal!"

"It's a very big fish," she allowed, staring down at it. She knew absolutely nothing about sport fishing, but she had to admit the marlin had been a beautiful creature, with striped markings in shades of blue that shimmered in the sunlight. "What did you do to it?"

Bariq's smile faded slightly. "I gave it a quick and painless death, as it deserved. I had no desire to see it thrashing in pain."

Well, that was noble of him. If he was so worried about the marlin's suffering, maybe he shouldn't have caught the damn thing in the first place. She pushed that thought away almost as quickly as it entered her mind. After all, she'd never been anything close to a vegetarian, so there wasn't any real reason for her to go all PETA on him now. "That was kind of you," she said.

He looked a little happier after she said that, so she guessed she'd hit the right note. "But there is no need to have it cluttering up the deck now." A wave of the hand, and the marlin disappeared.

Amber frowned. "Where did it go?"

"Back to the house, of course," Bariq replied. He went past her, into the interior of the yacht, where the galley was located. Now he stood at the stainless-steel sink, vigorously washing his hands —probably to get the fish and saltwater stink off them. "We'll have marlin steaks for dinner tonight."

"It's safe to eat?" she asked, trying to think if she'd ever seen marlin on a menu anywhere. She'd only ever heard of it being either caught and released, or mounted as a trophy.

He wiped his hands on a towel and tossed it on the pale quartz-stone countertop. "Of course. Perhaps once it was considered questionable, but there are no more toxins being dumped into the ocean, so anything I can catch there is perfectly safe."

Right. She supposed she should have thought of that. Maybe even the often-murky water off Southern California would be as sparkling as the Caribbean now that no one was around to dump oil and a host of other noxious substances into it.

Bariq went past her and on to the refrigerator, which he opened to reveal a pitcher of margaritas that Amber could have sworn hadn't been there when she fetched her bottled water a half hour earlier. "I thought you said you liked making your drinks from scratch," she said, hoping he wouldn't catch the distinct lack of enthusiasm in her tone.

"I do," Bariq said easily. "But I was otherwise occupied this past while, as you might recall."

"True." She watched as he got some glasses from a cupboard and poured the thick, slushy mixture into them. "Didn't you tell me we wouldn't be drinking on this trip?"

"I only said we wouldn't be drinking while I was fishing," Bariq replied. "But I am done now, and I think landing that fish deserves a cele- bration."

Any argument she offered would sound petty, so she gave an inner shrug and went to take one of the glasses from him. At least the yacht was big enough that she couldn't really notice the move- ment of the waves, so there probably wasn't much chance of the tequila making her feel woozy.

He went on, "Let's go out to the deck and sit in the sunshine for a while before we head back."

"Sure," Amber said, figuring that sounded relatively safe. Being out in the sun and the wind somehow felt a little less fraught than being inside one of the yacht's opulent lounge areas. She had absolutely no idea who had owned this vessel in the time before the Heat changed the world forever, but she would be shocked if someone told her the couches hadn't seen at least a little action in the past.

They went forward, to the sundeck at the front of the yacht. Was that aft? She couldn't really remember, since her family hadn't been into boat- ing. There were several sectionals bolted to the deck, along with matching tables and chairs. From what she had been able to tell, it looked as though the ship could sleep up to ten people, although obviously that wasn't something she and her companion needed to worry about. Clearly, the large decks could accommodate many more people than that for a party or fishing expedition.

Bariq sat down on one of the sectionals, and after a brief hesitation, Amber took a seat next to him. He might have raised an eyebrow if she'd chosen one of the chairs instead, and she really didn't feel like getting into an argument over something as silly as their seating arrangements. The sun beat down on them, warm and soothing, but bright enough that she was glad she'd remembered to slather herself with sunblock before they left the house this morning. Funny, the habits you forgot after spending so much time living underground.

For a moment, they were quiet, sipping their margaritas and breathing in the fresh ocean air. Then Bariq said, "You enjoy the ocean, don't you?"

"Yes," she replied. "I went to the beach when I had the time, but it's not the same as living right next to it, like we are here."

"Then I think we should probably go to Laguna Beach when we are done here in Costa Rica. Bel-Air is beautiful, but it is still miles from the water."

That made sense. If she had to start over somewhere, she might as well do it someplace that would be an entirely new experience. Living in

Bel-Air might feel a little too much like being back in San Marino, although Amber had to smile inwardly at the thought. If she'd ever said something like that to her mother, she probably would have sniffed and made a comment about all the "new money" and Hollywood types who lived in that exclusive suburb.

"That sounds good," Amber said, although she knew she probably didn't sound quite as enthusiastic as she should. Going to Laguna Beach felt so…permanent. While they were here in Costa Rica, she could pretend this was simply a sort of way station, a stopping place while they figured out what they were going to do next. Once Bariq had taken her back to Southern California, that would be the end of it. There would be no chance of anything turning out differently.

There isn't a chance now, she told herself. *You made your choice, and you can't change it. So stop acting like such a wet rag and get with the program.*

Bariq was looking at her with some concern, so clearly her lack of zeal had been obvious to him as well. To try to make amends, she shot her most brilliant smile at him and added, "It'll be fun to pick out a house with you. I hope there are still some good ones left."

Her comment made him lift an eyebrow at her. "Oh, I am sure there must be one or two that will suit our needs." He paused, then shifted on the sectional so he moved a bit closer to her. Amber could feel herself stiffen, but she told herself to relax. All this time, he'd been a perfect gentleman, so she had no reason to think he would behave any differently now. "And really," he continued as he set his margarita down on the table, "if we are so close to moving on to that part of our lives, do you think it necessary to continue to maintain this distance between us?"

"'Distance'?" she echoed, her body stiffening with tension even as she recognized that she was stalling by feigning incomprehension. It would have been obvious to anyone watching their interactions that she'd done her best over the past few days to make sure she didn't give him any mixed signals, didn't behave in a way that made it seem as if she was open to his overtures.

He put his hand on her bare leg, and she somehow managed not to flinch. "Yes, distance. I wanted to give you some time to become accustomed to me, to relax into our…situation. But if we are to go to Laguna Beach, to present ourselves to the djinn and their Chosen there, then would it not make sense to go there as a true couple?"

"Um…I suppose so," Amber replied, knowing how uncertain she sounded. If only his hand didn't feel so heavy resting there on her leg, his fingers almost too warm as they pressed against her flesh. More than anything, she wanted to pull away, to tell him she hadn't said it was all right for him to touch her like that, but she knew that sort of protest wouldn't go over very well. Besides, hadn't she given him tacit permission to do anything he liked by agreeing to come here? She knew what the relationship of a djinn and his Chosen was supposed to be; she hadn't signed up for this thinking they would be platonic house-mates and nothing more.

But now he seemed to be pressing her at last, and something within her was rebelling, was telling her this felt wrong, no matter what she might have been thinking a few days earlier.

"You suppose so," Bariq repeated. A frown creased his tanned brow, and he stared at her, greenish-hazel eyes almost golden in the sunlight. "That is all you have to say?"

"I—" Not caring how he might respond, Amber put down her margarita glass and stood. She didn't know exactly where she planned to go —locking herself in a stateroom probably wasn't an option—but at least by getting up like that, she'd forced him to take his hand off her leg. With a lift of her shoulders that she guessed didn't look terribly nonchalant, she said, "I guess I just hadn't thought we would go this soon."

"It is not 'soon,'" he argued, rising as well. Standing this close, he practically dwarfed her meager five feet, five inches, and she wished—not for the first time—that she was model-tall, five foot ten or even six feet. Then she wouldn't feel quite so overwhelmed. "We have been here for five days, Amber. Each night, I have allowed you to go to your own room, have not pursued you or touched you or tried to force you in any way. But the time for my patience is at an end."

Before she could move away, he'd reached out and taken her by the wrist, pulled her to him. When his mouth touched hers, she experienced a strange wave of despair. It should have been Idris kissing her like this, not Bariq...although she somehow knew that Idris would never force a kiss, would never take something that wasn't willingly given.

That despair quickly turned to anger, and she tried to pull away, although she couldn't get far with his hand still wrapped around her wrist like that. "Don't," she said once her mouth was free.

"'Don't'?" he repeated, and now he sounded almost amused, as though it had never occurred to him that a mortal woman might try to resist his charms. However, his expression darkened almost immediately, his tone rough as he continued. "Who are you to tell me what I may or may not do? Did you not come here willingly? Could you not comprehend what it meant to be my Chosen?"

"I did," she said. There was no point in trying to be disingenuous, but neither was she just going to roll over and let herself be manhandled. "Or at least, I thought I did. I thought—"

His eyes gleamed, harsh gold in the sunlight. "You thought what?"

The Amber from before the Heat, before the world changed, might have attempted to deflect, to do what was necessary to hide the truth from him. After all, she had plenty of experience talking down guys who'd gotten too handsy. Now, though, she realized she wasn't that Amber anymore...and she wasn't going to take Bariq's bullshit just because he happened to be a djinn.

"I thought eventually I'd be attracted to you," Amber said, feeling strangely excited by her boldness. Had she ever said anything that direct to a man before? "But I'm not. I don't want this after all. I want you to take me to Los Alamos."

Unnervingly, he began to laugh. His hand tightened on her wrist, and he pulled her closer, even though she struggled in his grasp, did her best to grind the rubber soles of her sneakers into the deck so he couldn't get any leverage. "You want me to take you to Los Alamos? My dear, you are in no position to make such a request. As you mortals liked to say, you have made your bed... and now you will lie in it."

A harsh yank and she was up against him, his arms around her even as his mouth sought hers again. He tasted of margaritas, which shouldn't have been so bad, but she still wanted to vomit anyway. Her hands pressed against the unyielding muscles of his chest, too-short nails trying to dig into his flesh, and yet it didn't seem to matter what she did. He held her captive, and there wasn't a goddamn thing she could do about it.

And then...then a strange, lightheaded sensation began to overtake her. If Bariq hadn't been holding her tightly against him, she might have stumbled or even fallen, but there was no chance of that happening. Along with the dizzy feeling came a rush of warmth, of desire. Why was she struggling? She wanted him to kiss her, wanted him to do much more.

He deepened the kiss, and Amber opened her mouth willingly, tasted him again, breathed in the sea-salt scent of his skin. Deep within her, though, she felt a sudden wash of confusion, as if she somehow knew she shouldn't be responding this way even though her body was telling her something very different.

What was happening to her?

The answer swam up from the depths of her mind like a swimmer trying to breach the surface before she ran out of air.

The djinn glamour.

Idris had told her about it, how the djinn would somehow use their powers to bend humans to their will. Bariq must be using it now, because Amber knew that otherwise, she would never have willingly let him kiss her, wouldn't be practically moaning from his touch now.

She planted both her hands against his chest and pushed as hard as she could. Caught off guard, he stumbled backward a pace.

It was enough. She was free.

Without pausing to think, she turned and ran down the length of the lower deck, pounding her way back to the spot where he'd battled with the marlin. She didn't know what she planned to do, exactly, only that she had to do whatever she could to keep some distance between them.

But there he was, already recovered from his stumble, pursuing her on his much longer legs. Amber didn't know why he hadn't blinked himself up next to her, except that maybe he wasn't quite sure where she planned to go and thought it would be easier to follow on foot.

She didn't know where she was going, either. And she was rapidly running out of deck.

"Stop this foolishness!" he called out. "What do you think you're doing?"

"Getting away from you," she responded, although she knew better than to look back at him.

The edge of the deck was very close. Five feet. Three. Two.

Until she dove into the water, she honestly hadn't known that was what she intended to do. Now, though, as she frantically kicked off her sneakers and then began heading toward shore, she realized that jumping off the boat had been the only possible solution to her dilemma.

Did djinn swim? She supposed she was about to find out.

As she cut through the water, thankful for all her summers spent by the family pool and the swimming skill they'd provided, she heard another splash and looked back. Bariq had dived in as well, was now cutting through the thick swells like an Olympic-trained swimmer.

Well, that seemed to answer her question.

Panic threatened to overwhelm her, but Amber made herself keep swimming. No looking back. That would only slow her down.

The splashing got louder, and then he was beside her, teeth bared in a ferocious grin, his golden-brown hair plastered to his head. "Foolish girl," he said, not even panting. "You never thought to ask which element I controlled. Well, it is this one."

And then it was as if the ocean around her became alive, roaring, holding on to her so she couldn't move. The massive swells propelled her toward the shore, carrying her along so she had no choice but to move with them, desperately trying to gulp in enough air to fill her tired and terrified lungs. She had the impression that Bariq was swimming beside her, or rather, was somehow riding the crest of that perpetual wave, coaxing it along until it eventually crashed upon the beach and deposited her on the wet sand.

Gasping and choking, Amber dragged herself up and away from the water. Her heart pounded and her ears rang, and she wondered whether maybe it wouldn't have been better if she had let herself drown after all.

A shadow fell over her, and Bariq grasped her by the shoulder and turned her over, apparently no worse the wear for their wild ride. He lowered himself onto her, pinning her in place on the sand.

Oh, God. Was he going to force her here and now, get it over with?

The horrible thing was, she thought she might be too exhausted and frightened to care.

"Do not cross me like that again," he said, leaning down so his face was scant inches from hers. "You've seen the power I can command. It is not the place of a mortal to defy a djinn. Understand?"

She stared up at him, chest still heaving from exertion. It probably would have been worth it to spit in his face, but she doubted she had the strength.

Then a new voice cut in, female, one Amber thought she'd heard before but couldn't begin to place.

"Are we interrupting something?"

At once, Bariq heaved himself off her, and she

somehow managed to get to her knees so she could see who in the world had just spoken.

Standing a few feet away was the female djinn elder—Istar—her long red hair blowing in the breeze. Next to her, his face a thundercloud, was Idris.

SIXTEEN

I<small>F</small> I<small>STAR</small> <small>HADN'T</small> <small>SPOKEN</small>—<small>IF</small> B<small>ARIQ</small> <small>HADN'T</small> immediately moved away from Amber—Idris felt sure he would have stepped forward and landed a blow on the bastard's chin. How dare he assault her like that? And Amber…he didn't know what had just occurred, precisely, but she was soaking wet in a tank top and shorts, shoeless, her hair dripping and her face white with fear.

"How dare you interrupt me in my territory?" Bariq thundered, no doubt trying to look and sound as impressive as possible.

However, Istar only raised her eyebrows a calculated fraction of an inch and said, "We are elders, Bariq al-Dawud. We do not 'dare' anything. And besides, since you have taken a Chosen, this is not, strictly speaking, your territory any longer. You are here on sufferance, no more."

Anger still flaring along his veins, Idris moved forward to Amber and extended a hand. With shaking fingers, she took it and got to her feet, all the while staring balefully at the djinn who was supposed to be her protector and partner.

"Are you all right?" Idris asked.

"I am...now," she responded. Despite her shaken appearance, the smile she sent him then was so warm, he nearly forgot the presence of the other two. Surely she would not have smiled at him in such a way if she felt nothing for him.

Bariq glowered at all of them, arms crossed. He was wearing wet human clothing, a pale blue T-shirt and some kind of beige swim trunks with large colorful flowers woven into the design, and looked vaguely ridiculous. Bristling, he said, "Still, I was not aware that it was your responsibility to interfere with the business of a djinn and his Chosen."

"Under normal circumstances, no," Istar allowed. She gave Idris the briefest of glances, and he nodded back at her. For the moment, he thought it better to let her speak, since he was certain if he gave his tongue free rein, he might say something he regretted later. "But these are not normal circumstances, and we must talk. That is your house up there?"

She pointed toward the enormous modern villa perched on the edge of the cliff, and Bariq nodded, looking sulky.

"Yes," he admitted.

"Well, then. You and Amber may change into dry clothes and meet us afterward in the courtyard. Ten minutes."

Bariq opened his mouth as though to protest, then seemed to think better of it. In the next moment, he vanished, leaving Amber standing there with Idris and Istar.

As much as he wanted to kiss her then and there, he knew this was not the proper time. "I will take you, since Bariq was so churlish as to leave you down here."

Her face lit up with gratitude, but then she looked down at her dripping clothes and said, "I'm soaking wet."

"It does not matter."

Before she could protest further, he went to her and took her in his arms, then brought her to the gracious courtyard hidden at the center of the house. At once, he released her, mostly because Istar had also appeared in the courtyard at the same time, and he did not want to do anything that might invite comment.

"Go ahead and change," Istar said, smiling a little. "And then come back here as soon as you are ready."

Amber began to nod, then seemed to stop herself and said, "What are you two doing here?"

"You will learn soon enough," Istar replied.

"Just go, and do not fear Bariq. You are under our protection now."

A brilliant flash of a smile, and then Amber hurried off. Idris waved a hand, and the wet splotches on his black silk robe disappeared.

"It appears we were just in time," he murmured, and Istar nodded.

"I fear you are correct. I truly had no idea that Bariq would behave in such an abominable fashion."

Neither had Idris, but in a way, he allowed himself some measure of relief. It had been clear enough that the other djinn was attacking Amber out of frustrated lust, which seemed to indicate they had not yet become intimate. Even if they had, such a thing would not have made Idris love her any less, but he was still glad they had not consummated their relationship. This should make everything much easier.

Or so he hoped.

A few moments later, Bariq came back downstairs, hair now dry, sodden human clothing replaced by a garish robe in an orange-gold shade with coppery embroidery around the sleeves. His eyes narrowed as he looked at Idris, but at least he seemed to have remembered something of his manners, for he said, "Some refreshment, elders? Water, or wine…something a bit stronger?"

"Nothing, thank you," Istar said. "You may have guessed that this is not a courtesy visit."

Bariq crossed his arms, his entire stance somehow a bit stiffer than it had been a moment before. "The thought had entered my mind. So to what do I owe the honor of your presence?"

"We will wait to explain until Amber joins us," Idris told him. "This concerns her as well."

The scowl was back. Bariq lifted his chin, saying, "I am not sure how that is possible. She is a mortal. She lives by our whim, nothing more."

"Nice of you to spell it out so clearly," Amber cut in as she descended the stairs into the courtyard. She now wore a pale blue lacy dress with thin straps, her feet in simple silver sandals. And although her hair was still damp, it had already begun to dry into the rippling waves Idris loved so much.

Had she ever been more beautiful? He didn't think so, although perhaps his admiration now was as much a product of their recent separation as anything else.

Her comment earned her a frown from her supposed partner, but she ignored Bariq and instead came across the courtyard to where Idris and Istar stood next to one another. In her expression was curiosity, but also an element of hope. Was it only that she wished for the two elders to take her away, or did her gaze linger on Idris for a moment because other, even more welcome thoughts lingered in her mind?

"You said this concerned me?" Amber asked.

"Yes," Idris said. "I fear that when we told you Bariq had wished to make you his Chosen, we did not offer you the full story."

"Idris," Bariq rasped then, clearly forgetting the etiquette that dictated no djinn should call an elder by their name unless given express permission. Angry color flared in his cheeks. "I do not see how this has any bearing on the current situation."

"Oh, we think it does," Istar said. Her full mouth thinned in disapproval for a second; clearly, after what she had seen him doing to Amber, her opinion of Bariq had dropped even lower. "I think Amber should know that you hesitated to claim her, and that is the true reason why she was left alone in those days after the Dying."

Amber didn't even look over at Bariq, as if she somehow wasn't entirely surprised by this revelation. Voice flat, she said, "He...what?"

"I can explain—" he began, but Istar lifted a hand.

"You have already explained yourself to us, and I have no further need to hear your excuses." Her gaze traveled back to the young mortal woman who stood before her. "He doubted whether he possessed the correct temperament to give himself over to only one woman for the rest of his lifetime, especially a human woman. Because he was unsure of himself, he waited several days before he at last decided to go in search of you. By then, of course, you had already gone into hiding, thanks to being attacked by the djinn who sought to cleanse the world of your kind."

"I was only alive because of Idris," Amber said then, her blue eyes warm with gratitude.

"Yes, I know," Istar replied. "He told me what had happened. Actually, he has told me many things." She paused then, glancing up at him as if asking for permission, and he nodded. Perhaps it was cowardly to allow his fellow elder to make such a revelation, but Idris still was not sure whether he would be able to speak the truth of his heart to the woman he loved. Tone growing gentler, Istar went on, "He has said he has feelings for you, Amber McCoy, and that is why he is here."

A surprised flush stole over Amber's face, and her lips parted. More than ever, he wanted to kiss that delectable mouth, but this was still not the time.

"This is preposterous," Bariq spluttered. He stared at the three of them as his face turned red with rage. "He has no claim on her. None! I was the one who chose her, not him."

"Yes, and such a fine job you did of it," Idris drawled, feeling it safe enough now to enter the conversation. "For that matter, have you actually truly made her your Chosen? For I sense a certain…estrangement…between you."

Amber looked puzzled, but Bariq now glanced down toward the ground as he muttered, "I would have gotten around to it."

"I don't understand," Amber said. "You mean me being here with him wasn't enough to make it official?"

"No," Istar told her with a smile. "There is a certain declaration a djinn needs to make to the universe in order to make such a commitment a true and lasting one. Just a few simple words, but still, without them, you are no more bound to him than he is to me."

"Thank God," Amber said, with such vehemence that Idris knew then and there that truly no attachment existed between the two of them.

Looking satisfied, Istar continued. "In the few instances where two djinn desired the same mortal woman for their Chosen, a duel would be fought between them. However, that particular solution is not feasible in this case, for Idris, an elder, is far stronger than any ordinary djinn. It would not be a fair contest."

"So…what do we do?" Amber asked.

"You must choose."

"What?" Bariq broke in. A few veins had begun to show on his forehead, in addition to the angry flush that still reddened his skin. "That is not how this is done! The djinn chooses the mortal, not the other way around!"

"That is how it *was* done," Istar said gently.

However, the smile she wore told Idris that she was quite pleased with how annoyed Bariq appeared. "But one might say that you do not seem terribly confident in your choice, not when you have had her with you for the better part of five days and still have not formally made her your Chosen...not when it was clear you were physically assaulting the poor girl just as we arrived."

"She was defying me—"

"A djinn and mortal partnership is just that," Idris broke in, cutting off the other djinn's angry retort. "These people are taken to be your partners in eternity, not master and slave. I think you forget how this was supposed to work."

Bariq glared at him, but Idris could tell he had no ready reply to that remark. Or perhaps he had realized that continuing to argue with an elder was never a good idea.

"So, then," Istar said. She turned back to Amber, who had been watching this exchange in some bemusement, as if she still couldn't quite understand what was happening. "You have two djinn here, both of whom have said they wish to be with you. It is your choice—one of them, or of course you can go to Los Alamos, if that is what you desire."

"But I thought Idris—" Amber paused there, her fingers playing with the folds of her gauzy skirt, as if somehow that might help to clear her thought processes. "I mean, he's an elder. Is an elder even allowed to be with a mortal?"

"He is an elder," Istar replied with a smile, "and therefore he makes his own rules. Or rather, we have both determined that there is no reason in the world for the two of you not to be together...if, of course, that is what you wish."

"Oh, I wish it," Amber breathed. Her expression was stunned, as though she still couldn't quite grasp that she might be given the one thing she had truly wanted all along. "I definitely wish it."

Istar looked pleased. "Then it is done. Idris, you may take her away from this place. And you, Bariq," she went on, skewering him with a piercing green gaze, "you get to remain here in Costa Rica, in this house you appear to admire so much. Perhaps at some point, you may be able to entice a woman of the djinn here...as long as word does not get out as to how you treated the woman who was supposed to be your Chosen."

The threat hung on the air, and Bariq suddenly looked a little pale beneath his tan. Idris could only hope the other djinn might have learned something from the mistakes he had made...but somehow, he doubted it. A long lifetime did not necessarily guarantee the gift of self-awareness.

For now, though, he cared little about the other djinn or his costly errors. He could only look at Amber, who'd taken a hesitant step toward him, then another, her lovely face a study in dawning joy.

"Come, my love," he said. "Let us go."

———

Was this real? She didn't know if what was happening was real, but she hoped it might be. Idris held her as the villa in Costa Rica disappeared, only to be replaced by the even more opulent surroundings of the Huntington mansion.

This time, though, he did not let go of her right away, as he had on the other occasions when they'd used the djinn form of travel. Instead, they stood there in the drawing room, his arms still around her, his body strong and warm and comforting.

He stared down at her, searching her face. "Are you sure of this?" he asked softly. "Because it is not too late to take you to Los Alamos, if that is your wish."

"No, it is *not* my wish," she said, her tone as firm as she could make it. She wanted to make sure there would be no more of that nonsense. "I mean, to go to Los Alamos. I want to stay right here with you. That's all I've ever wanted—or at least, it's all I've wanted for the past few weeks. So kiss me right now to make it real."

A quick, beautiful smile touched his lips, and then he bent and pressed his mouth against hers, warm, welcome, utterly unlike Bariq. She supposed it was a little funny that an action whose mechanics really didn't change all that much from person to person could be so completely different when you were with the right man. Her every limb seemed awash with heat, with desire, and she held on to him, tasting the sweetness of his mouth, of his entire beautiful soul.

When that life-changing kiss ended, he gazed down at her with such love glowing in his dark eyes, she almost wanted to cry. No one had ever looked at her like that before, as though she was the promised land and he a weary pilgrim who, against all hope, had finally crossed its border. "I love you, Amber McCoy," he said, and she held his hands and smiled.

"I love you, too, Idris."

His fingers tightened on hers. "I would like to make you my Chosen now."

A thrill went through her, mostly of excitement, possibly tinged with the slightest bit of trepidation. Yes, she knew she loved Idris, had never felt like this about anyone in her life, but was that love strong enough to endure for decades, centuries...who really knew how long? For just a moment, she understood why Bariq had hesitated to claim her, why he had suddenly been uncertain. Forever was an awfully big commitment.

But then she looked up at Idris, at his clean, finely etched features, at the shape of his lips and the lift of his brows and the sooty lashes that shadowed his eyes, and she knew she could be happy to look at that face from now until eternity, happy to hear the sound of his voice as he greeted her in the morning and just before she lay down to sleep at night.

"Yes, please," she breathed. "I want that, too."

Idris continued to hold on to her hands, looking down at her with those endlessly deep, dark eyes of his. Amber thought she could lose herself in their depths, in the wealth of knowledge and experience and love she saw reflected there. Once again, she wondered if she really deserved to be with someone like him, but then she told herself that he didn't seem to be experiencing any such qualms. She needed to trust this, needed to believe that the universe had brought her to this place precisely so they might be together.

His warm, deep voice was soft as he spoke. "Amber McCoy, you are my Chosen, and my protection is given to you."

So simple, and yet she could sense a thrill move through her, as though her body and soul understood what had just taken place even while her mind was still trying to figure it out. No longer would she have to worry about being alone. Now she and Idris were bonded in a way that she was only beginning to understand… although she looked forward to exploring the depths of that bond.

"And…that's it?" she asked. "I'm your Chosen now?"

"Yes," he said, a wonderful tenderness warming his dark eyes. "What would you like to do on this, your first day in this new life?"

"Honestly?" While Amber knew what was probably going to happen between them in the very near future, she also realized that she'd put this dress on after being dunked in the ocean, and she really wanted to get the salt off her skin and out of her hair. And, probably, remove the last lingering dregs of Bariq's touch.

"Honestly," Idris said.

"I need a shower," she told him. "I've still got saltwater all over me."

That reply made Idris smile and shake his head, but he seemed to understand because he said, "Go ahead and use the bathroom in my room. *Our* room," he amended, a cheerful light in his eyes as he seemed to realize things would be very different between them going forward. "I'll make sure all your things are moved to the closet there."

"But I left my stuff down in Costa Rica," she protested, realizing for the first time that every-thing she'd taken with her when she went with

Bariq must still be sitting in the closet of the room she'd been using.

"That does not matter. It is already taken care of."

There were definitely a host of pluses to being a djinn's Chosen. She went on her tiptoes and kissed him on the cheek. "I'll be as fast as I can."

"Meet me on the loggia when you're done," he said with a smile. "It is a fine day. We should enjoy it."

"I will."

Then she ran quickly up the stairs and went down the hallway to Idris's room...or rather, the room they would now share. One glance at the imposing, silk-hung bed, and she felt a little shiver of anticipation run through her.

Soon, she told that bed, then peeked into the closet.

Sure enough, all her clothes were hanging there, and she found her underthings in a pretty little lingerie chest in the corner. She selected the white lacy top she'd worn her first day here and her favorite pair of jeans, along with a white lace bra and panties, and hurried into the bathroom.

The shower at the villa in Costa Rica might have been even more opulent than this one, and yet Amber knew she enjoyed her shower here far more. She quickly washed her hair and soaped herself all over, then made sure every last bit of sea salt—and Bariq's loathsome touches—were rinsed away.

Her hair would dry quickly in the sun, so she blotted it, put a little serum in it to set the waves, and got dressed hastily. Idris was used to seeing her without much makeup, so she only put on mascara and lip gloss. A pause as she sent a quick grin to the picture of her with her mother and grandmother, which now adorned the highboy, and then she hurried down the stairs and out through the French doors, where the bright California sunshine greeted her.

Idris stood there, black robes shimmering in the breeze. He turned toward her, and she saw that he held a pair of champagne flutes.

"I thought we might celebrate," he said.

Champagne sounded like an awesome idea. Amber took one of the flutes from him, and they touched the fine crystal glasses together.

"To forever," she said, and he smiled down at her.

"To forever," he replied.

They drank champagne and stood there for a moment, gazing down at the magnificent gardens spread out before them. This felt perfect as well, just to be here next to him, to know that this man —this djinn—had somehow decided she was the only one for him.

Then she glanced up at him and asked a question that had passed through her mind more than once. "Do you ever wear anything except black?"

"No," he said, looking vaguely startled that she would ask such a thing out of the blue.

"Why?"

For a moment, he didn't speak, only seemed to be occupied with thinking of an appropriate answer. "I'm not entirely sure," he said at last. "I suppose it just seemed easier."

What could she do in reply, except laugh? Amber chuckled, then sipped some of her champagne. It was very good, but then, she supposed an elder of the djinn would conjure only the best. Cristal, maybe, or a very good vintage of Dom Perignon. "Maybe you should try branching out," she suggested. "Try dark blue or dark green. Or purple. Purple would look great with your dark hair and eyes."

"I am open to all possibilities," he said, and from the way his gaze met hers, she had a feeling he was talking about much more than the robes he wore.

Which was fine with her. She sipped some more champagne, and then it was as if they both realized they didn't want to wait any longer. The flute disappeared from her fingers, its contents now mostly consumed, and Idris's glass vanished as well. He bent down and kissed her, mouth tart with the taste of champagne, and she pressed herself against him, once again reveling in the strength of his body, the heat of his flesh.

In a flash, the bright autumn afternoon around them disappeared, and they were standing in the mansion's airy but imposing master bedroom. Idris touched her face, caressing her cheek, and then his hand moved down, brushing against her throat, going lower to cup her breast.

Amber released a sigh that was half a moan, feeling her nipple harden under the lace of her bra. He seemed to sense it, too, because he murmured, "This is all right? I can wait for you as long as you wish, but...."

"Don't you dare make me wait," she whispered fiercely. "Don't you dare."

He chuckled, and then he grasped the hem of her blouse and pulled it over her head. Both hands caressed her now, and she moaned outright. Still, that was better, but not exactly what she wanted. She reached back and undid the clasp of her bra, then took it off and tossed it onto the carved trunk at the foot of the bed.

His dark eyes gleamed. "You are utterly perfect, Amber."

With someone else, she might have made a sound of token protest, or made a flip comment about the boob job she'd been contemplating back before the djinn changed the world forever. Now, though, she knew Idris was being completely sincere, and she realized she needed to accept the gift of his admiration and love, and not try to downplay it or otherwise be dismissive of it.

"So are you," she said. She reached up and took hold of the collar of his robe, then pulled it down and away from him, revealing his broad shoulders, the muscular chest and stomach she'd glimpsed before but could now see in all their glory. Her fingertips trailed down that chest, went to the waistband of his trousers, which were a simple drawstring style.

Easy enough. She untied them, watched them fall. Although she'd expected he would be just as magnificent below the waist as he was above, she couldn't quite keep her eyes from widening.

"Damn, Idris."

He laughed and picked her up, then set her on the bed. With eager fingers, he undid the button and zipper of her jeans, pulling them down along with her panties. "I have been wanting you for quite some time," he said by way of explanation.

"Apparently."

No time for any more talking, though, because his mouth was on her nipple, tracing slow, luxurious circles with his tongue, and as she sighed and lay back on the bed, his hand went between her legs. She could already tell how wet she was, but apparently it came as something of a surprise to him, because he pulled in a little hiss of a breath before he began to stroke her, long, strong fingers seeming to find by instinct the place she wanted him to touch her.

Oh, God. She didn't think anyone else had ever been so deft, so skillful, even the guys she'd dated who thought they were players and knew everything about women. Normally, it would take her a while to come, but she could already feel the orgasm building in her, slow, delicious, rippling waves of pleasure moving through her body, making her moan even louder, before the climax hit and she cried out so loud, she was glad there was no one else within square miles who could hear her.

Idris didn't seem to mind, though. He made a low, growling sound of pleasure deep in his throat, and moved so he could kiss her again, tasting her as though she was some delicacy he'd been deprived of for years. In response, she reached down to take him in her hand, feeling how heavy and hard he was, how ready for her. This time, he groaned, and she trailed her fingers downward, running them over his sac before she returned to his cock. Normally, she would have moved lower, taken him in her mouth, but it seemed he didn't want to wait for that. His arms went around her, and he lifted her up, then lowered her so he could enter her.

Sweet Jesus. She cried out as he began to move his hips, pushing himself deeper into her, filling her like no one had ever filled her before. They found their rhythm, moving together, faster and faster, until she knew she was going to come again, was going to have an orgasm like she'd never had before.

It burst through her like a supernova, all heat and light and intense, pulsing, exquisite ecstasy. He moaned as well, and she could actually feel him climax, feel his own heat fill her. Her hands found his and held on until the last wave finally moved through her and she fell onto the mattress next to him, breath coming in quick gasps as she tried to find her way back to herself.

Right then, she thought she was okay with the thought of an eternity or so of that kind of sex.

She didn't even care that they hadn't used any sort of protection. While she'd never been all that eager to start a family, had never dated anyone who even seemed like good husband/father material, she knew it would be much, much different with Idris.

However, it turned out she didn't have anything to worry about, because he leaned over and kissed her on the cheek, so tenderly that she felt more loved, more cherished, than she'd ever been before. When he spoke, his voice was calm, quiet, betraying nothing of the passion they'd just shared. "There will not be a child," he said. "If you feared that might be the outcome of this afternoon."

Amber rolled over to look at him. A faint

sheen of perspiration touched his forehead, but that was the only real sign of the intimacy they'd just shared. His expression was serene enough for a Buddha. "You sound very sure."

"It is because we djinn have to consciously decide to have children. They are never accidental with us."

That was convenient. She couldn't help thinking of the time she'd had to take Kelly to the Planned Parenthood in Pasadena to get an abortion after her birth control pills failed her. It wasn't anyone's fault—the antibiotics she'd been taking for a sinus infection had interfered with the pill—but Amber had to think the djinn way was a hell of a lot better.

"Do you want children?" she said, genuinely curious. Maybe this was a hell of a time to be asking such a thing, but she wondered. After all, Idris had been alive for who knows how many centuries and had apparently never even been in a serious relationship, let alone one with kids.

"Eventually, I would like that," he replied, after appearing to ponder the question for a moment. "This is the first time I have ever been in a position to consider such a possibility." A pause, and then he asked, "Do you?"

She didn't even have to hesitate. "With you, yes…at some point. Right now I just want to be selfish and have you all to myself."

His mouth lifted in a smile. "I believe I can accommodate such a wish."

Then he pulled her to him and kissed her again, and she could feel him rouse against her leg. It seemed that djinn had a shorter refractory period than most human men.

And as he touched her once again, she thought she was just fine with that.

SEVENTEEN

This was, Idris thought, exactly what he had hoped for—to wake up in his bed and see the morning light filtering through the curtains at the tall windows, to look down and see the most beautiful, the most precious, woman in the world lying there next to him, her pale hair glistening against the white damask of the pillowcase. She still slept, her breasts beneath their covering of sheets rising and falling slightly as she breathed the regular breaths of deep slumber. While he normally would have gotten out of bed to go to the window and look at the new day and its promise, he stayed where he was, gazing at the marvel of the woman he loved and wondering how he had been lucky enough to get to this place.

They had made love again after that initial time, more slowly, more deliberately, touching, tasting exploring. At length, they had gone downstairs to a sumptuous feast he'd summoned to the dining room, and they'd shared more toasts and more food, eating until they were full, speaking of what had transpired in the days they'd been apart.

"I tried, I really did," Amber had said. She wore a rose-colored silk dressing gown he'd provided for her, and looked deliciously beautiful, with her Cupid's bow of a mouth swollen by his kisses and her wavy hair tumbling over her shoulders. "But there was something about Bariq that just rubbed me the wrong way. Also, I couldn't stop thinking about you. I knew it was crazy and pointless, but you were in my thoughts no matter what I did to try to forget you. I suppose after five days, he just couldn't take it anymore."

"That is no excuse for what he did to you," Idris said sternly, and she smiled.

"Oh, I know. I'm not trying to excuse what he did. He was a jerk. But I'm sure he would have been Mr. Nice Guy if I'd slept with him right away."

Thank God she had not. It would not have kept Idris from loving her any more than he did, but if she'd submitted to Bariq physically, even if she didn't harbor any deep feelings for him, the two of them still would have shared a connection that would have been more difficult to sever...

especially if their physical intimacy had led him to formally make her his Chosen.

"Luckily for both of us, Istar divined what was occupying my thoughts and suggested a solution to the problem," Idris said. "I am very glad we arrived when we did."

"Believe me, so am I." Amber had gone quiet then, expression not so cheerful. Most likely, she was imagining what would have happened if the two elders had not intervened. But then her shoulders lifted, and she said, "But you did. And here we are."

"And here we are," he'd echoed, and soon after, they had gone to the bedroom to make love for a third time before falling asleep in each other's arms.

And here they were now. As he gazed down at her, Amber stirred and stretched, then looked up at him and smiled. "Good morning," she said, a deliciously lazy smile touching her lips.

"Good morning, my darling." He kissed her on the forehead, then softly on the mouth. "What would you like to do today?"

"I don't know. Just be with you. Here in the house, or in the gardens."

"That sounds like a good plan."

They kissed again, then went downstairs and shared a leisurely breakfast before returning to the master suite to share a shower, one that turned into its own form of play, with her taking him in her mouth before he lifted her and held her against the marble wall while they made love. It was the first time he had ever done anything like that, and he thought it a fine way to spend a morning.

Eventually, though, they got dressed and went outside. For a time, they walked the paths and enjoyed the sunshine while they discussed possible changes to the property—he thought it might be a good thing to make an addition such as the glorious indoor swimming pool he had seen at the Hearst Castle in the northern part of the state—but eventually, he paused as they came back to the house and stood on the loggia, his eyes sweeping across the garden.

"You look like you're thinking deep thoughts," Amber remarked, following his gaze as he surveyed the property.

"I suppose I am," he admitted. Truly, he had spent a great deal of time contemplating the future of his people and of this world, thinking of what it might be like fifty, a hundred, several hundred years from now. In a way, that future meant even more to him now that he had such a stake in it, thanks to the woman who stood at his side.

"About...?" she prompted, apparently wondering if he meant to continue.

"About many things." He took her by the hand and led her over to one of the stone benches on the loggia. After they had both sat—and he had summoned sweetly spiced iced tea for the both of them—he continued. "I suppose I have been trying to imagine what this world will be, what will become of this new civilization we are trying to cultivate. And I am beginning to wonder whether we djinn have made a mistake."

Amber glanced up at him, a small frown plucking at the delicate arches of her brows. "A mistake?"

"We cannot change what we have done." With his free hand, he made a sweeping gesture, as if to indicate the greater world beyond the cloistered grounds of the Huntington. "But I think that perhaps we should look to a future where we combine our strengths. Ibram and Istar and I determined that the djinn and their Chosen should live apart in their own communities so that their paths would never cross with those djinn who participated in the eradication of humankind. However, I am not sure if such an arrangement can be sustainable in the long run. It is from a meeting of minds that change and progress occur. You humans already know that, I think, but we djinn have had a long-stagnant culture, and this initial arrangement is only more of the same."

"So what do you want to do?" she asked, looking genuinely curious.

"I am not sure yet," he replied. "But I think we

need to begin by loosening the rules. For one thing, the communities we set up are already beginning to expand, thanks to the djinn and their Chosen who live in them starting their own families. People should be able to move freely from one place to the other, or possibly set up new homesteads and communities if the ones they are in begin to feel crowded."

For a moment, she was quiet. She lifted her glass of tea to her lips and drank, her gaze also turned outward to the world beyond this estate. At length, she said, "But what about the other djinn—you know, like the one who tried to kill me. Wouldn't they attack those new settlements, or at least attempt to?"

"They might try," he admitted. "But they would be risking banishment to the outer circles —a form of djinn prison," he added in response to Amber's puzzled glance. "No djinn wants to face the wrath of the elders and risk that kind of punishment."

For some reason, she smiled. "You don't seem very wrathful to me, Idris."

"Because you have not seen me truly angry."

"Well," she said lightly, "I hope I never do."

He leaned over and kissed her on the cheek. "My love, I cannot see how you could ever do anything to make me that angry."

As he'd hoped, she smiled, but the sunniness of her expression faded a bit as she said, "What about the other elders? Do you think they agree with your view of things?"

"I'm not sure," he said honestly. "It is something I will need to speak with them about. In fact, there is even more I've been considering."

Amber tilted her head to one side as she angled a glance up at him. "I had no idea you were such a radical."

Her comment made him chuckle, even though the situation was serious enough. "I am fairly certain no one has ever called me that before. But no, it is more that I am trying to think things through to their logical conclusions. As time goes on, there will be more and more children of mixed djinn and human blood, more and more blurring between our two races. I was even thinking that we should extend an invitation to some of the survivors in Los Alamos, to ask them to bring their devices which protect them from the djinn to California so they might start a second settlement here. But again, I suppose it is my hope that with the passage of time, those devices will no longer be needed. The reaver djinn and those who agreed with them will, I believe, grow more accepting with the passage of time, since this world is now theirs and they will no longer have any reason to resent humans for taking it from them."

She didn't look terribly convinced; not surprising, since she knew firsthand what it was like to face a djinn reaver with murder in his heart. "That's kind of a big hope, don't you think?"

"I expect it is," he allowed. "But I am supposed to be one of the leaders of our people, and what kind of leader would I be if I did not imagine where we could go from here, how we could make all of our lives better?"

For a long moment, she was silent. Then she set her iced tea down on the bench next to her and reached over and took his hand. "And this is why I love you, Idris…and why I'll do everything I can to help you."

The Huntington's grounds could accommodate very large parties—Amber knew that, since she'd attended several of the Founders' Balls her mother helped to organize as part of the organization's Platinum Circle. Still, she couldn't help feeling a little nervous as she looked at the numerous round tables and matching chairs arranged on the loggia and the enormous party pavilion out on the lawn, and wondered if it still would be enough to accommodate everyone they'd invited.

To her surprise, both Ibram and Istar had seemed intrigued by Idris's suggestions and more than willing to let him give this a try and see how it all worked out. Not every single djinn and his or her Chosen was attending this gathering, but more than a thousand had agreed to come, along with a small group from Los Alamos, who would be accompanied by a contingent of the Santa Fe djinn and their companions in order to get them all safely here.

Amber had suggested a theme of a harvest celebration, since it was near the end of October, although it was a full Hunter's Moon that even now rose in the east, promising some extra illumination for the party. Bronze torches flickered at the edges of the lawn, and lights had been swagged across the loggia, casting a warm glow on the cloth-covered tables and the arrangements of chrysanthemums and warm-hued roses and ivy. By this point, she knew better than to ask where it all had come from, since Idris had already proved that he could pretty much make anything he wanted appear at his will.

All in all, thanks to those djinn powers, this had probably been the easiest party setup she'd ever been involved with. No worries about caterers running late or party-supply providers delivering the wrong color of tablecloth—just a snap of the fingers, and everything was done just so in a way that would have made Judith McCoy proud. In fact, it all looked so much like one of the charity functions her mother used to organize, Amber couldn't quite hold back a sigh.

"Is something the matter?" Idris asked,

appearing out of nowhere. He hadn't been standing there a moment earlier, but somehow he must have sensed that she was troubled.

"No," she said at once, and, despite her current odd melancholy, she couldn't help smiling at him, at how handsome he looked. "I like the purple robes."

"They feel quite...showy."

Amber chuckled. "You look great. This whole event is about trying new things, right? That also means wearing a color that isn't black."

"I suppose you are right." He bent down and kissed her—but on the cheek, so he wouldn't smudge her lipstick. "You are looking quite marvelous yourself."

She brushed a hand against her gown, a pale gold beaded Badgley Mischka piece that he'd magically made appear for her after she showed him a picture in a magazine of what she wanted. It was a duplicate of something Kate Mara had worn at the Emmys the same year the Heat swept over the world. For all Amber knew, it actually was the same gown, just altered to fit her, but she hadn't asked. At this point, what did it matter?

What mattered was the glow of admiration in Idris's eyes, the way he touched her hand. They'd been living under the same roof for just a little more than a week now, and she supposed they were still safely in their honeymoon period. However, she had a feeling that she'd always be this thrilled by the way he looked at her, by the little things he did, like finding all her favorite beauty products and stocking the bathroom with them, or allowing her to take one of the mansion's smaller rooms for an entertainment space, complete with an enormous wall-mounted flat-screen television and a digital library of pretty much anything she wanted. And when he asked why she wouldn't rather read than watch television, she said, "I actually like to read. I don't plan to stop anytime soon. But I went two years without a single movie or TV show, so...indulge me."

He'd smiled and said he understood, because of course he did. She loved everything about him, and yet she thought one of the things she loved the most was the way he accepted her without trying to change her. Yes, she'd survived two years underground, living in jeans and T-shirts and hiking boots, using pillaged beauty supplies from the local drugstore, but that didn't mean she didn't want her La Mer moisturizer and Bumble and Bumble hair gloss, damn it.

"Anyway," she went on, since Idris was still looking at her with a lifted eyebrow, obviously waiting for some sort of explanation for her sigh, "I suppose I was just thinking about my mother. I guess I'd like to think she would approve of all this."

"And approve of me, I hope."

Amber squeezed his hand. "Are you kidding? She'd love you. You have unlimited wealth at your disposal, and you're one of only three people who're running the world."

"And that is the only reason she would approve?" he asked, looking somewhat offended.

"No, that's just the beginning," she replied with a smile. "Because you're also handsome and smart and kind, and nothing like my father."

"Ah, well." Idris paused there, obviously considering her words. "You don't talk about either of them very much."

"What's to say?" Since Amber knew how brittle and off-hand that remark must have sounded, she went on, "My father was handsome and charming and a silver-tongued devil in the courtroom. My mother was beautiful and smart and came from old money, and their marriage sucked. He cheated and left, and she pretty much raised me on her own."

Dark eyes sad, Idris said, "After an experience such as that, I am surprised you would take a chance on me."

"Oh, well." She went up on her tiptoes and kissed him, but gently, so she wouldn't get lipstick all over his mouth. "I have a good feeling about you."

Her comment made him smile, as she'd hoped. However, he didn't have time to reply, because Ibram and Istar appeared then, both of them adorned in even finer versions of the djinn clothes they normally wore—Ibram in midnight blue robes stitched with silver, and Istar in a tight-fitting plum-colored silk long jacket embroidered in silver and gold and what looked like real amethysts, worn over loose, blousy trousers. More purple stones twinkled at her throat and her wrists.

"Welcome," Idris said, and Istar sent an approving glance around the grounds.

"Everything looks magnificent. You have outdone yourself."

"Amber provided a good deal of assistance and advice," Idris told her, and the djinn woman smiled.

"That does not surprise me. Are we your first guests?"

"Yes," Amber said. "We wanted to have you two here first, before everyone else arrived, just in case you saw anything that you thought needed to be changed."

Istar shook her head. "No, it is all quite lovely. It appears as though you are expecting quite a few people."

"Nearly twelve hundred," Idris said.

That comment made Ibram look pleased. "A very good number—and a good sign that many of our people are ready to hear what you have to say."

"I hope so." That was all Idris said, but Amber

knew he had been worried that everyone would be satisfied with the status quo. Once the responses to their invitation had started to arrive, though, it became clear that he hadn't been the only one who'd been pondering the direction their world should take next.

"We have wine and champagne," she offered. "Can I get something for you?"

"Oh, no, Ibram and I can fend for ourselves," Istar replied. "Your other guests should be arriving soon—we will leave you to greet them."

The two of them wandered off toward one of the many refreshment tables, even though Amber guessed the two elders could have simply snapped their fingers to summon the drinks they wanted. It seemed Istar's words had been prophetic, however, because almost as soon as they were gone, a group of djinn and humans Amber had never seen before appeared and approached the spot where she and Idris stood.

"A marvelous location for a party, elder," said the woman who appeared to be their leader. She had shimmering black hair that fell to her waist and the sort of figure Amber couldn't help envying, full-bosomed with an impossibly small waist. Her companion was a model-pretty mortal probably around Amber's age, and with them were another djinn man and his Chosen. The djinn looked enough like the woman who had spoken that she guessed he must be her brother, and the mortal woman at his side was equally beautiful, dark and exotic.

"Thank you, Fatima," Idris said. "Amber, this is Fatima, the leader of the Bel-Air community, and her Chosen, Adam. And also, Fatima's brother Malik, and his Chosen, Leila."

"It's very nice to meet you," Amber replied, and Fatima sent her a curious smile.

"And nice as well to meet the mortal who managed to ensnare our elder," Fatima said. "That is quite the feat, my dear, something that no djinn has been able to accomplish, although many have tried."

Many? Amber slanted a glance up at Idris, but he responded with just the smallest shake of his head…and possibly a bit of an eye roll, as if trying to tell her that Fatima might have been exaggerating just a little.

Leila said, "Like all of us Chosen, I'm sure Amber has something of a story to tell."

"You have no idea," Amber remarked, and they all chuckled.

"Perhaps someday, someone will write them down," Malik said, wearing the kind of warm smile that she immediately recognized, since she'd seen it often on Idris's face. "In the meantime, it is good to meet you, Amber. We offer thanks to you and to our elder for arranging this gathering. The message he sent was one I believe many of us wanted to hear."

"And I am glad to hear that," Idris said. His expression was still calm and friendly, and yet Amber could tell he was relieved by Malik's response. "Please, enjoy yourselves. There is food and drink, and the others should be arriving shortly."

The little party went off toward the refreshment tables, where Ibram and Istar already stood, glasses of wine in their hands and their heads bent toward one another, as if they were sharing some kind of confidence. As soon as the Bel-Air group approached them, however, the two elders turned and greeted the newcomers, and they all were soon involved in what looked like a lively conversation.

"So far, so good," Amber murmured to Idris, and he nodded.

"Yes. It's somewhat surprising to see Ibram and Istar so open to mingling, but I suppose they are also trying to embrace the spirit of this evening."

She leaned in and took his hand, squeezing it. This did mean so much to him—and to her as well, because she understood what he was trying to accomplish, why it was so important for the world to become more cohesive as time went on, rather than having the djinn with their Chosen isolated from one another in all their separate small communities.

More and more people began arriving then—a

pretty woman around Amber's age, her hair almost as fair, her companion a roguish-looking, sandy-haired djinn who exchanged a knowing glance with Idris as he remarked, "Looks like you succumbed, too."

"If you wish to look at it that way, Nasim," Idris replied without so much as a blink. "Like so many others of our kind, I came to realize that we djinn have much to learn from our mortals."

Nasim chuckled, and he and his Chosen went off toward the large party pavilion on the lawn, joining the large crowd that had gathered there.

And then another group appeared, mixed djinn and human—except Amber noticed right away one couple who had traveled with them, both obviously mortal. The man was tall and thin, with a beaky nose and glasses he pushed up into their proper position as he stared at the crowd around them, and the woman was much prettier than anyone Amber might have expected to be with someone as gawky as that. Unlike the finery worn by the djinn and their Chosen, the clothes this couple had on were much plainer, although it looked as though they'd done their best to dress up for the occasion, he in an ill-fitting black jacket over a white dress shirt and no tie, and the woman in a simple black dress that looked a little too tight around the midsection.

One of the djinn who'd appeared with them, an intense-looking man with shoulder-length black hair, approached Idris and Amber. The woman who came with him was stunningly lovely, her honey-blonde hair pulled up in a French twist, her gown a pale purple one-shouldered dress that wouldn't have looked out of place on the red carpet.

"Thank you for the invitation, elder," the djinn said, and Idris inclined his head ever so slightly.

"We are glad that you could come, Zahrias— and that you could bring representatives from the mortal community in Los Alamos with you."

Ah, so that was who the two out-of-place humans were. Actually, the woman was pretty enough that Amber was sort of surprised she hadn't been Chosen. Maybe, as Malik has said, there was a story to be written there.

The tall, thin man—who Amber could completely believe might have been a scientist in the days before the Dying—looked around, an expression of some astonishment on his sharp features. "They really all came," he said, a certain flatness to his tone seeming to indicate that he'd expected exactly the opposite.

"Yes," Idris said. "They are ready to move on to a new world...as I hope you are as well, Miles Odekirk."

The man's expression was guarded, but he seemed to relax as he spoke, warming up to an idea he'd obviously been pondering ever since he was first contacted about Idris's proposal. "Possibly. Or at least, what you've suggested is intriguing. Certainly there are far more raw materials to be obtained here in California. Construction of our devices could go quickly. The real problem is having enough skilled people to produce them. If we—"

Idris held up a hand, but a smile touched the corners of his mouth, as though he was pleased by Miles's enthusiasm. "Yes, there are many details that will need to be worked out. In the meantime, though, please—enjoy yourselves, and enjoy speaking with those who live in the other djinn and human communities."

"We will," said the woman who stood next to him, her hand on her husband's arm. Or at least, Amber assumed they were married, since a simple band of diamonds glinted on her finger, and Miles also wore a plain gold band on his left hand. "No champagne for me, though—we just had our son three weeks ago."

That would explain why her gown looked a little tight. However, the woman's face was so radiant that the fit of her dress hardly mattered. "Congratulations," Amber told her, and she smiled.

"Thank you. I wasn't sure whether I would come, since Dylan is so young right now. Luckily, Los Alamos has lots of eager babysitters."

That sounded nice and friendly. Maybe Los Alamos was the kind of small town Amber had thought didn't exist anymore. While she was perfectly happy being here at the Huntington with Idris, she was glad to know there was still a community of regular humans out there working together, looking after each other. If Idris's vision became a reality, then there might be many more towns like it in the not too distant future.

"We are all glad to be here," Zahrias said. Amber noticed how his fingers were entwined with those of the woman who stood next to him, and how his dark eyes lit up as he looked down at her; apparently, he wasn't quite as intense as his appearance seemed to indicate. "And apologies from Jasreel al-Ankar and his wife Jessica—she has just discovered that she is with child and did not wish to make the trip."

"My congratulations to them both," Idris said gravely. "I know they traveled a difficult road to get where they are now."

Zahrias inclined his head, and Amber noticed the way his gaze moved toward her, as though attempting to determine what it was that had brought her to Idris. "As have we all."

The group took their leave then, and Amber and Idris turned to greet the next batch of newcomers, and more after that. Eventually, though, it seemed that everyone who had said they were going to attend had arrived, and so the two of them were free to mingle and get some food and drinks for themselves, to stop and answer questions as they moved through the crowd.

Idris had decided against giving any kind of a speech, telling her just the day before as they finalized their plans, "I would prefer to talk to people individually, rather than stand on a dais and make pronouncements. For I believe it is the little changes we make in our hearts every day that will make the difference, rather than being stirred up by a speech that is soon forgotten."

She hadn't argued, mostly because she agreed with him. In a situation like this, it was better to affect hearts and minds gradually, to allow people to come to their own conclusions about what should be done.

And at the end of the evening, after everyone had gone and Idris had made all the leftover food and drink disappear—not wanting to attract any more wildlife than already roamed the Huntington's grounds—they climbed the steps to the loggia and were about to enter the house...only to find a strange djinn standing in front of the French doors, blocking their way.

Amber probably wouldn't have recognized him, except she saw the stranger's robes, a brilliant green, and sheer terror pulsed through her. Grabbing Idris's hand, she murmured urgently, "It's him. The djinn who attacked me."

Unruffled, Idris stared at the interloper and said, "What are you doing here, Mahmoud?"

The djinn made no threatening movements. He only stood there, hands at his sides, dark gaze meeting that of the elder who stood in front of him. "I wish to have speech with you."

"You are having it," Idris replied, his eyes narrowed. "What is it you want?"

Amber had never heard him sound so curt before—not even when he'd confronted Bariq—but then, she supposed he had reason. At least Bariq had never tried to kill her in cold blood.

To her surprise, the reaver djinn went down on one knee, head bowed. "I am here to give my apologies," Mahmoud said, and Amber startled, staring at him. What in the world...? The djinn lifted his head and went on, his gaze intense and his tone urgent, "I would never have attacked this mortal if I had known she was Chosen. I thought—"

"I can guess what you thought," Idris broke in. "And I understand the circumstances...which is why I and the other elders decided to let the matter go. If that is all you want—"

The djinn shook his head, then slowly got to his feet, although his overall posture was still one of supplication. "No, there is more. Word has come to us of what you are planning with these mortals. And...." He paused there, heavy brows knotted, as if he wrestled with himself, with the words he knew he needed to say. In fact, he looked so tortured, Amber couldn't help but feel a little sorry for him, despite what he'd tried to do to her several years earlier.

"And what?" Idris made an impatient gesture with one hand. Although he had spoken of tolerance and empathy earlier, it was obvious enough that he had very little to spare for the man who stood before him. "It is late, and Amber and I are weary. Tell me what you have come here to say."

Despite this obvious command, Mahmoud still hesitated. Driven by a sudden impulse, Amber took a step toward him and put a hand on his arm. "It's okay," she said quietly, now certain that the djinn meant her no harm, no matter what he might have done previously. "You can tell us."

He stared at her, deep-set eyes startled, as if he had never expected such magnanimity from a mortal. After clearing his throat, he said, "We have heard how you wish to transform this world. I cannot speak for all of us, but I know that there are many who would like to be a part of this transformation. We have seen how you live with your mortals, and…."

Idris's expression softened. "And…?"

"And we are sorry," Mahmoud said, his voice barely more than a whisper. "We thought we were doing the right thing, but now we are not so certain. We cannot change what we have done, but perhaps if we work with you, we can help to change the world."

A long, startled silence. Amber stared up at

Idris, then at Mahmoud. Idris's eyes were full of a terrible hope; Mahmoud's, filled with guilt and contrition.

But then Idris smiled and said, "We would like to work with you, Mahmoud. We would like that very much."

And as the two djinn looked at each other, the hope Amber had seen in her lover's face seemed to awaken in Mahmoud's as well. Although he didn't smile, he looked happier, if resolute. He nodded, as if confirming something to himself.

"I will see what I can do," he said, then disappeared.

Idris took Amber by the hand. "That was...unexpected."

"But good," she said.

"Yes." He stood there for a long moment, as if unsure whether he was ready to go inside.

Amber reached out for his other hand, twined her fingers with his. As always, his flesh felt warm and strong, even though the night had grown cool, and she was more than ready to go into the house and get out of her heavy beaded gown. "What is it?"

"Are we ready for this?" he asked. "That is, I want this world to move forward, but truly, I did not expect to have much cooperation from the other djinn, at least not this soon." Expression troubled, he gazed down at her, dark eyes scanning her face as though trying to gauge her reaction. "What I mean to say is…are you ready to forgive? *Can* you?"

She thought of the stricken expression Mahmoud had worn. Maybe that had been an act, but she didn't think so. Those other djinn had done terrible things, horrible acts that no sane person could possibly excuse. And yet….

"I'm not saying I want any of them for a best friend," she replied, still holding on to Idris's fingers, hoping he could feel some of her own resolve in her touch. "But if they want to try to live alongside us, then I think we need to let them. Maybe this generation won't be able to forgive them—not completely—but as time goes on, there will be more and more who were born after the Dying, who never suffered any personal losses because of the actions of the reaver djinn. You yourself said that we were doing this for those children, for all our futures. So…yes. We need to let them in. We need to do what we can, Idris."

He pulled her toward him then and kissed her, with something fierce and pure behind the touch of his lips on hers. "I love you," he murmured.

"And I love you," she said.

At last, he reached out and opened the door, and they went inside, into the warmth of the home they had made together. And if she and Idris could find love when so much had kept them apart, not only their races but the gulf of centuries that lay between them, then she knew there was hope for all the others, those who hadn't yet found their heart's desires, those who had yet to even understand what that desire even was. They would all work toward that goal together, to make this world what it should have been and still could be.

And that, she thought, was what would make a true happy ending...for them all.

The End

ALSO BY CHRISTINE POPE

PROJECT DEMON HUNTERS

(Paranormal Romance)

Unquiet Souls

Unbound Spirits

Unholy Ground

———

THE WITCHES OF CANYON ROAD

(Paranormal Romance)

Hidden Gifts

Darker Paths

Mysterious Ways

A Canyon Road Christmas

Demon Born

An Ill Wind

Higher Ground

———

THE WITCHES OF CLEOPATRA HILL*

(Paranormal Romance)

Darkangel

Darknight

Darkmoon

Sympathetic Magic

Protector

Spellbound

A Cleopatra Hill Christmas

Impractical Magic

Strange Magic

The Arrangement

Defender

Bad Blood

Deep Magic

Darktide

THE DJINN WARS

(Paranormal Romance)

Chosen

Taken

Fallen

Broken

Forsaken

Forbidden

Awoken

Illuminated

Stolen

Forgotten

Driven

Unspoken

THE WATCHERS TRILOGY*

(Paranormal Romance)

Falling Dark

Dead of Night

Rising Dawn

THE SEDONA FILES*

(Paranormal Romance)

Bad Vibrations

Desert Hearts

Angel Fire

Star Crossed

Falling Angels

Enemy Mine

TALES OF THE LATTER KINGDOMS

(Fantasy Romance)

All Fall Down

Dragon Rose

Binding Spell

Ashes of Roses

One Thousand Nights

Threads of Gold

The Wolf of Harrow Hall

Moon Dance

The Song of the Thrush

THE GAIAN CONSORTIUM SERIES*

(Science Fiction Romance)

Beast (free prequel novella)

Blood Will Tell

Breath of Life

The Gaia Gambit

The Mandala Maneuver

The Titan Trap

The Zhore Deception

The Refugee Ruse

STANDALONE TITLES

Hearts on Fire

Sympathy for the Devil

Taking Dictation

Night Music

Golden Heart

* Indicates a completed series

ABOUT THE AUTHOR

USA Today bestselling author Christine Pope has been writing stories ever since she commandeered her family's Smith-Corona typewriter back in grade school. Her work includes paranormal romance, fantasy romance, and science fiction/space opera romance. She makes her home in Arizona.

Christine Pope on the Web:
www.christinepope.com

facebook.com/ChristinePopeAuthor

twitter.com/ChristineJPope

pinterest.com/ChristineJPope

www.ingramcontent.com/pod-product-compliance
Lightning Source LLC
Chambersburg PA
CBHW020401260626
47156CB00007B/2199

Also by Victoria Webster

The Con Artist

PART ONE

CHAPTER ONE

In which Abigail gets a big surprise

ANDREW WAS UP to something. Abigail was sure of that. He was quieter than usual, and his routine had changed. Sometimes, he would leave the house late and arrive back early. As he was the boss of the company, he could come and go as he pleased but usually kept to a strict regime and was first in and last out so as to set an example to his employees. The real giveaway, however, was that for the last few Saturday mornings, he had announced he was going out. Weekends, now that they had the girls, were supposed to be sacrosanct family time and Andrew had broken this rule. *No doubt*, she thought to herself, *I'll find out soon enough what he's keeping from me.*

Abigail didn't have to wait long. The four of them – Andrew, Abigail and their two daughters, Francesca and Annabel – were sitting down to dinner when Andrew announced that it was about time they moved to a larger house, preferably to an area where there was less people and traffic.

'I don't want to move,' said Francesca. 'All my friends are here.'

'And I don't want to move either,' said Annabel. 'I like it here!'

Andrew turned to Abigail. 'And what do you think, Mummy?'

Abigail knew she had to choose her words carefully so as not to upset the girls nor undermine Andrew.

'Well, I like it here too and I've got a good group of friends. However, a bigger house and larger garden would be nice. But there's the question of schools. The girls are settled in their school and doing well. Can't we look for somewhere else in this area?'

'I fancied a change. Somewhere on the edge of the countryside with more of a community feel, but still easy access to London. One or two pubs and a restaurant, instead of chains and franchises. A small doctor's surgery where you get treated as an individual instead of a number, and perhaps even a golf or tennis club. Also, whilst we're on the question of schooling, have you forgotten that Miss Briars thinks that the girls would excel in an all-girls' school, where the focus would be on education without the distraction of such things as boys, which is bound to happen.'

At the mention of boys, Francesca's face lit up.

'See, that's what I mean, Abigail,' said Andrew looking at Francesca.

'I don't like boys. They're silly,' said Annabel.

'Excuse me! I'm a boy and I'm not silly,' said Andrew, laughing.

'You're not a boy, silly Daddy. You're a man,' replied Annabel.

Abigail had to agree with Andrew on this. An all-girls' school would be ideal so that their two could focus on the important things, without distractions. Abigail, who had gone to a mixed comprehensive, had been distracted numerous times. She clearly remembered one maths lesson which was about simultaneous equations where, instead of paying attention, she had spent the time drawing hearts and writing in her maths book *Trevor Forever, Maloney Only*. Needless to say, she was given a detention for not paying attention, and had to alter the words a week later so as to then read *Trevor Not*

Forever, Maloney Baloney, when he ended the relationship. Yes, indeed, Abigail could well remember the distractions. 'Sorry, girls, I'm with Dad on this one. So, when should we start house-hunting?'

Andrew had a sheepish look on his face. 'I already have.'

'Oh, so that's why your routine has changed, and you've been disappearing at the weekend. I thought you were keeping something from me. Naughty Daddy, isn't he girls?'

Both girls nodded, with glum expressions.

Abigail folded her arms and looked at Andrew. 'For the next viewing, the girls and I would like to come. Wouldn't we?' she said, looking at them both.

They both gave a reluctant nod.

'Mmm, there won't be a next viewing,' said a somewhat nervous Andrew.

Abigail narrowed her eyes. 'Why not?'

'Because I've found the perfect house, in the perfect location, and I've put an offer in with the agent.'

Abigail was astounded, and annoyed. 'Don't you think you should have involved me in this, Andrew? You can't just go ahead and buy a house without me having a say. What if I don't like it?'

'Yes, Daddy, what if we don't like it either?' said Francesca.

'You will like it. I promise. Wait until you see it!' replied Andrew excitedly.

Abigail had an ace up her sleeve. 'You're forgetting something, Andrew. We haven't put this house on the market yet.'

Andrew looked sheepish again. 'The estate agent is coming tomorrow morning at 10am. I won't be here as I need to show my face at the office, but I can leave it to you, can't I, Abi?'

Abigail knew when she was beaten and kept the ace where it was. Sighing, she said, 'I suppose so. When do we get to see this house then?'

'Saturday morning at 10:30. I promise you girls, and Mummy, you will like it'.

*

Andrew was right. They did like it. Aside from the fact that the house was 30 miles away from their previous home, which resulted in a few glum looks from Abigail and the girls, there was nothing not to like. A long gravel driveway, accessed by electric gates with an intercom, revealed a substantially sized house set back on a spacious plot. As the estate agent had left the front door unlocked earlier that morning, Andrew opened the bright red door. They stepped into a marble-floor hallway which was bigger than the utility room in their current house. A curving staircase on the right-hand side led to the upper floors, which Francesca and Annabel immediately ran up to explore the bedrooms. Alone with Abigail, Andrew showed her the downstairs living area. The living room was twice the size of their current living room, with a separate dining room through an archway. The kitchen was also large with a butcher's block in the centre, which also served as a breakfast bar. The kitchen also had an alcove set back in the corner which was spacious enough for a settee and TV unit, and there was still ample room for their existing kitchen table and chairs which could be placed near the bi-folding doors which led out onto the patio and the generously sized garden. As Abigail looked out at the garden, she let out a squeal of excitement. 'There's a swimming pool! Wait till the girls see this.'

Turning back to the kitchen, her eye was drawn to the turquoise-coloured fridge/freezer. 'Oh, look! It's got a dispenser for chilled water and ice cubes. Amazing!' She then noticed the oven, which caused her face to fall as it wasn't a conventional oven which she was used to, but one that looked very much like a range-style oven. Stunning though it was, because the colour was also turquoise and very eye-catching, Abigail hadn't a clue as to how they worked and immediately started to worry about how she would cook with it. Before she could voice her concern to Andrew, there were sounds of arguing coming from upstairs. Going into the hallway, they were greeted with a red-faced Annabel running down the stairs. 'Slow down, Annabel, you'll fall if you're not careful,' said Abigail, who was a natural worrier when it came to her children.

'I don't care! Mummy, Daddy, it's not fair. Francesca has taken the biggest bedroom and it's got its own bathroom. Why do I have to have a smaller bedroom just because I'm younger than her?'

'When you say "biggest bedroom", which one are you referring to?' asked Andrew.

'The one on the left. It's got its own bathroom and a separate dressing area.'

Andrew ran up the stairs, closely followed by Abigail and a grinning Annabel, because she knew Francesca was going to get a telling off. She had also locked the bedroom door, which Andrew now demanded she open. 'Francesca, open the door please. We need to talk to you.'

The door opened to reveal a sulky face.

Going into the bedroom, which was indeed very large and as described by Annabel, Andrew spoke sternly to Francesca. 'Francesca, this is mine and Mummy's bedroom. Come out of here, at once!'

Francesca came out and, as she passed by Annabel, she stuck her tongue out.

'Now girls,' said the ever-peace-making Abigail, 'don't argue. Andrew, show the girls their rooms. And me, too, because I haven't even seen all of the house yet.'

Andrew opened the door of a smaller bedroom with an en-suite which he said was Francesca's, and then a slightly smaller bedroom next door which shared the en-suite by a connecting door. This appeared to appease Annabel because the size wasn't that much different to Francesca's bedroom. Francesca was disappointed because she liked the idea of a separate dressing area, although she was happy to have an en-suite which both girls, at that exact moment, were making a dash for. Sensing another argument, Abigail stepped in front of them. 'Right, you two, I don't want any falling out over this. There are two hand basins. So, Annabel, if we move here, you will take the left side and put all your stuff there. Francesca, you take the right side. In the mornings, when it's time to get ready for school, you can use the bathroom at the same time. However, when one of you has to you-know-what,' which was said with a grin, 'be considerate and patient. Is that clear?'

Both girls nodded.

'Abi,' said Andrew. 'I think you're forgetting something.'

'Am I?'

'Our current house has one bathroom which we all share, and one downstairs loo. This house has two bathrooms and a downstairs loo, and so if either of the girls need to go at the same time, there's always the downstairs toilet.'

'Or,' said Francesca, with a hopeful look on her face, 'we could always use yours.'

'Don't even think about it,' said Abigail and Andrew in unison.

Andrew realised he was onto a winning streak as, already, the girls and Abigail were talking about a future in the new house. 'Now, girls, we've got something to show you which I think you will be very excited to see,' and they followed him downstairs with Abigail following behind.

Walking into the kitchen, Abigail went over to the bi-folding doors and opened them to reveal the large garden and swimming pool. 'Look, girls, a swimming pool!'

'Is it ours?' they exclaimed in unison.

'Yes, it's all ours. Or will be if Daddy's offer on the house is accepted.'

Caught up in the excitement of living in a house with a pool, all thoughts of leaving friends and their school behind were quickly forgotten.

Andrew put on a sad face. 'Erm, I've got something to tell you all.'

Three pairs of eyes turned towards him, one pair of which was filling up with tears.

'Now now, Annabel. There's no need to cry. Because… guess what? My offer was accepted. The house is ours!'

Everyone clapped and they joined hands in a happy family circle and danced round and round, until the circle was broken by the girls who ran into the garden to look at the pool.

Although Abigail was happy, she felt that she had been excluded from a decision which should have been talked through and shared. Also, there was the small matter of her clients who she saw on a regular basis at the health clinic where she worked part-time as a psychotherapist. Having studied psychology at UCL, Abigail had then trained as a psychotherapist specialising in cognitive behavioural therapy where, over the years, she had built up her own list of clients. With the move, she would have to say farewell to them and suggest alternative therapists. She felt sad about this, and that she would also be leaving her friendship group behind.

'Andrew?'

'Yes?'

'I don't want to be a spoilsport, but this house is quite a step up from our current one. Can we afford it?'

'Yes, we can. No worries, my dear Abi, on that score,' he replied grinning.

'But what if we can't sell ours?'

Andrew was getting exasperated as he felt this was typical of Abigail who always seemed to put a damper on things. However, he needed her on side and decided to be patient. 'We will sell ours. You have created a lovely family home. A home anyone would be happy to live in. In fact, Abi, if you hadn't trained as a psychotherapist, you should have been an interior designer.' He lent in and kissed her on the cheek. 'Now, didn't I tell you this house was perfect?' He turned with his arms wide open to show off the kitchen in its entirety.

Abigail knew when she was beaten. 'Yes, you did.' In a spirit of reciprocation, she stood on tiptoes and kissed him on the cheek. She still wasn't sure about the fancy turquoise oven. What she would have preferred was a Neff with a double oven, like her current one. *Still*, she thought, *beggars can't be choosers.*

CHAPTER TWO

In which Abigail feels at a disadvantage

AS ANDREW HAD predicted, their house did sell quickly and the girls were offered places at Knighton Grammar School, which was an all-girls' school, starting in September, and not too far away from where they would be moving to. The timing was perfect because the house-move coincided with the summer holidays, which meant that at least Abigail would have the help of Annabel and Francesca, seeing as Andrew would be going to the office as usual. Abigail had her last girls' night out with her friends, with promises to keep in touch and visits on occasion. She had seen all her clients and explained that, as she was moving some 30 miles away, she would be unable to continue seeing them and gave them each a list of alternative psychotherapists. It had not been easy, and she felt as if she was letting them down, particularly as a level of trust had been built up between them. But a change is as good as a rest – or so the saying goes – and Andrew explained that he needed a change.

From the brief experience Abigail had had with the area they were relocating to, she had the feeling that the "world" she was moving into was going to be very different from her old one. From a look at the other large houses on Green Park Road, where their new house was situated, and the luxury cars in the spacious driveways, it was clearly a big step up for her, Andrew and the girls. Also, the nearest place for shopping, which was not large enough to be a town, but too big to have village status, was Cornham. They had driven through it, and Abigail had noticed that most of the shops were of the independent variety. The boutiques looked exclusive, if the clothes on display in the windows were anything to go by. There was a delicatessen-cum-supermarket, a handful of independent cafés and an independent bookshop.

Abigail noticed a hairdressing salon with the name of André of Knightsbridge, which seemed odd to her seeing as they were in Cornham. When Andrew had slowed down due to a build-up of traffic in the high street, they had stopped outside a beauty salon bearing the name Naturally Beautiful which advertised botox, lip fillers and non-surgical face lifts. With the pretentiously named hair salon, and a beauty salon advertising treatments that were the opposite of anything "natural", Abigail wondered how well she would fit in here.

*

The move had gone smoothly, and Abigail was now busy unpacking boxes and getting the house organised. Depending on the weather, if it wasn't sunny the girls were getting their bedrooms organised. If the weather was good, Abigail had said they could swim in the pool and sunbathe, but only after they had at least helped her for a couple of hours. That particular morning, everything was going swimmingly well, and Abigail felt contented and happy. She had left the gates open, and from the kitchen she could hear footsteps on the gravel, followed by a ring on the doorbell.

Putting down the plates she was holding, she went into the hallway and opened the door. Standing at the entrance was a very pretty woman whose age was difficult to determine because it was obvious to Abigail that the woman had probably had some cosmetic work done to her face. Her forehead was completely smooth and shiny, her lips very plump and there were no signs of lines at the corners of her mouth or leading down from her nose to either side of her upper lip, which suggested that she had had fillers. Her eyebrows were perfectly shaped, and her eyelashes were long and thick. Abigail thought that they were definitely fake. Her cheekbones were pronounced and looked to be natural, and not surgically enhanced. She had arrived at this conclusion because the woman standing in front of her had blue eyes and naturally white-blond hair which was tied back tightly in a ponytail, thus giving her features akin to those people of an Eastern European ethnicity such as Polish or Russian.

If Abigail had to sum up the look of the woman, she would describe her as resembling a Barbie doll. Nevertheless, there was no denying that she was pretty and clearly kept herself in shape. In terms of what she was wearing, Abigail would say she was channelling sporty Barbie, as she was dressed in pink and black Lycra leggings and top, which showed off her shapely breasts and a perfectly toned figure. Abigail, who was wearing a beige tracksuit and was make-up-free, immediately felt frumpy and at a disadvantage.

The woman extended her hand and attempted to smile. Abigail wiped her hands on her top and shook the woman's hand. 'Hi, I'm Abigail. Pleased to meet you.'

In an accent that Abigail thought was probably not the one the woman had been born with, she introduced herself, 'And I'm Svetlana. I live next door, and I've come to welcome you to the neighbourhood and give you this as a welcome present.' The woman handed her a bottle of Provence rosé.

'Oh, thank you! That's very kind. I'd let the girls come and say hello, but they're in the garden.'

'Yes, I know. I can hear them. They're obviously very excited.'

'Mmm, well, they've never lived in a house with a pool before.' Abigail could sense that the conversation was leading somewhere and waited for a response. There was none.

'Well, thank you again for the wine. I'll let Andrew know where it came from. Now, I must get on. So much unpacking to do.' Abigail turned to go but was stopped in her tracks.

'The thing is,' said Svetlana, 'Sven and I don't have children, and so we live in complete peace and quiet. Are your girls very excitable then?'

'As I said, Svetlana, it is quite a big thing for them to have their own pool, and naturally they will be a bit noisy. No doubt they'll calm down once the novelty wears off. Now, I do have a lot to do, and again thanks for the wine.'

This time, Abigail did turn away and close the door. *Welcome to the neighbourhood*, she thought, and pressed the button on the intercom pad to close the gates once the Barbie doll – as Abigail now thought of her – had returned to her own house.

Later that afternoon, the intercom buzzer sounded and Abigail looked in the camera to see who it was. A woman with an elaborate hairstyle, and a heavily made-up face, was standing close to the camera.

'Hello, who is it?' asked Abigail.

'It's Juliana Hetherington. I've come to welcome you and your family to the neighbourhood.'

Here we go again, thought Abigail and pressed the "gate open" button to allow the woman in. Abigail opened the door with a smile. 'Pleased to meet you, Mrs Hetherington. I'm Abigail Thomas.'

'Yes, I know. The agent always tells us when we've new people moving into the road. And do call me Juliana. No formalities are required in this road. I've brought you this as a welcome present.' She handed Abigail a terracotta pot containing red geraniums. Abigail, who was now dressed in her usual "uniform" of jeans and a jumper, once again felt scruffy next to Juliana who was also wearing jeans. These, however, were fashionable in that they had rips in the knees, and sparkly dots scattered on the fabric. She was wearing white strappy shoes with a heel, and a pink and yellow bouclé jacket, with gold buttons, completed the outfit. Her abundant auburn-coloured hair was piled precariously high on her head and looked slightly unstable.

'Have you been somewhere nice?' asked Abigail.

Juliana looked puzzled. 'No. Why do you ask?'

'You're all dressed up. I thought that perhaps you'd been out somewhere, or perhaps you're going somewhere,' said Abigail with an expectant look on her face.

'Oh no. This is what I wear during the day. If I was going out, I'd be wearing something a bit more glamorous than this!'

Abigail felt wrong-footed and slightly disgruntled. 'Oh, apologies. It's just that – look at me,' she laughed, 'dressed in old jeans and a jumper!'

'But presumably you're unpacking, so...' Juliana shrugged.

Abigail was about to respond that this was her normal attire but thought better of it.

'Anyway,' said Juliana, 'welcome. Just so you know, Rufus and I are – I suppose – the "head honchos" in the road. Where we lead, others follow, so to speak.' She laughed loudly. 'Seriously, though, if you need any information or help or advice, come to us. Our monthly get-together is happening soon, and you and your husband will get an invite in your post box. It will be at ours this time. You can't miss our house. It's the largest in the road. Right, must dash. Things to do etc., etc.' And with a wave, she left.

Abigail went inside, shut the door and closed the gates. Going into the kitchen, she headed for the fridge and took out a chilled bottle of Sancerre. Taking a wine glass out of the cupboard, she poured herself a large glass of wine and took it outside. The girls were running around in the garden, laughing and squealing with happiness.

'Mummy,' shouted Francesca, 'you shouldn't be drinking alcohol. It's not 6 o'clock yet!'

'Mummy needs this! I might even have another one!'

'I'll tell Daddy,' shouted Francesca.

'I won't tell Daddy, Mummy,' piped up Annabel.

'You're such a mummy's girl, and a sneak,' replied Francesca, which made Annabel start to cry.

Abigail sighed and took a gulp of wine. 'Now look what you've done Francesca. You've made your sister cry. Why can't you just both be nice to each other?'

'Don't tell Daddy, will you?'

'Okay, I'll do a deal with you, Francesca. If you don't tell him about my drinking wine in the afternoon, I won't tell him about you making Annabel cry. Is that a deal?'

'It's a deal, Mummy,' said Francesca.

'Annabel.'

'Yes, Mummy?'

'You don't tell Daddy about any of this either, okay?'

'Of course I won't. I'm not a sneak,' and she stuck her tongue out at Francesca.

The afternoon was drawing to a close. Abigail finished her wine and told the girls to come inside. As she closed the patio door behind her, she wondered how much of the conversation her neighbour had heard because she was sure she had seen a flash of pink in the garden next door and very close to the fence.

CHAPTER THREE

In which Abigail finds herself living in
a house with a split personality

THE SUMMER WAS flying by. Abigail was gradually getting the house organised and, as they weren't having a summer holiday, she spent as much time as she could with the girls in the garden. It became clear to both Andrew and Abigail that the furniture from their previous home didn't really go with the new interior because the house was relatively new, thus their existing furniture looked out-dated and a bit shabby. Furthermore, as the house was substantially larger, it was obvious they would have to buy more furniture. As a result, their weekends were spent shopping together as a family, mostly in Knighton where there was a good selection of shops including two department stores which had, as part of their displays, a floor devoted to ready-made interior-designed living rooms. Abigail's taste lent towards rustic French-meets-English-countryside, which created a colourful, comfortable, and unostentatious interior, whereas the style on show in both department stores favoured a minimalist Scandinavian chic design in muted tones of taupe, grey and cream. The style of the displays aimed for uniformity and formalness; a design aesthetic which favoured "form over function".

The interior and ambience Abigail had created for their previous home was one where visitors felt they could kick off their shoes, curl up on the settee, or sit at the kitchen table drinking wine or tea and coffee, and have a good chat. There was no room for airs and graces in Abigail's home. It became clear, however, that this informal and charming style was not going to work in the new, ultra-modern, house. It was calling out for, almost demanding – if a house could demand, that is – totally impractical glass-top tables with wrought iron legs, leather settees with steel frames, and elegant lampshades without adornment. Definitely no painted furniture where the grain showed through, or stencilled patterns, or curtains with frills and tassels. In terms of palette, gone were the colours of summer, to be replaced with – if Andrew had his way – the exact muted colour palette she was now looking at.

Andrew, who was also a bit of a neat-clean clutter-free person, liked the style and the restrained colours but agreed to a compromise with Abigail who was showing signs of resistance. So, in order to avoid an argument in front of the girls in the department store they were currently in, it was agreed that he could choose the downstairs interior design, and she was allowed to dictate the upstairs. Thus, in the end, the house ended up with a split personality: downstairs was masculine, formal, calm and orderly; upstairs was frilly, flowery and feminine with soft creamy colours with a splash of turquoise, lavender and green for the main bedroom. Annabel predictably chose pink and white, whereas the more mature Francesca opted for turquoise, mint green and pale pink, much to Abigail's approval and delight.

Apart from the welcome visit by Juliana and Svetlana, Abigail hadn't seen much of their new neighbours. As it was the summer holidays, with no school traffic and many people away, everywhere was generally quiet. When Juliana had called by, she had mentioned that their end of the road met each month for a get-together, but Abigail had heard nothing further. That morning, going to the post box, she found a white envelope addressed to "Mr and Mrs Andrew Thomas". Inside was an invitation from Rufus and Juliana Hetherington, for the monthly get-together, at 7:30 pm, on Friday, 10th July. There was no landline or mobile telephone number, nor a house number. However, Juliana had said that their house was the largest in the road and so it should be easy enough to find. Going back into the house, she called up the stairs to tell the girls she was popping out to see one of the neighbours and wouldn't be long.

Closing the gate behind her, she took a walk up the road to see where Rufus and Juliana lived. She saw two large houses of the same size and architectural design. As one was for rent, and appeared to be empty, she reasoned that the Hetherington house must be the one next door. So, Juliana's statement that their house was the largest one in the road wasn't strictly true. As she walked up the driveway, Abigail chided herself for being pedantic over such irrelevant matters. There was no doorbell, but a large brass bell hung at the end of a thick rope which Abigail then rang. It was very loud, and she jumped back in surprise. The large oak door opened. Although it was only 10:30am, Juliana was in full make-up, wearing a short-sleeved navy-blue shift dress that had gold buttons down the front and stopped just below the knee. Instead of slippers, she was wearing navy and white peep-toe shoes with a stiletto heel.

'Oh, hello, Abigail. What can I do for you?'

Before she could stop herself, Abigail asked, 'Are you going somewhere nice?'

'No. Why do you think that?' replied Juliana looking perplexed.

'It's just that you're looking very smart, and so I wondered...' Abigail had a feeling of déjà vu, recalling the similar conversation she'd had with her not so long ago.

Juliana laughed, immediately making her seem more approachable. 'We've had this conversation before, I think. No. This is how I dress at home. Can I help you?' 'It's about the invitation. Thank you, by the way. It's just that it's only myself and Andrew who've been invited. You didn't mention the girls.'

'That's correct. It's for adults only. Of course, up until now we haven't had any children living in the road and so the issue hasn't arisen. Just this once, I suppose, we can make an exception. Normally though...' Juliana shrugged her shoulders.

'Ah, that explains it then,' replied Abigail. 'I'll see what Andrew says, and perhaps we could leave them at home. Well, have a nice day. Goodbye.'

Juliana closed the door, and Abigail made her way back to her new home which suddenly didn't quite feel like home at the moment.

*

The evening of the July get-together arrived, and Andrew and Abigail were getting ready.

'It's easy for you, Andrew. All you have to do is choose which shirt and trousers to wear, and that's it. I, on the other hand, if Juliana is anything to go by, am going to have to smarten myself up a bit.'

Having seen what Juliana considered "dressing down" during the day and realising that Svetlana was someone who proudly showed off her toned body, Abigail knew with absolute certainty that her uniform of jeans and jumper, or t-shirt, was not going to be suitable. So, she chose the safe little black dress that came out for functions, teamed it with black patent shoes with a small heel, and some gold jewellery. Putting on a coating of face powder, blusher, mascara and pink lipstick, she sprayed some Michael Kors Amber perfume on her wrists and asked Andrew what he thought.

'You look nice,' he commented. 'Can't go wrong with that little black dress of yours, can you?' he said with a grin. 'Do you think the girls will be okay on their own?'

They had decided to leave the girls behind as it was clear from the conversation Abigail had had with Juliana, that children were not really welcome. 'Yes,' she replied. 'They're both well behaved and we are only just down the road. Also, they know to call me on my mobile if there's a problem, and under no circumstances do they answer the intercom or open the gates.' Abigail and Andrew then shouted their goodbyes and made their way to the party.

The door was open and revealed a cavernous hallway, similar to the ones found in baronial stately homes. A suit of armour stood in one corner, complete with a halberd. A large grandfather clock stood in the other corner. A large threadbare Persian carpet covered most of the floor, on which sat a mahogany sideboard placed against the wall. On the top of the sideboard was a Chinese vase and a silver photo frame. On closer inspection, Abigail and Andrew saw that it contained a photograph of Rufus in top hat and tails, and Juliana wearing an enormous red, white and blue hat, and matching outfit, obviously in the Royal Enclosure at Ascot. Standing behind them, minor members of the royal family were visible. Abigail and Andrew looked at each other, gave a sigh, and walked into the equally spacious living room which spoke of "old" money or, at least, wanted to convey that impression. In terms of the interior design, it made Abigail think of British Colonialism meets South-East Asia, where the dark heavy-looking wood furniture of the former dominated over the decorative and colourful Asian furniture, which lent some relief to the overall imposing and masculine feel of the room.

Everyone was already seated. A tall, and striking, man stood up. Handsome, with a florid complexion, and a full head of silver hair, he was clearly the oldest of the group and, although Abigail disliked the expression, he was obviously the alpha male. That he had natural leadership qualities was borne out by the fact that the assembled group all turned their attention towards him when he began to speak. From the photograph in the hallway, Andrew and Abigail knew this must be Rufus, Juliana's husband.

He clapped his hands together. 'Right, everyone. Attention please. Before we go into the kitchen for our informal get-together, there are two things to deal with. The first is to welcome our new neighbours, Andrew and Abigail Thomas, who have moved into No. 10. Juliana and Svetlana have already met Abigail,' and here Rufus nodded at Abigail, 'but none of us have met Andrew. So, welcome Andrew. Now, let me introduce both of you to the group. I'm Rufus, and that lovely lady over there is my wife, Juliana. There's Sven and Svetlana sat on the chaise longue. And here we have Toby and Tammy, and Tommy and Trixie. If you think you're seeing double – don't worry, you don't need to go to Specsavers,' which was said with a laugh, 'because you're seeing two sets of twins!' The twins waved and smiled, revealing four sets of perfectly straight white teeth; Sven and Svetlana merely nodded. 'So, that's the introductions over with. Now, onto more pressing matters. Speeding in the road. It's become a racetrack, and now that we have children living here, something has to be done. I've been on to the council, and they're not interested. So, I suggest we buy two speed signs – one for each end of the road – and put them up. What does everyone think?'

There were general assents all round. 'Is it legal?' asked Sven. 'Can we do that?' he added.

'How much will it cost?' asked one of the male twins.

'In answer to your question, Sven, that's something I'll need to get clarification on. In answer to yours Toby, or Tommy – you know what, boys, you really should wear badges so that we can tell you apart – now, where was I? Oh yes, in answer to how much it will cost, I'll need to find that out as well. But, if we're all in agreement in principle, including our new neighbours, I'll get onto the matter straightaway. With any luck, we should have the signs installed by September once the summer holidays are over and the traffic builds up again. This, by the way, will be our last get-together until September. So, I declare this meeting over. Let's go into the kitchen for some food and, more importantly, alcohol!'

Everyone followed Rufus into the kitchen. Rufus took Andrew by arm, and Sven followed behind. The twins and their wives went and sat at the kitchen table, which left Abigail with Juliana and Svetlana. As Abigail had rightly predicted, compared to all the women present, she was, by far, the dowdiest. Juliana was wearing a leopard print jumpsuit teamed with chunky gold jewellery. Her shoes were black patent with gold stilettos and looked very expensive. Her auburn hair was piled high on top of her head, but Abigail knew it was a carefully contrived look. As for Svetlana, Abigail had to admit to herself that this was one woman who showcased her assets. Her very carefully applied make-up shone, shimmered, glistened and glimmered. Her lime green dress, with a plunging neckline, coated her body like a second skin, and ended just above the knees, displaying tanned legs toned to perfection. She wore gold shoes with a complicated arrangement of straps and buckles, with towering stilettos. Gold and diamond jewellery, which Abigail thought looked very much like the Tiffany jewellery she had seen featured in the *Vogue* magazine she had bought the other day, completed her carefully achieved "arm candy" appearance. Unlike Juliana's elaborate coiffeur, Svetlana's long white-blond hair was pulled tightly back from her face and styled in a French twist, which created a potent mixture of sophistication and sex appeal. Standing next to her, Abigail felt diminished, dull and depressed. Something made her look in Andrew's direction, possibly because there was loud laughter coming from Rufus, Sven and Andrew. She noticed that Andrew was looking at Svetlana. She also noticed that Rufus was taking a sly peek. The only one not to take any notice was Sven who was now talking, unaware that he didn't have the complete attention of the other two.

'You're looking very elegant tonight, Abigail,' said Juliana, perhaps sensing how Abigail was feeling. 'I've only ever seen you in jeans and a jumper.'

Abigail shrugged her shoulders. 'I was never one for glamming up; always felt comfortable in casual clothes, I suppose. Thought I'd better make an effort tonight though.'

'It suits you,' said Svetlana, matter-of-factly.

'Tell me,' continued Juliana 'who does your hair for you?'

'I do, at the moment. I need to find a new salon. There's been no time though.'

Juliana took Abigail by the arm. 'You must go to mine. André is simply the best. You'll find his salon in the high street in Cornham. It's called André of Knightsbridge. Tell him I sent you, and he'll give me a discount on my next visit. Now, I'm off to get more wine.' She wandered off, holding her wine glass up in the air.

Svetlana then grabbed Abigail by the arm. 'Whatever you do, don't go to Juliana's hairstylist. He can only do one style, and as you can see it's a cross between a '60s beehive and Marie Antoinette. You could bury a bird's nest in Juliana's hair, and you'd never find it.' Svetlana laughed throatily at her joke, and continued, 'Also, his name isn't André – it's Alan. He thinks a French-sounding name sounds more glamorous. Go to my hairdresser. Kellyanne at Cornham Cuts in South Street, just off the high street. She's very sweet and doesn't charge a fortune. Mention me, and I'll get a discount on my next visit. We'd better stop talking. Juliana's coming back.'

'What have you been telling Abigail, Svetlana? I could see you from across the kitchen.'

'I was just telling Abigail that she must go to Naturally Beautiful in the high street for her mani-pedis. I told her that they do excellent shellac acrylics. Don't you agree?'

Both Juliana and Svetlana simultaneously looked at Abigail's nails, which were short and polish-free. Juliana's and Svetlana's nails were long and pointed at the tips, with Juliana's painted a bright red and Svetlana's a neon pink. 'Mmm, I'll bear that in mind,' Abigail replied, not totally convinced.

'Also,' continued Svetlana, 'I suggested she try the microdermabrasion facial with fruit acid peel for dull skin. It's to die for!'

Abigail was beginning to feel even more depressed. Generally, she was an upbeat person, a bit low on the odd occasion, but not really the depressive kind. She didn't think the two women were being deliberately unkind, or somehow trying to make her feel inferior. What they were obviously trying to do was to change her appearance and image so that it fitted in with what they felt and thought looked good. Abigail didn't suffer from low esteem either, and neither did she lack confidence. In her old life she had been part of a group of women who dressed casually, wore very little make-up, and only had beauty treatments if they were going somewhere special. They were all university educated, had worked in professions such as accountancy, law and education, before becoming part-time so that they could still devote quality time to bringing up their children. Of the two women who had decided not to return to work, one volunteered at the Citizens Advice Bureau, whilst the other was volunteering for Age Concern. Thus, with this group of friends, Abigail had many shared cultural references and had worthwhile and meaningful conversations. Now, in Juliana's and Rufus' kitchen at this precise moment in time, she felt she had swapped a life with meaning and purpose for one that was shallow and lacking purpose outside of the home. Nevertheless, she knew she would have to adapt if she was to survive in this new world but be careful not to lose sight of herself and what she considered important either. So, she decided there and then, that once the girls were settled in their new school, and she had time on her hands during the day, she would look for voluntary work with a view, later, to returning to her profession as a psychotherapist. At the moment though, she felt distinctly discombobulated and out of kilter. She looked over to where Andrew was standing, with legs apart, and hands in his pockets. He was laughing at something that had been said, and saw Rufus clap him on the back as if they had been friends forever.

When Abigail turned back from where Andrew was standing, she saw that Juliana and Svetlana had wandered off, and she was left by herself. She looked over to where Tammy and Trixie were sitting at the kitchen table, their husbands having gone outside for some air.

They were a wholesome-looking pair. Expertly applied make-up but not overdone, healthy shiny light brown hair which was cut into matching bobs, and both wearing the current trend for athleisure clothing which was, in effect, a smarter version of the tracksuit. They looked approachable and so Abigail decided to go and introduce herself.

'Hi, girls. Thought I'd come and say hello.'

'Hi, Abigail,' they replied in unison. 'Take a pew.'

Abigail sat down and placed her wine glass on the table.

'How are you finding it here?' one of the twins asked.

Abigail took in their open friendly faces and decided to take a chance. 'Do you want an honest answer, or a dishonest one?' she said brightly.

The girls grinned. 'The honest one, of course!' And they laughed.

'I'm still finding my feet. I miss my old friends, and I haven't really made any new ones yet. I suppose that will change when the girls start at their new school, but in the meantime...' She shrugged her shoulders.

'Have Juliana and Svetlana been giving you a hard time seeing as you're the new girl on the block?' asked Tammy, or it could have been Trixie, because they were identical twins and were dressed in matching outfits.

'To be fair, not really. I get the impression, though, that their life seems to revolve around hairdressers, beauty salons and shopping.' Abigail stopped suddenly, as she realised that this kind of life might also appeal to Tammy and Trixie. This was because whenever she had seen them they had been going out in one of their matching white Range Rovers and had assumed they were either going shopping, or to a health club or beauty salon. Nevertheless, having never spoken to either of them before, only waved in passing, she didn't want to cause offence and decided to use flattery as a way out. 'By the way, I wanted to ask you which salons you use. You both look so effortlessly immaculate. How do you do it?'

Tammy and Trixie looked at each other. 'Shall we tell her?' one of them said.

'Can we trust you?' asked the other one.

'Absolutely!' replied Abigail.

'We're both trained hairdressers and beauticians. I'm Tammy by the way. We do each other's hair, and beauty treatments. Saves the boys a small fortune.' They both giggled.

'We even do our own teeth whitening,' said Trixie. 'But you mustn't tell Juliana or Svetlana, otherwise they will expect us to do their hair and treatments and, of course, expect to have it all done for free. Also, I probably don't have to tell you this now that you've met them, they are incredibly "high maintenance" and Tammy and I would no doubt be expected to be at their beck and call. Nope, we don't need that, do we, Tammy?' Tammy shook her head.

'I won't say a thing. I promise. How come you haven't set up your own business, then?'

'Because we don't want to,' they explained in unison.

'And because we don't need to,' said Trixie. 'We did that for a number of years after we'd finished our training. We enjoyed it, but it can be tiring and although most of our clients were very appreciative, some of them were a bit wearing especially those who were like you-know-who.' She nodded in the direction where Juliana and Svetlana were standing, having come back into the kitchen.

'Also,' said Tammy, 'Trixie's right. We don't need to work. The boys' company is doing really well, and we enjoy being able to do what we want when we want.

Also, at some point we will want to have babies, won't we Trixie?'

'Yes!' replied Trixie grinning.

'Actually, Abigail, if you want to get more involved in the community, then I do know that the care home at the end of the road is looking for volunteers to sit with the elderly residents and read to them, or talk to them or play games. It makes their day go quicker, and some of them don't appear to have many visitors. Tammy and I go there every month and do the elderly peoples' hair or give them manicures and pedicures. It gives them a bit of a lift,' said Trixie.

'We don't charge them. We do it voluntarily as we enjoy it and it means we're not losing our skills,' added Tammy.

Well, well, thought Abigail. *You can't always judge books by their covers.* 'Yes, I'd like that. I would feel there was some purpose in my life apart from being a mother to the girls and Andrew's wife.' She raised her eyes to the ceiling and back down again. 'Well, it was nice speaking with you. Hope to see you again soon.' Abigail got up and went to see Andrew to tell him she was going home.

It was obvious he was enjoying himself, and not yet ready to leave. 'Okay, I'll be along a bit later.' He turned back to Sven and Rufus.

Andrew arrived home an hour later in a very jolly mood, no doubt helped by the large glasses of red wine Abigail had seen him drinking. 'Great bunch, aren't they? That Rufus is a scoundrel. Essex boy, left school at 15 and found a job as a post boy in one of the large trading firms in the City. Worked his way up to the trading floor as he showed a natural flair with numbers and gambling and had the gift of the gab. He eventually ended up on the directors' floor. Made a mint, not the one with the hole, and not called Murray – ha-ha – erm, where was I? Oh yes!'

Abigail was looking at Andrew with a puzzled look on her face. 'Andrew, you're not making much sense. What are you trying to say?'

'Abigail, my dear, my darling wife, what I'm trying to say is that Rufus made a ton of money, sold up in Essex and moved out here. Still goes up to London every Friday for an old boys' get-together.' He tapped the side of his nose with his finger and winked.

'He didn't today though, did he?'

'What?'

'He didn't go to London today.'

'Obviously not, because he was hosting the get-together. What are you on about, Abigail?'

'You said that... Oh, never mind. I'm tired and I'm going to bed.' Abigail rose up from the settee and went upstairs to the bedroom, with Andrew following behind.

They were in bed. Abigail was about to go to sleep, but Andrew was wide awake, clearly feeling enlivened by the evening out. 'And that Sven, well he's a bit of a dark horse. Doesn't say much, but you can see he's thinking and processing things all the time. He's like a human computer. And that wife of his, she's a bit of a stunner, isn't she?'

'I wouldn't know,' Abigail replied huffily. 'Now, go to sleep. We're shopping in Knighton tomorrow with the girls.'

'Do I have to come? Rufus has said he'll take me to the golf club for lunch.'

'Yes, you do. Saturday is family day. Now, please let me go to sleep.'

'Oh yes, and evidently I have to go through an initiation ceremony as I'm the new boy on the block.'

Abigail was suddenly wide awake. 'What do you mean?'

'As the new man in the road, I have to go through an initiation ceremony. It's usually held in London, and all the men go – Rufus, Sven, Toby and Tommy. It'll be in a couple of weeks' time.'

Abigail didn't like the sound of it. 'What will it involve?'

'I don't know, but evidently I will like it.' And he fell asleep with a smile on his face.

Not for the first time, Abigail thought *Oh crikey, what have we done moving here?*

CHAPTER FOUR

In which Abigail comes to a worrying conclusion

THE NEXT TWO weeks passed quickly. Abigail and the girls took two further trips into Knighton and purchased new bedding, curtains, throws, cushions and lampshades in the colour schemes they had respectively chosen. On the second visit, they went to an "open afternoon" at the girls' new school to look round the classrooms and facilities, and to meet some of the teachers.

Abigail had also invested in a soup-making machine, slow cooker and George Foreman grill, so that she could at least serve up homecooked meals as she still hadn't got to grips with using the fancy oven. The new furniture Andrew had chosen for the living room had now arrived, and the house was finally taking on a finished look. At Andrew's insistence, the living room and dining room was to retain a pristine new "show home" appearance. In any event, Abigail and the girls preferred to be in the informal seating area in the alcove in the kitchen, which contained a small television they had brought from their previous home, together with their old comfortable settee which they could curl up on, and not worry about making a mess.

It was Friday morning, two weeks after the get-together. Andrew had come downstairs dressed in his best navy pinstripe suit, highly polished brown brogues, a crisp white shirt and his favourite bright yellow Hermès tie. The design was called *On Air* because it resembled hundreds of small microphones. Abigail thought they looked more like acorns and it made her dizzy when she looked at it.

'You're looking very smart,' she said, still in her dressing gown and slippers, and holding a large mug of coffee. 'You smell nice too. Is that your Cartier aftershave? Where are you off to?'

'Yes, it's my Cartier aftershave. Have you forgotten, it's my initiation ceremony tonight,' he said with a big grin on his face.

'Oh, yes, I'd completely forgotten about that. No wonder you're looking extra smart and wearing the expensive aftershave. So, you won't be home until late then?'

'Probably not. Don't wait up. Say goodbye to the girls for me.' Giving Abigail a quick peck on the cheek, he exited the kitchen and made for the front door.

'I'll give the girls your love. Have a good time!' she shouted. *Initiation ceremony, indeed,* thought Abigail. *Just an excuse to have a boys' night out, without the prying eyes of the wives.*

True to their word, Tammy and Trixie had spoken to the manager of the care home and Abigail had an appointment to see her at 11am. Finishing her coffee, she put the mug in the dishwasher and went upstairs to shower and get dressed. She could hear the television in Francesca's bedroom and opened the door. Both girls were sitting on the bed watching *Keeping Up With The Kardashians.* 'Morning, you two. Do you want any breakfast?' enquired Abigail.

'No thanks, Mummy. We're good. We can help ourselves anyway,' Francesca replied, and turned back to the programme.

'I've got to go out briefly this morning. Only up the road to the care home. Will you both be okay?'

'Yes, we'll be fine. Don't worry. We can look after ourselves, can't we, Annabel?'

Annabel nodded, engrossed in watching Kim and Kourtney engaged in a sisterly spat which involved some hairpulling and shoving.

Abigail sighed, 'Okay, then, I'll leave you both to it,' and she closed the door.

After her shower, she went to the wardrobe and, out of habit, took a pair of jeans off the hanger, and a jumper from the drawer. Then she realised that her old comfortable way of dressing, at least when she went out, was going to have to change and she needed to smarten herself up. Because she wanted to make a good impression with the manager of the care home, she chose her "colour block" navy and pale blue linen dress from Next and teamed it with navy sandals. Then, she applied some mascara, pale pink lipstick, and blusher, and dabbed on her Michael Kors perfume. Not to appear overdressed, she wore a simple gold necklace and bracelet.

As she walked out of the gates, which Andrew had left open, she heard the sound of a car horn coming from her left. Turning, she saw Svetlana in her sporty red Mercedes SLK coming out of her driveway. Giving Abigail a wave, she sped down the road. Abigail closed the gates and walked up Green Park Road. As she approached Juliana's house, which was on the opposite side, she saw a young man dressed in sportswear, carrying an Umbro sports bag, going into the driveway. *Mmm,* thought Abigail, *Juliana must be having personal training or a tennis lesson.* For a very brief moment, she felt slightly dissatisfied. She couldn't put her finger on precisely why, but something was amiss in her psyche and had been triggered by seeing Svetlana obviously out somewhere, Juliana clearly having a "session" with a young man and, lastly, Andrew very excited about his night out with the boys. *And what am I doing today?* she asked herself. *You're going to a care home, and then back home with the girls,* came the reply.

Well, at least if this meeting goes well, I'll be doing something good for the elderly. She then realised that talking to herself, and replying to herself twice, might possibly be the first sign of madness. Nonetheless, she couldn't shake off the feeling that her life had changed, and she wasn't sure if it was for the better or not.

The meeting went very well, and Abigail found herself committing to a couple of hours on Wednesday and Friday mornings. The care home appeared to be well run, with a structured daily routine, and a good rapport between staff and residents. She had met some of them, and they were a cheerful bunch. However, the manager had told Abigail that they had to have eyes in the back of their heads sometimes, and the ones they needed the most help with were those who preferred to stay in their rooms and only came out at mealtimes, or those who sat by themselves and refused to take part in the activities. Also, it was two or three residents of this kind who, when they thought no one was watching, would sometimes escape and try to evade capture. 'Gosh, I make it sound like a prison, don't I?' she had said with a laugh. 'Seriously, though, just very recently one of our female residents had packed a small suitcase and somehow had managed to get out without being seen. Fortunately, one of the staff members who was coming to do her shift had seen her walking along the pavement and coaxed her into the car. Then, there are those residents who are in the early stages of dementia, so your help would be very welcome and appreciated as they can be quite difficult.'

After her meeting, Abigail immediately felt in a happier frame of mind knowing that she would be helping others and that her time would be taken up doing some good out in society. She opened the gates and went inside. It was obvious by the mess left on the kitchen surfaces that the girls had eaten breakfast.

'I'm back,' she shouted upstairs.

'Hi, Mummy,' they shouted back.

'All good?'

'Yes, all good,' they replied.

Going back into the kitchen she poured herself a mug of coffee from the percolator and toasted a slice of bread, which she then spread with peanut butter. From out of nowhere, she once again felt slightly dispirited and preoccupied with various thoughts. Andrew was always telling her that she overthought and overanalysed things, but this was how Abigail worked through feelings such as this. On her way back from the care home, she had felt happy and that was because soon she would be doing something useful and worthwhile. Now, back at home, the girls were clearly happy and occupied, and had no need of Abigail for the time being. In her previous home, and particularly during the school holidays, she would be out with her friends and their children, or meeting up for lunch with friends if her two had been invited out. Now, she found herself with nothing to do and stood twiddling her thumbs with boredom until she had wound herself down into such an unmotivated state that when the girls finally came down and asked what was for lunch, she just shrugged and replied grumpily, 'Beans on toast.'

'Are you all right, Mummy?' asked Annabel. 'You seem a bit grumpy.'

'To be honest, girls, I'm a bit bored. I miss my friends. Don't you miss yours?'

'Yes, we do,' replied Francesca. 'But I have Annabel, and Annabel has me and so we keep each other company.'

'Haven't you made any friends yet, Mummy?' asked Annabel, looking sad.

'Not really. Everyone is always out and about, and I'm still settling in. But...' And here she forced herself to brighten up her mood because she didn't want to upset the girls, 'Soon I'll be going to the care home after I've dropped you both off at school and doing some voluntary work for a couple of hours. That'll give me something to do.' She immediately felt uplifted again, aware that she was now experiencing mood swings which was a new feeling for her.

'Now, the bad news is that it's beans on toast for lunch. The good news is that tonight we can have takeaway chicken wings and pizza for dinner because Daddy is out. Also, we can eat in the living room and watch a film on the big TV. How does that sound?'

Abigail thought that the girls would jump for joy at the suggestion because it was two treats in one: eating pizza and chicken wings and watching TV in the living room. Instead, Annabel asked if they could eat in the kitchen. 'We don't mind that the TV isn't big, do we Francesca?'

'No, we don't mind at all. Then, if we drop any food or spill our drink, it won't matter so much. It's more comfortable in the kitchen, Mummy.'

Abigail felt sad that the girls considered the living room not comfortable or relaxed enough to spend time in. A couple of things had happened to cause this. On one occasion, Annabel had accidentally spilt some orange juice on one of the glass-topped side tables and it had dripped onto the pale cream carpet. Abigail immediately went into the kitchen to get a cloth, but she could hear Andrew telling Annabel off for being clumsy. And then there was the incident with the chocolate button. The girls had been sitting on one of the new beige leather settees eating a packet of chocolate buttons. They were being silly and trying to throw them into each other's mouth. One button had been dropped and instantly forgotten about, until sometime later they had both got up and there was the chocolate button which had left a mark where it had started to melt. Thankfully, on that occasion, Andrew wasn't at home and Abigail managed to wipe off the mark. Nevertheless, it had made the girls so worried that they hardly ever went into the living room, unless it was to have essential bonding family time together, and certainly with no food or drink. Hence their preference for the kitchen which, in truth, Abigail also preferred. Abigail lamented how different it had been in their previous house. Not having a large kitchen with an alcove-cum-seating area, the only room they could relax in was the living room. Andrew would sprawl on the smaller settee with his beer, and Abigail and the girls would sit together on the larger settee. Sometimes, all four of them would eat their meals on trays on their laps and watch television.

Since moving to the new house, Andrew had suddenly become very formal and fussier. One instance stood out. Abigail and Andrew had gone into the living room after dinner, and Abigail had remained standing.

'What are you doing?' he asked.

'I'm standing up,' she replied.

'Why?'

'Because I'm afraid that if I sit down, I'll dent the leather on the settee.' She had grinned when she said this.

Andrew had frowned. 'Don't be so silly. Settees are meant for sitting on.'

Abigail had sat down and leant back against the plump cushion. At some point, she had got up to go into the kitchen to see if the girls were okay and had secretly watched Andrew when he thought she had left. He had stood up, patted down the seat on which she had been sitting, and then plumped up the cushion. Feeling in a rebellious mood, on arriving back in the living room, Abigail had deliberately plonked herself down on the settee and leant heavily against the cushion. She could sense Andrew looking at her but kept looking straight ahead with a grin on her face. This incident, however, revealed something to her. Andrew's personality was slowly changing and she wasn't convinced it was for the better.

After lunch, Abigail suggested that they could go for a walk in the woods which were nearby, and the girls agreed. They walked past Svetlana's and Sven's house, and Abigail noticed that Svetlana was still out. At the end of their road, they turned left, and Abigail saw that the house on the opposite corner had a 'For Rent' board outside. They walked to the end of the road and into the woods, where they spent a pleasant few hours picking wild flowers to take home. On returning, the girls immediately went into the kitchen to watch television, whilst Abigail caught up with some chores which she now felt motivated to do.

It was early evening. The food arrived and was put onto plates. Abigail poured orange juice for the girls, and a white wine for herself. After some discussion, it was agreed they would all eat in the living room. After further discussion, a film was chosen they all agreed on and the evening passed by pleasantly without any liquid spillage, food droppage or tears before bedtime.

Abigail was fast asleep and didn't hear Andrew creeping up the stairs at 2am having left his shoes in the hallway. Quietly taking off his suit jacket which he hung over the back of the chair, and then his tie, he took off his trousers and folded them neatly placing them on the chair seat. He then took off his shirt and tiptoed quietly into the ensuite and placed the shirt at the bottom of the laundry basket under other items to be washed. Coming back into the bedroom, he realised he still had his socks on. Leaning against the wall to steady himself, he took them off and left them on the floor by the chair. Carefully getting into bed so as not to wake Abigail, as he knew she would start asking him questions, his last thought before he fell asleep with a smile on his face was, *I never knew such things went on.*

CHAPTER FIVE

In which Abigail finds something
surprising in Andrew's jacket pocket

IT WAS SATURDAY morning and, as usual, Abigail was the first to get up. She noticed Andrew's suit on the chair which she thought would probably need dry cleaning. She picked his socks up from the floor and, going into the bathroom, she put them in the laundry basket. She was surprised to see that his white shirt was not in the basket, which made her suspicious. So she rummaged through the clothes and found it well hidden at the bottom. *Mmm*, she thought, *what's he hiding?* Pulling it out, she examined it and noticed a smear of red lipstick on the inside of the collar and a smudge of foundation. She also smelt perfume; something sweetly cloying and overpowering. *Well, well, Andrew Thomas, just what have you been up to?* She put the shirt back into the laundry basket, but this time so that it was visible on the top. This way, Andrew would know that she had seen it. Going back into the bedroom, she looked again at Andrew who was sleeping soundly. Next, she took the suit jacket off the back of the chair and sniffed at the lapels. There was the same strong smell of perfume. Feeling a touch guilty, but unable to stop herself, she put her hand in the breast pocket and could feel the shape of a business card. Looking to see if he was stirring, which he wasn't, she pulled out three small rectangular-shaped cards. From the bed, Andrew groaned, 'Oh, my head. Abigail!' he shouted, as he could see she was not next to him in bed, 'Where are you? I need some water.'

'There's no need to shout, Andrew. I'm right here. I'll be back in a minute with the water.' Putting the cards in her dressing gown pocket, she went downstairs to the kitchen. She could hear Andrew groaning, 'Oh, oh, my head. My head.'

Serves you right, she thought. In the kitchen, she laid the three cards out on the table and, picking up her mobile phone which she had left on the table overnight, she took photographs of both sides of the cards to look at later, and then put them back into her pocket. She poured a large glass of iced water from the dispenser built into the fridge and took it up to Andrew.

Whilst she had been downstairs, Andrew had got up and gone into the bathroom. This gave Abigail her chance to put the cards back in his jacket pocket. She put the water on his bedside table and went downstairs again to start preparing breakfast. It was a family rule that, on Saturday mornings, the family had breakfast together. Francesca and Annabel came down and sat at the kitchen table.

'Where's Daddy?' asked Annabel.

'He's still in bed,' replied Abigail. 'He had a late night and is feeling very tired.'

'I'll go and get him,' said Francesca, standing up. 'We always have breakfast together on Saturday.' And she marched out of the kitchen.

Always a stickler for the rules, that one. Takes after Andrew, Abigail thought with an affectionate smile.

Francesca came back down a few minutes later. 'Yuck! He's being sick in the bathroom. I can hear him retching.'

Abigail shrugged and sighed. 'Okay, just us three then.'

'Mummy, if Daddy isn't coming down for breakfast, can me and Francesca have our breakfast on the settee and watch television? We never get to see the Saturday morning children's shows.'

This gave Abigail a chance to look at the cards on her phone which she was itching to do, so she readily agreed. Pouring herself a mug of coffee, and taking a bite of her toast and marmalade, she called up the first photograph which was of a card with a glossy white background. Printed on the background was a picture of a pale pink cat wearing a black collar. On the actual card, the black collar had been a thin strip of velvet, in the centre of which a small diamond-like crystal had been affixed. Beneath the image, in bright pink italic writing, were the words *Pink Pussycat Parlour*. The second photograph was of the reverse of the front of the card, also with a white background. Printed in bold black italic text, were the words *For Your Purrlicious Pleasure!* There was no other information. No address, website, or telephone number.

Abigail looked over to where the girls were sitting. They were engrossed with whatever they were watching. She listened out for any signs of movement coming from upstairs. All was quiet, so she looked at the second card. This one had been fiddly to photograph because it consisted of two flaps folded over a rectangular piece of card which, when opened, formed a triptych. Abigail had noticed when she had held the actual card in her hands, that the left-hand flap had a small square piece of black leather affixed to it in the middle, whilst the right-hand flap had a small square piece of black lace affixed. When both flaps were opened, the underside of the flaps were black which matched the centre of the card. In the centre, was printed a single image in red, which looked to Abigail to be Oriental in origin, possibly Japanese or Chinese.

As with the first card, there was no other information. Abigail was completely baffled, and slightly concerned as to what Andrew had been involved in or, more importantly, with. It was all a bit too secretive in her opinion. The third card at least gave a person's name. In embossed gold lettering, on a sparkly black background, was the name "BRIANNA MORGAN, CEO". Beneath that was written *"Eve's Garden"* in red letters. On the reverse of the card, which had a white background, the words "Corporate Entertainment. Discretion Guaranteed" were written in black lettering. It was obvious to Abigail that the cards were advertising establishments that catered for men's desires and fantasies, with the Oriental-looking card hinting at darker desires.

Closing the photographs down, she put her mobile phone away for the time being and went upstairs to shower. Andrew had clearly drunk the water, as evidenced by the empty glass and had fallen back to sleep. Abigail took the clothes and underwear she needed and showered in the girls' en suite.

Andrew finally surfaced at 11am. He came downstairs and poured himself a large mug of coffee from the percolator and helped himself to cereal.

'How are you feeling?' asked Abigail.

'I've felt better. God, the amount of booze Rufus and Sven put away. Rufus doesn't hold his drink that well and gets quite loud and raucous. But Sven – well, he's one cool customer. That's for sure,' said Andrew, with a tone of admiration, which was rare for him.

'Okay, then, spill the beans. Where did you go, and what did you get up to?' asked Abigail, with a grin on her face because, for once, she was half a step ahead of him.

'Can't tell you. Sorry,' came the abrupt response.

'What do you mean you can't tell me?'

'What I said. Can't tell you, Abi. It's part of the initiation ceremony. What goes on tour, stays on tour.' This was said with a shrug, followed by a spoonful of cereal eaten with gusto with, it seemed to Abigail, a nonchalant look tinged with insolence.

Abigail was feeling irked. 'What are you on about?' she asked crossly.

Somewhat pompously, Andrew responded with, 'I cannot divulge what we did, and where we went. If I did, I'd have to kill you.' And he laughed.

Abigail decided not to be drawn into an argument in front of the girls, who had gone quiet and were obviously listening in to the conversation. 'Probably just some boring men's clubs, such as lap dancing and strippers,' she said sulkily.

'Mummy, what's lap dancing and strippers?' asked Annabel.

Abigail clapped her hands together. 'Right, girls, that's enough TV for a while. Go upstairs and tidy your bedrooms, then you can play out in the garden. Go on, chop-chop.'

The girls sighed, switched off the television and exited the kitchen.

'Oh, and leave the door open. I know what you two are like at listening in,' Abigail added with a grin.

Waiting until she could hear the girls go upstairs, she turned her attention back to Andrew, who was looking at her with half-closed eyes. 'Have you been going through my pockets?' he asked.

'No, I flipping well haven't. What do you think I am? A prying sneak?' she replied, colouring slightly.

'Now, now, Abi. Calm down. Look, I can't tell you. However, I did find out some very juicy information about our neighbours. Do you want to know what

I found out?' he asked in an effort to appease his wife and prevent any further interrogation from her.

For the moment, Abigail was duly appeased. 'Ooh, yes please. Let me top up our coffees, and you can tell all.' Abigail put the refilled mugs on the table. 'Right, spill the beans,' she said, grinning and rubbing her hands together.

'Well, you won't believe it! That Rufus is a bit of a rogue. Juliana was his secretary, and his "bit on the side" when he was still married. She started out in the typing pool and worked her way up, if you know what I mean,' Andrew said, winking.

Abigail frowned. 'I'm not sure I do know what you mean.'

Andrew shook his head. 'You're so naive sometimes, Abigail. Anyway, she ended up on the directors' floor working for Rufus, because he'd had his eye on her for some time. Anyway, she got pregnant and started making things difficult. To cut a long story short, Rufus had to divorce Sharon – that was his wife, by the way – and marry Juliana. His wife agreed to a quick divorce but only if he gave her an ample settlement. Also, Juliana may put on "airs and graces" now, and speak in that awful fake plummy accent, but she comes from the Isle of Dogs. What do you make of that then?'

Abigail was amazed. *Well I never*, she thought. 'Did Rufus tell you all of this when he'd had too much to drink?'

'No, Sven did.'

Abigail frowned. 'Wasn't Rufus annoyed with Sven for gossiping about him and Juliana, with him listening in?'

'Rufus wasn't there at the time.'

'Where was he then?'

'Oh, he was having a—' Then he stopped himself when he realised he was revealing too much information.

'Come on, Andrew, you might as well tell me. I'm not going to say anything, am I?'

Andrew sighed. 'He was having a private lap dance in one of the VIP rooms. Evidently, he's a regular there. All the girls knew him.'

Abigail rolled her eyes. 'And you, Andrew, did you have a *private lap dance?*'

'No, I most certainly didn't. What kind of man do you think I am, Abigail?' he said with more vehemence than was necessary. Abigail noticed that he had reddened slightly as well.

'Okay, what else did you find out?'

'Well…' He leaned closer to Abigail across the table and lowered his voice.

'Why are you whispering? There's only us here!'

'Yes, I know that. But they live next door.'

'Who? Sven and Svetlana?'

'Yes.'

Abigail was puzzled. 'They can't hear us, Andrew. We live in a detached house. Why are you being so odd, and please can you speak in a normal voice?'

Before speaking again, Andrew looked left and right as if someone might be eavesdropping.

'The girls are upstairs. You don't need to worry about them listening in,' said Abigail.

Andrew took a deep breath and let it out. 'Svetlana isn't her real name. It's Shirley, and she's from Croydon, not Russia.'

'I wasn't sure if she was from Russia. I thought perhaps she was Polish or Russian,' replied Abigail.

'Sven met her through an escort agency he used to use. He's a senior partner in a shipping law firm and is only interested in work and earning lots of money. He goes to a lot of corporate events which sometimes call for a *plus one*, and so he would hire beautiful escorts to accompany him as he didn't want all the emotional demands that come with having a permanent relationship.'

'Oh, thank you very much, Andrew! And what "emotional demands", to quote you, do I make on you? None, Andrew. None whatsoever!'

'Oh, for heaven's sake, Abigail, calm down. I'm not talking about you. I was talking about Sven.'

'Yes, I know, but you said that being in a permanent—'

'Abigail, do you want me to continue or not, because if you don't, I've got more important things to be getting on with,' and he began to stand up.

'No, no, don't go. Carry on.'

'As I was saying, he hired very attractive escorts to accompany him to the functions. One of these was called Svetlana. That was the name she used when she was working, because she looks Russian and it seems many men like to be seen with attractive Russian women because it gives them kudos in the business world.' Andrew stopped to take a slurp of coffee. 'Evidently, she was very good at what she did. Her looks, combined with that figure of hers...' Andrew looked wistful for a moment, until Abigail shot him a warning look. 'Well, unsurprisingly, she was so popular and in high demand that on one occasion when Sven wanted to hire her, she wasn't available. So, he married her. Simple as that. Rufus didn't go into great detail, but it seems that Sven made it worth her while, although it is a marriage of convenience which seems to work for them both. Also, she told him her real name was Shirley, but he told her to keep calling herself "Svetlana" because "Sven and Svetlana" sounded better.'

Abigail was amazed. 'And Rufus told you all of this?'

'Yes.'

'And where was Sven when Rufus was telling you all of this?'

'He was a bit tied up. Fuck!' He put his hands over his mouth.

'Andrew! Language, please.'

He removed his hands. 'Sorry, but now I've let the cat out of the bag.'

'What cat have you let out of the bag? You're not making much sense. You said he was "a bit tied up". A bit tied up doing what? Surely not having a lap dance? Svetlana probably gives him a lap dance for free.'

Andrew looked wistful again, then stood up. 'I'm going back to bed for an hour. All this talking has tired me out.'

Three thoughts sprang into Abigail's mind. One was to do with Svetlana's real name and her beginnings in Croydon, which seemed to Abigail to be a long way from where she had ended up. Another was to do with the card advertising the Pink Pussycat Parlour which was obviously a lap dancing club they had visited, and where Rufus had had his private session. Her third thought was Andrew's letting "the cat out of the bag" about Sven being tied up. The question was, what was he tied up with, or who? *All very puzzling*, she thought. Then she remembered the card with the name of Brianna Morgan, who organised corporate events. Instinctively, Abigail knew that this woman was central to everything, and she was determined to find out more. She also realised that Andrew hadn't revealed what his initiation involved, and that there had been no mention of Toby or Tommy.

Andrew came downstairs an hour later carrying his suit over his arm. 'Have you got a carrier bag, Abi? I'm taking my suit to the cleaners. I also thought I'd pop into the delicatessen whilst I'm in Cornham and get us something nice for dinner, to save you cooking. To be honest, I'm getting a bit fed up with stews cooked in the slow cooker, and grilled meat. What do you think?'

'Good idea. See if they've got one of those nice coq au vin meals and bring back some mashed potato and green beans. That'll do for us. The girls would probably prefer lasagna, so get one of those as well.'

'Okey dokey. See you later.' Somewhat uncharacteristically, he went over and gave Abigail a quick peck on the lips and then left.

Abigail decided to do some laundry and went upstairs to bring the laundry basket downstairs. She could hear chatter coming from Francesca's bedroom and knocked on the door.

'Come in,' the girls said in unison.

'I'm putting a wash on. Anything need washing?'

'No thanks, Mummy,' came the joint reply.

'What are you both up to?'

'We're looking at the curriculum of the school we're going to,' replied Annabel.

'It's really cool,' added Francesca.

'They've got fashion design, chef's skills, and entre... how do you pronounce it, Francesca?'

Francesca adopted an aloof air, as she was about to show off. 'Entrepreneurial and enterprise skills.' Then grinned, because she had been practising the correct pronunciation of "entrepreneurial".

'Wow!' remarked Abigail. 'In my day, we had needlework classes, domestic science and office practice. How times have changed.' She shrugged her shoulders.

'But that was a long time ago, Mummy,' said Annabel, which caused Francesca to burst out laughing and Annabel to blush.

'Well, thank you for that, girls. Your dear old mother will now leave you alone to get on with what you were doing.'

Abigail took the laundry basket downstairs to the utility room and sorted the washing into different piles according to the washing instructions for temperature, and whether the clothes were colours or whites. She realised that in the white pile, Andrew's shirt wasn't there. *Mmm, interesting*, she thought. *He's taken it to the cleaners and must have hidden it in his suit. Guilty conscience if there ever was one.*

With Francesca and Annabel upstairs, and Andrew out shopping, Abigail decided to make a start on her "research project". She'd drunk enough coffee, so made herself a cup of tea and sat down at the kitchen table. No sooner had she switched on her iPad, than she heard footsteps on the stairs and then the girls came into the kitchen.

'What are you up to, Mummy?' asked Francesca.

'Oh, nothing really. Just looking at things on my iPad,' Abigail replied. 'Why?'

'We're hungry. What's for lunch?' asked Francesca.

'It's not quite lunch time yet. Can you hang on a bit because your dad will be back shortly with food. Have a piece of fruit to tide you over.' Abigail was impatient to get on with what she wanted to do before Andrew came back, and so was a bit short with Francesca, who had pulled a face at the mention of something healthy like fruit.

'We're bored, and we miss our friends. Don't we, Annabel?'

Annabel nodded and looked glum. 'There's nothing to do here. We don't know anyone, and the pool is too cold to swim in,' she said.

They've got a point, thought Abigail. 'I know, it's a big change for all of us. But when you start at your new school, you'll make friends in no time.' Just then Abigail heard the sound of tyres on the gravel driveway. 'Ah! That's Daddy back.'

The front door opened and closed, and Andrew came into the kitchen carrying three olive-green shopping bags bearing the name *Cornham Delicatessen* which was in gold lettering with a distinctive typeface not dissimilar to a well-known luxury department store in Knightsbridge. Looking at the bags, Abigail rolled her eyes at the pretentiousness of it all, recollecting that there was a hair salon in Cornham called André of Knightsbridge.

'Crikey, Andrew, did you buy up the whole store?' asked Abigail, laughing.

'Not quite, but there's some lovely food in there. Not cheap, mind you. Anyway, the evening meal is all sorted,' he said as he gave himself a pat on the back.

I must remember to give myself a pat on the back every time I go shopping, Abigail silently thought. *I'd probably get a bruise though with all the pats.* She laughed.

'What are you laughing at, Abigail? Have I said something amusing?' asked Andrew, with a puzzled look.

'No, not at all. Just something that I thought of. Did you, by any chance, pick up anything for lunch? The girls are hungry.'

'I most certainly did! I bought sweet potato salad, a mixed salad of quinoa, rice and chia seeds, and a quiche Lorraine. How does that sound?'

'Bit of a mixture, but I'm sure it will be nice. Won't it, girls?' she said hopefully.

The girls both looked slightly dubious, but knew they had to be careful not to appear ungrateful in front of their father. The diplomacy was left to Francesca.

'It all sounds lovely, Daddy. Could Annabel and I perhaps just have some of that quiche, as we're not that hungry.'

'I thought you said you were hungry?' asked Abigail, and then realised what Francesca was doing. 'Would you like baked beans with your quiche, instead?' A pair of nods signalled approval at the suggestion. 'Great. Sorted then. The grown-ups will have the delicious salads and quiche, and the children can have quiche and baked beans.'

Before Andrew could complain, Abigail told him that the girls were bored and so would he mind taking them out for a couple of hours after lunch, as she had some chores she wanted to get on with.

'Sure.' He shrugged. 'Would you like that, girls?' he asked. Another pair of nods showed their agreement.

Lunch was over. Whether it had been a success foodwise, was debatable. Abigail didn't like the sweet potato salad as she found it too mushy, and too spicy, but she liked the more subtly flavoured mixture of rice, seeds and grains. Andrew, on the other hand, preferred the potato salad over the grains, with both of them agreeing that the quiche would have been just as nice served with a good old fashioned straightforward salad of lettuce, tomato and cucumber.

The girls had gone upstairs to change into outdoor clothes and came back down to say goodbye. They both gave Abigail a kiss on the cheek and waved goodbye.

'Bye, girls. Bye, Andrew. Have a nice time.'

Abigail felt conflicted. Saying goodbye to them made her feel a bit sad because she wasn't going with them, and Saturdays were supposed to be family time together. However, it did free her up so that she could get on with the task of finding out just what those cards in Andrew's pocket were all about, although she already had some idea about two of them. She only had a couple of hours, and so she switched on her iPad again and went to the Safari search engine. The first name she searched for was Pink Pussycat Parlour. Various references popped up, and some were of a very questionable nature. There was an advertisement for a pill that purportedly enhanced female sexual pleasure, followed by a review site; a reference to an Australian brothel, and further down the list, the sites became increasingly lurid, all of which made Abigail feel very alarmed. There was nothing, however, with a link to a London club with that name, which reinforced for her that it was probably a private and exclusive "members only" lap dancing club and almost certainly would not be advertised on the internet, being recommended by word of mouth only.

The next bit of research was to do with the Oriental-looking card. She instinctively felt that the card was for a Japanese club due to the unfussy and simplified design, using the two colours of red and black. She reasoned that if it had been Chinese, the colours would have been red and gold, and included an image of a dragon, Chinese lantern or firecrackers. So, deciding that it must be advertising a Japanese club, she did the obvious thing and typed in "Japanese leather and lace club London" into the search bar. A number of references came up, but nothing that was remotely Japanese or Oriental. Looking at the symbol on the card, she typed "Japanese symbols" into the search bar. A link to a very informative website popped up and Abigail clicked on the link. She discovered that the Japanese language had three types of characters: *Hiragana* and *Katakena*, which were described as phonetic symbols equal to letters of the alphabet. The third one was *Kanji* which was described as an ideogram.

Although she found this information interesting, without any knowledge or understanding of Japanese, and how the language system and sentence structure was constructed, she was at a complete loss. One thing she did learn, however, was that the red symbol on the card was an ideogram. Then she had a "light bulb" moment. She thought back to what Andrew had said about Sven being tied up and his remark that he had let the cat out the bag. So, in the search bar she typed "Japanese tied up". There was a link to an article about Japanese knotweed, another to do with Japanese proverbs, and then a website that purported to show how to say "tied up" in Japanese, which Abigail clicked on. One of the words for "tied up" was *shibari* with the symbols used for the word. Whilst not a perfect match for the symbols on the card, there were some resemblances. Abigail then typed in the word *shibari* which translated as "tied up" in English. There was a further reference to the word which gave a fuller translation of "the art of Japanese rope bondage", which caused Abigail to take a double look as she was not expecting this. The website also gave a link to a magazine which had featured an article about *shibari* rope bondage. Opening the link, she uploaded the magazine and then was able to go to the article which described *shibari* rope bondage as "functional and beautiful". Scrolling further down, she read that it had been used as an ancient Japanese method of restraining captives and a form of torture, but it had morphed into an erotic art form. The article also stated that it had links with the BDSM community. Not entirely sure what this stood for, Abigail closed down the magazine article and typed "BDSM" into the search bar. She was directed to an information site where she quickly found out what the initials stood for and was shocked again.

Getting up, she went to the fridge and brought out the bottle of Provence rosé. She then went to the cupboard where the wine glasses were kept and took out a large glass meant for red wine. She poured herself a large glass of wine, put the bottle back in the fridge and went and sat back down. Taking a hefty gulp, she reflected on what she had found out so far. She couldn't quite believe it. Of Rufus maybe, but certainly not Sven who was always in control emotionally and physically. He was always calm and cool, never laughed loudly, or showed anger or irritation. In fact, thought Abigail, he was very restrained. Yes, that was it, she thought and took another large gulp of wine. *He was always,* she reflected, *a bit tightly wound up,* and she began laughing uncontrollably, and didn't hear the girls and Andrew coming back into the kitchen.

'What are you laughing at, Mummy?' asked Annabel.

'Oh nothing. Just got myself tied up in knots over something,' she replied and began laughing again.

The girls and Andrew looked at Abigail, and then at the almost empty wine glass.

'Have you been drinking wine during the day, Mummy?' asked Francesca.

'Yes, I have. And so knot... oops, I meant so what.' That set her off again.

'Daddy, why is Mummy behaving so strangely?' asked Annabel.

'Yes, Mummy, why are you behaving so strangely?' asked Andrew. 'What have you been up to whilst we've been out, apart from drinking wine?'

'Oh, not very much. Just tying up a few loose ends.' She giggled, then turned off her iPad.

Andrew sighed. 'I'll have a cup of tea if that isn't too much trouble. Oh, and I've got the girls enrolled in tennis lessons at the local club for the rest of the summer. They start tomorrow morning. I'll drop them off, and then I'm going to the cricket club with Rufus. He's going to show me around and introduce me to a few people, and I'll pick the girls up on my way back. I thought we could all go to the local pub and have a carvery for lunch. How does that sound?'

'It all sounds good,' replied Abigail, who had stopped giggling. Once again, she felt conflicted. On the one hand she was glad the girls were going to have something to do, and that Andrew was making friends with the neighbourhood men, but she wasn't part of any of it and she momentarily felt a sense of loss. On the other hand, however, it meant that she had some free time again to try and find out more about the third card she had found in Andrew's pocket, which filled her with a mixture of excitement and trepidation.

It was Sunday morning, and everyone was up early. The sun had made an early appearance and the day promised to develop into a warm one, which made them all feel happy and energetic. After breakfast, Andrew and the girls left with kisses, "goodbyes", and "see you laters".

Abigail sat down at the kitchen table and switched on her iPad. She typed the name "Brianna Morgan" into the search engine and was surprised to see a link to a website for someone with that name. The website revealed two pages of information about the woman who was American but who had lived in London for many years. She ran an events company aimed at corporate clientele, and on the surface it all appeared to be above board and straightforward. There were a few photographs on the site. One showed a group of men in combat outfits on what was described as an "army roleplaying" event; another was taken at a black-tie event organised for hedge fund managers and venture capitalists where the entertainment was provided by a well-known irreverent comedian. Both photographs were obviously aimed at "men only" functions, as there were no women present at all. However, a third photograph showed a dinner and auction evening at a top London hotel, with guest appearances by a number of celebrities. The photograph showed groups of men and women sitting at tables. Some of the women were very attractive and clearly a lot younger than the older men they were sitting next to. Not knowing what Brianna Morgan looked like, Abigail had no way of knowing if any of the women in the photographs was the organiser of the event. There was a link to the company's Facebook page, Instagram and LinkedIn, but again the content was very businesslike and seemingly respectable. Again, there was no photograph and Abigail thought this was odd. Closing down her iPad, she reflected that, whilst, on the surface, her research had revealed some information, it was still shrouded in secrecy.

Andrew, Francesca and Annabel came back. The girls had enjoyed their tennis lesson and were keen to continue. Andrew said that he was thinking about joining the cricket club, and that Abigail could come and help the other wives with the cricket teas and that way she would meet people. Sunday lunch at their local pub went well, and Abigail went to bed feeling more positive and happier than she had in a while.

It was back to normal on Monday morning. Andrew went off to work, the girls occupied themselves and Abigail did some household chores. As it was warm and sunny, Abigail and the girls had lunch outside and then sunbathed. The girls went swimming, but kept shrieking with laughter, and Abigail was sure she had seen a flash of lime green through the garden fence and told them to keep the noise down.

Later, she remembered she hadn't checked the post box. On opening it, there was a letter from Mrs Collins, who was the headteacher at the girls' new school. It was an invitation for Mr and Mrs A Thomas, and their daughters, to come to an open evening where they could meet other new parents and pupils. Mrs Collins would be giving a talk, as would the head of the parents' association – Mrs C Smythe-Brown – which is how Abigail met Cassandra Smythe-Brown.

PART TWO

CHAPTER SIX

SANDRA SMITH'S LIFE had been mapped out by her solidly respectable and very ordinary parents from the day she was born: primary school, comprehensive school, a job in retail or office work rather than a factory or supermarket, marriage, babies, grandmother, die. Of course, with the latter two criteria, they would have no control over the matter, although that never occurred to them when they were mapping out her life plan. There was a minor blip when Sandra passed the eleven-plus, which gave her an automatic place at the local grammar school. Rather than being pleased, her mother – who worked as a part-time cleaning lady at the local bakery – burst into tears. 'You'll get airs and graces, Sandra, and we won't be good enough for you,' she wailed.

'Don't be silly, Maureen. Of course she won't forget about us. Will you, Sandy?' said her father, George, who worked in the local factory as a warehouseman and also acted as the union representative.

'Of course not,' replied Sandra. 'I'll always be your little girl.' This set her mother off crying again.

Later that evening, over dinner, Sandra made an announcement. 'Mum, dad, I've come to a decision. I'm not going to grammar school. I'll go to the local comprehensive instead.'

Her father frowned, but kept quiet, knowing that Sandra had come to the decision for her mother's sake. On cue, her mother started crying again; this time, however, they were tears of joy.

In due course, Sandra went to her local comprehensive and made her parents proud when she was placed in the "A" stream. She made them even prouder when she left school with five O-Levels and a Grade 1 Certificate in keyboard skills, office practice and book-keeping. These qualifications were sufficient enough for Sandra to find employment as a receptionist/typist in the local firm of solicitors in the small market town where she lived. Being very pretty, with a bubbly and confident personality, and a figure that was becoming curvaceous, it was no coincidence that she was placed on reception, where she quickly became a favourite with the male clients, which is how she began dating Derek Dickson.

Derek had been in the year above Sandra at school and had always had his eye on her. His father, Ted Dickson, was a client at the firm of solicitors where Sandra worked and would feel his spirits lift when he saw her and so, with his father's encouragement, Derek began to actively seek Sandra out. His chance came when he spotted her walking home from her job, in the rain. Derek worked as an apprentice car mechanic for his father's firm and had use of the company van. Although Sandra was grateful for his offer of a lift home, she was embarrassed as she felt that getting into a van was a bit beneath her. However, she thought that he was polite and not bad looking, if a bit spotty. When she got into the van, she saw that he was wearing overalls and, when she looked at his hands on the steering wheel, she noticed that he had grease under his nails. A series of sudden and unbidden images popped up in Sandra's mind: her and spotty Derek at the altar; at the christening of their first child, then the second child... at this point, she shut the images down before things got worse.

Nonetheless, he was passable, persistent and, more importantly, clearly worshipped her and paid for everything. Added to this was that he sometimes had the use of his father's Jaguar and wore a suit and tie whenever they went out anywhere. So, they began dating and became thought of as a couple. Sandra drew the line though when Derek wanted to put a decal on the back window of the company van which said *Sandra and Derek* and included an image of a red heart. Not to be thwarted in his attempt to advertise their coupledom, and much to Sandra's dismay, he dangled a pair of red dice from the mirror on the inside of the windscreen of the Jaguar, which had the capital letters "S" and "D" printed on the dice. This time, however, the thwarting came from Derek's father who told him to take the dice down as it conveyed the wrong impression for him and his business – Ted Dickson Motors.

Her mother, not surprisingly, approved of the relationship. 'Oh, Sandra! His dad's got his own garage and he'll probably be a co-owner soon. You won't want for nothing, and you won't do better than Derek Dickson. Just imagine, you'll be married to the son of Ted Dickson Motors!'

Sandra's father remained silent.

Time passed, and it was a foregone conclusion that Sandra and Derek were a permanent couple which would result in marriage. Thus, her mother began knitting baby clothes, drawing up a list of who should be invited to the wedding and reception, and pondering whether the latter should be held in the village hall or the Spread Eagle Hotel. The fact that Sandra and Derek weren't even engaged at this time seemed to have been forgotten by Sandra's mother, who had started making noises about wedding dresses, Sandra losing a few pounds to drop a dress size, and what flowers should be in the bride's bouquet, until Sandra's father put a stop to it all. Sandra had gone out with Derek for the evening, just to escape from her mother's relentless chitter chatter, which left George and Maureen alone.

'Oh, and George,' she said, having got to the bottom of her first to-do list, 'you'll need to buy a morning suit, and start thinking about your speech. Don't try and be too funny, and definitely nothing smutty. We don't want the Dickson family thinking we're common.'

George raised his eyes to the ceiling and back down again. 'Hold on, Maureen, you're jumping the gun a bit. There's been no talk of an engagement yet, let alone a wedding. If you're not careful, you'll jinx the whole thing,' which is what he was secretly hoping would happen and, in fact, did happen.

Although Sandra was genuinely fond of Derek, she didn't love him and she certainly didn't fancy him. He was beginning to get increasingly amorous and aroused, which made her feel queasy. She couldn't get the sight of his greasy nails out of her mind. It wasn't his fault; she knew that. It was just that the grease was so deeply embedded under his nails and surrounding skin that nothing removed it. Also, she disliked the way he kissed. It was too wet and sloppy. Furthermore, when he put his tongue into her mouth, she felt as if she was going to be sick. So, the thought of the inevitable sexual contact made up her mind for her. She broke up with him and broke his heart in the process. Now, she had to break the news to her parents.

Over dinner that evening, Sandra took a deep breath and said, 'Mum, Dad, I've got something to tell you.'

Her mother's hands flew to her face, then she removed them to reveal eyes wide with expectation and excitement. 'You're not...?' she asked.

'No, Mum, I'm not *with child*,' came the reply, and she rolled her eyes.

'Then, it must be that Derek has asked you to…?'

'No, Mum, he hasn't.'

Sandra's mother frowned. 'Then what is it you're wanting to tell us?'

Sandra took another deep breath. 'I've finished with Derek. I don't love him.' She could have added that she didn't like his greasy nails, slobbery kisses and the thought of having sex with him made her feel queasy, but she refrained.

Uncharacteristically, her mother stayed silent with disapproval and disappointment sketched on her face. Uncharacteristically, her father spoke out. 'Thank God for that!' he said. 'I never did like the Dickson family. A right oily, oiky lot, if you ask me. I never forgave that Ted Dickson for diddling me out of money when he did a shoddy repair on my car. Good on you girl.' He shot a warning glance at his wife to keep quiet.

With the best indignant attitude she could muster, Sandra's mother stood up and folded her arms. 'Well, that's that then. I best clear away the dinner things.'

'I've got something else to tell you.'

Sandra's mother sat back down. 'Out with it then.'

'There's no need for that tone of voice, Maureen,' said Sandra's father. 'Go on, love, what else do you have to tell us?'

'Well, I've got a new job. You know that I've been taking a secretarial course at the adult education centre?' They both nodded. 'Well, I applied for a job vacancy as a legal secretary at partner level for a large firm of solicitors in Oxford. It's a big jump up from my current job in terms of position and responsibility, and an increase in salary and – guess what – I got the job. I start in a month's time.'

'Well done, Sandy. Well done, indeed,' said her father. Her mother remained silent.

Sandra's parents, like many parents I suppose, think they know their children, not realising that they have a mind and a personality of their own and, unless the parent or parents exercise such control over their offspring so as to prevent them from becoming fully developed and independent beings in their own right, such children will inevitably go their own way. What Sandra's parents hadn't realised, because she had always been obedient and deferential, was that she fostered ambitions and aspirations, and a burning desire to escape from a small-town mediocre mentality and experience a more fulfilling and interesting life. So, when she applied for the job as a legal secretary to one of the tax partners at the law firm of Baker, Charles, and Simpson, whose head office was in London with branches in Oxford, Bath, and York, she saw Oxford as a stepping stone to the "bright lights" of London and beyond.

In order to make her curriculum vitae appear more impressive, and herself more appealing, she had to tweak it slightly. The first thing was a subtle change of name that wasn't so different from her real name. So, Sandra Smith became Cassandra Smyth. The next thing was to "upsell" herself. Whilst she didn't lie about her schooling and could truthfully list the excellent grades she had achieved, she was slightly concerned that the fact that she had left school at age 16 and not gone on to college to study for A-Levels, or even a secretarial course, might go against her. Therefore, under "any other relevant information", she wrote that she had to leave school after O-Levels to care for her ailing mother and had studied for secretarial qualifications at evening class. She had further explained that she was, by nature, ambitious and fostered a wish to study as a paralegal in the not-too-distant future.

Having submitted her curriculum vitae, she had then taken a day off from her current job and travelled into Oxford to see what the offices of the Oxford firm were like. Standing on the opposite side of the road, she took in the glass and steel modern architectural grandeur of the building, saw the dark-suited and white-shirted male and female employees, carrying black leather attaché cases, going in and out. She decided that these people were the legal executives such as solicitors, articled clerks and paralegals. When she saw a taxi pull up outside, from which two bewigged barristers exited in their flowing black robes, carrying bunches of files tied in pink ribbon, she felt a thrill of excitement well up. The gaggle of chatty girls she also saw emerging from the building at lunchtime were obviously the secretarial and administrative staff, and Sandra decided she needed to set herself apart from this group – at least, for interview purposes – should she be successful in securing an interview.

Much to her delight and surprise, she was given a date for an interview by the human resources department. She chose her outfit with care, choosing a V-neck navy-blue dress, teamed with a navy-blue jacket with gold buttons, black patent shoes with a kitten heel, and a black patent handbag not dissimilar in design to the black attaché cases she had seen. Appearance-wise, she had aimed to look like a cross between a young solicitor and an administrator at senior level. Her gambit paid off. The interviewer was impressed by her professional appearance and serious manner, and the fact that she was also attractive didn't go against her. Thus, she was sent to the upper floor to be interviewed by Angus Laidlaw Baker, one of the senior managing partners. Before going upstairs, the human resources person had warned Cassandra (as she was now known) that he could be difficult, with a tetchy and exacting personality, which not everyone could deal with. He needed someone who could organise his overflowing diary, complete his complicated timesheets, word process his legal documents speedily, and greet his important clients. What he really needed was a "right hand" to steady his "left hand", the interviewer had added. Did Cassandra think she could be his right hand?

'I'm sure I can,' Cassandra had replied. 'I don't flap, I work well under pressure, and am a bit of a perfectionist myself. I think we'll make a great team,' she had said with outward confidence, but had crossed her fingers behind her back as she really wanted this job. The grandeur of the offices, the fact that Angus Laidlaw Baker was not only a senior partner but one of the firm's three managing partners, was a big step up on her aspirational ladder.

That day, the gods were with Cassandra. Despite looking harried, the middle-aged solicitor with his frameless glasses perched on the end of his nose was in a good mood having secured the business of a large local firm which was going through a merger. He was sat back in his chair, with his hands linked behind his head, when Cassandra was brought into his office. Over the top of his glasses, when he saw her blond hair and heard her softly spoken voice when she introduced herself, he was momentarily transported back to his early carefree days at Oxford University and his youthful love for Philomena O'Brien, a blond-haired blue-eyed undergraduate from Cork who wanted to be a barrister. He also liked Cassandra's calm, reassuring manner, and the fact that she was pretty didn't go unnoticed either.

A month later, Cassandra joined the law firm of Baker, Charles, and Simpson, which is where she met Ingram Smythe-Brown.

CHAPTER SEVEN

INGRAM SMYTHE-BROWN came from a family of solicitors on the male side, and did not disappoint when he, too, decided to maintain the tradition and take up law. He did, however, incur disapproval when he chose to bypass Oxford University and apply instead to the University of Birmingham to read for a degree in international law and globalisation, which also offered an optional year abroad in either Singapore, Hong Kong or Japan. As Ingram had a yearning to visit Southeast Asia, a year in Singapore appealed to him. Achieving a First, he then decided to break with tradition again and study for a two-year MBA at Harvard Business School. Whilst at Harvard, he socialised just enough so as to take part in essential networking events and make the right contacts. In reality, though, he had little time or inclination for small talk as he was an intellectual heavyweight with a sharp analytical mind who liked nothing more than being in his own company reading weighty tomes on legal precedents, and international tax law. He had taken advantage of the year spent in Singapore to start learning Japanese and Mandarin and continued his learning at Harvard by taking two online courses. On his return to England, he began to apply to the top London law firms. Normally, these prestigious firms tended to hire from Oxbridge. However, the name of Smythe-Brown was well known in legal circles, and the fact that Ingram had an impressive set of qualifications, resulted in his being offered a position as a junior international tax planning solicitor at the firm of Baker, Charles and Simpson, at their offices in Blackfriars.

As part of Ingram's career development, and after spending time in the London office, he was seconded to the Oxford branch to be mentored by Angus Laidlaw Baker, which is how he met Cassandra Smyth. Keen to make a good impression with his serious-minded mentor who rarely smiled, Ingram likewise adopted this attitude. So, he was taken aback when a knock on the door of Angus' office caused his mentor to clap his hands like a child and, with a grin on his face, shouted 'Ah! Come in, Cassandra.' The door opened to reveal an attractive, smartly-dressed, young woman who was balancing a cup and saucer in one hand and a plate with two shortbread biscuits in the other hand. Walking over to the desk, she placed the cup and saucer, and plate, carefully in front of her boss. Still smiling up at her, he introduced Cassandra to Ingram who was transfixed. 'Cassandra, meet Ingram Smythe-Brown. He's on course to become the youngest ever junior partner in the firm, and I'll be sharing you with him. Ingram, meet Cassandra. She's my "right hand". Don't know what I'd do without her. She'll look after you, won't you, Cassandra?' said Angus Laidlaw Baker, turning away from Ingram to address his secretary.

'Of course I will, Angus. I will make sure Mr Smythe-Brown is not distracted by anything unimportant, so that he can focus on the important things.' Cassandra then turned her attention to Ingram. 'Anything you need, Mr Smythe-Brown, just ask. That's what I'm here for.' She flashed him a smile showing a perfect set of white teeth and two small dimples in her rosy cheeks.

At the mention of Ingram's double-barrelled surname, combined with the knowledge that he was on the fast track to make junior partner, it was love at first sight for Cassandra. Whilst she didn't find him overly attractive in looks, she did like his smart, conservative way of dressing, his well-groomed appearance and, of utmost importance, his ultra-clean hands and nails that had obviously never done a dirty day's work in their life. The fact that he was serious, almost bordering on stern, and hadn't even acknowledged her with a smile, didn't bother her and she was confident that with time she could break through his reserve.

For Ingram, who also liked what he saw – but for very different reasons – and who had been raised in a patriarchal household with a stay-at-home mother who made sure Ingram's father and Ingram's needs were always given priority over her own, saw – in Cassandra's deferential nature – an image of his mother; hence, perfect wife material with the added bonus that Ingram found her to be very attractive. However, relationships between employees – particularly those between support staff and professional staff – were discouraged and so Ingram decided to proceed with caution, even though Cassandra was completely unaware of his intentions.

Cassandra's charms were not making the remotest dent in Ingram's armour. He was always abrupt in his tone, remained unsmiling and rarely looked her in the eye. She would arrive at her desk each morning to find a pile of tapes to be transcribed, legal documents to be word-processed and a mound of filing, with instructions written in small, neat handwriting on coloured Post-It notes. As with Angus Laidlaw Baker, she would take Ingram in a cup of coffee each morning, minus the biscuits at his request. Without looking at her, he would tap his index finger on the top of the desk to indicate where she should put the cup and saucer. This behaviour went on for a while, until Cassandra could take it no more. She knocked on his office door and waited.

'Enter,' came the response.

'Mr Smythe-Brown, could I have a word please?'

'Yes, Cassandra. What is it?' he said, without looking up. 'Oh, and you can call me Ingram. You don't need to be so formal.' He looked up at her at last with an attempt at a smile, revealing a set of small white teeth. Cassandra was reminded of Foxy who had been her pet fox terrier when she was growing up. She almost had a yearning at the moment to go and pat Ingram on the head but restrained herself.

'What it is, Ingram, is that I get the feeling you're displeased with me in some way. Is it my work? Am I not efficient enough? Tell me how I can improve or make your daily life better. You do know that I tend to give your work priority over Angus', which is not how it should be.' All of this was said in a rush, as Cassandra was beginning to feel flustered and hot.

For once, Ingram looked at her with an intense expression on his face. 'Cassandra, you are the perfect secretary. I couldn't wish for a better one. The one I had in London was, well, to be honest, bloody useless. Your organisational skills are excellent and I'm well aware you put me first. In many respects, you remind me of my mo—' Ingram stopped himself from saying "mother", as he didn't want Cassandra to think he was a mummy's boy. Instead, he said, 'Why do you think I'm displeased with you?'

'Well, you never talk to me. Everything is done by Post-it notes, and well—'

Cassandra never got to finish her sentence because Ingram had leant across the desk towards her and blurted out, 'Cassandra, I love you!'

Which is how Sandra Smith eventually became Mrs Cassandra Smythe-Brown.

After Ingram's surprise declaration of love, three things happened in quick succession. The first thing was that

Ingram was called back to the London office, where he was informed that he would be going to Singapore to open up an office, as Baker, Charles and Simpson were expanding into Southeast Asia and Singapore was a perfect location as it was a financial hub. Also, because of Ingram's legal specialisation and his fluency in Japanese and Mandarin, and his familiarity with Singapore already, it was only natural and logical that he would be sent there.

The second thing that happened was that Cassandra, with some sadness, gave a month's notice as she was moving to London to be with Ingram. Unsurprisingly, Angus was not happy but when she told him why she was leaving, he grudgingly said, 'Well, Cassandra, you've been a brilliant secretary. One of the best I've had, and you'll no doubt be an attentive and caring wife. So, you go with my blessing.'

The final thing was that Cassandra had to go and see her parents. Over Sunday lunch, she said, 'Mum, Dad, I've got something to tell you.'

Her mother put down her knife and fork, sighed and folded her arms. Her father kept on eating. 'Out with it then, Sandra,' said her mother. 'What is it this time?'

Cassandra, whose parents weren't aware she called herself by that name, took a deep breath and exhaled. 'I'm getting married, and I'm going to Singapore.'

She was met with a wall of silence from both her parents. Her father spoke first: 'I think you'd better fill us in on the details, Sandy. There seems to be an awful lot of things we don't know about.'

'Well, she's always been a bit secretive, George. But, then again, we're only her parents. I think she sometimes forgets who's fed and clothed her, and put a roof over her head.' Cassandra's father shot his wife one of his warning looks. Cassandra explained how she had worked for this solicitor who had been seconded from the London office. She told them she had fallen in love with him and the love was reciprocated. Her mother frowned. 'How long has this been going on?' she asked. 'And why haven't we met him? In fact, since you moved to Oxford, we've hardly seen you, have we George?' she said, trying to get Cassandra's father into the conversation.

'It's true, Sandy. We've hardly seen you. The odd phone call now and then, and the visits back for Sunday lunch, but that's about it. We know you're busy with this job of yours which sounds very demanding, seeing as you're working for one of the top bosses, but this... well, suddenly you're in a serious relationship with someone we've never met, getting married and moving to London and then going to Singapore. It's a lot to take in. I know I'm a bit old-fashioned, but I always hoped that you would meet someone nearer to home who would ask me for your hand in marriage, and that I would then walk you down the aisle.'

'Well, if she'd married Derek Dickson, like I'd hoped, then both your wishes would have come true. Still, I suppose we're not good enough now. I always knew this would happen. Always had ideas above her station.'

'Now, that's enough, Maureen!' said Cassandra's father, raising his voice.

Cassandra's parents never argued except – it seemed to her – when the three of them were together, and she was wishing she hadn't come home. She had arrived feeling happy, although a bit trepidatious with the news she had to impart. Now, she felt downhearted because she had caused discord between her parents, and it had been her good news (for her) that had caused the atmosphere. She had to rescue the situation. 'Mum, Dad, I'm sorry. I really am. I've been very selfish. You both have done so much for me, and I'll always be grateful. In fact, if it hadn't been for your encouragement and support, I wouldn't be here now telling you that I'll be marrying Ingram Smythe-Brown who is going to be a junior partner very shortly and running the Singapore office.'

Maureen Smith looked up with a sly look on her face. 'So, you'll be Mrs Sandra Smythe-Brown, then?'

Cassandra reddened slightly. 'Yes, that's right.'

'And a junior partner, you said. It sounds very important, doesn't it, George?'

'Mmm, very important, Maureen,' he replied, nodding thoughtfully.

'So, you'll be the boss' wife then?' said her mother.

'Erm, yes I suppose I will!' Cassandra replied brightly.

'Oh well, then, George, she's done all right for herself, I suppose, hasn't she?'

'She has indeed, Maureen. She has indeed.' George turned to his daughter. 'Just one more thing, Sandy, and then perhaps we can finish our lunch. You haven't given your mother much time to organise a wedding. So, am I right in thinking you're not getting married in church?'

'Yes, that's correct. We're going to get married in the Chelsea Registry Office, and we're expecting both of you to come up. In fact, it's essential you're both there because I want Dad to give me away, and I thought it would be a nice change of scenery for you both. If you like, Mum, I can take you shopping for your mother-of-the-bride outfit. What do you say?' Cassandra had her fingers crossed in her lap that they would be happy with this.

Although it wasn't what her parents had hoped for, in particular Cassandra's mother who had made all sorts of plans when she thought her daughter would be marrying Derek Dickson, they nevertheless agreed to come up to London.

Later that night in bed, after their daughter had returned to her bedsit in Oxford, Maureen turned to her husband. 'Don't you think Ingram is a bit of a strange name, George?'

'Well, it's different. Perhaps it's a family name handed down through the generations. It certainly sounds a bit posh. I wonder what his parents are like. Anyway, she's done well for herself, hasn't she?' He said a private thank you to no one in particular that she wasn't marrying Derek Dickson.

'Yes, I suppose she has. I don't like Chinese food.'

'What's that got to do with the price of eggs?'

'They might want to go to a Chinese restaurant after the wedding because they're going to live in Singapore.'

George laughed. 'Maureen, you are funny sometimes. Singapore isn't Chinese. It's a very cosmopolitan place. There're all kinds of nationalities living there who eat all kinds of different food.'

'I don't want to go there. It's too far.'

'Don't worry, Maureen. I doubt we'll ever go there. Now, stop worrying and go to sleep.'

George thought that there wasn't a cat in hell's chance they would even be invited to Singapore, and in his heart he knew they had lost their little girl who was moving up in the world.

Maureen fell asleep wishing that Sandra was marrying Derek Dickson, living nearby, and having babies which she could knit clothes for and be a hands-on, doting grandmother.

*

The wedding day arrived. Ingram's parents weren't in attendance as they had already planned a long-distance trip away. Two of Ingram's colleagues acted as witnesses, returning to the office immediately after the ceremony. There was a slight awkwardness during the ceremony when the registrar asked Ingram Smythe-Brown if he was willing to take "Sandra Smith" as his wife, causing Ingram to look at his about-to-be wife with a puzzled look. "Cassandra" responded with an equally puzzled look and a shrug, and then it was all over when the registrar announced, 'You may now kiss the bride.' As Ingram bent down to kiss his new wife on the lips, he smiled revealing his small teeth. Once again, an image of Foxy sprang into her mind and, for a moment, she thought Ingram was going to bite her and she jumped back, leaving Ingram looking puzzled again.

After photographs were taken in a nearby park, Mr and Mrs Smythe-Brown took Mr and Mrs Smith out for dinner and drinks at The Ivy in Covent Garden, and then they each went their separate ways.

Later that night in the Premier Inn where George and Maureen were staying, Maureen turned to her husband and said, 'He's a funny-looking bloke, isn't he? Not half as good-looking as Derek Dickson. I hope the children take after Sandra in looks.'

'Maureen, looks aren't everything, you know. He's got a good career, obviously not short of money, and I'm sure he'll look after her. It's just all a bit quick though. They hardly know each other, and that's my concern. But, it's her life and we have to let her live it. Now, go to sleep. We can go sightseeing tomorrow if you like. Shall I book us in for another night?'

'No ta, George. I'd like to get home. London's too busy and noisy.'

*

After the wedding, matters progressed swiftly. Ingram and Cassandra flew out to Singapore where they were given a serviced apartment in the Orchard Road area, provided by the London office. Atypical of many of the upmarket high-rise blocks of apartments, this one had a concierge, gym, swimming pool, and a barbeque area.

Orchard Road was a major shopping area with designer stores, air-conditioned shopping malls, restaurants, bars and cafés. It even had a Marks and Spencer, which made Cassandra feel at home. In comparison to many parts of the United Kingdom, she couldn't believe how clean the streets were, no doubt helped by the fact that chewing gum wasn't allowed, neither was littering of any kind, nor cigarette ends thrown carelessly on the pavements. The buses and the MRT, which was the equivalent of the London Over- and Underground, were also spotlessly clean, ran like clockwork and had orderly queues. For journeys outside of the MRT routes, and where time was of the essence, the various taxi apps were invaluable for the efficient ordering of taxis and their speedy response.

Naturally, Ingram was very busy setting up the new office which left Cassandra by herself. So, she purchased a travel card from one of the booths at her local MRT station and spent the first few weeks familiarising herself with the different areas that made up central Singapore. She visited China Town, Little India and Arab Street, where the unfamiliar sights and sounds, different languages and nationalities all comingling excited her. Further afield, she caught the bus to the botanical gardens where she marvelled at the variety and beauty of the orchids in the orchid garden. She even took a taxi to the zoo but found the walking around exhausting due to the humidity. Singapore had an all-year-round tropical climate, hence the humidity and then the sudden downpours, which was something she was struggling to get used to. As a result, she made a point each time she went out to take an umbrella and a raincoat with her, and carry a small fan in her handbag to cool herself down.

All in all, though, she felt very alive and couldn't believe how much her life had changed in such a short time. As a child, she had only ever gone on one week's holiday each year with her parents and that was usually to Butlins Holiday Camp. Then, she had worked for a local firm on leaving school, moved on to Oxford, then London very briefly and now here she was in Singapore. It had all been a bit of a steep learning curve for her, but she felt she had coped very well. There was one thing she did find difficult to get used to, and that was the hectic nature of Singapore life. People were on the move all the time, and not always paying attention to where they were going as they were too busy looking down at their mobile phones. As a result, she had experienced one or two collisions but at least the people who had caused the collision had the decency to utter a quick apology. This was another thing she liked about Singapore. On the whole, people were very polite and considerate, particularly the younger generation towards the adults. One rule that she had to get to grips with involved crossing the busy roads. Jaywalking was illegal, and people could only cross the road when the flashing signal on the opposite side of the road indicated it was time to cross. Cassandra noticed that people remained on the pavement, and then everyone launched themselves into the road when the lights changed, and she found herself being carried along with the throng of people.

As Ingram worked late most days, he was often too tired to go out in the evenings. The weekends, however, were a different matter. If they wanted to have some fun, they went to Club Street which, on a Friday evening, was closed at both ends to cars and was like one big party. Or, they went to Clarke Quay where, on one occasion, Cassandra saw a side of Ingram she had never seen before. They had gone to a bar which played live music, and when the band played "Livin' on a Prayer" by Bon Jovi, Ingram started playing air guitar much to Cassandra's surprise and amusement. When the singer sang "Take my hand, we'll make it I swear", Ingram took Cassandra by the hand; this uncharacteristic gesture delighted her, and she felt that she really had made the right decision in marrying him. For somewhere more sophisticated, they headed to Marina Bay Sands Hotel for cocktails and then to eat in one of the smart restaurants.

For relaxation on a Sunday, they would take a walk round Dempsey which seemed to be an enclave for expat families, and then eat at the Open Market Café and Bakery. Or, if Singapore was beginning to feel a bit claustrophobic, they would head across to Sentosa and spend a day at one of the beach clubs. For these excursions, Ingram swapped his usual conservative attire of suit and tie, and wore a t-shirt, shorts and deck shoes. For both Cassandra and Ingram, these times spent together were the equivalent of a honeymoon period where they got to know each other better. Like all honeymoons, however, theirs came to an end and real married life began. As Ingram's hours became longer, it was essential that Cassandra made an effort to find a friendship group so as not to get lonely. Thus, she became part of the expat wives community and filled her time playing tennis, going to yoga and Pilates classes, and endless coffee mornings and lunch dates.

As Ingram's wife, it was also expected of her that she would entertain the corporate wives of the important clients and visitors to the Singapore office, during the day. She would take them to all the usual places that she, too, had visited during the early days and, depending on the personality of the wife she happened to be showing around, it could either be a chore or fun. The endless traipsing round one of the many shopping malls became a chore. However, one of the wives wanted to go to the famous Raffles Hotel and have a Singapore Sling. One drink turned into two or three, and Cassandra and the wife found themselves a bit tipsy and giggly. Such light-hearted moments as these, however, were rare and, after a while, if she had to go to the botanical gardens, or the Gardens by the Bay, one more time, she felt she would go mad. Similarly, the evening canapé and drinks gatherings, and the large formal dinners she had to attend, and which she initially met with enthusiasm, now simply bored her. In fact, it was at one of the larger events consisting of an international mix of people, that provided the straw that broke the camel's back – the straw being in the form of Mrs Takako Ito who was the wife of Ingram's contemporary in the Tokyo office, Mr Daizen Ito.

Like many Japanese women, Takako Ito was naturally slim and dressed elegantly in a simple shift dress, low heels and discreet gold jewellery. Her skin was flawless, her features small and delicate, and her long black hair hung straight with a healthy shine. Cassandra immediately felt out of sorts. She had always been curvy, and had built up muscle due to playing tennis, and was well-toned due to her yoga and Pilates classes. Standing next to Takako Ito, Cassandra felt big. Her hair didn't help matters either. It had always been slightly curly and, as a result of the humidity, over time it had become slightly frizzy which no amount of conditioner seemed to help improve. If Cassandra had to describe how she felt at that very moment, it would be that she felt fat and frumpy. It also didn't help that Mrs Ito spoke no English and so Cassandra couldn't even converse with her. Ingram, on the other hand, who spoke fluent Japanese, had engaged Mrs Ito in conversation and she had seemed enthralled by this tall Englishman speaking her language. Cassandra was not surprised because Mrs Ito's husband, Daizen, was not very tall and, even though he was of a similar age to Ingram, his hair was already prematurely grey. Having introduced himself and Takako to Ingram and Cassandra, he had wandered off and was currently talking business with a group of Japanese men. In the meantime, all Cassandra could do was to stand silently by Ingram's side, feeling like a spare part.

Matters didn't improve when Ingram was sat next to Mrs Ito for the meal. Whatever Ingram was saying to her, was making her languid almond-shaped eyes look up at him admiringly. At one point he made her laugh, and she immediately covered her mouth with her hand so as not to appear unladylike. Cassandra felt ignored and disgruntled. Also, of late, she had begun to feel queasy at the sight and smell of seafood and noodles. So, when the dishes of noodles, rice, prawns and lobster tails were placed on the table, Cassandra felt very nauseous. Getting up slowly from her seat, she made her way as ladylike as she could from the banqueting hall, and then made a dash for the ladies' powder room, where she vomited violently in the sink. *Right*, she said to herself, *I'm fed up with this*. Going back to the table, she tapped Ingram on the arm. 'If you can manage, just for a moment, to tear yourself away from Mrs Ito's scintillating conversation, I don't feel well and I'm going back to the apartment. See you later. Or perhaps I should say, *sayonara!*'

Ingram frowned at her, not particularly liking her tone, and even Mrs Ito looked at her strangely. This was because, unbeknownst to Cassandra, the real meaning of the word sayonara was "goodbye forever". Nevertheless,

Ingram said that he hoped she felt better soon, wafted his goodbye, and turned his attention back to Takako Ito.

The following morning, after Ingram had left for work with barely a word spoken between them, Cassandra went to her local pharmacy and bought a pregnancy test. Her suspicions were confirmed. She was pregnant. When Ingram came home, slightly earlier than usual, she said that she had something to tell him. He replied that he also had some news.

'You go first,' he said.

'No, you go first. I'm sure your news is far more important than mine.'

'Why are you being like this, Cassandra? This is most unlike you. And Takako was a bit puzzled when you said goodbye to me forever!'

'I didn't say goodbye to you forever. I said "sayonara" which means "goodbye" in Japanese.'

'I know what it means, Cassandra, but the real meaning is "goodbye forever" and is only used when a person probably won't be seeing another person ever again. It's rarely used in a general sense such as "goodbye, see you later" – that sort of thing.'

This pedantic side of Ingram really irritated Cassandra, and the fact she wasn't feeling well caused her to snap at him. 'Well, Mr Clever Clogs, I'm not as clever as you and I don't speak Japanese.' She might have added *so there*, but felt that was going slightly too far.

Ingram sighed. 'Let's not argue, Cassandra. We hardly ever have cross words.'

Cassandra might have replied, *Well whose fault is that, as I hardly ever see you?* Instead, she said, 'I'm pregnant. I took a test this morning, and it's positive.'

'Ah, that explains your change of mood and odd behaviour. Your hormones are probably kicking in.'

At that moment, Cassandra wanted to kick him. 'Are you pleased, Ingram?' she asked.

'Of course I am. Delighted that there's going to be a little Smythe-Brown on the way. Come here, let me give you a hug.'

Cassandra went over to him. 'Now, what's your news?'

'I'm being sent to the Tokyo office on secondment, and Daizen Ito is coming here.'

Cassandra wasn't expecting this. 'Oh! When?'

'Next month.'

'Well, this is news indeed. I'm not sure I'd cope in Tokyo, Ingram, and particularly now I'm pregnant. I think I'd rather be back in the UK. To be honest, I've been getting a bit fed up here in Singapore.'

'I was going to talk to you about the future. I had concerns that you wouldn't settle into Tokyo life. It's not like Singapore, and you've done amazingly well here, but Japanese culture with its strict hierarchies and social codes is not for everyone. Now that you're pregnant, it's the ideal time for you to go back to England. I'll get our human resources people to find a nice apartment for you to live in temporarily whilst you set about finding us a family home for when I'm back on visits. How does that sound?' This was said with a look of hope on his face, not knowing how Cassandra would take the news.

'That sounds like a perfect plan. I have one request though.'

'Ask away. I want you to be happy, especially now you're carrying the next generation of Smythe-Brown.'

'I don't want to live in London. I'd like to live somewhere where there's good schools, plenty of shops and things to do, and an easy commute into London for when you come home.'

Which is how Cassandra Smythe-Brown eventually met Abigail Thomas.

PART THREE

CHAPTER EIGHT

In which Abigail makes a potential new friend

TERM HAD STARTED and Annabel and Francesca had settled into their new school very quickly. They had already made friends with some of the other new pupils, it being well known that, for the "new" girls, getting accepted into well established "old girl" friendship groups took time and sometimes never happened. So, the new girls would form their own friendship groups.

Abigail, however, was still trying to get a handle on the groups of (mainly) women who arrived daily at the school gates to drop their girls off. From her observations, Abigail deduced that the working mothers were easily identified by their smart attire, and the speedy depositing of the daughter with a wave, sometimes accompanied with a quick peck on the cheek, and then a quick exit by car or a fast walk away from the school. The presumably non-working mothers, who were dressed casually or wore sportswear, formed small groups and stood around chatting long after the school gates were closed. Some of them then drifted off in splinter groups probably, Abigail thought, to go to a café or shopping, or to an exercise class or gym. And then there were the school buses which served the outlying areas ferrying the girls to and from school, which took away the responsibility of the parent doing a drop-off and pick-up for whatever reason.

Abigail's routine never wavered from the previous school. As they had lived near the school, Abigail would walk Francesca and Annabel to school, give them a hug and kiss on the cheek, wish them a good day, and either walk back home, meet up with some of the other mothers or go to work. Now, the difference was that she drove them to and from the school each day, and then returned home. This was what she was struggling with; she was missing her old friendship group. *All I need*, she thought, *is to make just one or two friends and then I'll feel a bit more settled.*

Abigail's wish was granted when, one morning, having just dropped the girls off, she got back into her car and immediately felt a bump as if something or someone had hit the back of her car. Looking in her rear-view mirror, she saw a flustered red-faced woman exit from the car behind, hurriedly give a young girl a quick kiss and a shove because the gates were closing. Coming round to the driver's side of Abigail's car, the woman motioned with her hand for Abigail to wind her window down.

'Oh my God. I'm soo sorry. I've gone into the back of your car. I was in such a rush because Bunty's almost late for school again, and I wasn't paying attention.' The woman rolled her eyes as she said this. 'All my fault, of course. Just can't seem to get to grips with the school's system. Completely different to Bunty's old school, which in hindsight now seems very laid back. I'm Miriam McTavish, by the way. Bunty's mum.'

Abigail closed the window and exited her car. Putting out her hand for Miriam McTavish to shake, she introduced herself. 'I'm Abigail Thomas. Francesca and Annabel's mum. Pleased to meet you.'

Miriam shook Abigail's hand. 'Oh! Bunty has spoken about Annabel. I think they're friends. Bunty talks about Annabel and Amy. That's Amy Murphy. Noreen's daughter.'

'Oh, right. Well, you're the first parent I've spoken to.'

'Yeah, I know what you mean. It's always difficult being a new mum at a new school. I've only met Noreen very briefly, and now you! By the way, I'm sorry about your car. Shall we inspect the damage?'

The two women walked to the back of Abigail's car. The only damage was a small dent in the number plate, which Abigail waved away with a "nothing to worry about" gesture.

Miriam McTavish had a round face with rosy cheeks, blue eyes and a mop of ginger curls. Although she was still looking anxious, Abigail could sense a person who, underneath, had a jovial and approachable personality, so she decided to take the plunge. With a hopeful look on her face, Abigail asked Miriam if she had time for a coffee because it would be nice to have a chat with someone "other than myself", and she laughed.

Miriam's face lit up, and she gave a broad smile, revealing a dimple in both cheeks. 'Yes! I'd love that. My shift doesn't start until one.'

'Where do you work?' asked Abigail.

'Knighton General Hospital. I'm a nurse in the paediatric unit. Part-time, which suits me at the moment. So, if it's okay with you, can we have coffee in Knighton?'

'Yes, absolutely. That works well for me.'

'Right, well, I can recommend Café Culture on the riverside. Do you know it?'

'No, never heard of it. Sounds good though.'

The two women got into their respective cars, with Abigail following Miriam for the journey from the school to the car park. It was a pleasant September morning, and they sat outside drinking their coffee and watching the ducks floating by on the river. Abigail had taken an immediate liking to Miriam, who came across as a decent down-to-earth, unpretentious person unlike some of her neighbours in the road where she lived.

Over coffee, and a chocolate brownie each, Miriam told Abigail that her husband, Hamish, worked at the same hospital as a senior clinician in ICU. Between them, they made sure that Bunty always had one of them to drop her off at school and collect her. Miriam also went on to explain that Bunty had been very happy and settled in her previous school and hadn't wanted to move. However, she was showing an aptitude for music and was excelling at maths, so they felt that she wasn't being stretched enough at her old school.

'So, against her wishes, we moved her,' she said with a shrug. 'Luckily for us, she was awarded a scholarship as, otherwise, we wouldn't have been able to afford the fees. But I'm not sure we've done the right thing for her and, in the long run, I don't know how she's going to get on. It was obvious when we went to the open evening that the school is all about league tables, and "friendly" competition between the girls.' This was said with an eye roll. 'My concern though is the requirement that every pupil should achieve at least one sporting accomplishment, which is so not Bunty's thing at all. Still, Hamish and myself want the best for her. I just hope the pressure isn't too much. Oh dear, I've gone on a bit, haven't I?'

Abigail, who in her profession as a trained psychotherapist knew when to listen and when to interject, replied, 'Not at all, Miriam. Andrew and I had similar concerns. The girls' last school was lovely, but they weren't being stretched academically and the headteacher felt that an all-girls' school, with consistently good results, would benefit them. What I want is for them to have a good all-round education, but one that isn't too pressurised, or results-driven, and that's my concern. I much prefer the European Baccalaureate education model, but there aren't many schools which teach this system, and certainly none in this area.'

Miriam looked at Abigail with raised eyebrows. 'I think we both may have chosen the wrong school then.' She shrugged. 'I presume, then, that you don't work?'

'What makes you think that?' said Abigail, smiling.

'Well, I was trying to work out whether you were a working or non-working mum and couldn't decide.'

Abigail laughed. 'Ha, so I'm not the only one trying to suss out the other mothers. So, what did you decide?'

'Mmm, well, you don't hang around after school drop-off chatting with some of the others, but that's possibly because, as you've now told me, you don't know anyone. You also don't dash off, either. So, I decided you were either non-working or, perhaps, like me, you worked part-time.'

'That's very perceptive of you. I'm still trying to settle in, you know – new school, new house, new area and new neighbours. I'm getting there gradually and now have time on my hands, so I've started doing voluntary work at the care home at the end of my road, and I'm glad I did because I'm feeling useful again.' Abigail laughed. 'Now, I've gone on a bit, haven't I?'

'Not at all,' responded Miriam amiably. 'This is why we're here. To chat and get to know each other. It'd be a bit odd if we sat here in silence. Anyway, I was thinking that when we have our next coffee morning, I'll invite Noreen. That's Noreen Murphy. Amy's mum. I think I already told you that. You'll like her. She's funny. Typical Irish sense of humour. Always got a mischievous twinkle in her eye, and a clever way with words so that you never know when she's being serious or joking. Very straight-up, though. What you see, is what you get.'

Abigail had been aware of a large woman at the open evening, who had not appeared remotely daunted at meeting either the other parents or teachers. The man by her side, who Abigail assumed was her husband, had stood silently by as his wife had held forth with anyone who came up to speak to them, including the headteacher. Abigail had been impressed at the time. 'So, which category does Noreen fit into?'

'She sort of works. Her husband is a successful builder. Constructs bespoke homes in the affluent area around Knighton.'

Abigail kept quiet, wondering if he had built in her area as there were at least two or three houses that were bespoke, including her home and that of her next-door neighbours; not that her and Andrew had experienced any problems with their house, but still it was a bit close to home.

'Noreen does all the admin. Deals with the architects, the clients, keeps a close eye on the budgets and timescales, planning permissions and so on. She's very astute and very tough.'

'Crikey, she sounds formidable,' said Abigail, pulling a face.

Miriam laughed. 'Talking about formidable women, have you been approached by Cassandra Smythe-Brown yet? She runs the parents' association.'

'I met her briefly at the open evening, which was clearly a networking event for her, but I haven't been approached by her as such.'

Miriam laughed. 'Oh, you will. Just give it time. I've heard she's always looking to recruit new members onto the association. Right, I must get going.'

'Can we do this again?' asked Abigail, almost pleading.

'Of course we can. And I'll get Noreen along. You'll like her. See you at the school gates tomorrow morning. Hamish is picking up Bunty from school today.'

Abigail sat for a moment, finally feeling that she may have made at least one friend, even though it was early days. She also reflected on the open evening and the speech given by the person called Cassandra Smythe-Brown. She had gone on about the importance of parental involvement in the school's activities, and how it was the duty of parents to give back to such a wonderful school who worked tirelessly to provide the best education and environment for the pupils so that they entered the best universities and professions. Andrew, naturally, was very impressed and Abigail found herself being irritated with him because he kept nodding and rocking back and forth on his heels, with his hands behind his back. To be fair, Abigail found nothing ostensibly to disagree with, but it was very different from the girls' last school. At this new school, however, there was certainly a culture and atmosphere of competitiveness, of the expectation of attainment at the highest level, which was borne out by the league tables pinned to the walls, and the shelves full of gleaming trophies. Nevertheless, she had left the café and returned home feeling happier than she had in a while.

Little did Abigail know, but Cassandra *was* looking for new recruits and the recruitment process and selection was based solely on a person's name, and their social standing.

CHAPTER NINE

NAMES WERE VERY important to Cassandra. They spoke volumes about background, parentage and, in her opinion, class. Hadn't she, in fact, upgraded her own name from plain Sandra Smith to Cassandra Smyth, which she was absolutely certain had secured her the interview at the firm of Baker, Charles and Simpson. Then, on her marriage to Ingram, she became Cassandra Smythe-Brown. Looking back, in a moment of honest reflection, she had to admit that it was his name and background she had fallen in love with rather than Ingram himself, although she did like him. Even her two girls' names had been carefully chosen involving some negotiation and compromise.

Convinced that their first born would be a boy, Cassandra – on one of her mid-afternoon phone calls to Ingram who was in Tokyo – trotted out a few suggestions: Florian, Tobias, Thaddeus. All three suggestions were emphatically turned down by him.

Knowing he had to handle his wife with care and tact, he had softened his response with carefully chosen words. 'Cassandra, my sweet, my dearest wife who I miss, it's a tradition in the family that the first born will be called Eustace if it's a boy, or Eustacia if it's a girl.'

'Oh, I see,' she had replied. 'So, I have no say whatsoever in the choice of name for the baby I'm carrying, and who I will probably have many hours of exhausting and painful labour to go through to give birth.'

Ingram could detect a note of grievance and theatricality in her tone but held fast. 'I'm sorry, Cassandra, but my hands are tied. It's been a centuries-old tradition, and you know what Ma and Pa are like with upholding traditions.'

Cassandra, who still hadn't met his parents because they were always travelling, and in fact had shown no inclination to meet her, wanted to respond with *No, I don't know what they're like*, but kept quiet. Instead, she sighed and replied, with some force mingled with resignation, 'Okay, Eustace it is, but I get to choose the next name.'

As it was 10pm in Tokyo due to the time difference of eight hours ahead of the UK, Ingram agreed because he was tired and had to be up at 6am the following morning. 'Okay, my sweet. You can choose the next name. Give "bump" a pat from me. Night-night.'

In the end, a baby girl was born and duly named Eustacia.

On one of Ingram's brief trips back to see Cassandra and Eustacia, who was now a toddler, Cassandra became pregnant with their second child. This time, she decided there would be no compromise or negotiation; Ingram had said she could choose the name, and she would hold him to his promise. To be fair, he had put up a fight and had lost.

Cassandra had plotted to perfection what was the best time to call him. Now back in Singapore, with a time difference of seven hours, she decided that 3pm was perfect as it would be 10pm at his end. No doubt he would have been out drinking with colleagues, or dining with clients, and would therefore be in a happy and sociable mood. More importantly, though, he would be tired and needing to sleep due to having to get up early. Hence, he would be keen to get Cassandra off the phone.

Although Cassandra loved being a mother to Eustacia, and took her to all the toddler groups such as Tumble Tots, Trampoline Tots, and Gym Tots, she decided she needed to do something for herself and to exercise her mind as she found conversations with some of the other mothers mind-numbingly boring. So, she had begun studying an online university course in English Literature and was currently taking the Shakespeare module, where she was working her way through the "tragedies". She had been gripped by this group of plays with their themes of sibling rivalry, greed, revenge, death and murder. Knowing already what the gender of the baby inside her was, she had drawn up a shortlist of girls' names based on the female characters in the plays. So, instead of using her mobile to call Ingram, she picked up the house phone which was rarely used and dialled Ingram's number in Singapore because she suspected that when he saw her name coming up on his mobile phone, it would perhaps explain why he sometimes didn't answer. She banked on him being half-asleep and not recognising the landline number, and so would answer.

Ingram had, in fact, gone to bed at 9pm due to an exhausting day and had fallen into a deep sleep. Takako Ito, with her long black straight shiny hair, and almond-shaped eyes which kept looking demurely up at him from beneath silky black lashes, was on her knees gently massaging his tired feet whilst he sipped green tea from a fine bone china cup decorated with bonsai trees. Suddenly, the noise of the brass Chinese gong, decorated with a dragon, caused Takako to abruptly stop her massage and jump up from the tatami mat on which she was kneeling. The abruptness of her actions caused Ingram to jump in his chair and spill his tea. The gong sounded again until Ingram, still half-asleep, realised that it was his mobile phone. At this time of night, it could only mean one thing – Cassandra was calling and he decided not to answer. However, the number was from a UK landline which he didn't instantly recognise, and so he answered.

It was Cassandra. 'I hope I didn't wake you, Ingram,' she said breezily.

'Cassandra,' Ingram replied sleepily, 'it's 10 o'clock at night. I was asleep.'

'Sorry, Ingram, but due to the time difference you're difficult to get hold of. If you're not at work, then you're out socialising, so for me this is the best time to call you. Anyway, I've had the gender of the baby confirmed and we're having a girl. I want to run some names past you, even though you said I could choose the name this time.'

Ingram had begun to fall asleep again. 'Ingram! Did you hear me?'

Sighing heavily, he propped himself up against the pillow, and put his mobile on loudspeaker and laid it on the bed. 'It's months away yet. Can't this wait?'

'No, it can't. Before you know it, I'll be going into labour without having chosen a name.'

'Okay, I'm all ears, fire away.'

'Well, seeing as I'm studying Shakespeare at university, I thought a female character out of one of his plays would be fun.'

Ingram remained silent, aware that Cassandra was trying to goad him into saying that studying an online course at an online university wasn't the real thing. However, not wishing to get into one of their long-distance bickering matches, he kept his mouth shut.

'Did you hear what I said, Ingram?'

'Yes, I did. You said you were studying Shakespeare at university.'

If Ingram could, at that moment, see Cassandra's facial expression, he would have seen that her eyes were half-closed with mistrust. She wasn't stupid. She knew when Ingram was trying to get one over on her. 'So, I thought Ophelia would be a nice name. It speaks of elegance, softness, and poetry. What do you think?'

If Cassandra could, at that moment, see Ingram's facial expression, she would see him sitting up straighter with a grin on his face. The verbal match was about to begin. 'You do know she's a character in *Hamlet*, which is one of Shakespeare's tragedies?'

Cassandra snorted. 'Of course I do! I'm currently studying the tragedies. They're marvellous. I get quite engrossed with the drama of plotting and revenge, and the gullibility and fallibility of human nature.' Cassandra stuck her tongue out at the phone, and grinned.

'Mmm, very impressive, Cassandra, but back to your suggestion of Ophelia as a name for our daughter. You do know that Ophelia was betrothed to Prince Hamlet, but eventually went mad and drowned, due in part to his actions?' Ingram was on a roll now. 'And there was that rather wonderful painting by the Pre-Raphaelite artist, Dante Gabriel Rossetti, who painted his version of the dead Ophelia surrounded by reeds and flowers. All very tragic, indeed'

Cassandra, who had never had any interest in art or the history of art, didn't know what Ingram was going on about, but decided that her next course would be an introduction to the history of art, and made a note mentally to look up the Rossetti painting.

'Cassandra, are you there?', he said with a grin, because he knew that she wouldn't know anything about the painting he was referring to and would be wanting to look it up. Also, she would now be thinking up another name to throw at him.

'Yes, I'm here. Okay, what about Goneril? Such a strong name. A woman who was not to be messed about; a leader, in fact.'

Ingram let out a deep sigh. 'Cassandra, Cassandra, Cassandra. Goneril was a principal villain in *King Lear*! She plotted to overthrow her father so that she could rule the kingdom of Britain. Hardly a good female role model, I would say. What on earth is your university lecturer…' and Ingram chuckled, 'teaching you?' Before Cassandra could respond indignantly, Ingram ploughed on, 'Also, the name sounds very much like a venereal disease.'

'*Ingram!* Don't be so disgusting. What on earth has come over you? Urgh, I've gone right off that name now.'

Thank God for that, he thought.

'Anyway, you said I could choose the next name and so I think Desdemona, from possibly Shakespeare's greatest tragedy, *Othello*, will be lovely. Desdemona Smythe-Brown will be the perfect name.' And she hung up before Ingram could point out that Desdemona was, in fact, murdered by Othello from whom she had been estranged at the time.

Yes, names were very important to Cassandra. They could open doors or, equally, have doors closed upon them. Eustacia and Desdemona Smythe-Brown would never experience closed doors, which is why the name of Abigail Thomas was causing her some concern. In her opinion, such a name was fairly ordinary, being neither of the kind that appears in magazines such as *Tatler* or *Country Life*, but neither was it like some of the American names that had found their way into – as Cassandra thought of them – the lower echelons of British society.

As head of the parents' association, Cassandra – who thought of herself as a general marshalling her troops to action – had her trusty lieutenants, and her foot soldiers.

Currently, there were only two lieutenants: Britt Mikkelson, whose twin daughters – Birgitta and Brigitta – were in Desdemona's year, as was Annabel Thomas, and Caroline Fortescue, whose daughter, Sapphire, was also in the same year. Usually, there were three lieutenants, so Cassandra needed a new recruit because they now had the extra responsibility of the end of term summer ball to organise, which followed on after the summer fayre, as well as the christmas fayre.

Being one of Cassandra's lieutenants entailed meeting once a month at their respective houses and deciding what tasks would be dished out to the "foot soldiers", which currently comprised Kelly Lewis whose daughter, Shaznay, was in the same year as Desdemona and Annabel, and Kylie Monaghan whose daughter, Kayleigh, was in Eustacia's class. In actuality, the title of foot soldier was a euphemism for being a dogsbody and doing all the donkey work of lifting, carrying, sorting, setting up the stalls, and clearing away. In comparison to Caroline and Britt, who were in charge of contacting the parents and asking for donations, producing flyers for the stalls, and organising the dates of collection of donated items, all of which could be done sitting down in the comfort of their homes, the responsibilities of the foot soldiers were a lot more onerous, time-consuming and tiring. Hence, she was now looking to recruit at least two more helpers – one to assist Caroline and Britt who were part of Cassandra's "elite" circle – and one to help Kelly Lewis and Kylie Monaghan. The "new" parents' open evening had provided the perfect place for finding new recruits.

After giving her speech, Cassandra had "worked" the room. From her time spent in Singapore, and being the wife of Ingram, who held an important position, Cassandra – out of necessity, and because it was expected of her – learnt very quickly how to "network" successfully, which was a skill in itself, and how to read people. Hence, she knew how to discern between those she met who would be of use and worth cultivating, and those who weren't worth the energy. Thus, when called upon, she could flatter and cajole. She had also acquired the confidence to move effortlessly between different social circles and groups of people. In fact, at one point, Cassandra reflected that she would have made an excellent politician's wife, as long as the politician was the prime minister of course. So, she introduced herself in a friendly and sociable way, all the while sizing up the new parents, particularly the mothers who would subsequently be placed into two categories: those who would be flattered to have been approached by Cassandra with the possibility of joining the parent's association and hence compliant, and those *she* wanted to get to know better as possible recruits into her "elite" circle, and might need some cajoling and flattering.

At home later, over a large glass of Merlot, Cassandra drew up her list of possible new recruits. She had earmarked Miriam McTavish as a possible foot soldier. Married to Hamish, a large man with a bushy beard and who had stood silently by whilst Cassandra had made friendly overtures towards his wife, she had found out that they were both nurses at the local hospital and were very proud of their daughter, Bunty, who had won a scholarship to the school. In Miriam, Cassandra saw someone from a modest background, who worked hard in a caring profession, and was neither pushy nor overbearing. Hence, Cassandra thought she would be happy to take orders and do her bidding. Furthermore, Bunty was a scholarship girl which meant that her parents probably weren't very wealthy. Also, she took after her mother as she was also slightly plump with rosy cheeks and a mop of curly ginger hair. Cassandra reasoned this might make her a target for the group of 'mean' girls that existed in the school. Thus, she would make sure that Desdemona was kind to her and befriended her when need be, which would undoubtedly get back to Miriam.

Another new mother, and who was in complete contrast to Miriam, was Noreen Murphy. She was a large Irish woman who was there with her daughter, Amy, who had confidently gone over to a group of girls and was introducing herself. Although Cassandra had thought Noreen was a possible recruit, on talking to her she had found her to be too outspoken and having a slightly domineering personality. Thus, Cassandra felt that Noreen would not be easy to push around and hadn't warmed to her; in fact, a thought crossed Cassandra's mind that Noreen Murphy could be a potential threat at some point for control of the parents' association.

Mavis Brown, a small woman with a shy personality, had stood in the corner holding her daughter Katy's hand, and had seemed grateful when Cassandra approached her. Mavis, then, would also make a perfect foot soldier. And then there was Abigail Thomas, mother to Annabel and Francesca. Cassandra couldn't decide whether Abigail was simply shy or reserved. She had maintained a watchful and cool distance when Cassandra had come over, and she appeared to be sizing up Cassandra as much as Cassandra was her. Her husband, Andrew, clearly took himself seriously and had little humour. He came across as confident and struck the typical masculine pose of a successful man, as he stood straight with his legs apart and his hands behind his back. It wasn't that Abigail was lacking in confidence; in fact, she seemed very comfortable in her own skin and did not appear at all daunted by being a new parent.

Cassandra just couldn't get a firm impression of her; couldn't read her. Thus, Abigail Thomas presented Cassandra with a dilemma as she was obviously not the type to take orders from anyone, but neither did she have the *presence* of Caroline Fortescue nor the authoritative personality of Britt Mikkelson.

Cassandra was able to make a decision a few days later.

*

It was Monday afternoon and the end of the school day. Cassandra was standing in the kitchen counting down from 5, 4, 3, 2, 1: front door opens, front door shuts with a slam, sound of school bag being thrown on hallway tiles, footsteps running across the floor, kitchen door flung open, and an out-of-breath, red-faced, Desdemona appeared in the kitchen. 'Mama, guess what? Annabel, the new girl—'

'Desdemona, how many times have I told you – no, asked you – to behave in a more ladylike manner and with some decorum?'

'Sorry, Mama, but—'

'Out you go. Let's try again, shall we?'

Desdemona sighed, hung her head and plodded out of the kitchen, closing the door quietly behind her. Cassandra waited for Desdemona's reappearance. However, this time, she was so quiet that her reappearance in the kitchen took Cassandra completely by surprise. 'Desdemona! Why are you creeping about? You startled me.' Desdemona knew when she was beaten and stood completely silent. 'Well done. That was a much-improved entrance. Now, what did you want to tell me?'

'Annabel, one of the new girls, is really nice. All the new girls had to stand up and introduce themselves and say something about their family. She said that she has an older sister called Francesca, also at the school, her father is called Andrew and runs his own company in London, and her mother used to work but is currently taking time off. Also, guess what? They've got a swimming pool. How cool is that?'

In Cassandra's mind, Abigail Thomas had gone up a notch. 'Thank you, Desdemona. That's very useful information. Now, run along upstairs and change out of your school clothes. Eustacia will be home shortly.'

Cassandra went and poured herself a glass of Chilean Merlot and waited. Very shortly, she heard the front door open and then quietly closed, followed by soft footsteps crossing the hallway, and the kitchen door opening to signal Eustacia's return from school.

'Mother! You're drinking wine at this time!'

'I've had a very trying day, Eustacia. Don't lecture me.'

Eustacia pulled a face. 'Not as trying as mine. Sometimes the teachers drive me mad with their pettiness, especially Mrs Collins. She's an old goat.'

'Eustacia! That's a very disrespectful way to talk about the headteacher. Anyway, what news from the school? Desdemona has been telling me about one of the girls in her class called Annabel.'

'Oh, ya. Her older sister, Francesca, is in my class. She's cool and super bright. Her father has his own IT consultancy in London, and her mother is a psychotherapist, but has taken a break for the time being.'

'Mmm, very interesting. Now, go upstairs and get changed, and I'll make a snack for you and Desdemona.'

Cassandra's mind was made up. Abigail Thomas would be approached with a view to becoming part of her trusted lieutenants, and Miriam McTavish would hopefully agree to joining the other group, with Mavis Brown as a possible back-up. Her girls would provide the perfect excuse for putting her plan into action.

Over dinner that evening, Cassandra suggested that Desdemona invite Annabel back for tea after school on Friday, and Eustacia was to invite Francesca, and to tell their mother that she would drop them back home later. That way, Cassandra could find out where Abigail lived and get to speak to her about joining the parents' association.

However, things did not go according to plan.

It was Tuesday afternoon, and Cassandra stood waiting for Desdemona's usual noisy entrance. But there was no Desdemona, which was unusual. Cassandra waited and waited. Still no Desdemona. Eustacia came into the kitchen, having made her usual quiet entrance.

'Mother, why is Desdemona standing outside looking glum? Have you two had an argument?'

'Oh! I wondered where she was. Go and get her for me, please.'

Desdemona came into the kitchen wearing a very long face.

'What's wrong?', asked Cassandra.

'Annabel can't come on Friday. She's been invited back to Bunty McTavish's house, along with Amy Murphy.'

'Mmm, I see. Eustacia, what about Francesca Thomas. Can she come back on Friday?'

'Yep, she said she'd love to come. Seemed pleased to be asked.'

Desdemona looked close to tears.

'Don't get upset, Desdemona. I'll sort this out. Now off you both go.'

Cassandra called up the new parents' contact details on her iPad and found the mobile number for Miriam McTavish, which she then rang. After a few rings, the mobile was answered. 'Miriam! Cassandra Smythe-Brown here. How are you?'

'...'

'That's good to hear. I've been meaning to call you for a catch-up since we met at the open evening. But you know what it's like, us mums are always busy!' She laughed. 'Now, the reason I'm calling is to invite Bunty back for tea on Friday after school. Desdemona has been nagging me for ages to invite her back.'

'...'

'Oh, I see. You've got Annabel Thomas and Amy Murphy coming to yours.'

'...'

Cassandra let out a deep sigh. 'Oh dear, Desdemona will be very disappointed seeing as she and Bunty are becoming such good friends.'

'...'

'Yes, I do see that it would be difficult for you because it would mean cancelling Annabel and Amy. Tell you what, I've got the perfect solution. They can come back here too! Desdemona has mentioned Annabel a few times, and her sister is coming back with Eustacia. So, problem sorted!' She laughed cheerily.

'...'

'Don't worry about that. I'll sort it out and drop them all back. Now, while I've got you on the phone, can I put your name down as one of my helpers for the Christmas fayre?'

'...'

'Brilliant! Thank you, Miriam. You're going to be a big asset to my team. Must dash. Homework to supervise, dinner to cook.'

Cassandra disconnected from Miriam and then called Noreen Murphy.

'Noreen! Cassandra Smythe-Brown here. How are you?'

'...'

'Yes, I'm good too. Very busy, what with the girls and, of course, having the responsibility of running the parents' association.'

'. . .'

'No, that's not why I'm calling but thank you for the offer. Much appreciated. It's to do with Friday. I've just spoken to Miriam McTavish and there's been a change of plan. As head of the parents' association, and as Desdemona and Eustacia are "old girls" at the school, we as a family have a responsibility to make the new girls feel welcome and settled in. So, I thought it would be a great idea to have Amy, Bunty, Annabel and Francesca Thomas back to ours on Friday after school for tea. Francesca will come back with Eustacia, and Desdemona will bring back your daughter and the other two. I do hope you're okay with that.'

'. . .'

'No, it won't be too much trouble at all. I love having the girls' friends back, and I'm sure they will amuse themselves. It will be nice for Eustacia and Desdemona to have some different friends.'

'. . .'

'No need. I'll drop Amy back off. I've offered to do the same with the Thomas girls and Bunty.' Cassandra disconnected from the call and clapped her hands with glee. *Not mission impossible, mission accomplished,* she thought to herself.

Cassandra was in a very good mood during dinner and didn't nag or criticise the girls and kept calling them "my darling children" and saying how lucky she was to have them, all of which made Eustacia and Desdemona look at each other with suspicious side-long glances. 'I can see you two looking at each other,' she said, laughing good-naturedly. 'Right, Friday is all sorted. I told you I would. Desdemona, you're bringing back

Annabel, Bunty and Amy. I've arranged it with their mothers.' She then realised she had forgotten to call Abigail Thomas. 'Blast! Right, eat up. I've got a call to make.' She picked up her mobile from the table and went into the living room.

Ringing Abigail's number, she got the engaged tone, so she rang the house number which went unanswered. Getting impatient, she rang the mobile number again and this time the call was picked up.

'Abigail, Cassandra here.'

'...'

'I'm good, thanks. Look, there's been a change of plan concerning Friday. I've just spoken to Miriam McTavish and Noreen Murphy, and it's been decided that all the girls can come back here. Desdemona will bring back Annabel, Amy and Bunty, and Eustacia will bring back Francesca.'

'...'

'No, no bother at all. They can all come back to mine and I'll drop them off afterwards. I wanted to have a word with you anyway. Must dash. Things to do!' And she hung up before any more questions arose.

In their respective houses, each woman was left reflecting on the recent phone call they had received from Cassandra. Miriam McTavish was aware that she had been subtly manipulated and flattered into agreeing to a change in Friday's arrangements, whereas Noreen Murphy knew that she had allowed herself to be coerced into agreeing to something achieved by underhand methods. She also instinctively realised that neither herself nor her daughter – her husband not being remotely interested in school matters – were going to fit in easily at the new school if this evening's devious shenanigans were anything to go by. Abigail was also aware that a form of "one-upmanship", or should that be "one-upwomanship", was taking place where the subtle, and not so subtle, hierarchies that exist in schools between the parents and children alike, was making an early appearance. With this realisation, she was left feeling again that the move was perhaps a mistake. The girls, however, were very excited when she told them of the change in plan for Friday and, at the end of the day, she concluded that was what mattered.

In the Smythe-Brown household, Cassandra was in high spirits partly due to having refilled her wine glass to the brim, but also because she was feeling pleased with her recent manoeuvres. She decided to call Ingram, even though it was 2am in Singapore.

Ingram was lying flat on his stomach, whilst the very lithe and supple female Thai masseuse called Boonsri (which meant "beautiful" in Thai) had climbed onto his back and was giving him a traditional Thai massage. She was currently kneading his shoulders and neck, and he was trying not to groan with pleasure. In fact, he was a bit concerned that she would soon be asking him to turn over as he was aware that his enjoyment would be all too obvious, and a persistent warning bell began ringing in his ears. Coming out of the dream, which had started pleasurably and was now one of anxiety, he realised it was his mobile phone. Groggily reaching for it on the bedside table, he knocked over a glass of water.

'Hello!' he shouted grumpily. 'Who's this?'

'Ingram, it's me. Cassandra. There's no need to shout.'

'Do you know what the time is?'

'Of course I do. It's 7pm.'

Ingram counted to ten and then breathed deeply. 'I mean here, Cassandra. Do you know what time it is here? No, don't answer. Let me tell you. It's 2am and I have to be up at six. What is it you want?'

'There's no need to be so unfriendly. It's not my fault you're so far away. Anyway, I wanted to tell you my good news. I've recruited two new members to my team and let me tell you it wasn't easy. Also, I'm very pleased with the way Eustacia and Desdemona are conducting themselves. They're a credit to this family.'

'Well, that's all very interesting. Now, is there anything else before I try and get back to sleep?'

'Yes, there is one more thing. Can we have a swimming pool?'

Ingram hung up.

Cassandra took a big gulp of wine and smiled.

CHAPTER TEN

In which Abigail meets a strange man

IF CASSANDRA'S WEEK was panning out nicely, then the same couldn't be said for Abigail. Her week had started off well enough, but since the phone call on Tuesday evening everything had begun to go downhill. On returning from her voluntary stint at the care home, the first thing she noticed was that the gates were open and she was certain that she had closed them. The second thing she noticed was that the side gate to the garden was open. Feeling wary, she closed the side gate and went into the house and through to the kitchen. Looking through the bi-folding doors, she saw a tall lanky man walking around the garden. Opening the doors, she called out, 'Excuse me. Who are you?'

'Ah,' the man replied, and walked over to Abigail. 'You must be the lady of the house. Unwin Trimble, at your service, ma'am.' He clicked his heels together and saluted.

Abigail, confronted by this man with thinning grey-blond hair, rosy cheeks and a nose to match, wearing a faded check shirt that had obviously been washed many times, beige trousers and Jesus sandals, was already irritated by his manner.

'Well, Mr Trimble…'

'Do call me Unwin.'

'Okay, well, Unwin, firstly how did you get in because I remember closing the gates behind me when I left this morning and, secondly, what are you doing here?'

'Did your husband not tell you?'

'Tell me what?'

'That I'm your gardener.' He smiled.

'No, he didn't mention you at all. How did you get in, though?'

'Your husband gave me the code.'

Abigail would have words with Andrew about this when he came home. In the meantime, she asked how he had met Andrew.

'I drink in The Royal Oak, and we just got chatting early one evening, as you do, and I was telling him how bored I am since retiring. He replied that he couldn't wait until he retired because he was too busy and had no time to do the garden.'

Abigail thought to herself, *well, he obviously has enough time to go to the pub for a drink before coming home*, but kept quiet. 'Oh, I see. Well, it's true. My husband is always working, and I don't have green fingers.' She shrugged her shoulders and gave a small smile.

Unwin grinned, revealing uneven teeth stained brown. 'Well, that's where I can be of help. I said to your husband that I have more than enough time on my hands. How about I come and do your garden? I can mow the lawn, trim the edges, water and deadhead the flowers. And he agreed, so that's why I'm here to have a look round.'

Abigail couldn't ostensibly see any objections to this very reasonable solution, and they did need help with the garden as it was definitely showing signs of neglect. So, she replied, 'Okay, that explains things then. What day are you thinking of coming, just so I know to leave the gate open?'

'You don't need to worry about that, Mrs Thomas. I can let myself in.'

VICTORIA WEBSTER

'Please don't take this the wrong way, Unwin, but for the time being it's best I let you in if I'm here, which I am most mornings. On a Wednesday and Friday morning, I do a two-hour voluntary session at the care home up the road, and I can leave the gates open for you. I will be back by 12 o'clock, by which time you will have probably finished and I can then close the gates. So, when do you think you'll be coming?'

Unwin Trimble shuffled his feet. 'Wednesday or Thursday morning would be best for me. How does that sound?'

'That's fine by me. Now, what about payment? Presumably Andrew said he would deal with that?'

'No, he said that you would pay me. That if you're not here, I should leave a note of my hours in the post box and then you would pay me the next time. Or, if you are here, you would settle up on the day. I prefer cash by the way,' he said with a hopeful smile and waggled his eyebrows up and down.

Abigail nodded her head, feeling irked by the way Andrew had organised this but had left her with all the practicalities to deal with. *Bloody typical,* she thought. 'What about equipment? Will you bring your own, or are you using ours because, if you're using ours, I will need to leave the items out for you.'

'Your husband said I could use your lawnmower and strimmer.'

Abigail sighed. 'Okay, I'll make sure everything you need is left at the back of the house. Now, I must be getting on. Can you let yourself out please?'

Unwin Trimble clicked his heels, saluted, and walked briskly away.

Abigail waited until she had heard the side gate close, and his receding footsteps on the gravel driveway. Going into the hallway, she closed the gates using the intercom

115

button. She had the beginnings of a stress headache but needed to call Miriam McTavish as her intuition was telling her all was potentially not well regarding the change in plan for Friday, so she decided it would be a good idea to meet up for coffee before then, which only left Thursday.

Miriam had answered immediately and agreed to meet up the next morning, at Café Culture. She had also said, 'We'll meet you there.' When Abigail had queried who the other person or persons joining them were, Miriam had answered that Noreen would be coming.

It was Thursday. As usual, Abigail dropped the girls off at school, and then drove into Knighton. She parked in the same car park as last time and made her way to the café. It was cooler than the last time and so she went inside. She spotted Miriam talking to a large woman who she recognised from the parents' evening and realised that this must be Noreen Murphy.

'Hello! Am I late?' she asked.

'Not at all,' replied Miriam. 'We've only just arrived, haven't we, Noreen?'

The woman nodded and then smiled warmly at Abigail. 'I'm Noreen Murphy. Amy's mum. Pleased to meet you.' Noreen had a broad Irish accent, and an open friendly face, making Abigail immediately warm to her.

The waitress came and took their orders for coffee. When she had left, Noreen asked Abigail how Annabel was getting on at school, as she was in the same class as Bunty and Amy. Abigail could truthfully reply that both her daughters were enjoying their new school and appeared to be making friends.

Noreen looked at Miriam, who nodded. 'That's what we want to talk to you about,' said Noreen.

Uh-oh, here it comes, thought Abigail, her intuition being correct once again.

'When was Annabel invited to Desdemona's house on Friday?' asked Miriam.

Abigail had a sense of where this was leading. 'Tuesday. She was invited by Desdemona on Tuesday morning but said that she couldn't go because she was going back to Bunty's on Friday. Is there a problem?'

'Mmm,' said Noreen. 'Not so much a problem, but the thing is, on Tuesday evening both myself and Miriam were called by Cassandra Smythe-Brown who gave us little option but to cancel Friday's arrangement with Miriam and for the girls to go instead to her house on Friday. Presumably she called you as well on Tuesday evening?'

Abigail nodded. 'Yes, she did. She said there had been a change of plan and all three girls were coming back with Desdemona. I'm sensing something amiss here, but not sure quite what.'

The waitress appeared and put their coffees on the table, then left.

Miriam picked up her coffee cup and took a sip.

'The thing is, Abigail, neither Amy nor Bunty were invited by Desdemona on Tuesday morning to go back to hers on Friday.'

'That's true,' added Miriam, who put her cup down. 'Bunty told me that on Tuesday, at break time, Desdemona had come up to Annabel and invited her back on Friday. Bunty was with Annabel and Amy at the time, and only Annabel was invited back. Annabel told Desdemona that she had been invited back by Bunty on Friday and couldn't come to hers. So, you see what it looks like, don't you?'

Abigail chewed her lip. 'Yes, I think so. What you're saying, if I've understood correctly, is that only Annabel was invited back but not your two. Desdemona must have told her mum on Tuesday after school that Annabel was coming back to yours, which resulted in the Tuesday evening call by Cassandra. Coincidentally, Francesca has been invited back on Friday by Eustacia. So, the point of Cassandra's call was to reorganise things to suit whatever agenda she had, which meant that Amy and Bunty were also included in the invite, even though they hadn't been initially. Have I got that right?' Her headache had come back, and she took a big gulp of her coffee in the hope that the caffeine might ease it a bit. Miriam and Noreen replied to the effect that she had understood correctly. Abigail sighed. 'Okay, what do you want me to do about this?'

'We don't want you to do anything,' replied Noreen. 'It's not your fault. Just be aware, though, of some "game-playing" going on.'

'By the way, has Cassandra asked you to be on her "team", as she puts it?' asked Miriam.

Abigail replied that Cassandra hadn't mentioned anything about that, and she had the feeling she was going to be asked on Friday. She then enquired of the two women if they had been asked.

Miriam replied that she had. Noreen laughed. 'Nope. I offered but was told politely that she had sufficient help. I think I've had a lucky escape.'

All three women finished their coffees, each deep in thought. Abigail was thinking that she was about to be caught up in something not of her making, and that her fledgling friendship with Miriam and possibly Noreen was on the verge of being scuppered.

She wasn't wrong.

CHAPTER ELEVEN

In which Abigail feels out of sorts

IT WAS FRIDAY evening and, as promised, Cassandra dropped the girls off at their houses. Amy was deposited at the end of her driveway, at the top end of which Cassandra could see a large sprawling house which looked in need of renovation. She had learnt from Amy that her father was a builder and property developer, but never seemed to have the time to work on their own house. This was said with a smile, but Cassandra could detect a note of sadness beneath it and felt slightly sorry for her. She also spotted what looked like an old black Rolls Royce, and a number of other vehicles including a digger and cement mixer. She gave an involuntary shudder and drove off.

Next was Bunty's home. She pulled up alongside the kerb of a small, detached house, with a driveway big enough for one car. Net curtains were hung in the windows, and two small hanging baskets of flowers, which hung from hooks either side of the beige-painted front door, brightened up the drab outside. *All very ordinary, as I suspected*, she thought. Cassandra waved Bunty goodbye and then drove to the Thomas house. The gates were open and Cassandra drove in, feeling satisfied and reassured at the crunching sound of gravel on the driveway. *This is more like it*, she said to herself, when she saw the large house, the double garage, and two terracotta pots filled with red and white geraniums placed either side of a glossy red front door. Francesca and Annabel exited the car and rang the doorbell. Cassandra also got out of the car.

Abigail opened the door. 'Thank you so much, Cassandra, for dropping the girls off. Would you like to come in?'

'No can do, Abigail. Sorry. Must be off, as I've left my two at home alone. However, can I count you in as part of my team? You'd be an invaluable asset.'

Abigail knew when she was being flattered, but agreed to helping out because she felt that she couldn't say no.

Cassandra clapped her hands. 'Brilliant! Thank you so much. The first meeting, which is to begin organising the Christmas fayre, will be at Caroline Fortescue's house next Wednesday. We start at 10 and are usually finished by 12. I'll text you her address later. Now, I must dash. See you then!'

Francesca and Annabel had already gone inside, and Abigail closed the door behind her. Once Cassandra had driven out, she closed the gates and the three of them went into the living room. 'Did you have a nice time?' she asked.

Both girls nodded and said that Desdemona and Eustacia were very nice.

'Mummy?' asked Annabel.

'Yes, Annabel?'

'Are you going to Sapphire's house on Wednesday?'

'Who's Sapphire?'

'Sapphire Fortescue. Caroline Fortescue is her mum.'

'Oh! I didn't know that. What's this Sapphire like, then? That's an unusual name.'

Annabel thought for a moment. 'She's very pretty and she knows it. She tells everyone she's going to be a model when she leaves school. Evidently, her mum was a model. She doesn't mix with many of us, except Desdemona but they're not best friends though. She tends to hang out more with Willow Barrington and her group who are in the parallel class.'

'Mmm, very interesting. I've joined the parents' association which Cassandra is head of, and I'm going to help organise the school's Christmas fayre. That's why I'm going to Sapphire's house on Wednesday.'

Annabel shrugged, having already lost interest. Francesca too, it seemed, as she yawned.

'Right, you two. Bath, bit of TV, bed.'

On Saturday, after breakfast, and when the girls had left the kitchen, Abigail took Andrew to task for his employing Unwin Trimble as their gardener without discussing it with her first. He had responded with, 'Well, I don't have time, Abigail, and you don't have much interest in the garden. So, what's the problem?'

Because Abigail couldn't think of a reasonable objection, she realised that Andrew was correct but nonetheless she was still niggled by it.

The weekend passed by uneventfully. On Saturday, Andrew had risen early and gone to play golf with Rufus, and the girls had gone to their tennis lesson at the nearby club, which left Abigail home alone. In her previous life at the old house, and because it had been within walking distance of the town centre, she would often pop into town and browse the shops with the girls. Or, if Andrew said he would look after the girls, she would go in by herself and enjoy a few moments of "me" time. Sometimes, they would all go in together and have lunch out. Here, in her current house, a trip into either Cornham or Knighton had to be done by car due to an infrequent bus service. As Abigail drove every day during the week, the last thing she wanted to do was drive at the weekend.

Also, because the house was much larger than their previous one, the housework was taking longer to do, and Abigail was feeling fed up. The monotony of wiping down one more surface was broken by the sound of her mobile phone pinging, alerting her to the arrival of a text. She opened it up and it was from Cassandra, with Caroline Fortescue's address:

Knighton House, Higher Knighton Road, Knighton. U can't miss it. Big black wrought iron gates with gold pineapples. 2 pillars with lion heads. C u Wed x

Andrew had come back in a jolly mood, no doubt helped by the drinks he had had with Rufus in the clubhouse, and the girls came back famished and asked what was for lunch. As Abigail hadn't even made a start on the ironing, her abrupt reply was, 'Cheese and crackers, and you can do it yourself.' This caused the girls and Andrew to look at each other and shrug. Sensing that all was not right with Abigail, Andrew suggested she leave the ironing for another day, and that they all should go for a walk in the woods as it would be nice for all four of them to spend time together.

On Sunday morning, Andrew suggested going to the local pub for the carvery so that Abigail didn't need to cook. Andrew's thoughtfulness had the effect of lifting Abigail's mood, and she happily tackled the pile of ironing until it was time to leave for the pub. Then, it was back home for a bit of TV and bed. Abigail sighed as she got into bed, and wondered what kind of week she would have, as her weekend had been a bit up and down. She also realised that Andrew had taken up golf, rather than cricket, and so his earlier comment that she could help with the cricket teas and get to know the other wives had obviously been forgotten. As a result, Abigail fell asleep with mixed feelings. One thing was clear, Andrew's and the girls' lives were moving forwards; her life, she reflected, had stagnated.

CHAPTER TWELVE

In which Abigail feels out of place

IT WAS WEDNESDAY morning and Abigail had just dropped the girls off at school. She had swapped her morning shift at the care home for the afternoon, so that she could attend the parents' association meeting. She was about to get back into her car when she saw Miriam McTavish pulling up at the kerb. The passenger door opened, Bunty got out, gave her mum a wave and headed into school. Going up to the driver's side, Abigail tapped on the window and smiled at Miriam, who subsequently put her window down.

'Hi, Miriam. Glad I caught you. We've a bit of time before the meeting. Do you fancy a quick coffee?'

Miriam looked blankly at Abigail. 'What meeting?'

'The one at Caroline Fortescue's house at 10 o'clock this morning. It's the first meeting to discuss preparations for the Christmas fayre.'

Miriam shook her head. 'I know nothing about such a meeting. In any case, I'm on mornings this week at the hospital and so I wouldn't have been able to come anyway. Let me know what gets discussed. Must dash, or I'll be late for work.' Miriam blew Abigail a kiss, put up her window and sped off.

A puzzled Abigail got into her car and, because she had time to spare, decided to see where Caroline Fortescue's house was, so that she knew where to go when it was time for the meeting. Driving up the main Knighton Road, she turned left into Higher Knighton

Road, which was tree-lined on both sides with road bumps to maintain the 30-mph speed limit. All the houses were large and built on substantial plots, and Abigail drove slowly down the road looking both ways as she searched for the address. About halfway down, she spotted the black wrought-iron gates which, as per Cassandra's description, were decorated with pineapples painted gold, and spearheads across the top of the gate also painted gold. The imposing gates were flanked by two stone pillars, with a carved lion's head sat atop each pillar. Subtly carved into the stonework of the left-hand pillar, were the words *Fortescue House*. In Abigail's opinion, gates and an entrance such as this spoke of wealth, luxury and, she thought, a certain showing off, until it dawned on her that the very road she lived in, which was also tree-lined and consisted of large to middling size houses, was a smaller version of Higher Knighton Road, so who was she to pass judgement. However, she also reflected that Green Park Road was nowhere near as "showy" where the conspicuous display of wealth, such as the entrance she was parked outside of, made Abigail feel irrationally intimidated.

Glimpsing through the imposing wrought iron gates, Abigail could see – at the end of a very long driveway – an equally imposing large house constructed in the style of a Palladian mansion. She then noticed a very discreetly placed black security camera tucked away on the right-hand side of the gate, with a blinking red dot. Abigail realised she was being surveilled, and so she drove off down the road, turned back into Knighton Road, and parked outside a bakery. Exiting the car, she went into the shop and bought a coffee and Danish pastry which she ate in the car, and then made her way back to Caroline Fortescue's house.

Driving back into Higher Knighton Road and approaching the house, she noticed that the gates were now open. She drove along the driveway, which had lawns on either side, bordered with shrubs and colourful hydrangeas. Abigail almost expected to see male peacocks parading regally on the grass, showing off their beautiful jewel-like feathered fantail, as it would have been fitting for such a setting. At the end of the driveway, she noticed that there were two garages on the left-hand side of the house, and two on the right. She stopped driving for a moment as she had a decision to make. On the left-hand side, was parked a black Bentley, a green Aston Martin DB8, and a black Range Rover with tinted windows. All the cars had personalised number plates. On the opposite side, and sitting forlornly alone, was a small blue Fiat. Abigail, who drove an Audi A3, instinctively felt that the small car needed some company and so drove to the right and parked up. As she got out of her car, two other vehicles came down the driveway and, without any hesitation, parked on the left hand side. Cassandra exited from a white BMW, and a woman who Abigail didn't recognise got out of a dark green Land Rover Defender. She was tall and slim, her short blond hair cut in a style that needed little maintenance, and she was wearing riding clothes. This, thought Abigail, must be Britt Mikkelson, mother to Birgitta and Brigitta.

'Abigail!' Cassandra shouted. 'Come and park over here.'

Walking over to meet the two women, she replied that she couldn't be bothered to move the car.

'Come and meet Britt. Britt, this is Abigail Thomas. Annabel's and Francesca's mother. Abigail, this is Britt Mikkelson. Birgitta and Brigitta's mother. Right, that's the intros over with. Shall we announce our arrival?' She smiled brightly and knocked on the door using the big brass knocker shaped like a lion's head.

The door was opened by a woman of mid-height, wearing a maid's uniform. Although there were some grey strands in her naturally fair hair, her age was difficult to determine. Her features, however, were distinctly Eastern European and she reminded Abigail of an older version of Svetlana. They were ushered into a spacious hallway with cream marble flooring and a sweeping staircase on the right-hand side. Apart from a chaise longue which was covered in maroon velvet material in one corner, and a small ornate table with a cut-glass vase containing red roses on the table-top in another corner, these were the only two pieces of furniture in the large space. What caught Abigail's attention, however, was the oil painting on the back wall showing a standing man and woman, and two girls standing in front of the couple. Cassadra noticed Abigail looking.

'That's the Fortescue family. Darius, Caroline, Sapphire and Apollonia. Impressive, aren't they?'

Abigail was thinking that they looked formidable, but before she could reply Cassandra took her by the arm and they followed Britt into the kitchen. Confronted by the sheer size and opulence of the kitchen, with its cream gloss units, black marble work surfaces, and gleaming copper pots and pans hanging from hooks in the ceiling, in that precise moment, Abigail was transported back to her roots as a "country mouse" who belonged in a small gap in the skirting board. Her feelings of being overawed weren't helped by the series of framed front covers that graced two of the walls. They looked very much like the front covers from high-end, glossy magazines. Britt and Cassandra, who were obviously familiar with the house and surroundings and felt comfortable, were busy talking. Consequently,

Abigail took the opportunity to take a closer look at the framed pictures, as their host hadn't yet made an appearance. Two photographs showed a young woman with blond hair styled in a sharp bob, high cheekbones, blue eyes, an aquiline nose which gave her face an aristocratic look, and full lips which hinted at a sensuality lying just beneath the surface. Abigail was reminded of a young Grace Kelly, with a hint of Brigit Bardot. Both front covers were from *Vogue*, with the byline "Caro wears Chanel" on one front cover and "Caro is Coco!" on the other cover. This, thought Abigail, must be Caroline when she was a young model.

On the opposite wall was a framed front cover from *GQ* magazine. The image featured an attractive middle-aged man with a mane of wavy black hair which was swept back off his forehead, revealing a few grey hairs at the temple and at the sides. He was wearing a white shirt unbuttoned at the neck, revealing black chest hair, and black jeans and black loafers. Abigail found him very attractive in an overt masculine way, and he was someone who was clearly confident and, probably, she thought, ruthless. A slight smile played on his lips and the photograph had captured his impenetrable dark brown eyes. In Abigail's profession as a psychotherapist, she had considered that a person's eyes were the "windows to the soul" and she could sometimes quickly assess a person's character from their eyes. Darius' eyes gave Abigail the impression that he could look out, but did not allow anyone to look in. Beneath the image of Darius, printed in large black capital letters, were the words "In Convo with Darius Fortescue. GQ's Hedge Fund Manager of the Year!".

Adjacent to the *GQ* framed front cover, was a front cover from *The Tatler*, which featured an older-looking Caroline Fortescue, with her two daughters standing either side of her. The younger one had blond hair, like her mother, and had also inherited her mother's sophisticated and sleek appearance. Abigail knew that this must be Sapphire Fortescue. The other daughter, however, had clearly taken after her father. Her jet-black hair was deliberately styled in an unkempt "just got out of bed" look. Her brown eyes were rimmed with kohl and had a slightly defiant look, which was obviously contrived. This, thought Abigail, must be Apollonia. The caption to the photograph read "The Model Family. Britain's Next Generation Top Models".

Abigail felt a "squeak" coming from the invisible mouse on her shoulder, and suppressed it. She had been born into a lower middle-class family with parents who had little aspiration other than to work hard, be good upstanding citizens, and bring their daughter up likewise. Her father was a tenant farmer, and her mother a housewife. For social outings, he would attend the weekly livestock sales in Barnstaple where he met up with other farmers, and her mother would go to Bingo. Other than that, they had no social life and seemed perfectly happy. Depending on how good the year had been financially, her father would take Abigail and her mother on a week's holiday to Ilfracombe where they stayed in a caravan park.

Abigail had gone to a comprehensive school and had shown academic ability. Her parents were approached by the school to suggest that she should transfer to the local grammar school but, unbeknownst to her, they had declined the suggestion and wanted her to stay where she was. Nevertheless, she achieved excellent O-level results, was encouraged to go to the local college to study for A-levels where she achieved 3 As, one of which was in psychology. Although they never showed it, her parents were very proud of her

VICTORIA WEBSTER

and when she said she wanted to apply to university to do a psychology degree, they gave their blessing but said she would have to fund herself. So, she found two part-time jobs, applied to those universities that offered psychology degrees, and was accepted by all of them. One of the universities was University College London, and Abigail had visions of her life suddenly becoming more interesting and exciting, and decided to accept the place offered. She applied for a grant and was successful. Her parents were dismayed to learn she was moving to London as they had hoped she would choose a university in Devon such as Exeter or Plymouth, so that she could come home at the weekends. Realising, though, that she had aspirations beyond their life, they had to let their "little bird" fly the nest.

London was expensive, and Abigail worked all through her university years in various part-time jobs at the weekends and during the holidays. This ensured that she had just enough money to live on and to pay her share of the rent on the property she shared with four other students. Achieving a high 2:1, she went on to train to be a psychotherapist, and then joined a small private practice in Regent Street. It was on one of their nights out that she went to The Thistle in Vigo Street, which was just off Regent Street, where she met Andrew who worked in the IT department of Lloyds & Scottish which was opposite The Thistle. Then, as the saying goes, the rest was history. After a few years working for the company, Andrew decided to start up his own IT company because he had realised there was a gap in the market for niche IT specialists. The company became successful and expanded, taking larger office space in Central London. By this time, Abigail was working for a larger practice in Harley Street and so both her and Andrew were doing very well. They decided to get married and buy a property outside of London where prices were cheaper, the air cleaner, and the quality of life less frantic. A bustling market town was decided upon. The commute into London was easy for Andrew, and Abigail had decided to set up her own psychotherapy practice in the town centre. There were decent schools for when they decided to have children, a park, plenty of shops, pubs, cafés and restaurants. Eventually Francesca and Annabel were born. They were living a comfortable and happy life; at least Abigail thought they were, until Andrew had decided they should "move up" in the world and they ended up in Green Park Road, which was as high as Abigail was prepared to go. Now here she was in this huge kitchen in a huge house where the occupants clearly had celebrity status, and she felt out of place.

She looked at her watch and it had already gone past 10 o'clock. She was about to ask Cassandra when the meeting was going to take place, when the kitchen door opened and in swept Caroline Fortescue. Older, of course, but still effortlessly sleek and elegant, dressed simply but expensively in beige linen trousers and a pale blue cashmere jumper. Abigail took a quick peek to see what shoes she was wearing. They too were beige and trimmed in black. Abigail noticed that in black on the front of the pumps the letter C was intertwined so that one C was facing forwards, and the other C was facing backwards. Abigail knew then that these were Chanel pumps, because she had seen them advertised in *Harrods* magazine at the doctor's surgery.

Caroline air-kissed Cassandra and Britt, and then came over to Abigail and extended her hand. 'You must be Abigail. I'm Caroline. Pleased to meet you.' She smiled with genuine warmth, which surprised Abigail as she thought she would be snooty, so she silently chastised herself for being so judgemental.

Cassandra clapped her hands to get everyone's attention. 'Right, come on, ladies. It's gone 10 and we need to make a start. Have you all brought pen and paper to take notes?'

Britt, Caroline and Abigail nodded yes. Abigail put her hand up. 'Don't we have to wait for the others?'

'What others?' queried Cassandra.

'The other team members. Miriam—'

Cassandra interrupted Abigail before she could finish her sentence. 'They don't come to these meetings, Abigail. This is my "elite" team. We use these meetings to discuss ideas, practicalities and the like, and then we give the others instructions as and when. Right, let's start.'

Before Cassandra could start the meeting, Caroline called out to the woman who had let them in. 'Karlinka!' she shouted, making the other women jump. Karlinka came hastily into the kitchen. 'I'm dying for a coffee. Can you prepare the coffee for us and put some biscuits on a plate as well?' she requested.

Karlinka nodded and went over to the yellow Gaggia machine to make the coffee.

Crikey, thought Abigail, *and here's me with my percolator, which I thought was posh.*

Whilst the very professional-looking, and no doubt expensive, coffee machine hissed, spluttered and gurgled, Cassandra began laying out her ideas for the Christmas fayre. 'So, this year, I thought it would be easier and less work for us if we keep to the format for last year's fayre.'

Karlinka called across the kitchen. 'Madam, shall I use the frother?'

'I don't know. Let me ask the others,' she replied. 'Do you all want frothy coffee, or normal?'

'Frothy please,' they answered in unison.

'Frothy please, Karlinka.'

Cassandra was showing signs of impatience, and then a phone rang somewhere in the house and the maid stopped what she was doing to go and answer the phone.

'As I was saying, this year's format will—'

Cassandra was interrupted by the maid coming back into the kitchen. 'Madam, that was the photographer on the phone. He wants to know if 9am is too early to come on Saturday to do the shoot.'

'Tell him nine is way too early and to make it 10,' Caroline replied.

Cassandra tried again. 'As I was saying, this year's format will run along the lines of last year. We will still have our "bring-and-buy stall" which is always very successful, and also our "books and toys" stall, but—'

Cassandra didn't manage to finish her sentence because Karlinka came back into the kitchen, made a thumbs-up gesture to Caroline, then proceeded to use the frother again because the milk had gone flat. She then put everything on a tray and brought it over to the kitchen table. No sooner had she done this than the phone rang again and she made a hasty exit.

Cassandra sighed heavily and threw her hands up in the air. 'Caroline, why don't you just take the calls on your mobile?'

Caroline looked at her with a slightly puzzled expression. 'Because, Cassandra, I didn't want us to be constantly interrupted, that's why.'

Cassandra couldn't think of a polite response and kept quiet. Britt bent her head to hide the smile on her face, and Abigail looked discreetly at her watch which showed that an hour had nearly passed by without anything being discussed or achieved.

Whilst Karlinka was dealing with the second phone call, everyone helped themselves to biscuits and coffee and awaited her return, so as to avoid yet another interruption. Coming back into the kitchen, she asked Caroline if it was okay for the wardrobe people to bring the clothes and accessories on Friday morning. Caroline replied that the timing was a bit tight, but to tell them yes.

'What's all this about, Caroline? I know you're dying to tell us,' asked Cassandra.

Caroline grinned. 'I thought you'd never ask! I'm very excited. Sapphire and I are going to grace the front cover of *The Lady*, and a double spread inside with photographs and an article, with the heading "Like Mother, Like Daughter. At Home With Caroline and Sapphire Fortescue". Of course, Apollonia is a bit put out, but the school won't release her for the weekend as a punishment for some infringement of the school's rules. Very petty of them if you ask me,' she said and she rolled her eyes.

'Right, thank you for sharing that. Now *please* can we get on?' said Cassandra, with emphasis on the word "please".

Britt spoke up. 'Yes, can we? I've got the farrier coming at one and Pepe has the afternoon off, so I've got to do the mucking out myself.'

Cassandra shot a "don't ask!" look at Abigail and Caroline in case they were going to ask who Pepe was. 'So, back to the reason we're here – the Christmas fayre. The "bring-and-buy" and "toys and books" stay. Unfortunately, what we can't have this year is the "cakes and biscuits" stall. Too many complaints from parents about the lack of information concerning ingredients.' Cassandra turned towards Abigail and explained. 'Last year, we had an unfortunate incident. Someone brought in biscuits which contained nuts, but weren't properly labelled, and a pupil bought the biscuits and ate one and suffered an anaphylactic shock. Luckily, she had her EpiPen with her, but nevertheless an ambulance was called. It rather put a damper on the afternoon. Also, with certain parents and pupils now wanting gluten free, wheat free, nut free and egg free, I've taken the executive decision to not have a stall this year. However, I thought that we could instead have a homemade goods stall, excluding food of any kind, which might appeal to those parents and girls who are creative. Like, for example, Christmas decorations, table decorations, cards and so on, and perhaps have a competition for the best creative idea. Then they could all go on sale and the proceeds, along with the proceeds from the other stalls, would go to the school. What do you think?'

Abigail, Caroline and Britt all nodded their approval.

'Right, that's it for today as we've run out of time. The next meeting will be in a month's time, second Wednesday of the month. Can you host, Britt?' asked Cassandra.

Britt replied that she could, got up from the chair and made to go. 'Must dash. Time critical!' She blew air kisses round the table. Said it was a pleasure to meet Abigail and dashed out.

The remaining three women also got up and went into the hallway.

Caroline stopped Abigail in the hallway. 'It's Sapphire's birthday party in two weeks' time. I'll get her to give Annabel an invite tomorrow at school. One for Francesca too. Apollonia will be home for the weekend and she's bringing some of her mates, so it'll be a lively affair no doubt,' she said, laughing.

Abigail was taken aback. 'Oh! Thank you. They will be pleased.'

Cassandra and Abigail said their goodbyes to Caroline, thanked Karlinka, who had also appeared in the hallway, for the coffee and biscuits, and made their way outside. Once the door had closed, they stood for a moment in the driveway.

'I'm a bit cross,' said Cassandra. 'We didn't get to discuss much today, which is a bit of a nuisance, but that's what happens when you're dealing with a celebrity family. Constant interruptions. By the way, Eustacia and Desdemona will be going to the party, so your two will have someone to talk to.'

'What do you mean? Won't the other girls be going from the class then?'

Cassandra shook her head. 'The Fortescues move in different circles from us mere mortals, and Sapphire is no exception. She doesn't mix with many of the girls in her class, preferring to hang out with Willow Barrington and her lot in the parallel class. Apollonia is a handful as well. By the way, it's probably best if your two don't tell the others they've been invited, particularly Annabel. We don't want to start a class divide. You know, a "them and us" situation.'

Abigail thought there was already a class divide but kept quiet.

'Well, must be going. Thanks for coming. Hope it wasn't too daunting.' Cassandra kissed Abigail quickly on both cheeks and walked briskly to her car.

Abigail drove away, aware that she had been given an insight and introduction to a world of glamour, luxury and abundant wealth. Her neighbours in Green Park Road were all wealthy to varying degrees, as were her and Andrew, but the Fortescue's wealth was of a different kind altogether, and Abigail felt out of her depth. Furthermore, although she felt privileged that Annabel and Francesca had been invited to the birthday party, even though Annabel had little to do with Sapphire at school, she was concerned that her daughter's developing friendships with Amy Murphy and Bunty McTavish, who were obviously considered to be of a different social class to Sapphire Fortescue, might be jeopardised. This caused Abigail to realise that her own burgeoning friendships with Miriam and Noreen might also be compromised. She then realised that the cause of all this was Cassandra Smythe-Brown who seemed to be pulling the strings. *Oh, why does life have to be so complicated?* she asked herself as she drove away.

CHAPTER THIRTEEN

In which Abigail does a good deed

ABIGAIL HAD LEFT the gates open for Unwin Trimble because he had said the previous week that he would come today, being Wednesday, to do the garden. Also, she had taken the lawnmower and strimmer out of the garage and taken them round to the back of the house. She was surprised to see a small white van in the driveway. Thinking that perhaps this was Unwin Trimble's vehicle, she parked her car and went to have a look at the signage because it didn't look like it was anything to do with gardening. She was right. Instead of advertising gardening services, large capital letters in black advertised "BARNEY AND BILLY BRIGHT. VISUAL TECHNICIANS". This was followed by the words *"We aim to make your world cleaner and clearer"* written in black italic lettering, followed by a mobile number. On the van's doorway was a red and blue decal of two cartoon men dressed in overalls, with one of the figures carrying a bucket, and the other a ladder. Abigail gave a big sigh and went through the side gate.

She was greeted by the sight of a stocky middle-aged man dressed in denim overalls, holding onto the sides of a tall ladder. Abigail looked up and saw at the very top, a younger version of the man at the bottom of the ladder, also dressed in denim overalls, cleaning the bedroom windows with a yellow squeegee in one hand and holding onto the ladder with his other hand. A small window/shower screen wiper was hung on the right-hand side of the ladder, and Abigail could just make out a plastic bottle filled with blue liquid hanging on the left-hand side. She shook her head in amazement, not quite believing what she was seeing. When the older man suddenly turned at the sound of Abigail's footsteps behind him, he jumped, causing the ladder to wobble.

'Fuck's sake, Dad. Keep a hold of the ladder,' came a shout from above.

'Watch your language, Billy. There's a lady here. You'd better come down.'

Billy placed the squeegee in his pocket and descended carefully down the ladder. Having reached the bottom, he went and stood by his father's side.

Abigail waited for one of them to say something, but they stood there in complete silence. Sighing again, she introduced herself. 'I'm Abigail Thomas. I live here. I wasn't expecting window cleaners today, or visual technicians. I was expecting the gardener.'

'Ah, hello, Mrs Thomas. I'm Barney Bright and this is my son, Billy. Pleased to make your acquaintance, aren't we Billy?' He gave Billy a nudge.

Billy nodded. 'Yes, Dad.'

'There's been no one here except us, has there, Billy?'

Billy shook his head. 'No, Dad.'

Abigail realised this was going to be hard work. 'Okay. So presumably my husband, Mr Thomas, has asked you to come?'

'Yes, that's right. I got talking to him in The Royal Oak the other evening and he said he was looking for a window cleaner, and here we are.' This was said with a hopeful smile. 'Your husband hasn't mentioned us, then?'

'No, he hasn't. But we do need the windows cleaned. Did he say how often and when? Because I'm not always here in the morning.'

'He said that once a month would be sufficient. Any morning would suit us, wouldn't it, Billy?'

Billy nodded. 'Yes, Dad.'

'Lad's a bit shy, aren't you, Billy?'

'Yes, Dad.'

Abigail smiled at Billy. 'Okay, Mr Bright. Once a month is good. Can you come on a Tuesday morning, as I'm usually here then?'

Father and son smiled. 'Yes, that's good for us, isn't it, Billy?'

Billy grinned. 'Yes, Dad.'

Abigail now had to set some ground rules as she had been alarmed at the lack of safety measures in place. 'Just one thing, Mr Bright...'

'Please call me Barney.'

'Okay, Barney. Just one thing. Are you insured?'

Barney Bright looked puzzled. 'What do you mean, insured?'

'For accidents, personal injury, that sort of thing. You know, if people fall off wobbly ladders, or drop something from a height onto someone's head.' Abigail gestured at Billy, who blushed.

'See, the thing is, Mrs Thomas...'

'You can call me Abigail.'

'Right, see the thing is, Abigail, we've only just started doing this father and son business. Billy's just left school, and well I was laid off recently and was finding it difficult to get alternative employment, so...' He shrugged his shoulders in a gesture of defeat.

Abigail picked up on something that spoke of difficulty, sadness even, but she couldn't risk having any accidents or problems on her and Andrew's property. She decided to try a softer approach. 'I did wonder if your business was new, because your van looks new and your advertisement is very eye-catching.'

'It is! Only bought the van a few weeks ago and had the signage done last week. Very pleased with it. Hoping that people will see us out and about and give us a ring.'

'Look, Barney. You and Billy can clean our windows, back and front, once a month on a Tuesday morning. But you must get some insurance in place and, perhaps more importantly, because you're sending your son up the ladder to clean the top floor windows, you should invest in a window cleaning kit that has an extendable pole, so that your son doesn't have to climb so high up. In fact, I'm making that another condition of you cleaning for us – insurance, and an extendable cleaning kit. You can buy an inexpensive one at B&Q.'

Barney Bright let out a deep sigh of relief. 'Thank you, Mrs Thomas. In fact, me and Billy will go to B&Q right now and buy one of those kits you mention, then I'll get the insurance sorted.'

Abigail smiled and nodded her head. 'Good. All sorted. Now, what about payment? I suppose my husband said I would settle up with you?'

'Yes, he did. Can you pay cash?' Barney screwed up his face when he said this and told her how much she owed for today.

Abigail was surprised how reasonable it was and guessed it was because they were just starting out. She decided then and there, that if they did a good job, she would spread the word round her immediate neighbourhood. 'I don't suppose you've got any leaflets handy, have you?'

Barney looked puzzled again. 'Leaflets? For what?'

Abigail counted to five. 'For your window cleaning business. If you've got some leaflets, I can take them round the neighbourhood and put them through some doors.'

Barney looked embarrassed. 'Haven't got round to that yet. Didn't realise there would be so much to do. If I put an idea together, would you take a look at it for me, if that's not asking too much?'

Abigail said that she would be happy to do that, because she realised that he hadn't thought things through properly and she was guessing that they were probably going through some financial and possibly some personal difficulty.

Abigail waved to them as they drove away, and then went into the house and closed the gates. As to Unwin Trimble's no-show, that was another matter to be dealt with. If he didn't turn up the next morning, she'd be having words with Andrew as she didn't have a contact number for Unwin.

It was Thursday morning and, as usual, Abigail dropped the girls off at school and returned home. She had closed the gates and was surprised to see Unwin Trimble standing outside as he hadn't made any contact with her or Andrew to say that he was coming. He was dressed the same as the first time she had met him, and still not wearing a coat despite the weather having turned chilly. For some inexplicable reason he both exasperated her and yet made her feel concerned for him. Here was an elderly-ish man, who obviously took little care of himself, stood outside in the cold. Furthermore, it crossed her mind that if it had been raining, he would have got wet because neither was he carrying an umbrella, and it seemed that he didn't have a vehicle either. *This really won't do*, Abigail thought to herself, and she opened the gates from inside her car and drove in. Unwin Trimble followed behind on foot.

Exiting from the car, she closed the car door and waited for him to come up to her. She was about to speak, when he cut in. 'I'm sorry I'm late, Mrs Thomas.

I couldn't get in. The gates were shut, and the code didn't work.'

Abigail didn't know which statement to comment on first. 'I expected you yesterday, and I left the gates open and all the equipment round the back. The code won't work because we've changed it.'

Unwin shuffled his feet on the gravel and clasped his hands in front of him. 'I came yesterday but there was a van in the driveway and two men were cleaning the windows, so I went away again.'

Abigail reasoned that this was a fair answer. 'Right, I see. My husband had arranged for the window cleaners to come.'

'I can clean windows too, Mrs Thomas,' he replied and wiggled his eyebrows up and down and grinned.

'Thank you, Unwin but I think the garden is quite sufficient for you. Can't have you going up and down ladders.' She wanted to add "at your age" but decided not to.

'Oh, it wouldn't be a problem, Abigail. Can I call you Abigail? No, it wouldn't be a problem for me at all. I clean my own windows and I've got one of those long-handled telescopic gadgets that do away with ladders.'

Abigail realised she was entering tricky territory here and she must make sure that Andrew – who obviously and secretly frequented The Royal Oak before coming home – wasn't persuaded by Unwin to use him to clean their windows instead of Barney and Billy Bright. So Abigail stood her ground and in a firm tone said, 'No, no, it's okay, Unwin. Let's leave it as it is. I've already organised for the window cleaners to come once a month on a Tuesday morning, and on my schedule I've got you down to do the garden on a Wednesday or Thursday. However, Wednesday is best for me and I can leave the gate open for you and put the mower and strimmer round the back. I can then pay you, as I'm sure you'll still be here when I get back at 12. That is, if you come at 10. I think two hours will be sufficient time for you to do the garden.'

Unwin shuffled his feet again. 'Yes, Abigail. I could do Wednesday. But what if I needed to come on a different day, and you're not here. How would I get in?'

Abigail chewed her bottom lip. 'Why would you want to come on a different day? Does Wednesday not suit?'

'Yes, Wednesday suits me very well. It's just that, what if something else came up and...' Unwin tailed off because he didn't know what else to say.

Abigail realised she needed to assert herself with Unwin Trimble, so she took a deep breath and then expelled it. 'That's not how it works, Unwin. I need someone to work a set day so that I know what's happening. However, I do understand that things can arise. Can I have your mobile number then?'

'No.'

'Why not?'

'I don't have a mobile. No need for one.'

Abigail sighed and counted to five. 'Landline, then.'

'Nope, don't have one.'

Abigail was losing patience. 'Well, how do people get in touch with you? Oh, let me guess. The Royal Oak!' Unwin grinned. 'Well, Unwin, I don't have the luxury of conducting my business in the pub. So, seeing as there's no way for me to contact you, as agreed between us, I'll expect you here on Wednesday mornings at 10 o'clock. Seeing as you're here now, and that we've wasted quite a bit of time already, you get on and do what you can in the time left, and ring the front doorbell when you've finished.'

Unwin smiled. 'Okey dokey. If you don't mind me saying, Abigail, you're a formidable woman to do business with.' And he made his way to the side gate.

Abigail went inside and made her way to the kitchen. She made a percolator full of coffee and sat down. She reflected on Unwin Trimble's comment. No one had ever described her as "formidable"; "easy-going", "placid", certainly, but "formidable" never. Andrew clearly didn't think of her as formidable and the image of a doormat sprang into her mind. She suddenly felt quite pleased. Perhaps she was, finally, becoming an assertive and less of a people-pleaser type of person.

CHAPTER FOURTEEN

In which Abigail realises she's a spoilsport

FRANCESCA AND ANNABEL were excited. Saturday had arrived; the day of Sapphire Fortescue's party. They were in Francesca's bedroom getting ready and playing music downloaded from Spotify so loud that Andrew and Abigail could hear it downstairs.

'I'll go up,' said Andrew. The volume had been turned down and Andrew came back down the stairs and into the kitchen. 'They're very excited. Who's this Sapphire Fortescue, anyway? And who on earth calls their daughter Sapphire? Seems a bit poncy to me.' He pulled a face.

Abigail laughed. 'The other daughter is called Apollonia and she goes to boarding school. The mother is an ex-*Vogue* model, and the father is Darius Fortescue; someone big in the City by all accounts.'

Andrew stood up straighter. 'Darius Fortescue! I've never met him, but I've heard about him. Runs a very successful hedge fund and venture capital firm, and our two have been invited to the party? Well, well, well. Tell you what, Abi, to give you some time to yourself I'll take the girls and pick them up.'

'Oh, you don't usually offer to do such things. Why the sudden generosity with your time?' Abigail knew exactly why Andrew had offered. It was because he wanted to see where they lived and what the house was like. She also suspected that he was hoping to meet Darius.

'Don't be like that. To be honest, I want to see where they live and what their house is like.' Andrew was clearly excited as well, because he had started whistling which was a very rare thing indeed. 'I'll go and tell the girls that I'll be taking them and picking them up.' He left the kitchen and Abigail could hear him running up the stairs, still whistling.

The time to leave for the party was approaching. Annabel and Francesca came down the stairs and went into the kitchen. Andrew had gone into his study, which left Abigail to deal with the problem standing in front of her. Francesca had gone into the dressing room in Andrew and Abigail's bedroom and used some of Abigail's make-up. This presented Abigail with two problems: the first was that Francesca hadn't asked permission, and the second was that Abigail didn't approve of Francesca wearing make-up, so she was in for a telling-off. Abigail looked directly at her eldest daughter. 'Firstly, Francesca, you do not go and help yourself to my make-up without at least asking me first. Secondly, you are wearing far too much and you're far too young.'

Francesca had her "don't mess with me" look on her face which she had picked up from somewhere recently. 'If I'd asked you if I could of used your make-up, you would of said no.'

'Quite right, I would have said no. And it isn't "would of" and "could of", by the way. That is poor English.'

Francesca rolled her eyeballs. 'I don't see why I can't wear make-up. It is a party we're going to.'

Abigail stood her ground. In her newly found assertive and "formidable" manner, which she was still trying to get used to, she told Francesca to go back upstairs and remove the make-up. The order didn't go down well. Francesca shot Abigail a defiant look, turned on her heels, stomped out of the kitchen, stomped up the stairs and into her bedroom slamming the door behind her. Annabel had stood silently by and then began to cry.

'Why are you crying, Annabel?' asked Abigail.

'Because I said to Francesca that she shouldn't go into your bedroom, and that you would be cross. Now, I suppose we can't go to the party, and I've been looking forward to it.' The crying started again.

Abigail went upstairs to Francesca's bedroom and tried to open the door. It was locked. 'Francesca, open this door at once!'

'No, I won't,' came the reply. 'I'll ask Daddy if I can wear make-up. He's taking us to the party anyway.'

'Fine by me. He's in his study. I'll shout for him to come up and sort this out. You need to be leaving soon, so have a think.'

The door opened and a make-up free Francesca came out. 'Okay, you win, *Mother*. You're such a spoilsport.'

'I don't think you're a spoilsport, Mummy,' said Annabel who had followed her mother up the stairs to witness the telling-off. 'I think you're—' Annabel was prevented from finishing her sentence by Francesca, who had given her sister a push.

Abigail sighed and then was very grateful to Andrew for offering to take them to the party. This meant she had a bit more time to herself. 'Right. Let's go downstairs and tell Dad you're ready to go.'

Abigail stood at the door and waved the three of them goodbye. Andrew would be back in about an hour, so she got herself ready and went to the supermarket to get the ingredients for a fish pie she was making for dinner. She had finally decided to get to grips with her fancy oven and had recently purchased two books from the bookshop in Cornham. One was called *A Beginner's Guide to Cooking with Agas*, and the other was a recipe book with the title *Easy Recipes for Aga and Range Appliances*. She had also looked online which is how she found out that her beautiful, eye-catching oven was no less than a limited edition "Tiffany Blue" with an eye-watering price tag. This made Abigail all the more determined to start using it, and she had read the instructions. The two large circular rings on the top were called "plates". One was a boiling plate and the other was for simmering. There were three cast iron doors which, when opened, revealed ovens. She found out that one was for roasting, one for baking and then a simmering oven. Her Aga was electric and, according to the information in her book, the temperature would be pre-set. It all seemed straightforward enough, and she decided that she would attempt an "easy" fish pie from a recipe in the second cookery book.

Having returned from shopping, she awaited Andrew's return. She heard the crunch of tyres on the gravel and knew this was Andrew back from dropping the girls off. The front door opened and then Andrew burst into the kitchen. 'Crikey, that's some house they live in, isn't it?' he said excitedly. 'And you should see the cars. I spotted a Bentley, Aston Martin, BMW, Mercedes… oh, and a small blue Fiat which was parked on the opposite side of the driveway.'

'That's Karlinka's car.'

'Who's Karlinka?'

'The maid.'

'They've got a maid! Mmm, and our two were invited. Still, I suppose all the class were invited, weren't they?'

Abigail knew that Andrew was fishing and was probably secretly hoping that not all the class were invited, making it special that their two were. Disliking this kind of thing, she did however truthfully reply that not all the class were invited, adding that, 'Our two were only invited at the last minute, though, because I was at Caroline's for the parents' association meeting.'

'Ah, that explains it then. But she didn't have to invite them, though, did she?'

Abigail had to admit that this was true and nodded in agreement. 'So, what did you think of the inside? Impressive, isn't it? Must have cost a fortune.'

Andrew shrugged his shoulders. 'Didn't go in the house. Just dropped the girls off, and they went inside as the door was open. It was very noisy. Lots of shouting and squealing. Anyway, here I am Abi. We've a few hours before I need to pick them up. Do you fancy going for a walk, or a browse round the shops in Cornham? I'm all yours!' he said grinning, opening his arms out wide.

Abigail was a bit taken aback, but nonetheless pleased. 'Well, let's go into Cornham and browse round the shops. Perhaps have a coffee out.'

Andrew then noticed the books on the butcher's block and picked one of them up. 'What's all this? *Easy recipes for Agas and Range Appliances.* Does this mean we're going to have a proper meal tonight cooked in the Aga?'

'Yes. I decided it was ridiculous having such a beautiful piece of equipment and not using it, so I'm going to attempt a fish pie.' She looked up at her husband with her fingers crossed.

'I'm sure it will be a success. Talking about beautiful pieces of equipment... come here.'

Abigail felt very happy at the attention she was suddenly getting from Andrew. Only recently a phrase had been popping up in her thoughts which went something like *the poverty of your attention dismisses me,* so she decided to make the most of it while it lasted.

The trip into Cornham was very pleasurable. The clothes shops were all very upmarket with those selling menswear stocking designer brands such as Hugo Boss, Tommy Hilfiger and Armani, as advertised by the display in the shop fronts. Abigail knew that Andrew bought suits and shirts by Hugo Boss and was partial to Hermès ties. Now, from the prices on display, she realised how much he spent on his clothes which was way more than she ever spent. In contrast to the menswear shops, the boutiques catering for women also stocked designer brands but didn't display the prices in the windows. In Abigail's opinion, this was making a subtle, or perhaps not-so-subtle, statement that if you had to ask the price of something, that is if you were brave enough to go into the boutique in the first place, then you probably couldn't afford it. Both Andrew and Abigail detested this kind of snobbery. Andrew dared Abigail to go in and ask the price of a dress that was in the window.

'No way,' she replied. 'Not dressed like this!' Abigail was in her uniform of jeans and jumper.

Andrew looked Abigail up and down. 'Mmm, you've got a point.'

'Andrew!' she shouted.

'But you said you couldn't go in there dressed like that. Seriously, though, Abi, you do need to buy some new things. Instead of wearing the same old clothes and the same old style, there's enough money for you to go and update your wardrobe. In fact, I quite like that Armani suit we saw just now. I might go back next weekend and treat myself.'

Abigail could feel an argument coming on, even though it might spoil the nice time they were having together. 'Andrew! Did you see the price of that suit? That's more than I would spend in a year on clothes.'

'Exactly, Abigail. That's my point. You need to smarten yourself up a bit and invest some time and money into your wardrobe, and your appearance.'

'I suppose you want me to dress like Svetlana?'

Andrew gave a wistful smile. 'Well, she does have a particular eye-catching style. But, then again, she has the figure for it.' He smiled, then realised he had opened a whole box of trouble for himself.

'Well, thank you very much for that, Andrew. First you tell me that I dress scruffily and now you've said I'm fat.'

'Firstly, Abigail, I did not say you dressed "scruffily". Secondly, I most certainly didn't say you were "fat". I merely said... oh, never mind. I can't be bothered to argue with you. Look, go into Knighton in the week and buy whatever you want. But, and I do mean but, no jeans, jumpers, trainers, or long flowered skirts.'

'I haven't got any long flowered skirts,' Abigail replied.

'Exactly! Keep it that way. I've never said this before, but some of your friends where we lived previously were obviously part of the long flowered skirt and unshaved legs and armpits brigade.'

'Now that's just being rude, Andrew. I had a good group of women friends in that "brigade", as you call them, and they weren't bothered by how they looked. They had more important things to think about, like doing good in society and helping those less fortunate in the community.'

Andrew was getting cross and becoming bored. 'Okay, I apologise. The offer is there though. Go into Knighton and have a good spend-up. Let's go and have a coffee at the café over the road as we'll need to get back soon as I have to collect the girls.' Andrew, in a gesture of appeasement, took Abigail's hand and they crossed the road.

The café was of the independent variety. Although it was getting late in the year, the sun was out, and they sat outside. They both chose a flat white and enjoyed a few rare moments of tranquil togetherness. Abigail thought that she really was lucky to have married someone who was generous with money, although stingy with his time and affection. Then, it was time to return home. Andrew dropped Abigail back, gave her a quick kiss on the lips, which surprised and delighted her, and drove off to collect the girls.

Abigail had a spring in her step. Going into the kitchen, she switched on the Aga to warm up the ovens and then she put the final touches to the fish pie she was making. Once the required temperature had been reached, she would put it into the baking oven as this was the oven for stews, casseroles and pies. The carrots and broccoli, however, she would cook in her steamer. *One thing at a time*, she told herself, and awaited the return of Andrew and the girls.

*

Abigail heard the sound of a car coming into the driveway and went into the hallway to greet them. The front door opened, and Abigail was confronted with three faces all showing different emotions and expressions. Andrew was very excited and was almost bouncing up and down, Annabel was grinning but also wore a slightly worried expression, and Francesca was quiet and morose.

Andrew spoke first. 'You'll never guess what, Abi. I met Darius Fortescue and what a guy he is!'

Abigail needed to deal with the girls first as she could sense something was amiss, particularly with Francesca. Also, she needed to tackle Annabel who was wearing far too much make-up. 'Sorry, Andrew. Can this wait? I want to talk to the girls.'

Andrew wasn't happy, and his expression turned sulky. 'The girls always come first, and I've got something very exciting to tell you.'

Abigail turned to Annabel and Francesca. 'You two go into the kitchen. I'll be along in a minute.' She waited until they had left and then turned to Andrew. 'That's not very fair, Andrew. I always make time for you when you're here.' Abigail put a stress on the words "when you're here". 'As soon as I've spoken to the girls, because I detect all is not well with Francesca, I'll come and see you. Is that okay? By the way, thanks for today. I appreciated your help.'

Andrew nodded. 'Fair enough. I'll be in my study.'

Right, now the girls, thought Abigail to herself, not relishing the task of telling Annabel to remove the make-up she was wearing. She found them sitting on the settee in the alcove watching television. 'Turn off the TV, please.'

The TV was turned off without any argument. 'So, first things first. Did you both have a good time?' In reply, Abigail received a "yes" from Annabel and a "no" from Francesca. Abigail sighed. 'Looking at your face, Annabel, I can see there was a make-up session at the party.'

Annabel grinned. 'Yes, Mummy! The theme of the party was "Knighton's Next Top Model".' This was greeted with an eyeroll from Francesca, and a warning look from Abigail aimed at Francesca. Annabel was oblivious to all of this. 'It was a really cool party. Sapphire's mum hired a professional make-up artist who came and gave a demonstration on Sapphire how to apply make-up. She's so pretty...' Annabel looked momentarily glum, and then brightened up again. 'And then we were all allowed to use the make-up, and we had to make each other up, and there was a prize for the best made-up face. I didn't win. Sapphire's "bf", Willow Barrington, won.' Annabel pulled a face, making it obvious her dislike of the girl. 'Then, we had a lesson in deportment and how to do the "catwalk" walk, and then there was a professional photographer who took photos which would be put into a... I can't remember what it's called. But it's like a book with lots of photographs in it that models have to have. I might get to be a top model!'

Oh no you won't, thought Abigail, but kept quiet. 'Right, well I can see you enjoyed yourself, Annabel. Unfortunately, you're now back at home and I need you to go upstairs and take off that make-up.'

Annabel frowned. 'Do I have to? I think it makes me look sophisticated.'

'It makes you look like a clown,' said Francesca, who was getting gloomier by the minute.

'No it doesn't!' shouted Annabel. 'Just because you didn't enjoy the party, there's no need to spoil it for me. I don't look like a clown, Mummy, do I?'

Abigail needed to tread carefully, because the make-up had been applied very badly. 'No, Annabel, you don't. But you do need to take it off. It's only fair. I wouldn't let your older sister wear any, so it's only fair that you now remove it.'

Annabel got up and stomped out of the kitchen, with the parting words, 'You're such a spoilsport.'

Abigail then turned her attention to Francesca. 'Right, Francesca. What's the matter? You don't look at all happy and you've been a bit mean to Annabel. Did you not enjoy the party?'

Francesca chewed on her bottom lip. 'You've got to promise me, Mum, that you won't tell anyone about what I'm going to tell you. Not Dad or anyone.'

'Of course I won't, if you ask me not to. What on earth is the matter? I thought you'd like that kind of party seeing as I wouldn't let you wear make-up.'

'The next top model thing was for Sapphire's group. Eustacia and I were expected to hang out with Apollonia and her friends from boarding school. In fact,

I don't really know why I was invited. All we did was stay in her bedroom listening to music. Also, I didn't like her or her friends. They were very stuck-up.' Francesca paused. 'Also, and you mustn't say anything. Promise?'

Abigail was getting exasperated. 'For heaven's sake, I said I wouldn't tell anyone. What is it?'

'They were smoking a funny cigarette. Apollonia had a piece of white paper and some brown flakes which she then put in the paper and rolled up in the shape of a cigarette. Then she lit it and they passed it around to each other. It smelt funny as well. And they all got very silly and giggly, and started rolling about on the bed and the floor. So, I said I was leaving and Apollonia said, "Yeah, whatever, square," and they all started laughing. So, I went to see where Annabel was and she was having her make-up done. They were all being silly as well, so I went and sat by myself.'

Abigail frowned, not liking what she was hearing. 'Where were the parents?'

'Dunno. Somewhere in the house, I guess.'

'So there was no supervision? What about food?'

Francesca shrugged. 'They have a housekeeper. She has a funny name. She was there. Food and drink were laid out on the kitchen table, and we just helped ourselves.'

Something then occurred to Abigail. 'You said that you left the bedroom and came and sat down by yourself. So where was Eustacia?' Francesca chewed her lip again. 'I won't say anything,' said Abigail.

'She stayed in the bedroom with the others. Then, after a while, she came out but was acting weird. She kept giggling and wandering about pretending she was a zombie. Honestly, Mum, all I wanted to do was to come home. Eventually, she calmed down. I asked her if she had smoked any of the funny cigarette and she said she had, but only because when she leaves Knighton High she's going to board at Apollonia's school, and she didn't want to be uncool like me. I was so pleased when Dad came to pick us up, but he bumped into Sapphire's dad and was invited in. It seemed ages before he came to get us.' Abigail could see that Francesca was completely deflated by the experience. 'I don't want to go there again, Mum. I didn't like it.'

Abigail was shocked by all she heard. Her first instincts were to tell Andrew and then Cassandra, but she had promised not to. 'Okay, Francesca, we'll keep this between us. Go up and see your sister and see if she's calmed down. Make sure she's taken that make-up off. Between you and I, she did look like a clown, but don't you dare tell her.' Abigail put her finger to her lips in a "shush" gesture. 'Now for Andrew,' she said out loud to herself, and made her way to his study.

The door was closed and so she opened it without knocking because there was not a cat in hell's chance she was going to give him the excuse to say in the pompous voice he sometimes used, 'Enter.'

'Right, Andrew. I'm here and I'm all yours. What did you want to tell me?'

'Just a moment, Abigail, I need to finish what I'm doing.'

'Andrew! Stop with this attitude. Did you not notice anything wrong in the car going home?'

'Nope. Francesca was a bit quiet, and Annabel was her usual excitable self.'

'Well, I've sorted it out anyway and I need to serve up dinner. So, what did you want to tell me?'

'What I wanted to tell you is that I met Darius Fortescue. Now there's a man who's at the top of his game. Very successful. Quite a name in the City. Those Fortescues must be loaded. Have you seen the cars? And the home? They've got an indoor swimming pool, home cinema, and a gym. He gave me the tour.'

Andrew, who was usually calm, cool and had a tendency to be supercilious, was behaving like some starstruck fanboy. 'Andrew, you're a bit overexcited. You're like a child who's just met his hero.'

Andrew turned his cool emotionless gaze on her. 'Don't be such a spoilsport, Abi. Anyway, I've got some good news. Two bits of news, actually. Darius said he could probably put some business my way, as he's got lots of contacts who are looking for niche IT specialists. I was thinking that perhaps I could buy myself a Bentley or maybe an Aston Martin.'

'Andrew, I think you're getting a bit carried away. What's the other bit of news?'

Andrew was brought back down to earth by Abigail's dismissive comment. 'Oh, they've invited us to dinner next Saturday.'

Abigail shook her head. 'No way. I'm not going. I'm not that keen on them. Anyway, there's no one to look after the girls.'

Andrew exploded. 'For heaven's sake, Abigail. They don't just invite any old people. We're going, so you'd better go and buy something new to wear and get your hair done. I caught a glimpse of Caroline Fortescue. You can see why she used to be a model. Very classy lady. Right, that's sorted, then. Is dinner ready because I'm famished.'

Abigail exited the study and shouted for the girls to come down. They all assembled in the kitchen and went and sat down. The fish pie was a success, although it seemed to Abigail that it took far longer to cook than in an ordinary oven.

As she got ready for bed that night, she remembered that she had been accused of being a spoilsport on no less than three occasions that day. If this is the price she had to pay for her newly found assertive and formidable personality, so be it.

CHAPTER FIFTEEN

In which Abigail breaks with protocol

IT WAS MONDAY morning and, after dropping the girls off at school, Abigail drove into the centre of Knighton to go shopping for some new clothes, including a dress and shoes for Saturday evening. She had thought that it would be nice to go with someone and so had called Miriam on Sunday, but both calls had gone unanswered. She had left two voicemails, but there had been no response from her. She hung about outside the school gates hoping to catch her, but when there was no sign of her, Abigail realised that she had either dropped Bunty off early or that Hamish had done the school run.

Abigail parked her car and made her way to M&S. She found the clothes and shoes to be well-made, fairly priced, with a good cross-section of sizes and styles, and she always managed to find what she wanted. On entering, and out of habit, she headed to the "casual" area where jeans and jumpers were located. *No, Abigail, don't you dare go there,* said the voice inside her head, and she changed direction and made her way to the *Classic* range. Unlike Andrew, who obviously thought nothing of spending hundreds of pounds on his clothes, Abigail was very price-conscious, and was conservative in her choice of outfits, preferring a timeless style over whatever was trending at the time and would, no doubt, go out of fashion as quickly as it came in. Such a long-held mindset of hers, which had served her perfectly well in her old life, she now realised had to change and needed updating. Similarly, she always chose dark colours such as black, dark grey or navy as she didn't want to draw attention to herself. This was partly due to her training as a psychotherapist where the wearing of dark colours was perceived to be professional-looking and reassuring. However, *Rome wasn't built in a day*, she reminded herself and headed for the trouser rails which had the usual selection of black, navy and grey. Abigail knew she was an M&S size 12 and chose two pairs of "ankle grazers", one in navy and the other in pale grey, and put them in her basket.

She then broke protocol and headed to the selection of stylish *Autograph* jumpers. She preferred round neck sweaters with long sleeves, and soft to the touch. She baulked at the expensive price tag for pure cashmere, even though the feel of it was luxurious, and selected instead a pale pink blended wool mix. Also, and which was very adventurous for her, she chose a lime green jumper with black polka dots and put it in her basket. Both would work well with her choice of trousers. Her eyes were then drawn to a rail of mid-length flowered skirts in the *Per Una* section. She knew that Andrew disliked flowery things. However, the mannequin on the display was wearing one of the skirts teamed up with a pale blue twin set which perfectly matched the colour of one of the flowers in the skirt. Also, Abigail realised the pink jumper would go as well. So, she took a size 12 skirt off the rail, and a size 12 twin set hanging nearby and put them in her basket. She felt very uplifted. *Perhaps this is what is meant by retail therapy,* she said to herself.

Abigail then made her way to the shoe department. Trousers that ended at the ankle had become popular and made more of a fashion statement than those of a traditional length. The ankle grazer style looked particularly effective when worn with a shoe that had a higher heel and Abigail decided to treat herself. She was a size 4 and bought two pairs: a dark grey patent with a three-inch stiletto, and a leather navy court shoe with a three-inch chunky heel. She knew that she would never see Juliana or Svetlana wearing these styles, but neither would she wear the kind of shoes they wore as Abigail considered them too showy and impractical. The basket was beginning to get heavy and full, and she wished she'd taken a trolley, especially as, on her way to the payment desk, she had seen a pale grey jersey blazer with navy edging and silver buttons and added that too. After the cashier had rung up all the items and told Abigail how much it all came to, she wondered if she should put the blazer back. It then occurred to her that Andrew's penchant for expensive clothes meant that what she had spent on her basket full of clothes was still relatively frugal when compared to what he spent on a couple of items, so she talked herself out of it.

Abigail left M&S carrying two large carrier bags and feeling very pleased with her purchases. Now for the tricky part – the dress and shoes for Saturday evening. As a rule, she steered clear of anything sparkly or figure hugging, as she had a typical pear-shaped figure. That morning, as he was leaving for work, Andrew had instructed her to not buy another black dress. 'Anything but black, Abi. Be a bit more adventurous. *Comme moi!*' He was wearing a bright blue linen suit, white shirt with lemon stripes, and a pale blue tie with lemon-coloured spots. Abigail had merely stared. 'Why are you staring like that? I'm the boss. I can wear what I like.' Then he had blown her a kiss and waved goodbye.

Abigail headed for John Lewis and went up the escalator to the first floor to the womenswear department.

They were now stocking the beginning of their Christmas outfits and Abigail went over to the store's own brand of party wear. Ignoring the rails of black and silver, and black and gold outfits, she went over to the black and plum section. There was a mix of tops, trousers and skirts, and dresses in Christmassy fabrics of taffeta and velvet. She saw a lovely dress that ended just above the knee. It had a square neckline and was sleeveless. The skirt section was in black velvet, and the bodice was a plum colour in a taffeta fabric. The two halves were brought together by a wide plum-coloured sash with black velvet polka dots, which could be tied either at the front or the back. Because the cut of the skirt was an A-line, and the bodice close fitting, she took a size 12 and 14 into the fitting room. She was pleased when the 14 was too big, and that the 12 fitted her perfectly. The dress, however, needed a pair of shoes with high heels and so, after paying, she headed over to the shoe department. The easy and safe option would be to buy black. However, in the Kurt Geiger concession, she spotted a plum-coloured pair of suede shoes with a stiletto. The price was a bit on the high side for her, but she felt they would complete the outfit and decided to splash out.

Buoyed on by the success of her shopping trip, she went down the escalator to the cosmetics and perfumery department and made her way to the Bobbi Brown counter. She showed the Bobbi Brown consultant the dress and shoes, and was advised to buy a deep shade of lipstick and a darker shade of blusher. Abigail, who rarely wore make-up and was grateful for the advice, popped the two items in her John Lewis carrier bag.

With time still to spare, and because she was in need of a coffee, she returned to the car park and deposited her bags and then headed for Café Culture. On entering, she could see that it was busy and she scanned around for a vacant table. Then, she caught sight of two people deep in conversation. It was Miriam and Noreen. *Oh, so that's how it is,* she thought with disappointment. Before they looked up and spotted her, she made a hasty retreat. Of course, she told herself, there could be a perfectly good reason why she wasn't invited and why Miriam hadn't returned her calls. However, her intuition told her that something was wrong and, whatever it was, she wasn't privy to it. The thing was, she would have to approach Miriam at some point because she was her contact in the pecking order of the parents' association, and it was Abigail who would have to tell Miriam what her tasks were for the Christmas fayre.

Abigail woke up on Tuesday morning in a good mood. On Monday evening, she had engaged in a "show and tell" of her shopping trip in front of Andrew and the girls. Everything was met with approval – well, almost. Andrew had raised his eyebrows at the sight of black and sighed when he saw the colours of the trousers she had bought. However, he did show a pleasantly surprised look at the colourful jumpers and grudgingly admitted that the dress looked elegant. So, there was no reason why Abigail shouldn't feel in a good mood.

Today, she had decided to go into Cornham and see about making an appointment to get her hair cut and styled. At Juliana's insistence that she should go to the salon she used, which was André of Knightsbridge, that's where she went first. The salon wasn't large inside. There were six chairs, with only one occupied by an elderly lady with curlers in her hair who was sitting under a dome-shaped dryer. The reception desk was at the back of the salon, adjacent to a metal staircase leading up to the first floor.

Abigail crossed the salon floor until she came level with the receptionist behind the counter, whose name, as depicted on her badge, was Chelsea. Abigail rarely went to hair salons and felt nervous, which she told herself was ridiculous. 'My neighbour, Juliana Hetherington, recommended this salon. I'm looking to get my hair cut and restyled this week with André if possible.'

Chelsea looked at Abigail as if she was mad. 'Impossible, I'm afraid. André is booked up solidly for months and he has a waiting list.'

'Oh, I see. I didn't realise. My neighbour said I should try here.' Abigail had hoped that by mentioning Juliana's name, it might have helped. She looked over to the occupied chair. 'Is there another stylist here who has availability?'

'Well, there's Barry,' replied Chelsea. 'He's just popped out for a sandwich. Let me have a look at his appointments.' She flicked through a few pages. 'Nope. Sorry. He's fully booked for the next two weeks.'

Abigail looked over again at the elderly lady. She had a feeling that Barry was the go-to stylist for the "shampoo and set" brigade and suddenly felt relieved. 'Oh well,' she said brightly. 'Never mind.' She turned to leave and made her way back towards the entrance.

However, she turned back when she heard footsteps coming down the stairs. A slim man of indeterminate age, with shoulder length blond hair, wearing black leather trousers and a purple shirt on which was a design of red poppies, had reached the bottom and was standing on the opposite side of reception. 'Chelsea, love, just popping out for a fag. Keep an eye on Lady C for me. She's being a right pain today!' The accent Abigail heard wasn't remotely French; it sounded more West Country to her. Abigail left the salon feeling that she'd had a lucky escape and decided to try and find the salon that Svetlana had recommended.

Cornham Cuts was down a side street just off the high street. Abigail went inside and made for the reception desk. The salon was busy and noisy, with the sound of hairdryers and chatting competing with music emanating from invisible speakers. Apart from a young receptionist, there was also a trainee who had just finished sweeping up some hair and was now asking a client if they wanted a drink, and three stylists. Abigail approached the reception desk and saw that the young girl was called Kirsty. 'Can I help you?' she asked.

'I hope so. My neighbour, Svetlana Johansson, recommended this salon. I'm looking for an appointment this week, if possible, with Kellyanne.'

Kirsty shook her head. 'Sorry but Kellyanne is fully booked.'

At the mention of Svetlana's name, a woman with long, jet-black hair and dressed all in black, and who was standing nearby cutting her client's hair, stopped what she was doing and spoke briefly to her client who merely nodded. The hairstylist came over to where Abigail was standing. 'Did I hear you mention Svetlana?'

Abigail smiled. 'Yes, she's my next-door neighbour and suggested I come here because I need my hair seeing to.' She grinned and pointed her finger at her head. 'The thing is it's for Saturday. Your receptionist has said you're fully booked. I realise it's a bit short notice,' said Abigail shrugging.

'Kirsty's right. I am fully booked. I'm Kellyanne, by the way. This is my salon.'

'Pleased to meet you. I'm Abigail Thomas.'

Kellyanne turned her attention to Kirsty. 'Kirsty, be a sweetie and let me have a look at my appointments.' Kirsty turned the appointments book towards Kellyanne who began to look at her appointments. She turned back to Abigail. 'Mmm, I'm chock-a-block. Svetlana is a good customer though and you've probably realised she's not one to take "no" for an answer.' She grinned and then looked at Abigail's hair. 'You have lovely thick hair, with a nice healthy bounce. I don't think I'd need to take much off. Just a tidying up of the ends and a bit of styling. There isn't enough time to put in any highlights, and that's an option for the future if you decide to brighten up the colour. If you can get here for 11:45 on Friday, I'll get Stacie to wash your hair and then I'll cut it in my lunch hour. How does that sound?'

Abigail was taken aback at how accommodating she was being. 'I can't expect you to give up your lunch hour! I'd feel awful.'

'Don't be silly. I've offered, haven't I? Anyway, me and Shirley – that's Svetlana's real name, did you know that? – go way back.' Abigail nodded. 'Well, I'm not one to gossip, but we've known each other for years. Ever since we left school together. Anyway, as I said, I'm not one to gossip. If I didn't fit you in, she'd give me some stick!' She laughed. 'Right, I must get back to my client. Get here for 11:45 on Friday, and I'll see you then. Kirsty, be a poppet and put Abigail in the appointments book.'

Kellyanne returned to her client, and Abigail left the salon feeling happy again and made her way home. After parking her car in the driveway, she went round to see if Svetlana was in. Her Mercedes SLK was in the driveway so Abigail presumed that she must be at home and rang the doorbell. Svetlana answered the door. She was dressed in a pale grey tracksuit, and matching pale grey fur slippers, and was make-up free. As Abigail had only ever seen her when she was dressed up and wearing make-up, she thought that Svetlana looked lovely in a natural way. 'Hi, Abigail,' she said brightly. 'What can I do for you?'

Abigail smiled. 'I came to tell you that I went to the salon you recommended and met Kellyanne. She has very kindly squeezed me in for an appointment on Friday.'

'Did you mention my name?'

'Yes, I did, and that's why she fitted me in. So, I thought I'd come round and thank you.'

'Well, Kellyanne and I go back a long way and I'm always sending people to her. Why the haircut all of a sudden? Are you going out somewhere?'

Abigail nodded. 'Yes, we've been invited out for dinner on Saturday evening and I thought I'd better smarten myself up.' Abigail lingered on the doorstep.

'Is there anything else?' Svetlana asked, as she could see Abigail wanted to ask something.

Abigail hesitated. 'I need a favour.' She chewed her bottom lip. 'Are you and Sven home on Saturday evening?'

'Yes, we are. No plans at all. What is it?'

'We don't have a babysitter and, for reasons I won't go into, I don't want to take the girls – not that they've even been invited. But, if we leave them on their own, can I tell them to call you if there's a problem? I wouldn't normally ask, but I haven't got round to finding a sitter because we don't go out that often.'

To her surprise, because Svetlana had never shown the slightest interest in anything pertaining to children which was why Abigail was nervous of asking her, she said, 'Yes, of course. No problem. In fact, why don't you put the girls in their PJs and bring them round to us and we'll look after them.'

Abigail's face must have registered surprise, because Svetlana laughed. 'Sven and I may not have children, but that doesn't mean we don't like them. As long as we can give them back.' She laughed again. 'One thing, though, we don't like to be too late to bed and so can you be back by 10 or 10:30 at the latest?

'Yes, perfect. That suits me, and thank you so much, Svetlana.'

'No probs. See you on Saturday.' Svetlana turned and closed the door, and Abigail returned home feeling that she was finally, albeit very slowly, becoming part of the community of Green Park Road.

CHAPTER SIXTEEN

In which Abigail found out something amazing

IT WAS WEDNESDAY and Abigail went to the care home to do her usual morning session as a volunteer and asked the manager if it was all right if she swapped her Friday morning session for Friday afternoon. She explained that she had managed to get an appointment to have her hair done, as they were going out on Saturday evening.

'Of course, Abigail,' came the reply. 'We are so lucky to have you. You're very popular with the residents.'

After her session had ended, Abigail made her way back home. The gates were open, as was the side gate into the garden, which told her that Unwin had arrived. She opened the front door and went into the kitchen and made a pot of coffee. Opening the patio door, she called out to Unwin who was busy trimming the edges of the newly mown lawn. 'Morning, Unwin!' she shouted.

Unwin turned at the sound of her voice. 'Morning, Mrs T,' as he had now begun to call her. 'How are the old folks?'

Abigail laughed. 'They're fine. Would you like a cup of coffee?'

'Well, I wouldn't say no. I'm a bit parched. I'm nearly finished here.'

Abigail went and poured two mugs of coffee, adding milk to both and two sugars for Unwin. Taking it out to him, she told him that the garden was looking good. 'A great improvement on how it was.'

Unwin grinned at the praise, revealing his neglected teeth, which had the effect of making Abigail immediately feel sorry for him. 'When you're ready to leave, knock on the door and I'll pay you.'

Unwin rubbed his hands together. 'Oh goody. I can go to the pub now.'

Whilst Abigail had been talking to Unwin, someone had put a piece of paper through the door. It was from Barney Bright with his ideas for a leaflet to advertise his window cleaning business. Abigail called the mobile number on the piece of paper. 'Barney, it's Abigail Thomas. I've got the leaflet. I'll take a look later and get back to you.'

'...'

'No problem, at all. Glad I can help.'

She wondered whether she should try and make contact with Miriam but decided against it. In any event, there was something else she wanted to do. Whilst she was genuinely happy being a wife and mother, she was aware that she did very little for herself and neglected her own needs and interests. True, she had begun to pay more attention to her appearance having bought new clothes, but she needed internal stimulus and to nourish her brain. Thus, she had decided to return to her profession as a psychotherapist and knew that she would have to undergo some retraining, with an updating of her skills. She even thought that she might train in some new aspects of therapy and decided to do some research. Logging onto the website for the British Association for Counselling and Psychotherapy, she scrolled through the various types of therapy. Having trained in cognitive behavioural therapy, Abigail thought that it was logical to find a therapy that complemented it. She had often considered training in neuro-linguistic programming which was a combination of cognitive behavioural and humanistic therapies. This appealed to her and she made a note to explore it further to find out exactly what was involved. She was also drawn to play therapy which was primarily used with children whose behaviour was deemed problematic and she felt this might be worth exploring. Her research had left her with a lot to think about but at least she had made a start and she felt positive and energised about returning to her career. Now, it was "mummy" time and she had to collect the girls from school.

*

Friday arrived. Abigail kept to her usual routine and then, at 11:30am, made her way into Cornham for her hair appointment. She parked her car and went into Cornham Cuts. She was greeted with a smile and a wave from Kellyanne who was just finishing up with a client. Kirsty put a gown around Abigail's shoulders and led her to the wash basin, where Stacie briskly washed Abigail's hair, applied conditioner which she massaged in, and then rinsed it out. She then took Abigail over to where Kellyanne was waiting.

'This really is kind of you, Kellyanne.'

'Think nothing of it. Now, I'm going to take off a couple of inches all round which will make it shorter, but you'll still have plenty of bounce left. I can see that your hair wants to fall naturally with a left parting, so I think it's best to keep that style. Very elegant and chic.'

Abigail laughed. 'In my dreams,' she said and rolled her eyes.

Kellyanne frowned. 'No, seriously, you have wonderful bone structure and very clear skin. Your hair is thick and has a natural healthy shine. It's a little bit frizzy though. What conditioner do you use?'

Abigail looked down. 'Erm, I don't.'

'Well, I told Stacie to put conditioner on today and I think you'll see the difference. Try and include that now in your routine at home. Also, you should capitalise on your looks. Just like Shirley. Oops, I meant Svetlana.' Kellyanne grinned and winked. As she began to comb Abigail's hair in preparation for the cut, she chatted away. 'I suppose she's told you her story?'

Abigail shook her head. 'Not really. We're neighbours, but don't see that much of each other. Although, she's very kindly offered to look after my two girls when we go out on Saturday evening.'

'I'm guessing you were a bit surprised by that. Am I right?'

'Yes, totally. I was quite taken aback, to be honest.'

Kellyanne nodded thoughtfully. 'Svetlana is a perfect example of "what you see is not what you get". I can tell you her story if you're interested. You'll perhaps understand her a bit better after.'

Abigail was intrigued by her statement and although she didn't like to engage in gossip, she nevertheless nodded.

'Give me a minute,' said Kellyanne and she went into the back room, coming back a few minutes later with a champagne flute which she handed to Abigail. 'Here, you drink the prosecco whilst I set about cutting your hair and I'll tell you about Svetlana.' Abigail sipped at the surprise glass of prosecco and settled down. 'Shirley, as she was then called, went to the same comprehensive school as me in Croydon. We both left school at 15. Me, because I was told there was no point staying on as I wouldn't get decent grades, which suited me as I was bored at school, and Shirley because her mum needed the money. Shirley's dad is Polish, although she doesn't know if he's still alive because he sodded off when she was very young, and that was the last she and her mother saw of him. That's where she gets her looks from. From her dad's side. Looks nothing like her mother. Also, we both lived in the same tower block in Croydon and, although we weren't friends in school, we became friends when we ended up at the same hair salon in Croydon, called Croydon Cuts, as apprentices. I enjoyed it. Still do, otherwise I wouldn't be here now doing your hair.' Kellyanne grinned. 'Shirley didn't really enjoy it. Sweeping up, making tea and coffee, and washing hair wasn't her thing. She wanted to be cutting and colouring straightaway without doing all the legwork first and had ambitions to work for a London salon and be a hairdresser to the *stars*.' Kellyanne did an inverted quote sign with her right and left index fingers. 'Me, I was happy to do all the legwork. It's part of the training, and I got to know the regulars who might in due time become clients of mine.'

She stopped what she was doing and took a step back to look at Abigail's hair. Pleased with what she saw, she continued. 'Anyway, she kept turning up late. Got the timings wrong in the appointment book which caused a few problems and was on the verge of getting the push by Christian, who owned the salon, when she had what some might say was a "lucky break".' Kellyanne pulled a face and shrugged. 'Oh, let me top up your glass.' She took the empty champagne flute from Abigail and disappeared into the back room to get a refill.

She handed Abigail another full glass and continued. 'Now, where was I? So, our salon had entered the competition for "best local hair salon", the winner of which would go on to the regional finals. The big prize was an awards ceremony at the Park Lane Hotel for the overall best salon. One stylist from the overall salon winner would then have the opportunity of further training at either Toni and Guy, Daniel Galvin or Vidal Sassoon, in either cutting or colouring. The salon would also get a year's supply of well-known branded salon products, a year's worth of free advertising and a trophy to be displayed in the window. Runners up would get a year's supply of salon products and free advertising. Oh! I'm digressing, and I need to dry your hair now and there's still so much to tell.' Kellyanne sighed and picked up a can of mousse and sprayed a small amount in the palm of her hand and spread it through Abigail's hair. She then picked up the hairdryer and began to blow dry Abigail's hair with one hand and style it with the brush in the other hand. She had left it to fall naturally because Abigail had said she preferred a natural look. In Kellyanne's skilful hands, and from the products she had used, Abigail's hair looked smooth and shiny. 'So, what do you think?'

'It's lovely. It really is. I don't recognise myself,' said Abigail smiling. 'From now on, I'll start using a conditioner.'

The salon door opened. It was Kirsty back from lunch followed by another of the stylists, both of whom went out to the back room. Kellyanne drew up a chair and spoke in a conspiratorial tone. 'The others are coming back in now, but I want to finish the story. I think you'll be amazed; shocked, even. I've got about 15 minutes left before my next client arrives. Are you okay for time?'

Abigail nodded.

'Right. I'll continue. So, on the day of the competition, we were all excited and nervous. Even me, and I was only a trainee. Two out of the three models had turned up, the make-up artists were ready, and the photographer had already been taking some background shots. Then the phone rang. It was the third model to say she was unable to come. As you can imagine, everyone was in a panic. Christian was having a meltdown and waving his arms around. One of the stylists started crying because she thought this might have been her big break.' Kellyanne rolled her eyes. 'Then, Shirley saved the day or, rather, the photographer saved the day. Even without make-up – she didn't wear make-up in those days – she was very pretty. Pale unblemished skin, blue eyes, small nose, high cheekbones and that white-blond hair of hers. Her features had caught the attention of the photographer and he had taken some photos of her which he showed to Christian and suggested that she would make an ideal model. So, it was, "Oi, Shirley, get your arse over here. You're going to be a model today. And Kellyanne, stop what you're doing and get on reception". Anyway, she was a photographer's dream as she was very photogenic. The brief was female icons of the '50s, '60s and '70s. So, because of her hair colour, the stylist knew exactly who she wanted to recreate and the make-up artist, under the direction of the stylist, transformed Shirley into Marilyn Monroe, Dusty Springfield and Debbie Harry. Unfortunately, her hair, being very straight, didn't take easily to being curled or backcombed, which made it difficult for the stylist to recreate the look of Monroe or Springfield. However, with the skills of the make-up artist her transformation was still amazing.'

Kellyanne picked up a can of hairspray, quickly sprayed Abigail's hair, then continued with the story. 'The salon didn't make it to the regional finals as the competition was fierce, but Christian had posters produced of Shirley as the three female icons and put them in the window. Also, the photographer added her photos to his portfolio which he then took to a few of the London modelling agencies and one of them saw her potential. Like Kate Moss, her face was like a blank canvas which meant she was ideal for various clients and shoots. She was also on the short side but nothing that a pair of high heels couldn't sort out. So, she started a modelling career but didn't like it.' Kellyanne rolled her eyes again. 'Typical of Shirley, thought she could straightaway become a supermodel and pick and choose who she modelled for. Didn't occur to her that she'd have to start at the bottom and claw her way to the top. She'd kept in touch with me. This is how I know all of this. The agency would send her out on "go-sees" where she'd be competing with tons of other models. She told me that the atmosphere was competitive and bitchy, and some of the more successful models acted superior and were unfriendly. She also disliked the rejections and began to lose confidence. The other thing was the parties she was expected to attend. She described them as being like "a cattle market", where wealthy older men would proposition her for sex, and where drugs and alcohol were readily available. But she needed the money to survive and support her mother who was in poor health. She realised that she wasn't cut out for the modelling world but that she had "assets" – that was her word – she could capitalise on and so she joined an escort agency that catered to VIPs and wealthy businessmen.'

Kellyanne turned to speak to a woman who had just had her hair washed and was taking a seat. 'Be with you in a minute, Mrs Webb. Just finishing up here.'

She turned her attention back to Abigail. 'Evidently the money was good, and she was in demand. She told me that she never crossed the line into being a high-class call girl and I believe her. One of her repeat clients was Sven Johansson. She liked him well enough, and he always asked for her. Then, he wanted her exclusively which the agency didn't condone and got difficult when she wasn't available. So, he made her an offer she really didn't want to refuse, and she became Mrs Svetlana Johansson because Svetlana was her escort name and they both felt it sounded better than Shirley. So, that's her story and I must now go and see to my next client. Will I see you again?'

Abigail nodded. 'You most certainly will. I'm going to make an appointment now for a cut and colour in a month's time.' Abigail stood up and went over to Kirsty to pay and make her next appointment.

Abigail was amazed at what she had been told, and still a bit conflicted about the convenience of the arrangement between Sven and Svetlana, because she had been brought up to believe that you married for love. However, fair dos, if it worked for them, good luck. Who was she to judge? As she made her way back home, she remembered that she had forgotten to ask Kellyanne how it was that she ended up in Cornham near to where Svetlana lived, and thought that she'd ask that question at her next appointment, because it couldn't be a coincidence – could it?

Abigail arrived back home, parked her car and then walked up to the care home. As she wasn't normally there in the afternoon, she was surprised and pleased to see Tammy and Trixie who were in the lounge giving two elderly ladies manicures.

'Hello, Abigail!' they said brightly. 'We don't normally see you here at this time.' Both statements were uttered in unison and Abigail marvelled at how in tune they were with each other; it was as if they were one person divided into two.

'You look lovely, doesn't she, Tammy?' said Trixie.

'Yes, she does. Have you just had your hair done?' said Tammy.

'Hi, girls. Yes, I've just been to Cornham which is why I switched shifts.'

'What's the special occasion?'

'Trixie! Don't be so rude,' said Tammy.

'What do you mean? I wasn't being… oh, I see.' Trixie laughed. 'Sorry, Abigail. I didn't mean that you only have your hair done for a special occasion,' replied Trixie looking momentarily embarrassed.

Abigail laughed. 'It's true, though. I only go to the hairdressers for a special occasion. Andrew and I have been invited out to dinner tomorrow evening and Andrew said I had to smarten myself up because the hosts are quite a glamorous couple. The wife is an ex-*Vogue* model, and the husband is a well-known figure in the City. The whole family has appeared on the front covers of magazines. So, I've bought a new dress and shoes, and had my hair done. I've even bought a new lipstick and blusher.'

The two elderly ladies were listening intently, but one of them was tapping her fingers impatiently on the table. 'Have you got somewhere to be, Elsie?' said Tammy. 'Are we holding you up?' She winked at the other lady.

'Yes, in fact, you are. There's bingo at 3 o'clock and it's a rollover this week. I'm feeling lucky.'

Tammy sighed. 'Okay, point taken. Give me a minute. I've nearly finished anyway. Do you want *Racy Red* again, like last time?' Elsie nodded. 'I can do your make-up for you as well. Free, of course. It won't take long, not with your natural good looks. I've heard Eric is doing his Elvis impersonation in the lounge later.' She winked at Trixie.

'Oh, go on then,' said Elsie. 'I'm partial to a bit of Elvis.'

'More like you're partial to a bit of Eric,' said the other elderly lady, which caused everyone to laugh.

Tammy and Trixie looked at each other, clearly engaging in a telepathic moment. Looking at Abigail, one of the twins said, 'Come round to us at five tomorrow. Bring the dress, and we'll do your make-up. Won't we, Tammy?'

Tammy clapped her hands. 'Yes! We'd love to glam you up. It'll be fun. We might even have some champagne to get you in the party mood.'

Abigail was taken aback at the generosity of the gesture. 'Are you sure?'

The twins nodded and then turned their attention back to the two elderly ladies, and Abigail went to find the resident who she usually read to on a Friday morning.

After her shift had ended, she went back home and left to pick the girls up from school, both of whom told Abigail that her hair was lovely. Even Andrew, when he finally returned home, exclaimed that it was a "great improvement" and she should go to the hair salon more often.

*

On Saturday, at 5pm, Abigail came downstairs carrying her new dress and a small make-up bag. 'I'm off now. I'll be back at six,' she shouted.

Three voices, from two different parts of the house, shouted back, 'Where are you going?'

'I'm off to see Tammy and Trixie.' She quickly opened the front door and made her way to the twins' houses before there could be any more questions.

Their gates were open and she walked up the path and rang the doorbell of the first home, as she didn't know which house the wives would be in. The door opened and Abigail was greeted with a smile by one of the wives. 'Come in, Abigail. Tammy, Abigail's here,' she said, revealing herself to be Trixie.

Tammy came out into the hallway, holding a glass of something bubbly which she handed to Abigail. 'Right, Abigail, follow us.'

Holding her dress and make-up bag in one hand and the champagne glass in the other hand, she carefully made her way upstairs. Tammy and Trixie took Abigail into a room which resembled an at-home beauty salon. A large mirror, illuminated by bright lights around the outside, was propped up on a dressing table which had an array of cosmetics and accessories arranged methodically. Make-up brushes of varying sizes and thicknesses were on one side, and sponges and cotton wool pads were on the opposite side. Eye shadow palettes, an array of eyebrow pencils, lipsticks, mascaras, and numerous other tubes and pots, were laid out in orderly rows. Abigail noticed that most of the cosmetics were by Bobbi Brown and MAC, which brought a memory back of a shopping trip with her mother many years ago when they went into Fenwick's. The go-to cosmetic counters at that time were Revlon and Coty, and Abigail remembered that her first ever perfume was Revlon's Charlie Girl.

A separate half-moon-shaped table was placed in one corner with all the implements required for manicures and pedicures, with three shelves on the wall full of pots of nail varnish of just about every colour imaginable arranged in precise lines. In the opposite corner was a small table and chair, with a mirror on the wall. A trolley stood at the side which contained scissors, brushes, curling tongs and hair straighteners. There were also pots of gel, hair putty, and cans of mousse and hairspray. Abigail was astonished. 'This is amazing!' she exclaimed. 'No wonder you two always look so well-groomed.'

'Thanks, Abigail,' said Trixie. 'Now, we have to get on as time is limited. Can you quickly get changed into your dress so that we can make a start.'

Abigail realised she hadn't brought any tights. 'I've forgotten to bring tights. Sorry!'

'No worries. Just the dress will be fine.'

Abigail took off her trainers and changed out of her jeans and jumper and put on her new dress.

'That's lovely, Abigail. Really suits your figure and colouring,' said Tammy. 'So, I'm going to do your nails and I need you to sit at the table in the corner. You said that you'd brought your own lipstick, so can I have a look to get a good match for the nail varnish?'

Abigail took the lipstick from her handbag and handed it over. Tammy took the lipstick and went over to the bottom shelf where the colours ranged from pink through to red, plum and purple. She picked out a dark plum colour, which was a shade darker than the dress and lipstick. 'This is perfect! What do you think, Trixie?' Trixie was standing at the make-up table, getting organised, and turned to give Tammy a quick thumbs up before returning to her task. 'What do you think, Abigail?'

'Erm, isn't it a bit dark? Won't it look a bit dramatic? Especially with the dark lipstick, which I'm having second thoughts about.'

Tammy laughed. 'There's nothing wrong with being dramatic, at least once in your life, Abigail!' She winked. 'Wait and see the end result. You'll be very happy, particularly once Trixie's done your make-up. We know what we're doing, don't we, Trixie?' Trixie put up her hand and gave another thumbs up. 'Right, I'm going to crack on and do the best I can in the time we have. When did you last have a manicure?'

Abigail shook her head, and looked a bit shamefaced.

'That long, eh?'

Abigail nodded.

'I'll give your cuticles some attention, give your nails a shape – square or round?'

'Round please.'

Tammy tidied up the cuticles on Abigail's left hand, shaped the nails, applied a base coat, two coats of varnish, a top coat, and finished off with a quick hand massage. 'How does that look?'

'They look great. Thank you, Tammy.'

Abigail felt truly pampered. In fact, she felt quite tearful as she'd never had such a lot of attention in her life. *Don't be ridiculous,* she told herself, and picked up her glass of champagne with her free hand. Tammy then did the same on the other hand and, 30 minutes later, she had finished. 'What do you think? Are you happy?'

Abigail looked at her nails. They were nicely shaped, her cuticles were tidy and the plum-coloured varnish matched the plum colour of her dress, even though it was a shade darker. Tammy had been right. It was perfect. 'I'm very happy. My nails have never looked so good. Thank you!'

'Right, over to Trixie now. I'll arrange a date and time with you later to come over and I'll give you a more thorough manicure and Trixie can give you a pedicure.'

Abigail went over to Trixie and sat down. First, Trixie put a cape over Abigail's shoulders and tied it at the neck, explaining that it was to protect the dress from the cosmetics. Then, she placed a fabric band over Abigail's head to keep the hair off her face. 'Don't worry. I'll make sure your hair is back in place once I've finished. I'm assuming you've CTM'd?'

Abigail looked puzzled, and then realised Trixie was asking her if she had cleansed, toned and moisturised. She hadn't, and decided to lie. In any event, it wasn't as if she was wearing any make-up. 'Yes, I have,' she replied, and hoped that she hadn't gone red in the face, as she suddenly felt hot.

Abigail realised she was in the hands of a professional make-up artist when Trixie opened up a little pot and scooped out an opaque substance, using a tiny spoon. 'First, I'm going to apply this primer as this will smooth out any open pores or wrinkles, not that I can see any, but it will enhance the foundation and help your make-up stay looking fresh.' She coated her fingers with the primer and worked it efficiently over Abigail's face, massaging it in. Next, she took a triangular-shaped sponge and squirted a light-coloured foundation onto it from a tube and applied it quickly, and then blended it in with her fingertips. 'Because we're short of time, you might have noticed that I haven't applied any concealer. That's because you're very lucky in that you don't need it, as you don't have any blemishes or dark circles.'

Abigail laughed. 'I don't even own any concealer!'

Trixie kept quiet, but Abigail noticed a slight raising of her eyebrows. She then applied a translucent setting powder with a circular sponge and, picking up a large brush, dabbed on some of the blusher Abigail had brought with her and smoothed it over Abigail's cheeks. Next, and using a smaller brush, she applied a pale pink highlighter in a sweep over Abigail's cheekbones, creating a subtle shimmer. Abigail could see that her face, indeed her whole look, was slowly being transformed into a more groomed and glamorous version of her usual self, which she considered to be on the plain side. Trixie picked up a pair of tweezers and tidied up Abigail's eyebrows before using a brow pencil to enhance their shape.

Then it was time for the eyeshadow, and Abigail could see that the shades Trixie had chosen had been carefully thought out. Trixie took a small sponge brush and dabbed it on a pale beige eyeshadow that had a slight shimmer and applied it to Abigail's brow bone.

Then, she took another small brush and dabbed that onto a plum-coloured eyeshadow which she smoothed onto Abigail's eyelids and into the crease line, which she then blended in. A small amount was added just beneath the bottom lashes, and then finished off with a sweep of black eyeliner and two coatings of black mascara. Because Abigail either usually didn't wear mascara, or only applied one coat, she was amazed at how thick and long her lashes now looked. Finally, it was the turn of her lips. She had naturally plump lips and so Trixie decided not to add lip liner. She took the lipstick that Abigail had brought with her and applied it. The make-up session was complete. The hair band was removed, Abigail's hair was given a quick brush and fortunately it fell back into its style.

Whilst Trixie had been doing Abigail's make-up, Tammy had been quiet so as not to distract her sister. Now, she clapped her hands. 'So, Abigail, what do you think? Isn't my sister great?'

Abigail was stunned at her transformation. She had never looked, nor felt, so good in her whole life. 'I think you're both great! I don't recognise myself. Honestly, I love it! Thank you both so much.'

The session had run over a bit and Abigail needed to get going. She picked up her jeans and jumper and quickly put on her trainers. 'I'm sorry, I've got to dash. Otherwise, Andrew will be pacing up and down. I can't thank you enough.'

'We're glad you're happy, Abigail,' said Tammy.

'You look stunning,' said Trixie.

They went downstairs, and Trixie handed back Abigail's cosmetic bag containing the lipstick and blusher. 'Don't forget this. Just in case you need to apply more lipstick.'

After Abigail had left, Tammy and Trixie did a high-five. 'The boys will be home soon. We'd better start dinner,' said Tammy, and they both went into the kitchen.

Abigail went across the road to her house. Francesca and Annabel were in the kitchen watching television and came into the hallway when they heard the front door shut.

'Mummy! You look beautiful,' said Francesca.

'You look like a princess!' said Annabel.

'Thank you, girls. Where's Daddy?'

'I'm here,' came a voice from the top of the stairs. Andrew came down the stairs and into the hallway.

'Daddy, you look amazing,' said Francesca.

'You don't look like Daddy,' said a solemn Annabel.

Andrew was wearing a pale grey linen suit which fitted him perfectly. He had teamed it with a dark grey shirt and black, tasselled loafers, and was sockless. 'Well, what do you think?' he asked Abigail.

Abigail thought that he, too, had undergone a transformation. 'You look... well, you look very, very smart and not like your usual style. A more fashionable version of yourself. Have you forgotten to put your socks on?'

Andrew gave Abigail a withering look and shook his head at her. 'Right, girls. Mum will drop you round next door, and I'll get the car out.'

'Daddy, haven't you forgotten something?' asked Francesca.

Andrew looked nonplussed. 'I don't think so,' he replied.

'You haven't said how beautiful Mummy looks.'

'Yes, Daddy. She looks like a princess and you could be her prince,' said Annabel.

Andrew looked at Abigail. 'Sorry, girls. Sorry, Abi. You look lovely. You really do. I've never seen you look so glamorous. Only one thing, though.'

Abigail frowned. 'What thing is that then?'

'Tights, Abigail. Have you forgotten to put on tights? Also, those trainers don't go with the dress. I hope you're putting on different shoes,' he said, smirking.

'Oh well, touché to you, I suppose.' Abigail ran upstairs to put on a pair of sheer black tights, and then came quickly down the stairs carrying her new shoes.

'Mummy, don't come down the stairs so fast. You might trip. That's what you're always telling me and Annabel.'

'Right, thank you for that, Francesca. I sometimes wonder who's the mother and who's the child in this home.' This was said with good humour, and Abigail had to admit her eldest daughter was right. She put on the new shoes and ushered her daughters out of the house and went next door.

The door was opened by Svetlana who was make-up free, and wearing sparkly jeans and a pale pink jumper that had a large silver star on the front. 'Hello, girls. Come in. Sven's in the kitchen.' The girls said goodbye to Abigail and disappeared inside. Svetlana looked Abigail up and down. 'You look great, Abigail. I didn't know you were so good with make-up.'

Abigail wasn't going to let on that Tammy and Trixie had helped her in case Svetlana told Juliana, and they would have expected the twins to attend to them. Instead she said, 'Thanks, Svetlana. I cheated a bit. I found a website which gave a step-by-step class on how to apply make-up. It was very easy to follow.'

Svetlana nodded, not entirely convinced Abigail was telling the whole truth because it looked as if it had been done by a professional make-up artist. 'Well, you'd better be going. I can see Andrew waiting for you.'

'Thank you again for having the girls. They're really excited. Any problems, just ring me.'

Svetlana smiled, which softened her features revealing an almost imperceptible mask of vulnerability. 'There won't be any problems. We've got lots of things for the girls to do. Off you go, and enjoy yourselves.' And she closed the door.

CHAPTER SEVENTEEN

In which Abigail feels out of her "comfort zone"

ANDREW AND ABIGAIL made their way to the Fortescue house. The gates were open, with the driveway lit up on either side which Andrew remarked was like an airport runway guiding aircraft in for landing at nighttime. They parked next to a dark blue Rolls Royce. As there were no other cars in the driveway, they assumed they were in the garages. Exiting the car, they walked to the door and rang the doorbell. They were greeted by Karlinka who was wearing her maid's uniform. She led them into the lounge and, although they weren't late, all the other guests were assembled.

Cassandra was there with a tall man dressed conservatively in a navy suit, white shirt and navy tie. His black lace-up shoes were highly polished and he looked as if he had just come from a meeting. His hair was cut short and had once been black, but was now showing a fair amount of grey which, together with his horn-rimmed glasses, gave his face a stern demeanour. Standing next to Cassandra was a tall, very thin woman who Abigail thought looked to be borderline anorexic. Wearing a long black dress, which covered her neck and arms, an image sprang up in Abigail's mind of a stick of liquorice causing her to stifle a giggle which earnt her a sharp, but discreet, poke in her waist from Andrew. Abigail realised she was nervous. The woman's hair was jet black, parted precisely in the middle and falling to her shoulders in a straight line. A slash of scarlet lipstick completed the Morticia Addams look. As Abigail was soon to find out, this was Felicity Barrington who had been a contemporary of Caroline Fortescue in the modelling world.

Standing next to her was a well-built man with a florid complexion, and thick silver hair swept off his forehead in a leonine style. Somewhat incongruously dressed for an elegant dinner party, he was wearing a pale pink shirt, white jeans, no socks and tan loafers with tassels. He wouldn't have looked out of place on a yacht or at a beach club. The man was introduced as Hugo Barrington, Felicity Barrington's husband. Darius, Caroline's husband, was also casually dressed in a white shirt, also unbuttoned at the neck which allowed just enough dark chest hair to show through, denim jeans, and black velvet slippers with a monogram stitched on in gold thread. Abigail noticed that he also wore no socks. However, out of all the men present, Abigail felt with some pride and affection that Andrew was the best dressed, being neither too casually dressed nor too formal.

And then there was Caroline, wearing a black velvet sleeveless dress which stopped just above the knee, accessorised with diamond jewellery that sparkled. With her natural-looking "barely there" make-up, she had an undeniable and understated elegance and poise. Then Abigail realised she was the only woman who was wearing a dress that wasn't all black. If there had been a text or email about the dress code for the women, Abigail hadn't received it. She also concluded that her one and only little black dress would have been quite acceptable.

Once the introductions were over, the group split naturally into the men in one group and the women in another. Karlinka came into the room carrying a silver tray on which were flutes of champagne. Abigail was the designated driver that evening, and so would have to limit the amount of alcohol she drank having already had a glass of champagne earlier. Not wishing to appear boring, she nevertheless took a glass of champagne as there was nothing else on offer and she wasn't feeling assertive enough to ask for a soft drink. She could see that Andrew was enjoying himself, and envied his ability to immerse himself into groups where he didn't know anyone. Abigail was a mixture of reserve and detachment, an observer rather than a participator. Also, not adept at making small talk, she didn't know what to say. Cassandra, Caroline and Felicity were talking about school matters, and generally gossiping about some of the parents whom Abigail didn't know. Picking up on Abigail's quietness, Cassandra made an effort to draw her into the conversation by turning the discussion to plans for the Christmas fayre. Then, Karlinka entered carrying a brass dinner gong and striker, both of which looked to be antique, and announced that dinner was ready.

Karlinka led the way from the living room, across the spacious hallway and into the dining room, where they were met with such a show of opulence and conspicuous wealth that the invisible mouse on Abigail's shoulder gave a small squeak. It had already squeaked when Abigail took the flute of champagne off the tray, because Andrew had whispered to her to be careful because the glassware looked very much like Baccarat crystal and hence very expensive. Coming from the understated chic living room with its delicately patterned beige and cream silk wallpaper, cream silk curtains, pale wood furniture and cream velvet settees and chairs which Abigail thought probably reflected Caroline's sophisticated personality and taste, she was unprepared for the dramatic impact of the dining room. No doubt the others present tonight had seen it before, but for Abigail

– and also Andrew, she suspected, who had *loved* the design aesthetic of the living room – the appearance of black walls with unframed abstract expressionist paintings, black dining table edged in gold, and matching chairs covered in black velvet, was all a bit over the top for her. As she drew closer to the table, she noticed that the chairs had the same monogram on the back as the gold monogram on Darius' slippers.

There was a seating plan which placed Caroline and Darius as the heads of the table at opposite ends. Andrew was seated opposite Abigail, and between Caroline and Felicity. Abigail was seated next to Hugo Barrington, who was placed opposite his wife. Ingram and Cassandra were seated opposite on either side of Darius. No one had sat down yet and were standing and chatting, so Abigail took the opportunity to go and look at the paintings because she recognised the artwork and, apart from seeing works by the same artists in Tate Modern in London, she had never seen original paintings by Mark Rothko and Clyfford Still in someone's house and, once again, was reminded that she was in the presence of serious wealth.

Caroline and Darius made their way to their seats and everyone followed suit. Chairs were pulled out and the guests sat down and began making small talk. Abigail looked at the matching dinner service, the gleaming cutlery, and the glassware which glimmered and sparkled as the light from the large crystal chandelier glinted on the various sizes of glassware. Her attention was also drawn to the side plates which had a heavily decorated border in the colours of gold, red and black, with an image in the centre of the plate which was of a female head with what looked like writhing snakes in place of hair. Each red place mat had a black linen serviette placed on top. The colour scheme reminded Abigail of something but she couldn't exactly put her finger on what it was. Next came the cutlery placed either side of the placemat in a long row. *You work from the outside in,* Abigail told herself when she was confronted with so much cutlery. Black-stemmed glassware and cut-glass tumblers were clustered together to the right of the red placemats, thus completing the highly distinctive design of the dinner table.

In Abigail's opinion, it spoke of too much money and very little taste. She realised she was being judgmental, but the dining room was in complete contrast to the elegant and refined living room and she concluded that this was Darius' taste rather than Caroline's. There was also something else niggling away at her which was to do with the image on the side plates. So, seeing that everyone was making conversation with those they were sat next to, apart from herself who was sitting there quietly, she lifted up the side plate and took what she hoped was a discreet peek at the bottom of the plate. The name of a very famous fashion designer was printed on the plate and she then realised that the female head was that of Medusa, which was a trademark motif of the designer. She then realised that the monogram on the chair backs and Darius' slippers were those of the same designer.

Everyone stopped talking at the sound of Karlinka wheeling in a trolley containing dishes for the first course. Following behind was a smartly dressed man in a black suit, white shirt and black tie, also wheeling in a trolley on which sat two buckets of ice in which were two bottles of champagne, and a large jug of water. It was obvious to Abigail that the food and accompanying wines that evening were going to be equivalent to a fine-dining experience in a Michelin star restaurant. Everything was finely tuned to impress, astonish and showcase the wealth and prestige of the Fortescue family. Squeak went the mouse on Abigail's shoulder, and she wished she could go and hide in the skirting board, except there wasn't one.

Karlinka began serving the first course which consisted of oysters served in their shells, placed on a pile of crushed ice in the centre of a small red plate. At the farthest left of the row of cutlery was a small silver fork to prise the oysters from their shells. The smartly-dressed man followed Karlinka around the table and expertly poured Bollinger champagne into each guest's champagne flute.

'Thanks, Charlie. Has Karlinka fed you yet?' asked Hugo.

'Yes, sir. She has. Thank you,' replied the man.

Hugo turned to Abigail. 'Charlie's our driver,' he said by way of an explanation, 'so that we don't have to worry about drinking and driving.' He took a big gulp of the champagne and raised his glass. 'Cheers, everyone. And thank you to our wonderful hosts for what will no doubt be a first class dinner and fun evening.'

Everyone followed suit and raised their glasses, then proceeded to grapple with getting the oysters out of their shells.

Karlinka came in and cleared away the plates, returning very quickly with the trolley which this time was carrying bowls of what turned out to be a delicately flavoured tomato and fennel soup, served with a selection of seeded bread rolls and small pats of butter. The accompanying wine was a chilled Sancerre, and when Charlie went to pour some in Abigail's wine glass, she caught Andrew looking at her. This was his way of reminding her that she was driving, and so she put her hand over the glass and asked for some water instead.

In-between taking mouthfuls of soup and eating bread, people were chatting. Abigail could pick up the odd word of Darius' and Ingram's conversation which seemed to be about matters pertaining to tax and global finance, and then the conversation appeared to turn to art when Abigail heard Ingram comment on the paintings.

'Haven't got a clue, Ingram,' was Darius' reply. 'Don't understand this modern stuff, but the art consultant at Sotheby's said they would be a good investment, so who am I to argue.' He shrugged his shoulders.

Andrew was saying something to Felicity and Caroline which was making them smile, and to Abigail it seemed as if the smiles were a touch too much on the polite side and not sincere. To her right, Hugo was talking to Cassandra about boarding schools, which left Abigail twiddling her thumbs as she was the only one to have finished the second course.

Without being summoned, Karlinka seemed to instinctively know when the second course was finished and she came in unobtrusively and took the empty bowls away. Then it was back with the trolley and the main course consisting of a large joint of roast beef, dishes of mixed vegetables and roast potatoes, and two large jugs of gravy. The vegetables and gravy were placed down the centre of the table for the guests to help themselves. Charlie was carving slices of rare roast beef, which Karlinka then put onto the large dinner plates, which had the identical design as the side plates, and served them to the guests. When it came to the wine, a large decanter of red wine had been placed on a small side table near to where Darius was sitting. Getting up, he went over and picked up the decanter. 'This wine, my friends, is a 1945 Chateau Mouton Rothschild, which was given to me as a gift from a grateful client when I made him a ton of money. I hope you enjoy and savour the intense bouquet and masculine top notes of leather, wood, and cigar. To fully appreciate this rare wine, let the silky and velvety richness roll around on your palate before you swallow.'

Before he could go on, he was interrupted by Caroline. 'For heaven's sake, Darius, the food is getting cold and Karlinka has gone to a lot of effort. Just pour the wine so that we can eat.'

Darius rolled his eyes and made his way around the table pouring the wine into the large wine glasses. When he came to Abigail, she could sense Andrew looking at her and deliberately ignored him, gesturing to Darius that she would like some but only a small amount. 'Because I'm driving,' she added by way of explanation, and then realised how dull and boring this made her sound. She noticed that both Ingram and Cassandra were partaking of all the wines on offer.

Cassandra must have seen her looking and said, 'You and Andrew should have organised a taxi, like myself and Ingram, and then you could have relaxed and enjoyed yourself.'

That explains it, thought Abigail, wishing she was back with her former group of unpretentious friends, and took a sip of the wine. Preferring to drink a nice dry white wine, although she had declined the Sancerre, she understood wine etiquette sufficiently to know that red wine accompanied red meat. This outrageously expensive red was not to her taste at all. She found it too full-bodied and knew that a headache would follow at some point, and so took only small sips so as not to seem completely unappreciative. Andrew, on the other hand, having been to many wine tastings in London, was sticking his nose into the glass and breathing deeply before making a noisy slurp as he no doubt had witnessed at such tastings. *Silly prat*, Abigail thought somewhat uncharitably and then caught Hugo looking at her.

'Tell me, Abigail, are you gainfully employed, or are you like these three here,' – he gestured at Caroline, Cassandra and his wife – 'who spend their days playing tennis, having coffee mornings which then turn into long lunches?'

Abigail didn't quite know how to reply because, in truth, she didn't work, but she did go to the occasional coffee morning but they never developed into long lunches. So, her response was along the lines of, 'Occasionally I go out for a coffee and lunch, but I'm thinking of returning to work as soon as I've retrained in a couple of things.' She caught Andrew looking at her with a look of query on his face, as she hadn't yet told him of her plans.

'And what is it you do, if you don't mind me asking?' continued Hugo.

'No, I don't mind you asking at all. Before moving into the area, I had my own practice as a psychotherapist but took a break to get the girls settled into their new school. Now that the girls have made friends and appear happy, I've decided to return for a few hours a week but need to learn some new skills and retrain in a couple areas.'

Hugo grinned and looked at his wife. 'Did you hear that, Fliss? Abigail here is a psychotherapist. Perhaps you should book a session with her to discuss your addiction to buying shoes and handbags.' He laughed loudly and took a large gulp of the wine.

'And perhaps you need to see Abigail to discuss your addiction to *Babestation*,' was his wife's rapid response, causing Hugo to splutter out the wine. All chatter ceased as all eyes turned to Hugo, who was now dabbing the front of his shirt with water and looking shiftily around the table.

Darius was clearly amused as he laughed out loud. 'Hugo! I didn't know you knew about such things!' This resulted in a glare from Caroline.

Ingram reddened slightly as he remembered his recent exploration of the Asian *Babestation* channel and bent his head to avoid Cassandra's interrogative gaze. Only Andrew looked puzzled, which made Abigail feel a sudden affection for him as he was obviously unaware of what Hugo's wife was referring to. The only reason Abigail knew, was because she had seen a reference to the website when researching the cards she had found in Andrew's jacket pocket after his initiation ceremony.

After a brief moment of silence, the chatter ensued again. The main course was cleared away, then cheese and biscuits were brought out, followed by a selection of desserts accompanied by a sweet white wine. Abigail was feeling very full and a bit queasy. The talk was getting louder and when Darius suggested they should now depart to the orangery for some after-dinner port and brandy, and then the cinema room to watch a film – which was said with a wink – Abigail took her chance and signalled to Andrew, by tapping her watch, that it was time to go and stood up. Explaining that they had a babysitter, who had a time limit, they said their thank yous and goodbyes and left.

Once in the car, Abigail let out a loud sigh of relief and started the ignition. Andrew, who had drunk too much, wasn't happy. 'You're such a spoilsport, Abigail. I was enjoying myself. Why did we have to leave so early? I wonder what the film would have been. Do you think it might have been a "you-know-what" kind of film?'

'I haven't the foggiest idea of what you're going on about, Andrew. You've had too much to drink and I suggest you drink a large glass of water before you go to bed.'

'You're so boring, Abigail.'

'Yes, I know I am. But if you remember, Sven and Svetlana were happy to look after the girls as long as we were back by 10-ish. We're already going to be a bit late. Also, I was getting bored, and the food was a bit too much of a mixture for me. In fact, I feel a bit sick.'

The rest of the journey continued in silence. They arrived home. Andrew went inside, and Abigail went next door to get the girls. She rang the bell, which was answered by Sven and Svetlana.

'Sorry we're a bit late. Were these two well behaved?' she asked, looking at Annabel and Francesca, who were grinning.

'They were brilliant. We've had a nice evening, haven't we?' said Sven.

Both girls nodded. 'We played games, Mummy, and we watched *Finding Nemo*,' said Francesca.

'And we had ice cream in the living room,' added Annabel.

'Oh! I hope they didn't drop any?' asked Abigail.

'No, not at all. If they had, we would have wiped it up. No problem,' replied Sven.

'Well, thank you once again. Goodnight.'

Sven and Svetlana closed the door, and Abigail and the girls returned home, with the girls immediately going upstairs to bed. Abigail could see a light on in Andrew's study, and guessed what he was up to. First, though, she went into the kitchen and took a large tumbler from the kitchen cupboard and poured iced water from the dispenser. She went back into the hallway and opened the study door. 'Oh no you don't, Andrew Thomas. Don't even think about looking up *Babestation*. Here's the water by the way. Drink it before you go to bed.'

Andrew at least had the decency to look sheepish as he closed the lid on his laptop, just like a naughty child caught out doing something he shouldn't. 'You're just like my mother,' he said, and he trudged upstairs taking large gulps of water. Abigail followed on behind with a smile on her face.

Lying in bed, and on the verge of falling asleep, Abigail suddenly remembered what the red placemats and black napkins reminded her of. It was the Japanese card for the *shibari* club.

CHAPTER EIGHTEEN

In which Abigail finds herself amused

ABIGAIL COULD NOT believe that it was already November, but the central heating now coming on first thing in the morning confirmed this. The pool had been covered over and, after the initial excitement, the novelty had worn off because they'd all found it too cold to swim in. Andrew was being pressured to heat it but was being resistant due to the cost. Unwin had finished a few weeks ago after all the autumn leaves had fallen, and he had used a leaf blower to sweep them all up. They had said their goodbyes, and Abigail said if he was interested in continuing to do their garden, he'd be welcome back in the spring and she'd leave it up to him to get in touch. Unwin had nodded, and smiled. 'God willing, Mrs T. See you next year then.'

It then occurred to Abigail that he might miss the money and felt guilty. 'What will you do about money, Unwin?' she asked.

'Oh don't you worry about me. I start at Aldi next week. Just a few hours a week to tide me over.' He had purchased a bike and put on his trouser clips and helmet, and wheeled the bike out of the driveway, waving as he went.

Abigail felt that she had achieved a lot in a short space of time, and that her life was finally taking shape. They would be spending Christmas at home, just the four of them, and she was looking forward to it. No long drives to Devon to see her parents, or Anglesey to see Andrew's parents. At some point she would have to begin her Christmas list. However, her focus at the moment was on the school Christmas fayre which she had allowed herself to be roped into helping with.

It was Monday, the second week of the month, which meant that the meeting was on Wednesday, and this time at Britt Mikkelson's house. Abigail had already informed the manager of the care home that she would need to do her voluntary shift in the afternoon instead of the morning. So, after dropping the girls off at school, she made her way home. She had very little planned for the day and, after pouring herself a coffee and eating a bowl of muesli, she began to read through the literature she had received from the British Association for Counselling and Psychotherapy, and then made a start of working through some of the online questionnaires in preparation for her return to the profession.

The time flew by and she had to collect Annabel and Francesca. As Andrew was going to be late again, they decided to eat in the kitchen. Over dinner, Abigail told them she was going to Britt Mikkelson's house on Wednesday and asked Annabel what Birgitta and Brigitta were like, as they were both in Annabel's class. Annabel had thought carefully before answering. 'They're okay. A bit silly, I suppose. They're always whispering to each other in class, and sometimes they speak Swedish, so you never know what they're saying. The thing is, they're identical twins and they think it's funny to play tricks on the teachers by pretending to be each other.' Annabel screwed up her nose. 'I don't dislike them, but they're a bit odd.' With this, Annabel shrugged her shoulders and carried on eating.

Wednesday came round quickly. Abigail said goodbye to the girls, and put the postcode that Cassandra had given her into the satnav. The directions took her out of

Knighton and into the countryside. Cassandra had told her a bit about Britt and her family. She was from Sweden and had come over to England to work as a stable girl. At some point, she had met and married Magnus who was older than her, and came from a wealthy Danish family, but had made his home in England. No one knew exactly what he did, except that he consulted for well known auction houses specialising in antiques and fine art. She had added, somewhat conspiratorially, that they were "old money" unlike the Fortescues who were "new money", with the unspoken inference that the Fortescues were *nouveau riche*. It crossed Abigail's mind that perhaps this was the reason the Mikkelsons hadn't been invited to the Fortescue dinner party. Cassandra also told her that they lived in the middle of nowhere and that the house was impressive.

Thus, Abigail found herself driving down narrow country lanes with only a handful of passing places. Fortunately, there weren't many other cars, only a couple of slow-moving tractors. However, she knew that she was going to be late because the satnav had taken her down some "no through roads" and she'd had to turn back. Very soon, she was instructed to make a left turn in 100 yards, and then at 50 yards she had to take a sharp left down an unmarked single-track road with tufts of grass growing down the centre. Eventually, she came across a double gate bearing a sign which said *Mikkelson Estate and Equestrian Centre. PLEASE DRIVE CAREFULLY. Dogs and Horses.* The gate was closed, so Abigail switched off the ignition and exited the car. There was a green button on the gate post which she pressed. The gates opened slowly and Abigail got back in her car and drove carefully down a grass track which had fields on either side, and horses grazing in both of them. The track became wider and ended in a courtyard, on which sat a beautiful house with a distinctive design. To the right of the house, and in the near distance, she could see a barn and a stable block. Two dogs, an Alsatian and Golden Labrador, came running towards her car, barking, but were called back sharply by someone out of sight. Cassandra's white BMW pulled into the courtyard, followed by a silver Mercedes driven by Caroline. Abigail got out of her car and went to join them. As she drew close to the house, she noticed a blue plaque on the wall dedicated to "Sir Edward Lutyens. English Architect and contributor to the Arts and Crafts Movement". *Ah*, thought Abigail, *that explains the distinctive architecture.*

Cassandra rang the doorbell but there was no answer and so the three women stood in silence. Caroline began tapping her foot impatiently. 'She's always bloody late!'

Then, in the distance from the direction of the lane, a fast, thumping noise could be heard and then a chestnut-coloured horse came galloping into view. The rider was wearing full riding gear: black jacket, black riding hat, beige jodhpurs and black riding boots. It was Britt Mikkelson. She gave the reins a tug and the horse came to a halt. 'Good boy, Naughty Boy,' she said, patting the side of the horse's neck before executing a balletic flying dismount in the manner of Frankie Dettori. Holding onto the reins, she gave Naughty Boy another pat and then whistled. The Alsatian and Labrador came rushing out to greet her, their tails wagging. 'Good boy, Cameron. Good boy, Osborne.' She bent down and patted them both on the head, and shouted to someone in the yard. 'Pepe, llama a los perros, por favor.'

A loud whistle summoned the dogs back to the yard, and then a slim, wiry man came walking towards them. He was olive-skinned, had short black hair, and was neither young nor old. He was wearing a check shirt, jeans and trainers, and grinned revealing white teeth.

'Pepe, toma a Naughty Boy, dale un poco de agua y dale de comer, luego ponto en su puesto para des cansar.'

'Si, Señora Britt.'

'Gracias, Pepe.'

Pepe took the reins and led Naughty Boy away.

'Your Spanish is coming along nicely, Britt,' remarked Cassandra.

'Yes it is, isn't it! I've been having private lessons seeing as Pepe's command of English isn't very good. So, he's teaching me Spanish and I'm teaching him English.'

A look passed between Cassandra and Caroline, with the hint of a smile.

Abigail was getting impatient. They hadn't even gone inside the house yet and it had already gone past 10am. This meant she would be late getting back and so she coughed, which caught Cassandra's attention, and Abigail tapped her watch. 'Right, let's get cracking with this meeting. Britt, can we make a start please?'

Britt led them into the house. Despite the architectural grandeur of the exterior of the house, Abigail was surprised that the interior didn't match up. The hallway was laid with grey flagstones which looked to be original from the signs of much use. Padded jackets, wax jackets, and riding jackets were hanging from hooks in the wall. On a lower shelf sat riding hats, and then on the floor were riding boots, wellingtons, and trainers. Against the right-hand wall, was an old carved oak settle which had a crest in the centre of the backrest. Cassandra caught Abigail looking at it and whispered, 'That's the Mikkelson family crest. "Old money" unlike you-know-who.' She pointed in the direction of Caroline who was following Britt into the kitchen.

The kitchen was large and typical of a farmhouse kitchen which served as the hub of the family for mealtimes. A dark green range cooker with four ovens provided heat and, from its well-worn appearance, looked to be used a lot. This made Abigail think of her Aga which was still in pristine condition, even though she was now cooking with it. Dark-red floor tiles, again well used, together with a long rectangular-shaped oak kitchen table, and high back carved chairs, created a kitchen that had a certain rustic grandeur. Again, Abigail couldn't resist comparing it to her shiny ultramodern kitchen, and admitted to herself that she preferred the kitchen she was standing in.

Unlike Caroline, Britt didn't employ a housekeeper and so quickly made two pots of coffee which she put on the table with milk and sugar. Opening up a cupboard, she took out four mugs which had images of horse heads on both sides of the mug. She then opened another cupboard and took out a packet of chocolate digestive biscuits. Her actions were brisk, efficient, and unfussy. Her blond hair was cut short, she wore no make-up and was still wearing her riding clothes. Furthermore, even though she lived in a house of historical importance, and ran an equestrian centre, she was unpretentious and down to earth. Abigail liked her for this and, for once, felt at ease.

Cassandra started with Abigail first, and asked her how she was getting on with organising the toy and book stall. Abigail was able to report back that she'd had a good response so far and expected more donations over the next few weeks. She also advised that she would begin collecting some of the smaller items which she would store in her garage, and asked if Cassandra could talk to the headteacher about some of the larger items being stored in the school over the coming weeks, with drop-offs preferably during weekends. Cassandra said she would ask, and didn't think it would be a problem, but that Abigail would need to coordinate with the parents. Cassandra then mentioned that Abigail seemed to be doing a lot of the work, and that was why they had "helpers" to do some of the more onerous tasks. Abigail explained that Miriam McTavish had said she would help setting up the stall on Friday evening, and help with the running of it on Saturday. However, as she worked shifts at Knighton Hospital, and then had to look after Bunty when Hamish was at work, she wasn't available to do collections and there wasn't enough room to store things in their garage. So, Abigail asked Cassandra if she could have another helper. Cassandra replied that she had already sounded out Mavis Brown because, 'Desdemona is very fond of Katy, and so I thought I'd involve Mavis to make her feel a part of school life. Can you liaise with her please, Abigail?'

Next, Cassandra turned her attention to Caroline. 'How's it going with Kylie Monaghan? Any moans this time?'

Caroline shook her head. 'She's on board and I've given her a list of things to do. But you know what she's like. When her and Kelly get together, that's when we have a problem. They think they should be part of the committee and not relegated to "helper" status. Look, I was thinking, perhaps a sweetener would help. Seeing as Kayleigh is in Eustacia's class, any chance you could invite her back after class one day? Also, what about getting Desdemona to ask Shaznay Lewis back?'

Cassandra grimaced. 'Well, if it helps, I suppose so. I'll have to bribe both of mine though. Now, what about the raffle prizes? Have you managed to get any?'

Caroline beamed. 'I thought you'd never ask! I think you'll be happy. I've wangled a gift voucher for a spa day at Urban Retreat. Since the double page spread in *House and Garden*, it's become the go-to place. Of course, they were very accommodating because I've always been a good customer of theirs. I've also arranged for a photographic shoot at Models One in London. I do think, Cassandra, that these prizes should be the top raffle prizes, don't you?'

Cassandra nodded and thanked her for her efforts. Just as she was about to ask Britt what she had to report back, there was a knock at the door and Pepe came in looking anxious. 'Señora Britt. Is problem with Big Boy. Is limp.'

Britt frowned. 'Is lame, Pepe. Is that what you mean?'

'Si. Lame.' Pepe walked across the kitchen floor with a pronounced limp. 'Lo siento, madame.'

'Okay, Pepe. Tranquile. Use Toy Boy.' Pepe nodded and left. Britt uttered an expletive and abruptly stood up. 'Sorry, ladies. I need to phone the vet *toute suite*. Was going to ride Big Boy at Hickstead on Saturday. Now, we'll have to get Toy Boy up to speed.' With that, she walked quickly out of the kitchen mumbling under her breath.

Cassandra sighed. Abigail was thinking what a waste of time all of this was and that she could be at the care home doing something really useful.

Caroline reached into her handbag and brought out a small bottle of perfume which she sprayed on her wrists and then a quick squirt in the air. The scent was slightly overpowering.

Cassandra sniffed the air. 'What are you doing?'

'I'm putting on perfume,' replied Caroline.

'Why?'

'Because it smells of horses in here. Don't you think Britt smells of horses?' She looked at Cassandra and Abigail when she said this.

'Well, yes, a bit. But she's around horses all day so she's bound to smell of them,' replied Cassandra.

Caroline turned to Abigail. 'You're very quiet, Abigail. Don't you think Britt smells of horses?'

Abigail didn't want to be drawn into this conversation, but actually did think there was a pervasive horsey smell. She shrugged. 'Yes, a bit.'

'Well, I don't like the smell very much.' Caroline folded her arms, wrinkled her nose and shuddered.

'It's very strong perfume, Caroline. What is it?' asked Cassandra.

'Tom Ford. Black Orchid. My favourite.' She put the perfume back in her handbag. 'Now, about my raffle prizes being joint first and second…'

Before Cassandra could respond, Britt came back into the kitchen. 'What's that smell?' she asked, sniffing the air.

'Black Orchid,' replied Caroline.

Britt grimaced. 'Mmm, bit strong. I prefer something more spicy and earthy.'

Cassandra stifled a chuckle behind a cough, whilst Abigail lowered her head so that Britt couldn't see her grinning. Only Caroline remained straight-faced.

Time was running out and so Cassandra asked Britt how Kelly Lewis was coming along. Britt confirmed that everything was proceeding nicely, and that Shaznay was helping, which drew a smirk from Caroline. Abigail began to sense that there was some possible rivalry between the two women which might be another reason why the Mikkelsons weren't invited to the Fortescue dinner party. Matters deteriorated further when Britt announced that, for the raffle, she had secured two rather wonderful prizes which should probably be joint first prize. The first was entry to *Glorious Goodwood* for two people, with reserved seating in the Members' section which overlooked the racecourse, plus a table for two in the Double Trigger restaurant. The second prize was for entry for two people in the Royal Enclosure at Royal Ascot. Cassandra could see that she was now presented with a difficult decision, and would need to tread very carefully as she was dealing with two alpha females and couldn't risk alienating either of them when it was getting so close to the Christmas fayre. So, she decided to call the meeting to a close. 'Okay, well that's about it, then. Thank you, ladies for all your efforts so far. Next meeting is in December to finalise everything before the big day. Are you okay with hosting, Abigail?'

Abigail nodded, but not enthusiastically.

'Oh, before we all go, I've decided that we should invite the helpers. Is that okay with you, Abigail? It does mean that there will be eight of us.'

Abigail again nodded, thinking that she had just been taken advantage of. They all said their goodbyes and went their separate ways.

*

It was evening time, and four households were having dinner. In Cassandra's house, there were just her and the girls as Ingram had returned to Singapore. When Cassandra called her youngest daughter "darling", Desdemona knew she was about to be coerced into something.

'Desdemona, darling,' said Cassandra sweetly.

'Yes, Mama?'

'A little bird told me that Katy Brown looks to you for guidance and inspiration, and I thought it would be nice if you invited her for tea one day next week. Also, Shaznay Lewis.'

Desdemona was puzzled, because she had hardly spoken to Katy who spent most of her time with Bunty

McTavish and Amy Murphy. She was even more puzzled by the request that she invite Shaznay back, as they had nothing remotely in common. 'Do I have to?' she asked. 'I don't mind Katy, I suppose, but Shaznay?', and she grimaced.

Cassandra smiled affectionately at her daughter. 'I always have your best interests at heart, Desdemona. I thought it was about time that you mixed with those class members who are of a different social class. When you go out into the wide world...'. She was stopped mid-sentence by her daughter, who knew when one of her mother's long winded lectures were about to take place.

'Okay, mother. I'll do it. Just this once though.'

Cassandra noticed that Desdemona was becoming more like Eustacia, in that she was proving less pliable these days. She would need to change tactics. Smiling sweetly, she thanked Desdemona for being so helpful and asked her to invite them back on Tuesday, and to be collected by 7pm. She then turned her attention to Eustacia and smiled sweetly. 'Eustacia, dear...'

'Whatever it is, Mother, the answer is no.'

'Don't be like that, Eustacia. Try to be a bit more accommodating like your sister. I wouldn't ask if it wasn't important.'

Eustacia sighed. 'Okay, what is it?'

'When you see Kayleigh tomorrow, ask her back on Tuesday as well.'

'Do I have to? We're not even in the same friendship group. It will seem a bit odd. Her and her friends are a bit *meh*.'

'What on earth do you mean? What's *meh* mean?

'It means they're boring and ordinary.'

'Well, just this once. As a favour to me. Pretty please,' said Cassandra, grinning.

Eustacia sighed again and shrugged her shoulders. 'Okay, no worries.'

Not for the first time, Cassandra wondered what kind of English they were teaching the girls at school these days.

In the Thomas household, all four were sat down to dinner as Andrew had come home early for once. Abigail was doing a bit of research. 'Andrew, if you had to choose between a raffle prize for a day at the races at Ascot or Goodwood, or a photoshoot at a modelling studio or a spa day, which would you choose?'

Andrew looked at Abigail as if she was mad. 'What are you on about? What sort of question is that?'

'Please, Andrew. Just answer the question. I'll tell you afterwards.'

Without hesitation, Andrew answered horse racing.

'What about you two? Annabel?'

Annabel didn't need to think and chose the photoshoot.

'Francesca?' asked Abigail.

'Photoshoot,' came the reply. Abigail sighed. It was as she expected.

Andrew turned to Abigail. 'Your turn now. What would you choose?'

Without hesitation, Abigail grinned and chose the spa day to which the girls changed their choice to spa day.

Andrew wasn't happy. 'Oh, thank you very much!' he said grumpily.

Abigail then explained why she had asked. With Andrew now sulking, and the girls realising that it was only a question and not something that might actually happen, the meal continued in total silence.

The Fortescue household was silent. Darius was out doing whatever Darius did when he was out, and

Sapphire was in her room doing whatever she got up to when left alone. Caroline, on the other hand, was plotting and planning. She was plotting to knock Britt off the number one spot for raffle prizes and for this she needed to upgrade her own. She planned to drive to New Milton in Hampshire and visit a well-known luxury hotel and spa, and blag a spa weekend for two people using her contacts in the modelling world and Darius' connections in the City. The hotel also had a cookery school headed up by a well-known chef and she decided to get a full day's cooking experience as a back-up prize. She was determined to succeed, even if it meant paying for the spa and cooking experience herself as a last resort. Feeling less stressed and more relaxed having made the decision, she poured herself a flute of champagne and sat back, relishing the peace and quiet before Darius came home inebriated, full of himself and demanding attention.

In the Mikkelson house, dinner was going very well until one of the twins asked, 'Mamma, du har halmi håret?'

Britt patted her hair on both sides and pulled a strand of straw from the left side just above her ear.

'Thank you, Birgitta. I've been mucking out today in the stable.'

'Har du bråkat med Pepe?' asked Brigitta, and both girls giggled.

Britt glared at the twins, and gestured with her eyes towards their father. 'What have I told you both about speaking Swedish in front of your father? It's very rude of you.'

Magnus, who was browsing through *Antiques Weekly* whilst eating, looked up at his two pretty blond-haired, blue-eyed daughters, which made them giggle again.

'Can we be excused, please?' they both asked.

Magnus said yes and told them to run along. Britt sighed, 'Don't you sometimes wish that we'd had boys, Magnus? So much easier.'

Magnus, who was very easy-going, replied that they were at that silly age and they would grow out of it. He looked at his lovely wife, of which Birgitta and Brigitta were carbon copies, and reached across her back and removed a piece of straw from the back of her head and laid it on the table. Then, he went back to his meal and *Antiques Weekly*. Britt blushed, remembering the "mucking out" session in the stables and smiled.

CHAPTER NINETEEN

In which Abigail is let down

DECEMBER HAD ARRIVED too quickly and already it was Abigail's turn to host the last meeting before the Christmas fayre took place on Saturday. She had not had to swap her session at the care home, as it was the home's annual Christmas party from 2-4pm. Francesca had surprised her by saying that she and Annabel would get the train home so that Abigail didn't have to leave the party early.

'Are you sure?' Abigail had asked. 'You've never caught the train before.'

Francesca replied that they were excited about getting the train as it would make them feel grown up, and part of the group of girls who walked to the station together after school.

On the one hand, Abigail was pleased because she was looking forward to the party. On the other hand, she felt a bit sad because it made her realise that her daughters were already showing signs of independence and it wouldn't be too long before they didn't need her so much.

Because she was hosting the meeting, she decided to dress a bit smarter as Caroline and Cassandra were always smartly-dressed. So, she swapped her jeans and jumper for a pair of navy trousers, pink jumper and black patent pumps. Adding a touch of make-up, and pearl earrings, she felt very presentable. She needn't have bothered though. Cassandra had messaged her just before 10am to say she couldn't make it because Ingram's flight into Heathrow was arriving early. Caroline messaged to say that she was sorry but she had to go to Apollonia's school to see the headteacher to sort out yet another infringement of the school's rules. At least Britt had the decency to phone and explain she couldn't come to the meeting because the vet was on his way to de-worm Toy Boy.

When the doorbell rang at 10am, she was greeted by two women she didn't recognise who were both wearing jeans and jumpers, and trainers. They introduced themselves as Kelly Lewis and Kylie Monaghan. Miriam turned up in her nurse's uniform, explaining that she had to head straight to the hospital for her shift after the meeting. Abigail recognised the woman standing behind her as Mavis Brown who was aptly dressed for her name as she was wearing all brown. Thus, Abigail felt overdressed and slightly awkward. She led the four women into the kitchen, where she was aware they were all taken aback by the house she lived in. She knew they would be forming opinions and making judgments about her. She poured coffee into mugs, added milk and sugar for those who wanted it, and put some Millie's cookies on a plate. Whilst Kelly, Miriam, Mavis and Abigail went and sat at the table, Kylie Monaghan walked over to the bi-folding doors and looked out at the garden.

'You've got bi-folding doors. I've always wanted them. And you've got a swimming pool! Must cost a fortune to heat and maintain.'

'It isn't heated and it's very easy to maintain,' explained Abigail.

'Mmm. Very nice indeed to have one, though.' Kylie came and joined the others at the table and helped herself to a mug of coffee.

'How many bedrooms?' was the next question.

'Four.'

'Bathrooms?'

'Two and a downstairs loo.'

'Mmm.'

'Don't be so nosy, Kylie,' said Kelly. 'You have a lovely home, Abigail.'

Abigail thanked her and was about to start the meeting when Kelly asked, 'So, where's the triumvirate then?'

'Bloody hell, Kell,' said Kylie. 'You swallowed a dictionary, or what?'

Kelly laughed. 'I've been doing an OU course to stimulate my mind. I've chosen to study classical civilisation and I'm currently on the module dealing with leaders of the Roman Empire. This week it's Julius Caesar and his two generals.' She took a sip of her coffee, and bit into one of the cookies. 'Mmm, very nice,' she said, aiming for a nonchalant tone.

'I don't understand,' continued Kylie. 'What's this "trium" thing?'

Kelly sighed. 'Because it means three people, duh! Cassandra, Caroline and Britt, all of whom aren't here.' Kylie still looked puzzled. Kelly sighed again. 'Cassandra is Julius Caesar, and Caroline and Britt are the generals.' This statement broke the ice as they all laughed at the description.

Kelly turned to Abigail. 'So, what was their excuse for not being here? We're not usually invited to these meetings, so I'm not surprised they cancelled. Anyway, if this was in Roman times, we'd be the slaves, wouldn't we Kylie?'

'Yes. Abigail wouldn't though. She'd be a general.'

These comments didn't go down well with one member of the group, going by the look on Miriam's face who, because she was one of Cassandra's helpers, would also be deemed a slave.

Abigail stood up. 'Will you excuse me for a moment. Help yourself to more coffee and cookies. I'll be back shortly.' She left the kitchen and went upstairs to change into jeans and a jumper, but kept the pumps on. Coming back down, she went into the kitchen and sat down. 'Right, that's better. I feel more comfortable now. We'd better crack on and discuss the Christmas fayre.'

The meeting went well and everyone knew what they had to do. As Kelly and Kylie were old hands at this, they knew what was expected of them. Miriam and Mavis needed a bit more guidance, but were on board with everything. Finally the meeting came to an end with "goodbyes" and "see you Saturday". Abigail reflected that she definitely felt more comfortable in their presence. It was obvious that Kelly and Kylie were clearly very good friends, Miriam seemed a bit offhand, and Abigail realised that the flowering friendship had been nipped in the bud. Mavis was very quiet; possibly shy, but Abigail thought she had hidden depths.

Before heading off to the party at the care home, Abigail decided to make a quick call to Cassandra to update her. She expected to hear a lot of noise as Cassandra said she would be at Heathrow airport collecting Ingram. Yet, for an airport, it sounded suspiciously quiet as there was no background noise at all and Abigail couldn't rule out the possibility that Cassandra had been fibbing.

The Christmas fayre was well attended. There were no dramatic incidents such as anaphylactic shocks caused by food allergies, the toy and book stall was a success, as was the bring-and-buy stall. The biggest success by far was the sale of raffle tickets which surpassed last year's takings. In order to avoid any difficulties, Cassandra had decided to do away with labels of "first prize", "second prize" and so on, and instead did a "top table".

This meant that Britt's and Caroline's raffle prizes had equal importance. Multiple tickets were bought, and the prize winners went home very happy indeed.

*

It was the end of term and the run up to Christmas Eve followed by Christmas Day. Green Park Road was like a ghost town, as all their neighbours had gone away. Sven and Svetlana were on a cruise which also took in the New Year, the twins and their wives were spending Christmas Day with the boys' parents and New Year's Eve with the girls' parents. Juliana and Rufus went to Antigua with their daughter and her two girls, India and Chynna.

Andrew, Abigail and the girls spent their first Christmas in their new home and were as happy as any family could be. They spent New Year's Eve playing Scrabble and Charades, after having takeaway pizza and chicken wings which Andrew had agreed to as a treat, as long as they ate in the kitchen. Then, they had joined hands and formed a circle, counting down to midnight. On the stroke of 12, they shouted, 'Happy New Year!'

Andrew and Abigail toasted each other with a glass of champagne and Andrew said to Abigail, 'I wonder what the new year will bring?'

'Yes, I wonder too,' she had replied and, in that moment, although she was feeling happy, she suddenly shivered even though the heat from her beautiful Aga made the kitchen warm.

PART FOUR

CHAPTER TWENTY

In which Abigail is surprised twice in one day

THE NEW YEAR brought two surprises for Abigail in quick succession. The first was when Annabel and Francesca came home from school on the first day of the new term, having decided that they were happy to continue catching the train home on the condition that Abigail would still take them in the morning, and Annabel announced that Amy Murphy and Bunty McTavish had left the school, and a new girl had joined. She was Indian and called Anaisha. When she had to introduce herself to her new classmates, she revealed that her mother was called Indrani and used to be a Bollywood actress before she married Anaisha's father. He owned a large company involved in steel production and had just acquired offices in London. Abigail replied that it was all very interesting and instinctively knew that Cassandra would make a beeline for both Anaisha and her mother. She was, however, more interested in why Amy and Bunty had left the school, and wondered if it was not so much the girls who were unhappy, but Miriam and Noreen who had never really fitted in. *Then again*, she thought, *have I?*

The next surprise came a few days later. Andrew's car had disappeared before Christmas and, when Abigail asked him where it was, he had replied that he was trading it in. Any further questions were met with a "wait and see" response. She had just returned home when a big delivery vehicle pulled up on the opposite side of the road bearing the logo Aston Martin. Abigail wondered who was taking delivery of such a car. *Someone with too much money*, she decided and obviously someone with no children as an Aston Martin sports car was a two-seater. She therefore assumed it was either being delivered next door, or perhaps to one of the twins. So, she was surprised when a man wearing overalls came and pressed the buzzer on her gates. Abigail opened the gates and went to greet the man. He was holding a piece of paper.

'Is this the Thomas residence?' he asked.

Annabel replied that it was.

'Right, I've got a delivery for Mr Andrew Thomas.'

'Are you sure?' Abigail asked, completely nonplussed.

'Yes, look, here's the delivery note.'

Abigail saw that it was for a British Racing Green Aston Martin DB8. 'Right, well this is a surprise. Will you be driving it into the driveway?'

The man nodded. Pressing a button on a small hand-held gadget, the back door of the vehicle slid up and Abigail watched as a ramp came down. Walking back to the vehicle and climbing up the ramp, the driver disappeared into the back. From inside the vehicle, the car engine made a deep throaty sound when the ignition was started. The driver expertly manoeuvred the car down the ramp and drove into the driveway, parking it in front of the house. Handing Abigail the keys, he asked her to sign the delivery note and then returned to the vehicle and drove away.

Andrew Thomas, said Abigail to herself, *you've kept this a secret. I wonder how many more secrets you're keeping from me.*

Andrew arrived home early and literally bounced into the kitchen where Abigail and the girls were watching television. Before she could say anything to him about his new car, he impatiently asked where the keys were.

'Where's the keys? I'd forgotten the car was being delivered today. Where's the keys, Abigail?'

Abigail didn't like his tone. 'You might have told me you were getting a new car. It must have cost a fortune! Also, it's a two-seater. There's four of us in this family. And what about if you need to take the girls somewhere?'

Andrew shrugged. 'We can use your car when needed. Now where's the keys? I want to take my new toy for a spin.'

'Daddy,' piped up Annabel. 'Seeing as you've bought yourself a new car, can we have a puppy?'

'No. Abigail, give me the keys please.'

Abigail could see that he was getting annoyed and threw them at him which, on reflection, was a childish gesture to do in front of the girls.

Andrew caught the keys in both hands. 'Right, I'm off. Who wants to come for a spin? Abigail?'

'No thank you. I've the girls to look after and an evening meal to prepare.'

'Annabel?'

'No thank you,' came the sullen reply.

'Francesca?'

Francesca hesitated because she felt it would be very exciting to go in such a flashy sports car. However, the daggers coming from Abigail and Annabel made her reply 'Sorry, Daddy. It's a no from me.'

'Oh well, suit yourselves. I'm off.' And he bounced back out of the kitchen, not letting any of them dampen his excitement.

Later that night in bed, Abigail confronted Andrew. 'Andrew, don't you think you should have consulted me before splashing out on such an expensive car?'

'No,' came the curt reply. 'Why?'

'Because it's not very practical and it's an awful lot of money.'

Andrew sighed. 'It's my money. The company is doing well. So I thought I'd treat myself. Darius has got a Bentley and an Aston Martin.'

Abigail was feeling annoyed. 'What's Darius got to do with this?'

'Well, I was speaking to him just before Christmas and he said he knew someone at the Aston Martin dealership and could possibly get me a slight discount. So I thought, why not? Anyway, I'm tired and I'm going to sleep.' With that he turned off the light and turned on his side.

Abigail realised she was not going to win this argument. She turned off the light on her side of the bed, but was unable to sleep as so many thoughts were swimming around in her head.

CHAPTER TWENTY-ONE

In which Abigail experiences déjà vu

ABIGAIL WAS EXPERIENCING déjà vu, as if she'd been here before. Andrew was up to something. She knew the signs. He was still in bed even though it was a weekday. When she asked him why he wasn't going into work, he replied that he was taking the day off which was something he hardly ever did.

As usual, she had driven the girls to school and found Andrew in the kitchen waiting for her upon her return. 'Right, I'm all yours,' he had said. 'Let's go for a drive, find a nice country pub and have lunch. What do you say?'

Abigail was taken aback. This was not like Andrew at all, as he lived and breathed for the company, and this made her suspicious. 'But what about the office?' she asked. His reply was that the staff were capable of running the office without him for one day and, as the weather was nice, he thought he'd take the day off and treat his lovely wife to a day out in the new car. Abigail should have been pleased, but this thoughtfulness was so out of character it crossed her mind she was being manipulated. However, they'd gone out, had a nice walk, followed by a pub lunch and Abigail had to admit that she felt good being in the Aston Martin particularly when she saw admiring glances from people in the pub car park.

Her suspicions were heightened when, a few weeks later, Andrew suggested that they should have a weekend away. 'Just the two of us,' he had said.

'What about Annabel and Francesca? We can't just leave them.'

'Look, Abigail. We hardly spend any time together. The girls will be okay.'

'Absolutely not! No way. I'll see if Mum and Dad can come up and look after them. It's been ages since they've seen their granddaughters and they've never been here either.'

'Neither have my parents.'

'Well, ask your parents then.'

'No. It's okay. You ask yours.'

So, Abigail rang her parents who now lived on the outskirts of Exeter, her father having retired from farming, and asked if they could come and look after the girls so that she and Andrew could have some time away. She then told the girls that Granny Hilary and Grandpop Bill were coming to look after them because Mummy and Daddy were going away for the weekend.

The grandparents came, oohed and aahed over the house and swimming pool, and waved their daughter and her husband off.

'He must be doing well, Hilary. Those cars cost a small fortune. And I bet this house cost a tidy penny as well!'

'Yes, you're right, Bill. Can't see the point of having a swimming pool though. Far too cold to swim in I would have thought. Right, girls, what do you want for tea?'

Pizza and chicken wings came the reply and Coca-Cola. *Thank heavens*, thought Hilary, who didn't have a clue how to use the kind of oven Abigail had.

Later in bed that night, Hilary turned to her husband. 'Andrew's done all right for himself, if this home is anything to go by.'

'Yes, he certainly has. But he wouldn't have been able to do this without Abigail's support.'

'Mmm, you're probably right. She looks after him, the girls, and the house and, knowing her, she probably puts herself last.'

'That car's a bit flash, isn't it? The sort of car a single man "about town" without any responsibilities would drive. Hardly the type of car for a married family man.' This was Grandpop Bill's last comment before turning off the light and going to sleep. His wife's last thought was to do with her daughter, and if she was truly happy.

*

Andrew wouldn't tell Abigail where they were going, but he assured her that she would like it. So when they drove into the grounds of the luxury hotel and spa in New Milton, a bell rang in Abigail's head and she remembered that this was one of the raffle prizes that Caroline Fortescue had secured for the Christmas fayre. An alarm bell then began to ring when it occurred to her that perhaps Darius and Caroline would be there.

Andrew had sensed what she was thinking. 'Don't worry. They're not here, although I don't know what you've got against them. Darius is a splendid fellow.'

Andrew parked the car next to the row of other luxury cars and they entered into the foyer. It was certainly impressive and Abigail's invisible mouse gave a little squeak, although over time the squeaks were becoming less pronounced.

They checked in and were given keys to their room. It was decorated and furnished in a style befitting an upmarket hotel but was neither ostentatious nor intimidating. Although Abigail would have preferred a bit more splash of colour in the choice of décor, she realised she was being too fussy because the view of the parkland from their bedroom window was very pleasant to look at.

After they had unpacked the few things they had brought, Andrew surprised Abigail by saying that he had booked them both an hour's massage because, he said, 'You do so much for myself and the girls, you deserve a treat.' Although Abigail felt grateful, she couldn't help but think that, yet again, she was being manipulated by Andrew because this thoughtfulness was so out of character. However, who was she to turn down a massage in such a beautiful place?

Putting on the thick white robes they had found in the wardrobe, and the slippers bearing the hotel logo, they walked across to the spa and wellness centre. They hadn't packed swimwear but took a look at the pool area. They had to admit that they'd never seen anything quite so luxurious and sophisticated. Not for the first time, Abigail wondered how much all of this had cost, and she decided to look it up when she got home. They went into the reception area and waited until they were collected by the beauty therapists. Abigail's massage consisted of an exfoliating body scrub, followed by a full body massage with warm, scented body oil and finished off with a scalp massage. She felt totally relaxed and pampered. Meeting Andrew in the reception area, they walked back to the hotel and up to their room. As Andrew's hair was short, the scalp massage hadn't made much of a difference. However, Abigail had to wash her hair because it was oily. Afterwards, they both fell asleep until it was time for dinner.

Andrew had told Abigail to pack something smart for the evening and so she had packed the dress she had bought for the Fortescue dinner party and the plum-coloured shoes. Andrew was looking smart in his pale grey linen suit, a pale grey shirt and a tie Abigail hadn't seen before. It was black and she could just make out a repeating pattern of gold embroidered letters that looked like a forward facing "G" and a backward facing "G". 'Is that a new tie?'

'Yes! Do you like it? It's Gucci. I treated myself,' he said grinning.

'Mmm, very nice. Bet it was expensive.'

Andrew took Abigail by the hand and they walked into the chic lounge for pre-dinner drinks. Andrew ordered two flutes of Dom Perignon champagne. Abigail had looked at the price list and baulked at the cost. 'Andrew! Have you seen how much just a glass of champagne costs?'

He wafted her question away with his hand and replied that it was of no consequence, and raised his glass at her.

The first disagreement came shortly after sitting down to dinner. Looking at the menu, they both decided to have the Isle of Orkney scallops for their first course. Then Abigail said she fancied the fillet steak and chips.

Andrew had looked at her in astonishment. 'Abigail, you're in a fine dining restaurant at one of the best hotels in the United Kingdom and you're choosing steak and chips.'

'It's hardly just any old steak and chips. It's a prime piece of fillet steak, with mushrooms, gremolata and triple-cooked chips. Anyway, it's what I want.'

Andrew signed. 'Oh well, it's your choice I suppose. It might work though because I'm going for the smoked loin of Wiltshire venison served with celeriac, red cabbage and Sichuan pepper.' He had grinned and rubbed his hands together. 'So, seeing as you're having steak and I'm having venison, I'll order us a nice bottle of Burgundy then.'

'You're forgetting something, Andrew. I don't like red wine. I only drink dry white such as a Sancerre, Pinot grigio or Sauvignon blanc.'

Andrew looked at her with an unreadable expression. 'You can't drink white wine with red meat. It's just not the done thing, especially in a place like this. The waiter will think we're a couple of oiks.'

Abigail knew that Andrew was a stickler for food and wine etiquette, but this was ridiculous. She folded her arms across her chest and looked at him. 'I don't care if the waiter does think we're a pair of oiks. I'm not drinking red wine. It gives me a headache. How about we compromise and find a nice dry Provence rosé which we both like?'

Andrew shook his head. 'Nope. I'm drinking red.'

The waiter came to take their order. Andrew ordered the scallops for both of them, and then the waiter turned to Abigail for her main course. Much to Andrew's surprise, and her delight because she had wrongfooted him, she ordered the grilled Dover sole, sauté potatoes and vegetables, even though she had really wanted steak. Before Andrew could order the wine, the waiter suggested that they might like to have another glass of champagne to accompany their starters. Andrew ordered two more glasses, this time choosing a less expensive one. Before he could then order the wine, Abigail ordered a glass of the blended Chardonnay as she couldn't see any of her favourite dry white wines on the menu. Andrew glared at her and ordered a glass of Burgundy.

After the waiter had left, he had said grumpily, 'You do know, Abigail, that to drink wine by the glass is a false economy as it works out more expensive in the long run?'

Abigail, who had seen the price of the bottles of Burgundy, replied 'Only if you drink four glasses, Andrew.'

The waiter returned with two glasses of champagne, and they sat in silence whilst they waited for their first course, which was also eaten in silence. The waiter came with the wine for their main course. In preventing Andrew from ordering a bottle of Burgundy, Abigail realised she had deprived him of showing off his wine tasting skills in front of the waiter. Just like Darius, Andrew would stick his nose in the glass, take a loud sniff, swill the wine around in his mouth and then swallow it, pompously pronouncing it "splendid" and "excellent year". Instead, when handed the glass by the waiter, he had given the wine a brief sniff and nodded his acceptance without enthusiasm. The main course was then brought out, followed by the second disagreement.

Andrew reached across and took Abigail's hand. 'Sorry, I've been a bit grumpy, haven't I?'

Abigail wanted to reply, *no more than usual*, but replied instead that she was sorry that she didn't like red wine.

'The thing is, Abigail, we spend so little time together that it feels as if we're leading separate lives. So I thought it would be nice if we could spend more time together. Maybe even do a bit of travelling. The company is doing well, and I was thinking that I could take a break from going into the office every day, and I can work from anywhere as long as I have internet access and a computer. Maybe even sell the company and then the "world can be our oyster". Haha – perhaps it should be the "world can be our scallop" seeing how we've just had them. How funny.'

Abigail didn't see the funny side of it and took a gulp of her Chardonnay grimacing slightly because she wasn't fond of the "oaky" taste. 'You're forgetting something, Andrew. Well, actually you're forgetting two things.'

'What's that then?'

'Annabel and Francesca. Our daughters who are still at school.'

Andrew took a mouthful of Burgundy and swallowed. 'Mmm, I was coming to that. I was talking to Darius and he said that the boarding school Apollonia... don't look at me like that! Let me finish. Darius said that Apollonia's boarding school is very good and achieves respectable academic results. She goes there during the week and comes home most weekends. Cassandra...'

Abigail didn't like the way the conversation was going. 'The answer is no, and when were you speaking to Cassandra?'

'At the Fortescue's dinner party. She told me that Eustacia will be going to Apollonia's school to do her A-levels and I thought that perhaps Francesca would like to go there.'

'I doubt it,' replied Abigail.

'Why's that then?'

'She doesn't like Apollonia Fortescue or her friends, and she's hardly best friends with Eustacia. So the answer is no, Andrew. And you're forgetting Annabel.'

'Well...'

'No, Andrew. That's my final word on the matter!'

The rest of the meal passed in silence. Andrew ordered the poppy seed and citrus slice, with Limoncello and crème fraiche sorbet. Abigail said she was full and declined dessert.

They awoke in the morning, showered, dressed and packed up their few belongings. After breakfast they set off back home. They had begun speaking to each other again, making small talk about how lovely the hotel was and how nice it was to have some time together.

They arrived back and were greeted by two very happy daughters. 'We missed you,' said Francesca. 'But we've had a lot of fun with Granny and Grandpops.'

'I like Granny Hilary and Grandpops Bill makes me laugh. Can they come again?' asked Annabel.

Abigail, Andrew and the girls went into the kitchen to find Abigail's parents having coffee before setting off.

'You'll have to come and see us next time,' said Hilary. 'I think the girls would love to go to the seaside. We could take them to Budleigh Salterton which is very quaint, or Sidmouth which has a sandy beach. Anyway, must be off. It's a long journey.'

They all kissed, said their goodbyes and once the front door was closed it was all back to normal.

CHAPTER TWENTY-TWO

In which Abigail gets annoyed twice in one day

ANDREW DIDN'T RAISE the topic of boarding schools again and so Abigail assumed he'd shelved the idea. In any event, she had something else to think about. Their local estate agent had paid her a visit and asked if she would agree to becoming the local representative for welcoming new people into the area, particularly those from overseas who would need information regarding schools, doctors, dentists and so on. Abigail had said she would think about it and get back to him shortly. She was curious as to why she had been chosen and asked the agent, who told her that the manager of the care home had recommended her.

She was continuing her twice weekly volunteering at the home, going to the yoga classes at the village hall, and forging ahead with her studying in preparation for recommencing her profession as a psychotherapist. So she felt that she was busy enough. However, if she did take up the position, it would mean that she would get out a bit more into the community and widen her circle of acquaintances.

On Monday, the girls had arrived home from school and announced that they'd both been invited back by Eustacia and Desdemona after school on Friday, and asked if they could go. Abigail said it was fine by her, and they were to tell Cassandra that she would collect them.

It was Friday and Abigail was at Cassandra's house to get the girls. Cassandra asked Abigail if she would like to come in and have a glass of wine. Abigail said yes, but only one as she was driving. Cassandra poured two large glasses of white wine and they sat at the kitchen table. 'So, what did you think about Amy and Bunty not coming back this year?' asked Cassandra.

Abigail replied that she was a bit shocked as the girls seemed to be doing well, although she knew that Bunty didn't enjoy the sports element and was struggling a bit with the competitiveness.

'That's partly true,' added Cassandra. 'She wasn't very sporty at all, in fact. If she'd lost a bit of weight, and I did try tactfully to suggest it to Miriam, that might have helped I suppose. I don't think she took it too kindly though. Anyway, from what I heard, both parents thought the school was too competitive and driven by results. Isn't that what we pay for though?' She took a sip of her wine and shrugged her shoulders.

Abigail sipped her wine. It was chilled and very dry; just how she liked it. 'I suppose so,' she replied, but secretly agreed to some extent with Miriam and Noreen.

'Anyway, the McTavish's took Bunty out and I think she's gone into the state system now. Of course, between you and I, I think they would struggle to afford the fees as Bunty's scholarship was only for one year.'

Abigail sighed. 'It's such a shame, though, because Annabel was friends with Bunty and Amy, and now they've both left.'

'To be honest, I have to say I'm not sorry Amy has left. I liked her well enough, but her mother! Very loud and, you know me, Abigail, I'm no snob but she was a bit – how can I say it diplomatically – she was NOCD.'

Abigail thought that Cassandra was a bit of a snob and sometimes lacked diplomacy. She was puzzled though. 'What do you mean? What is NOCD?'

'Not our class, darling.'

'Oh! I hadn't heard of that before. Well, I met Noreen a couple of times. I found her to be very approachable. In fact, very down-to-earth and friendly.'

Cassandra pulled a face. 'Mmm, well there's warm and friendly, and then there's pushy and overbearing.'

'You didn't much like her then?'

'Not my kind of person, Abigail. What more can I say? Anyway, look on the bright side. Your two always have my two. Eustacia and Desdemona are very fond of Annabel and Francesca.' Cassandra smiled and lifted her glass to clink it with Abigail's glass, which Abigail reciprocated back albeit with some hesitancy. Again, as with the recent experience with Andrew, Abigail's intuition began to sound a warning bell.

Abigail drove home reflecting on the fact that she had almost found two possible friends in Miriam and Noreen, which appeared to have been scuppered by the machinations of Cassandra. There was also something else niggling her.

'Girls?'

'Yes, Mum?' they replied.

'Do you get on with Eustacia and Desdemona?'

Francesca replied first. 'Yes, we get on okay. We're not besties though, although she has been making a bit more effort lately.'

'Annabel, what about you and Desdemona?'

Annabel screwed up her face whilst she thought how to reply. 'Well, I miss Amy and Bunty. But I like Katy Brown. She's really nice and funny, and Shaznay Lewis. She's always getting into trouble though and Desdemona has told me not to get too friendly with her in case I get tarred with the same brush. I don't know what that means though.'

'What that means, Annabel, is that if Shaznay is always getting into trouble with the teachers, you might also get into trouble if you're seen with her when she's doing something she shouldn't. Anyway, you haven't answered my question.'

'I've forgotten what you asked me.'

Abigail sighed. 'Are you and Desdemona friends?'

Annabel screwed up her face again, which Abigail saw her doing when she looked in the rear-view mirror. 'Can you stop doing that please. Just answer my question.'

Annabel and Francesca looked at each other, wondering why their mother appeared to be in a bad mood.

'Sorry, Mummy. No, we're not besties but she has also been making a bit more of an effort recently.'

Abigail nodded and thought, *there's something going on here.*

They were having dinner. Just the three of them as Andrew hadn't yet come home, which was becoming a bit of a regular occurrence.

'Mum?' said Francesca.

'Yes, Francesca. What is it?

'Am I going to boarding school?'

Abigail stopped eating and put down her knife and fork. 'Most certainly not. What made you ask that question?'

'Well, Eustacia said she was going to board at the same school as Apollonia Fortescue when it's time to study for A-levels. She showed me the brochure. It looks very posh and they have all sorts of things like tennis courts, swimming pool, dance studio and a huge gym. But I don't want to go to boarding school. I want to stay here.'

'Mummy?'

'Yes, Annabel?'

'If Francesca goes to boarding school, can I have a puppy?' she asked with a hopeful look on her face.

Abigail was getting annoyed, which she rarely ever was but felt herself becoming more and more exasperated of late. 'The answer is no, you can't have a puppy.'

Not to be deterred, Annabel continued, 'But if—'

'Right, listen to me, you two, because I'm losing my patience. Francesca, you're not going to boarding school, and neither are you, Annabel. So if Desdemona starts going on about going to boarding school, just ignore her. She probably will go, as will Sapphire Fortescue, but you're not. Now, both of you eat up and we can get into our jimjams and watch TV together. We can also have ice-cream and sit in the living room. Now, I don't want to hear any more about boarding schools and puppies. Is that clear?'

The girls looked at their mother and nodded.

Abigail went to bed earlier that night still feeling frazzled and annoyed. It was bad enough when people tried to manipulate her, but to try and do the same with her daughters was totally out of order and unacceptable. She would have words with Andrew when he finally came home.

In the end, he must have arrived back very late because she saw him emerging from the spare room when she went downstairs in the morning to get a cup of tea. When she came back up, he was having a shower and then getting ready to go into the office and so she didn't get a chance to talk to him.

That morning, after taking the girls to school, she decided that she would be the "welcome representative" for new people moving into the area, which is how she met Cliff and Marnie Mitchelson.

CHAPTER TWENTY-THREE

CLIFF MITCHELSON'S REAL name was Mitch, Clifford being the name of his deceased father. Mitch and, to some extent, his wife, Marnie, because she was complicit in everything he did, was a con artist. For him, it was a business pure and simple to earn just enough money for him and Marnie to live comfortably on, and not draw too much attention from people. He was unscrupulous in his dealings and everyone was fair game, particularly those women he targeted for his "romance" cons. Apart from one time when he almost became emotionally involved, he was as cold and calculating as could be. In his time, he had conned his cousin out of money, adopted the personas of a wealthy Turkish restaurateur, a rich Arab sheik, and a small-time actor. As far-fetched as some of his cons sounded, such was the vulnerability of lonely women that he was successful most of the time.

As his confidence and feeling of infallibility grew, he decided to up his stakes and move away from romance cons and turn his attention to wealthy enclaves and target whole groups of people. He was taking a risk, but Mitch was methodical in his research and, as the saying goes, "a fool and his money are soon parted". Well, Mitch was banking on there being at least one or two "fools" in the area he had chosen. From the preparatory excursions he had taken around the neighbourhood he was interested in, taking note of the large houses on large plots, with luxury cars in the driveways which were behind electric gates, he had chosen Green Park Road. Luck was on his side as there was a house for rent on the corner of the road and so he had traded in his old car, rented a Mercedes, and signed a six-month rental agreement for the house. He and Marnie moved in, which is how they met Abigail Thomas.

CHAPTER TWENTY-FOUR

In which Abigail extends a hand of friendship

IT WAS EARLY evening. The girls were doing their homework, and Abigail was putting the finishing touches to a shepherd's pie. She then remembered that she had an appointment to go and welcome the new couple who had just moved in nearby. She was about to go upstairs and put on some smarter clothes, as she was dressed in her usual jeans and jumper, when Andrew rang to say he was on his way home, so she decided to go as she was.

'Girls, I'm just popping out for a minute. Won't be long.'

'Okay, Mum,' came the joint reply.

Abigail rang the doorbell and was greeted by an attractive man, dressed casually in jeans and a button-down shirt. 'Good evening. Sorry to disturb you. I'm Abigail Thomas and I live at number 10, just round the corner from you. I'm your neighbourhood welcome representative.' Abigail extended her hand for a handshake.

The man smiled. 'Well, that's a very neighbourly thing to do. I'm Cliff Mitchelson. Come and meet my wife, Marnie.'

Abigail followed the man into the living room where a dowdy woman, wearing a browbeaten expression, sat in an armchair. 'Marnie, this is Abigail Thomas. She's a neighbour come to welcome us into the area.'

Marnie stood up and did a little dip. 'How nice to meet you,' she said in what was clearly not her real accent, and clearly aiming at coming across as well-spoken.

Abigail went on to give the couple all the relevant information she thought would be helpful for them, such as schools, doctors, dentists, and general information about the area. She glanced briefly around the room and could see no photographs or any other personal touches. The agent had told them that they were looking to permanently relocate to the area and had rented the house for the time being. Yet, Abigail thought that even when people were only renting, they usually tried to make the place feel like home with some personal items. She saw no such attempt in this house. 'Well, I've probably taken up too much of your time, and I've left my girls home alone. So I'll say goodbye. You know where I am if you have any questions. Oh, I should tell you that once a month we have a neighbourhood "get-together" to discuss any issues and have a few drinks. You'll probably get an invite within the next few days.' Abigail smiled and told Cliff that she would see herself out.

'I'm back,' she shouted, and went into the kitchen.

'Mum,' said Annabel. 'I don't understand simultaneous equations.'

Abigail laughed. 'Neither do I. Wait until Dad gets home. He won't be long.' In that instant, Abigail realised that their two children were growing up. The terms "mummy and daddy" had gradually been replaced with "mum and dad". It was a small change, but in Abigail's mind a significant one because it marked the beginning of the process of the young child slowly maturing and then the gradual separation from the parent into a fully-fledged independent thinking person. The first to go would be Francesca as, once she had finished her GCSEs, she would start preparing for A-levels and then leave home to go to university. Annabel would be next, although in temperament she would always be the more dependent one. Still, it left Abigail with a feeling of sadness.

Andrew finally came home and they were sitting in the living room having a glass of wine.

'I met the new people today.'

'Oh, what are they like?'

'Well, he's very attractive. Slim. Friendly. Bit of a charmer, I think. His wife is quite plain and dowdy. Quiet. She seemed a bit ill at ease. Odd match, in my opinion. Anyway, you'll meet them at the get-together next Friday. No doubt the others will want to look them over,' she said and rolled her eyes.

*

Andrew and Abigail made their way to the Hetherington's house, as they had decided to host again. The girls were instructed not to open the gates to anyone, or to answer the intercom. 'Of course we won't,' said Francesca. 'Don't worry. Go and enjoy yourselves.'

This comment, coming from their eldest daughter, made Abigail and Andrew laugh because it sounded very parental and reinforced what Abigail had been thinking earlier.

Apart from Rufus, who was standing in the middle of the room, everyone else was seated, waiting for the Mitchelsons to arrive. On their entry into the living room, they were beckoned by Rufus to come and stand next to him so he could introduce them to the group. Abigail was struck by how good-looking Cliff Mitchelson was; dressed in beige chinos and a pale blue button-down shirt, he exuded an aura of confidence and an easy-going manner. To Abigail, however, in spite of his charming demeanour and his easy smile, his eyes were expressionless which, for her, made him difficult to read or get a sense of what lay beneath the surface charm. In complete contrast, Marnie appeared nervous and withdrawn. She was wearing a faded floral dress that looked very much like a dated Laura Ashley, flat brown shoes, and no make-up. Abigail could easily imagine what Juliana and Svetlana were thinking, and she immediately felt some sympathy for the woman, particularly as she could see Cliff Mitchelson giving Svetlana discreet glances. That evening, she was wearing a figure-hugging pale pink dress which showed off her toned body, accessorised with chunky gold jewellery and pink stiletto shoes with the usual complicated arrangement of straps and buckles. She had pulled her white-blond hair back into a tight ponytail which showcased her cheekbones which shimmered. Abigail also noticed Andrew giving her a sneaky peak and she jabbed him in the arm with her finger.

As usual, when they migrated to the kitchen, the twins and their wives sat at the kitchen table, whereas Andrew, Rufus and Sven went into their huddle, this time taking Cliff with them. This left Juliana, Svetlana, Abigail and Marnie. As was par for the course, Juliana and Svetlana dominated the conversation, whilst Abigail and Marnie stood silently by. Abigail asked Marnie how she was settling in, in an effort to get her to open up. Before she could respond, Abigail's phone rang.

'Sorry, Marnie. I've got to pop home briefly.' Abigail left the kitchen, but not before she saw Juliana and Svetlana wandering off leaving Marnie standing alone.

A short time after, Abigail returned to find Marnie just about to leave.

'Leaving already?' she asked.

Marnie replied that she was a bit tired and decided to go home.

'I suspect these kinds of gatherings aren't your thing. Am I right?' asked Abigail.

Marnie smiled, making her face light up. 'Spot on. I'd much rather be at home with a cup of tea watching *Coronation Street* or *Emmerdale*.' She shrugged her shoulders.

Once again, Abigail found herself feeling some sympathy for the woman because hadn't she also been thrust into an environment that had taken a while for her to feel more comfortable in, and with people that she had very little in common with? So, she decided to extend a hand of friendship. 'If you're free on Monday afternoon, come to mine for a cup of tea and a chat. I have to leave at 3:30 to pick the girls up from school, so how does 2 o'clock sound?'

The smile on Marnie's face told Abigail she'd done the right thing, although she felt it was a pity that the visit couldn't be for longer. This was because there'd been talk of local train strikes starting on Monday which was why Abigail was collecting Annabel and Francesca from school.

The gathering at the Hetherington house came to an end and Abigail and Andrew made their way home. The girls had taken themselves off to bed, again a sign showing their maturity and independence. Andrew and Abigail did the same, but before going to sleep Abigail asked Andrew what he thought of Cliff. He replied that he seemed pleasant enough and friendly. He also told Abigail that he ran a yacht timeshare business and had invited all the men on a day out on one of his yachts to see what it was like, and if they might be interested in investing in a timeshare.

'What did you say?' asked Abigail.

'I said that it sounded interesting and to drop some information in. Sven and Rufus were also interested, and Rufus is going to ask the twins.'

With that, he turned off the bedside light and they went to sleep.

CHAPTER TWENTY-FIVE

In which Abigail feels short-changed

AS PROMISED, CLIFF Mitchelson (alias Mitch Mitchelson and Daniel Simpson), dropped off the yacht timeshare leaflets to his neighbours, and it was fast approaching the day of the boys' day out on one of his yachts.

Andrew was up early on the Saturday morning, after bringing Abigail a cup of tea in bed. This was an unusual gesture by Andrew, and he was clearly excited by the prospect of spending a day out at sea with the others. He had dressed for the occasion. Gone was his formal suit and tie; instead, he was wearing navy blue chinos, cream polo shirt and tan loafers with navy blue piping.

'Right, I'm off,' he had shouted and bounded down the stairs. Abigail heard the throaty sound of the Aston Martin's engine and the crunching of tyres on the gravel.

Whilst she was drinking her tea, she reflected on his appearance and behaviour. There was no doubt he was spending more money on clothes and taking extra care with his appearance. He was also in a good mood these days, which made him easier to live with, in that he wasn't being so dictatorial with her and the girls. This, in turn, made the atmosphere much more relaxed. However, he had come home late a few nights, but that was par for the course as he had never been one of those husbands who kept regular "going home" hours. It was just that this morning, he was so excited it was as if he couldn't wait to leave. Furthermore, he had splashed on far too much aftershave.

Francesca came into the bedroom. 'Where's Dad gone this early?'

'He's gone out with the other men for a boys' day out.'

She frowned. 'Oh, okay. Doesn't he like being with us anymore? It's Saturday. We usually spend Saturdays together.'

Abigail thought her daughter had a point but replied, 'Of course he likes being with us. He works all week and so he's taking a day off. It's just that it's not with us.'

Francesca shrugged. 'Okay. Can we go shopping then?'

'Of course we can. If that's what you both want to do.'

She's right, though, thought Abigail. *He's late home most evenings, and sometimes after the girls have gone to bed. And when he does come home at a reasonable time, he goes into his study after dinner, so he hardly spends any time with us at all.*

Andrew had come back in a very happy mood. Before Abigail could start asking questions, he pre-empted her by saying that it had been a great day out, but he was tired and was going to have an early night. He also said that he was probably not going to invest in Cliff's timeshare because he didn't think they would make enough use of it. Abigail felt a bit short-changed because she wanted to ask what it was like being on a yacht, and also because he hadn't even consulted her on whether to invest or not.

*

It was Tuesday morning, three days after the boat trip. Andrew was still in bed, which surprised Abigail.

'How come you're still here at this time?'

'I thought I'd take the day off for a change. If you lend me your car, I'll take the girls to school.'

Abigail was really taken aback by this uncharacteristic offer. 'Oh, well, if you're sure. That's great because I'm meeting up with Marnie and we're going for a jog around the block.'

Andrew clapped his hands. 'Great! I'll get the girls up. Oh, and, by the way, I'm going for a proper run in the woods when I get back, not a jog around the block. So, don't come in the woods and slow me down.' He grinned, leaving Abigail wondering, not for the first, second or third time, just what he was up to this time.

Marnie and Abigail were jogging down Green Park Road towards Abigail's house when they saw Cliff coming towards them. He greeted his wife and Abigail and said that he'd come to meet them. 'Oh! That's nice of you, Mitch,' said Marnie, and then she had put her hand over her mouth.

Abigail noticed that Cliff had reddened slightly, and he abruptly turned to her to ask how she was. 'Erm, I'm very well,' she replied, 'but I'm a bit puzzled. Marnie just called you Mitch, or did I hear wrong?'

Cliff was clearly flustered, but composed himself to explain that Mitchel was his father's name and, as he resembled him, people who'd known him from the old days always called him Mitch. To anyone else, his given name was Clifford shortened to Cliff. He then quickly changed the subject and asked Abigail if Andrew had enjoyed himself on the yacht, to which she replied that he had come back in very high spirits. He then asked her if Andrew was at work, to which Abigail replied that he'd taken the day off and gone for a run in the woods. 'Do you want to see him, then?'

'No, no, that's okay. No need to mention it either. Just making chit-chat.'

With that, Cliff and Marnie headed back home, leaving Abigail wondering about a few things. *Something's not right. There's something going on and I'm not privy to it,* she thought.

CHAPTER TWENTY-SIX

In which Abigail hears some disturbing news

A FEW WEEKS had gone by and Abigail had noticed a change in Andrew. There was definitely something amiss. He had been getting up very early and leaving before Abigail had even stirred. Furthermore, he was coming home late and disappearing into his study, and had even taken to sleeping in the spare room. When Abigail had asked him about this, he had replied that he didn't want to wake her up. She had also asked him if everything was okay, and he had replied, 'Of course. Just a few things on my mind at the moment to do with work. Nothing to worry about, Abigail.'

Nevertheless, she felt as if he was avoiding her and he was not the only one. The neighbours had also gone underground, as it occurred to Abigail that she hadn't had much contact with any of them lately. She saw the usual cars coming and going but there seemed to be an atmosphere of silence. Then, one morning she'd had a visit from Rufus who had asked Abigail if she had seen Marnie lately because he knew the two of them were friendly.

In fact, since Marnie had become friendly with Abigail she had come out of her shell. She'd been attending the yoga and Zumba classes at the village hall, which had toned up her figure, and begun volunteering at the care home where she was proving a hit with the residents. She had also been gradually improving her appearance by having her hair restyled and highlighted, and updated her wardrobe. Recently, there'd been a get-together of all the Green Park Road women at Juliana's house, which was ostensibly an excuse to grill Marnie about her and Cliff's background. Abigail and Marnie both knew that whatever information was gleaned would go straight back to the men who were considering investing in Cliff's timeshare. Not surprisingly, Svetlana had been extremely interrogative with her line of questioning and received a rebuke from Juliana. Abigail had been duly impressed, though, with how Marnie had handled herself and came away with the feeling that perhaps Marnie wasn't quite the timid mouse she'd first seemed. Abigail then realised that she hadn't seen Marnie for a while and decided to pay her a visit.

There was no car in the driveway which meant that Cliff was out. So she rang the doorbell. There was no answer. Abigail assumed therefore that they were both out. She tried the side gate. It was unlocked, so she went to the back of the house and peered in through the windows. She could see no evidence whatsoever of anyone living there. In fact, the house looked deserted, although she remembered that when she first visited them there were no personal items on show. It was all very odd. Deciding to go back home, she saw Svetlana's car in the driveway and, on the spur of the moment, decided to call in and see her.

Abigail was taken aback when a very gloomy-looking Svetlana opened the door, dressed in black leggings and a baggy black jumper. 'Are you okay, Svetlana?' asked Abigail.

'You'd better come in,' she replied.

Abigail followed Svetlana into the kitchen. 'Would you like coffee, or tea?'

Abigail said coffee would be great, and Svetlana put a pod into the Nespresso machine and made the coffee, and they went and sat at the kitchen table.

'The reason I've called by is because I've just been to see Marnie and she wasn't in, and neither was Cliff. In fact, the house looked totally empty.'

'You won't find them in. They've gone. You obviously don't know what's happened, so I'd better fill you in. I know you always thought that Juliana and myself were mean to Marnie, but the pair of them just came out of nowhere and were such an odd pairing. He was accommodating enough...' Svetlana blushed when she said this and her eyes sparkled. 'But Marnie was... I just didn't see the attraction and both Juliana and I saw another side to her that afternoon. Something was off. I know you liked her, but you'll change your opinion when I tell you what's happened. Basically, they've done a runner with all the timeshare investment money. Thousands and thousands of pounds. All the men are furious that they've been taken in by a conman and woman!'

Whilst Abigail was shocked by what she had just been told, she was also relieved because Andrew had told her that he had decided against investing. She wasn't going to tell Svetlana, though. 'I don't know what to say. I'm shocked. They seemed such a nice couple.' Secretly, with hindsight, Abigail always thought that there was something a bit suspect about Cliff, if indeed that was his real name, as she remembered the time Marnie had called him Mitch.

'Well, there you have it. I'm very disappointed. Sven and I were going to cruise the Med for two weeks. Of course, it's worse for the twins because they'd invested double the amount!'

Abigail didn't know what to say and so she bid Svetlana goodbye and made her way home. She tried ringing Andrew on his mobile, but it went straight to voicemail. So she rang the receptionist and was told that he was in a meeting. She then decided to see if any post had arrived. There had been a postal strike recently, so she wasn't surprised to see a lot of mail. Amongst it was an envelope, with a second-class stamp, addressed to her and marked "Personal and Private". She opened it up to find a single sheet of white paper on which was typed:

Dear Abigail,

Firstly, sorry. Nothing personal. Secondly, ask Andrew why he was not on the yacht with everyone else, and who was the woman he was with in the woods on his day off.

Cliff.
Ps: Marnie sends her love

Abigail was stunned. Her intuition, niggling doubts and suspicions had been spot-on. Now she knew almost for certain that Andrew was having an affair; she just didn't know who with and for how long. She would tackle him about this in due course, but for now would keep quiet whilst she formulated a plan. Then, when she had come to a decision, she would give Andrew a chance to explain himself. However, the next shocking piece of news that arrived on her doorstep meant that Abigail had to act quickly and pull the rug out from under Andrew's feet.

*

Abigail and the girls had finished dinner and were in the kitchen alcove watching television when the intercom sounded in the hallway. Abigail got up and went to see who it was because it was 7:30pm and Andrew wasn't home yet. She could see Rufus and Juliana peering into the camera, and so she opened the gates and went to greet them at the door. 'Hello! This is a nice surprise,' she said by way of welcome.

'Hello, Abigail,' said an unsmiling Rufus. 'Sorry to disturb you. Is Andrew home?'

'No, sorry, he isn't. Can I help you? Why don't you both come in.' She opened the door wider to let them in.

The three of them walked into the living room, and Rufus and Juliana sat down on one of the settees. 'Can I get you both something to drink?' Something was wrong. She could tell. They both asked for gin and tonics and Abigail went into the kitchen. 'Girls, Rufus and Juliana are here. They're in the living room. If you need me, I'm in there.'

Francesca and Annabel nodded and turned back to watching a re-run of *Friends*. Abigail could never quite understand the appeal of the hugely popular series with its canned laughter, contrived storylines and faux camaraderie between the housemates. Still, it was keeping the girls occupied whilst she went back into the living room to find out what was behind the visit.

She placed the tray on the coffee table and handed Rufus and Juliana their drinks, and took the glass of white wine for herself.

'Cheers,' she said brightly, instinctively aware that she was probably going to hear something she'd rather not, as her guests weren't looking at all happy.

'The thing is, Abigail…' began Rufus, then stopped to take a big gulp of his drink. 'It's a pity Andrew isn't here. This is so awkward…'

Juliana interrupted her husband. 'Abigail, we have nothing against you. In fact, we like you very much but this recent turn of events just isn't right.'

Abigail was puzzled. 'Are you talking about Cliff and Marnie, and the fact that they've run off with all the timeshare money?'

'Well, that's part of it, but…' Rufus threw his hands up in the air. 'Juliana, can you tell her please. You're more forthright than me.'

'The thing is, Abigail, Andrew owes Rufus for his share in the yacht. £30,000 to be precise.'

Abigail was dumbfounded. 'I don't understand. Andrew told me that he had decided not to invest.'

'Is that what he told you?' asked Juliana.

'Yes. He said that he thought it was too expensive and that we'd probably not use it enough to warrant the expense.'

'I'm very sorry to tell you this, Abigail, but Andrew has lied to you. He asked Rufus to buy him a share and promised to pay Rufus back. He was obviously doing this behind your back. Why he would do such a thing, I don't know. You'll have to ask him. Also, even though that dreadful couple – clearly a couple of con artists who we were all taken in by… well, perhaps not Svetlana. She always had her doubts about Marnie – have disappeared with all the money, Andrew has to pay Rufus back. I'm sure you agree.' With that, the couple finished their drinks and stood up to leave.

Abigail was nearly in tears. 'I'm so sorry this has happened. I had no idea. I hope you believe me. Let me show you out.'

Francesca and Annabel went to bed, and Abigail sat in the living room waiting for Andrew to come home. At 1am, she heard the front door open and close very quietly. She went into the darkened hallway and could just see Andrew taking off his shoes. He jumped when he saw her standing there. 'What are you doing up so late?' he asked.

'Waiting for you, Andrew. We need to talk.'

'Can't it wait until morning. I'm very tired.'

'No, it can't. We need to talk now, and I mean it.' Abigail was furious and not about to back down or be browbeaten by him. Abigail went back into the living room with Andrew trailing reluctantly behind her.

All was revealed. Andrew was indeed having an affair. He wouldn't say who with or how long it had been going on for. When confronted, he admitted that he hadn't gone on the day out with the boys, and also that he had met the woman in the woods on his day off. He was puzzled, though. 'But how did you know about those two things?'

'Cliff Mitchelson told me.'

Andrew exploded. 'What! That conniving dishonest conman. Told us nothing but a pack of lies, and that wife of his. And you were friendly with her. Always thought you were a poor judge of character.'

Abigail stood her ground and folded her arms. 'Don't you dare start trying to wriggle out of this by being mean to me. Talk about being dishonest and telling lies, I think you fall into that category as well.'

Andrew then noticed the three glasses on the coffee table. 'Have you had visitors?' he asked.

'Oh yes. I nearly forgot. I had a visit tonight from Rufus and Juliana. You've been caught out in another lie. It seems that, unbeknownst to me – silly me for being so trusting – you did in fact decide to invest in the yacht timeshare scheme and got Rufus to pay for your share so as to keep it a secret from me.' Abigail was on a roll, preventing Andrew from interrupting her. 'Well, I've got news for you. You need to pay that money back immediately. Now, I'm going to bed. You can sleep in the spare room and we'll try to be amiable with each other for the girls' sake.' With that, Abigail got up from the settee and went upstairs to bed, leaving a shell-shocked Andrew feeling as if he had just had the rug pulled from under his feet.

The following morning, Abigail got up earlier than usual so that she could speak to Andrew before he left for work, knowing that he would try and avoid her after last night's revelations. She asked him in as much of an unemotional voice she could muster, even though she felt distraught, what it was he wanted. His pompous and arrogant reply was like a kick in the teeth.

'What I want, Abigail, is to come and go as I please and be answerable to no one.' With that, he had picked his briefcase up from the hallway floor and left, which is how Abigail, Francesca and Annabel found themselves living in Knighton.

PART FIVE

CHAPTER TWENTY-SEVEN

In which Abigail has to start over again

LEAVING THEIR HOME in Green Park Road had been an emotional experience for Abigail and the girls and, in terms of practicalities and readjustment, quite an upheaval. After Andrew had come out with his pompous statement, showing no regard for Abigail's feelings or how this would affect their two daughters, she decided that he could indeed "come and go" as he pleased and be "answerable to no one", but not whilst they were living under the same roof. However, Abigail knew that the house was far too big for her to manage on her own and came with too many responsibilities, so she took legal advice to find out what her rights were if she left the family home. Based on the advice given, she offered to leave the house on the condition that he paid for whatever alternative accommodation she found, and made no difficulties.

'Because, Andrew,' she had said, with her arms folded, 'you can't have it both ways. You can't be a free agent with no responsibilities, and then expect to come home when you feel like it and play "happy families" for the sake of appearances. Also, something else to bear in mind. You come home to a clean and tidy home, home-cooked meals, and washed and ironed clothes. In fact, all your needs and wants are catered for. From now on, though, you're on your own. Oh, and by the way, you may not want to be my husband any more, but you're still the girls' father and I expect you to have them every other weekend. Oh, and another thing, I'm starting up my psychotherapy practice again and will hopefully soon start earning some money. However, I expect a monthly allowance from you for Annabel and Francesca, and some maintenance for myself for the time being.'

With that, she had calmly given him her front door keys (although she'd had a spare set cut, but he didn't need to know that), loaded the suitcases in her car along with a few boxes containing essential items, and left him standing in the hallway with his mouth open. Only, then, once she was in the car and driving away, did the tears flow.

*

Not surprisingly, the girls were very upset when Abigail said they were moving. She didn't tell them why because Andrew was still their father, and she didn't want them to think badly of him. So she had told them that they were having problems and decided to have a trial separation to give them both space to work things out. Annabel had asked three times if they could now get a puppy, to which Abigail replied each time, 'No, no,' and, 'no.'

'I hate you,' shouted a red-faced Annabel and stomped up the stairs slamming her bedroom door shut. Then, she immediately came down, looking ashamed at her outburst. 'Sorry, Mummy. I don't hate you. I love you!'

'I know you do. It's going to be a big change for us, but it's still "no" for a puppy,' and kissed Annabel on the head.

Francesca had been a lot more "cool" about the whole thing. When Abigail had asked her if she was okay, she had replied matter-of-factly and with a shrug of her shoulders, 'Yep. All good for me. It's not as if Dad spent much time with us, is it?'

You can't argue with that, thought Abigail. However, she knew that Francesca was very hurt and was just not showing her feelings.

*

Abigail drove to what was going to be their new temporary home until she had decided what to do in the long-term. She had found a three-bedroom, nicely furnished riverside apartment in Knighton. She had taken the girls to see it and, somewhat unenthusiastically and understandably in the circumstances, they had said that it was nice but it wasn't home. Abigail knew it was a big adjustment for all of them. They had gone from a large house with a large garden, and swimming pool, four bedrooms, large living room and kitchen, and two bathrooms, to an apartment that had an integrated living/ kitchen area, one bathroom and one shower room, and a balcony. Even the previous home they had lived in before moving to Green Park Road had been bigger, and so Abigail completely understood how they felt. She felt it too. Yet, she was determined to make a go of it and look at the positives.

*

Abigail was beginning to feel settled and getting into a routine. After she had dropped the girls off at school, which was one positive because the school was now much nearer and hence a quicker drive, she would return to the apartment and, if the weather was nice, would sit outside on the balcony having her morning coffee and watch the rowers from the nearby rowing club pass by, and the ducks and their ducklings, gliding along on the water. It was peaceful and restful, and she was able to get some feeling of calm back into her life. She felt some guilt at what she saw as the abandonment of Unwin, and Barney and Billy Bright, as she had forged a good rapport with the three of them. *Oh well, they'll have to deal with Andrew now. Good luck with that!* she thought. *He's not the easiest of people to deal with.*

Her biggest sadness was leaving the care home where she had made friends with the other members of staff, and the elderly residents. The manager had been very understanding and, giving Abigail a hug, said that she would always be welcome back. That was something Abigail couldn't understand. She had arranged for Marnie to volunteer at the home, where she had become a firm favourite with the residents. In fact, she was a natural with them, and showed a genuine caring side. So her absconding like that was a complete mystery to Abigail, and she wondered how it was that she had misread her so badly.

CHAPTER TWENTY-EIGHT

In which Abigail finds herself feeling sad

WHEREAS FRANCESCA WAS her usual confident and happy-go-lucky self, Abigail detected that her youngest daughter was not happy. She assumed it was because she had taken her away from her home and her father, and decided to discuss it further. Over dinner that evening, she broached the subject.

'Look, girls, I know this has been an upheaval for you and I wish it hadn't happened, but your dad and I need time and space away from each other to think things through.'

'I know, Mum,' responded Francesca, 'you told us.'

Annabel remained silent.

'Anyway,' said Abigail brightly, 'you'll be seeing Dad at the weekend. He's coming to get you on Saturday morning and will take you to school on Monday. That will be nice, won't it?'

Francesca: 'S'pose so.' Shrug.

Annabel: silence.

Abigail, with forced brightness because she had never been alone on a weekend for a very long time, replied 'Well, it'll give me some time to myself. I might treat myself to a facial or a trip to the hairdresser. By the way, is everything okay at school?'

Francesca nodded and replied, 'All good.'

'Annabel? Is everything okay at school?'

Annabel looked sad.

'Francesca, what's wrong with Annabel? Can you tell me seeing as she won't speak to me?'

Francesca nudged her sister. 'Tell Mum. Go on.'

Annabel looked close to tears. 'Desdemona doesn't include me in her group anymore.'

Abigail didn't like hearing this. 'When did this happen?'

'After you and Dad separated. She started hanging round more with Anaisha and I found out that she had invited Sapphire, Willow and Anaisha back to hers last weekend, but I was left out.'

'So, who's your friendship group now?'

Annabel looked glum. 'I don't really have one now. Before, it was Amy and Bunty, and then Desdemona began to include me in hers and so Amy and Bunty drifted away. I want to change schools. I'm not happy.'

Abigail's heart was hurting at what she was hearing. It seemed so unfair. 'What about you, Francesca? Are you still friendly with Eustacia?'

'We were never bfs. She was just someone I hung out with as part of a large group. She was very silly at Sapphire's party. Also, she's going to be leaving the school to study for her A-levels at the same boarding school as Apollonia. Sapphire and Willow are going there too, at some point.'

'It doesn't bother you, then?'

'Nah, don't bovver me.' Francesca grinned cheekily, knowing her mum would not like her speaking in such a way.

'Well, all I can say, Annabel, is that I'm sorry this has happened. I'm sure it will sort itself out. Unfortunately, changing schools isn't an option.'

Abigail felt powerless as there was very little she could do about the situation. What she could do, though, was hopefully make someone feel awkward and perhaps a bit guilty about what their actions had caused.

When the girls had gone to bed, Abigail called Cassandra.

'Hi, Cassandra. How are you?'

'…'

'That's good. Look, we're settled in the apartment now and I wanted to invite Eustacia and Desdemona over after school on Friday.'

'…'

'Oh, I see… They've already been invited out on Friday.'

'…'

'I see. Yes, I quite understand, and it makes sense I suppose. Eustacia will be spending more time with the Fortescue girls because she'll be boarding with Apollonia, and Desdemona needs to make sure the new girl is made to feel welcome.

'…'

'Yes, I do see. Whilst I've got you on the phone, when will the first meeting be to begin discussing the summer fayre? I've not heard from you for a while.' There was no response from the other end. 'Are you there, Cassandra? You've gone quiet.' Abigail tapped her foot whilst she waited for a reply.

'…'

'Oh, I see. It was last week. Did I miss the text, or the call? I didn't have any missed calls on my phone.'

'…'

'So, you don't need me then for the summer fayre? But you'll keep me in mind for the summer ball in a helping capacity?'

'…'

'Right, along with Mavis, Kelly and Kylie.'

'…'

'Oh, yes. I understand, Cassandra. I can see quite clearly how the situation is. Well, thanks very much for making the position clear.'

Abigail disconnected. *Bloody Cassandra. Bloody Andrew,* she thought. *Typical bloody narcissists.* She was furious, but at least she now knew where she stood. As she had long suspected, Cassandra was nothing but a social climber who dominated her children and manipulated those around her to get what she wanted even if it meant causing difficulties or upsets for other people. *She'll get her comeuppance one of these days,* Abigail thought uncharitably. *And maybe, just maybe, Andrew will realise he's made a huge mistake.* With these consoling thoughts lingering in her head, Abigail went to bed.

*

Abigail's return to work happened quicker than she thought it would, and it was all as a result of the actions of Cassandra Smythe-Brown. It was a typical case of "out of every negative, there was a positive". No longer part of Cassandra's "elitist" team, meant that her time had been freed up in that she no longer had to attend the time-wasting meetings. Having completed the required refresher courses, Abigail was now working her way towards a Diploma in Neuro Linguistic Programming, and had decided to start up her psychotherapy practice as soon as she could find somewhere to rent. A few days after her talk with the girls over dinner, and her phone call to Cassandra, she had bumped into Mavis Brown outside the school gates. Mavis asked Abigail how she was doing and particularly asked about Annabel, as Katy had said that she seemed a bit down. Abigail replied truthfully and told Mavis what had happened. Mavis immediately said she was sorry to hear that and invited Annabel over after school on Friday.

'That's very kind of you, Mavis. Are you sure?'

'Of course I'm sure. When Amy and Bunty left, Katy was a bit lonely and Annabel was very kind to her. She tried to get her included in a few things but it didn't work out, if you know what I mean?'

'Mmm, yes. I think I do. Thank you. That will cheer her up.'

'And how are you doing?', she enquired sympathetically.

'Thanks for asking. I'm bearing up. To be honest it's been a bit of a shock. My focus has been on the girls, and now I'm going to sort myself out and start up my own psychotherapy practice just as soon as I can find somewhere to rent.'

Mavis smiled. 'I just might be able to help you there.'

*

So it was that Abigail dropped the girls off at school and made her way to her new place of work, which was called Heavenly Healing. It transpired, in the course of their conversation, that Mavis was a qualified reiki master and reflexologist, and had a room at Heavenly Healing, which was located in what used to be a church. It offered holistic and traditional forms of therapy and treatments. Alongside Tibetan sound healing and Tibetan head massage, the centre also offered reiki and reflexology. Mavis told Abigail that they were currently looking for a counsellor or therapist to join the practice, and they had a room to rent. Would she be interested?

Abigail couldn't believe her luck and said, there and then, that she was indeed. The upshot was that Mavis introduced her to the owner who had discussed Abigail's specialisms and then offered to rent her a room. The owner had added Abigail to the website, and now all she had to do was wait for people to contact her. She had also been proactive and spoken to the receptionists at the three doctors' surgeries in Knighton and given them some leaflets. She had also visited the relevant departments at Knighton General Hospital. Whilst there, she decided to see if Miriam was on duty that day. Much to her surprise, she was told that both the McTavishes had left the hospital and moved away. Abigail thought it was a pity because she had hoped to rekindle their friendship.

Everything was falling into place. Annabel was happier at school because she was now part of Katy's friendship group which comprised Shaznay Lewis, Chelsea Kimble, who had recently joined, and, sometimes, Birgitta and Brigitta Mikkelson. The last two were still bearing a grudge because they hadn't been invited to Sapphire Fortescue's birthday party, or to the "get-to-know-you" gathering at Desdemona's house which Cassandra had organised for Anaisha, and to which Annabel hadn't also been invited. *Things are looking up*, Abigail thought to herself. She also had a weekend off, as Andrew was collecting the girls on Saturday morning. She wasn't looking forward to being alone, but she would just have to get used to it. So, she had booked an appointment with Kellyanne for a cut and colour, and then she was going shopping for some new work clothes, hoping this would cheer her up.

CHAPTER TWENTY-NINE

In which Abigail hears some unwelcome news

THE FIRST WEEKEND went well. Andrew had been forced to buy a second car that seated four people so that he could keep to his end of the bargain, as Abigail had flatly refused to accommodate his request that she drop them off and pick them up. She had gone to Cornham Cuts and Kellyanne had cut Abigail's hair and put in some blond highlights. Kellyanne had asked Abigail how she was feeling, because Svetlana had told her that Abigail had left Green Park Road. She was a good listener and sympathetic, which made Abigail feel emotional, so she decided to change the subject. 'I meant to ask, how is it that you've ended up in Cornham near Svetlana? Was that a coincidence?'

Kellyanne told Abigail that, when her marriage ended, she decided to move away from Croydon and start afresh. She was still in touch with Svetlana, who told her that premises had become available in Cornham suitable for either a hair or beauty salon. Svetlana had spoken to Sven who had said he would invest in the business. 'So here I am!' said Kellyanne jovially. 'All thanks to Sven and Svetlana. Best thing I ever did.'

Abigail thanked Kellyanne, said she would see her next month, and made her way back to the apartment.

As Andrew had kept the girls until Monday, she collected them from school and, whilst she was waiting for them, had been coaching herself not to ask them any nosy questions. It didn't last.

'How was the weekend?' she eagerly asked.

'It was good,' came the replies.

'How's Dad?'

'He's good,' came the replies.

'What did you do?'

'Mum, can you please stop asking us questions. It was fine.' This was from Francesca.

Abigail got the message.

The second visit was a carbon copy of the first. The third visit didn't go so smoothly. Abigail was awaiting their return late Sunday evening, as Andrew's offer of taking them to school on Mondays wasn't working. Abigail was watching from the window that looked down on the street below, when she saw the car pull up. The girls exited the car, slamming the doors behind them. Then Andrew had driven off at speed. The girls had their own keys and she could hear footsteps thudding along the corridor. She opened the door and was confronted by two very cross-looking girls. They'd been fine when they had left, so something must have happened.

'Whatever is wrong?' asked Abigail.

'You tell Mum,' said Annabel to her sister.

'No, you tell her,' replied Francesca. Then with a sigh, 'Oh don't bother. I'll tell her.'

'Tell me what?' Abigail was becoming concerned.

'A woman was there,' Francesca said.

'A woman?'

'Yes. Dad's girlfriend.' Francesca stood with her arms folded, tapping her foot, which reminded Abigail of herself when she was annoyed and she involuntarily smiled.

'Mum! Why are you smiling? It's not funny. We didn't know he had a girlfriend. If we had, we wouldn't have gone, would we, Annabel?'

Annabel shook her head. 'Doesn't Dad love us anymore?' she asked sadly.

'Of course he does, silly.' *It's just me he doesn't,* she wanted to say, but couldn't as the thought was too painful to speak out loud.

'Then why has he got another woman there?' asked Francesca.

Abigail didn't know how to respond and was willing herself not to ask any questions and keep calm. 'Was she there the whole weekend then?'

Francesca nodded. 'She's living there.'

'What!' Abigail shouted. 'What do you mean, she's living there?' Abigail was furious. She had agreed to vacate the family home, and it was a house she had grown to love and it had been a wrench leaving it, but she most certainly hadn't agreed to Andrew's "bit on the side" moving in. 'What's this woman's name? What's she like?'

Francesca and Annabel looked at each other with raised eyebrows. 'I told you she'd be cross,' said Francesca. 'Her name is Brianna. She's American and has lived in England for a long time.'

The name rang a bell, and then Abigail remembered the business card she had found in Andrew's pocket the day after his initiation ceremony. Brianna Morgan, the CEO of some events company which Abigail couldn't recall the name of, and made a note to look it up on her phone later.

'What's she like?'

'Okay, I suppose. Very friendly. Said we're to call her Bri,' replied Francesca.

Abigail laughed, and before she could stop herself, said 'Ha, just like the smelly French cheese.'

Realising what she had said, it was too late to take it back, but it had the effect of breaking into the gloom that had descended. The girls starting chanting "smelly French cheese" and the three of them joined hands in a circle and began to skip around repeating over and over again "smelly French cheese", until Abigail remembered she was the adult and stopped. However, the mood had lightened considerably and equilibrium was momentarily restored.

Later that night, Abigail found the picture of the card on her phone. *Well, well, well, Andrew Thomas. So this is the woman who's turned mine and your daughters' life upside down. I hope she's worth it.* Abigail turned off her bedside light and fell into a restless sleep, where she dreamt she was on a sailing raft in stormy seas, hanging onto the mast to stop herself from falling overboard.

*

Matters began to go further downhill on the girls' fourth weekend visit. Andrew had collected them as per the arrangement on Saturday morning and was supposed to keep them until late Sunday evening. Abigail was now getting used to having time alone and was using it productively to prepare for the clients she was seeing at Heavenly Healing. People were trickling in and she had three female clients who were all struggling with what might be deemed a diminishing sense of self; a woman who always came immaculately turned out but had stopped looking in mirrors because she thought she looked ugly, and so Abigail was seeing her for body dysmorphia; a "high-flyer" who had won awards during her career as an investigative journalist, but upon marriage had given her career up to become a full-time mother and felt a resulting loss of identity. 'I'm someone's wife and someone's mother,' she had said. 'But who am I? Where have "I" gone?'

Lastly, a mild-mannered, painfully shy, woman who felt she was invisible. 'No one listens to me. Not my husband. My children. No one. I think perhaps I'm invisible. Can you see me?' Out of the three, Abigail felt this was going to be the most challenging and wanted to be fully prepared for the session.

So it was with some annoyance and frustration when Abigail heard the simultaneous slamming of three car doors on Sunday afternoon, and looked out to see who was making such a noise. It was Andrew, Francesca and Annabel. A few minutes later, the girls came in, red-faced, followed by an equally cross-looking Andrew.

'What on earth is the matter? I thought you were staying longer?'

'Ask Dad,' came the reply and both girls pushed past Abigail and went into the living room and sat down.

'Can I come in, Abigail? We need to have a talk,' said Andrew belligerently and he, too, pushed past Abigail, who sighed.

'Girls, can you go into one of the bedrooms so that I can talk to your dad.' They got up huffily, throwing dirty looks at him as they went past. Abigail turned towards her husband. 'What on earth has happened this time? They were perfectly happy when they left here!' She threw her hands up in exasperation.

Andrew looked sternly at Abigail. 'They have been unbelievably rude to Brianna. I don't know what you've been saying to them, but she's only ever been nice to the pair of them.'

Abigail wasn't having this, knowing that there's always two sides to any story. 'Excuse me, Andrew Thomas, but I don't talk about that woman, Brianna, or whatever her name is, to the girls. And I doubt very much that you're telling me the whole story. So, I'd like to know what has happened and I want the truth.' Abigail folded her arms defensively across her chest and looked Andrew in the face.

Andrew sighed. 'Brianna thought it would be a nice gesture if she redecorated the girls' bedrooms to make them a bit more grown-up-looking and less girly. Especially as they are both now getting older.'

Abigail was taken aback. The woman hadn't been in the house for five minutes and already she was making changes and putting her imprint on the place. 'Were the girls consulted about this? It is their bedrooms after all, and they chose the colour scheme. Although I must admit Annabel's is a bit Barbie-ish.' Abigail was keen not to get caught up in a WAG war, so was attempting to take a non-combative approach.

'No, they weren't consulted. As I said, Brianna wanted to surprise them.'

'Okay, what has she done so far?'

'Well, she's had the walls painted white. And she's bought some new curtains and bedding.'

'What colours?'

'Cream for both bedrooms.'

'Mmm, very boring. Bit too grown up in my opinion.'

'Well, you would say that, wouldn't you.'

'The whole idea, Andrew, was for the upstairs to have some colour to reflect mine and the girls' taste and the downstairs to be how you wanted it to be. Now, it seems as if the upstairs is going the same way.' *It's as if we're being erased*, she thought, feeling sad. 'Look, let me have a word with them. Perhaps a compromise can be reached.'

Andrew appeared pacified by this suggestion and said he would speak with Brianna. However, he wasn't prepared to give in yet. 'There was no need though for the girls to be rude to her. They need to apologise.'

'Okay, I'll have a word.'

Andrew left and Abigail called the girls into the living room. She asked them to compromise and suggested that they apologise and then politely ask "that woman", as Abigail couldn't bring herself to mention her name, if they could add some colourful accessories. The suggestion didn't go down well.

'But, Mum,' wailed Francesca, 'cream is so boring. I really liked my bedroom the way it was.'

'So did I,' said an equally upset Annabel. 'I like pink and white. I don't want cream. It's yuck. 'I'm not going back there.' She stamped her foot in annoyance.

Abigail sighed and wondered what had happened to her peaceful Sunday. 'Okay, what about if we make your two bedrooms here the same as your old ones? We can go shopping one day after school this week and look for similar colours. How does that sound? You're only at Dad's every other weekend so it's not as if you are spending a lot of time there.'

The two girls nodded reluctantly. 'Can we choose whatever we want?' Annabel asked.

'Yes, of course.'

'I was thinking, Mummy,' said an appeased Annabel, 'that perhaps pink and white is a bit babyish now. Seeing as I'm getting older.'

'And I can always get some orange and yellow cushions to brighten up the room,' said a less grumpy Francesca.

'Great, girls. You've made the right decision.'

'Can we still go shopping though and get things for our bedrooms here?'

'Yes, of course.'

'And can we get...'

'No, Annabel, we cannot get a puppy.'

So, peace and tranquillity was once again restored. It didn't last long.

CHAPTER THIRTY

In which Abigail becomes suspicious

ABIGAIL HAD JUST finished with a client and given her some visualisation exercises to do at home before their next session, when there was a knock at the door. It was Mavis Brown. 'How are you getting on? Are you settling in okay?'

'All good, thanks to you, Mavis. What can I do for you?'

'Well, I just had a reiki session with this woman. She came directly to me after a Tibetan sound healing session with Thekkla. She explained that her chakras need realigning and her aura needs a reboot, so thought that reiki could help with that. She also said that she was having some self-esteem issues and could I recommend anyone. She'd noticed that there was someone here who was a qualified CBT practitioner and did I know her. Well, of course I know you and so I recommended you. Then she asked if this person was any good, to which I replied that there had never been any complaints. When I gave her your name, she said, "Well, let's hope she's as good as you say and then I won't have to complain," and she winked at me! There was definitely something a bit off about her.'

'Thanks, Mavis. Did you get her name?'

'Well, her appointment was booked under the name of Beverley Masters, so look out for that name.'

Abigail had her suspicions. 'What did she look like?'

'She was quite tall, shapely figure, and she had that kind of hair that I associate with successful, confident women. Very luxuriant, with a mass of tight corkscrew curls. You know, you see the hair first and then the person. It was reddish in colour. Oh, and she had a slight American accent.'

Abigail had an idea who the woman was. It was the mention of the American accent that gave it away. She was almost certain that it was Brianna Morgan who had come to check her out. 'Right, thanks, Mavis. On another matter, I was thinking of inviting Katy over. Okay with you?'

'Yes, of course. Can I ask a favour?'

'Yes, of course. What is it?

'Can you invite Chelsea Kimble. Katy tells me she's being bullied a bit by the "alpha pack", if you know who I mean.'

'I do indeed. No problem. Leave it with me. Also, can you give me Kelly Lewis' number as I want to invite Shaznay.'

Another positive outcome of moving to Knighton was that they now lived near a number of restaurants within walking distance. That evening, Abigail decided to take the girls out for dinner. 'Right, girls. What's it to be? TGI Fridays or Pizza Express?'

TGI Fridays had been the resounding choice. The girls were drinking Coca-Cola and Abigail had ordered a mojito.

Mum! You're drinking a cocktail,' said Francesca. 'You're not becoming an alcoholic, are you?'

Abigail laughed. 'Of course not. Am I not allowed a cocktail?'

'Of course you are. But you always drink wine.' She whispered something to Annabel, who nodded in reply.

'What did you just say to your sister?'

'I said that you were acting a bit weird.'

'Well, thank you very much! Oh look, here comes our food.' Abigail then asked the waiter for a large glass of Pinot grigio, and two more cokes "for my parents". She gestured at her daughters, and grinned.

Francesca was momentarily embarrassed. 'Mum! Stop being weird.' She looked at her sister and grinned.

In that instant, Abigail knew that they were a happy little family, until she had to go and spoil it all. 'It's Dad's weekend this weekend,' she said cheerily.

'Do we have to go?' asked Francesca.

'I don't want to go,' was Annabel's response, and gloom descended on the table.

Why did I have to go and open my big mouth? Abigail silently chastised herself.

'Yes, you do. Now, who wants sticky toffee pudding with salted caramel ice-cream for dessert?'

Two pairs of hands shot up, and happiness was restored.

Just before Andrew came to collect the girls on Saturday morning, Abigail remembered that she needed to ask them something. 'Francesca, what does Dad's girlfriend look like?'

Francesca thought for a bit, knowing she had to be careful what she said as she didn't want to upset her mum. 'She's not as pretty as you, Mum, and she's not as slim. She's attractive but wears far too much make-up. And her hair is all bushy. It looks as if she doesn't comb it.'

This last comment made Abigail smile. From Francesca's description, the woman seemed very similar to the person who had been to see Mavis Brown and who was called Beverley Masters – the same initials as Brianna Morgan. Annabel, who didn't want to be left out, added, 'She's got a weird accent – like the actors in *Friends*.'

This confirmed it for Abigail. The woman was definitely Brianna Morgan, and she made a note to tell the receptionist at Heavenly Healing that if someone called Beverley Masters rang to make an appointment to see her, she was to say she was fully booked for the foreseeable future. There was no way she was going to let this woman give her the "once over".

As arranged, Andrew collected the girls. Abigail had organised a facial and a massage for herself, and then planned to relax for the rest of the day with some wine, a takeaway and the new series of *Vera* with Brenda Blethyn.

Sunday morning was spent catching up on domestic chores, and then Abigail planned a leisurely afternoon preparing for her client sessions. At 2pm the apartment door opened to reveal Annabel and Francesca looking very upset. Andrew had already driven away.

'What's up, girls? What's happened this time?'

The girls went into the living room and sat down. 'Dad and Brianna want to send us to boarding school, and I'm not going! I'll run away.' Annabel was almost in tears.

'Annabel, be fair. It was more Brianna than Dad. Anyway, I'm not going either!' added Francesca.

Abigail was furious. She thought she'd heard the end of talk about boarding schools when she'd made it clear to Andrew it wasn't happening. 'Neither of you are going to boarding school. Where has this come from? I'm going to ring your dad now and get this sorted out, once and for all.'

'No, don't! It'll only cause another argument.' Francesca looked downcast.

Abigail sighed. 'What do you mean, another argument?'

'We were in my room and we heard Brianna say—'

Before Francesca continue, she was interrupted by Abigail. 'Francesca, if you were in your room and Dad and Brianna were downstairs, how come you could hear what they were saying? Were you eavesdropping?'

Francesca reddened. 'Well, a little bit. When we heard them arguing, we might have crept downstairs to listen.'

'Mmm, I see. Okay, carry on.'

'Well, we heard Brianna say, "Andrew, I'm not putting up with such difficult behaviour. I didn't sign up for this. They'll have to go to boarding school, or else I'm leaving. Also, we agreed we'd go travelling in the summer and if the girls are going to continue to be disrespectful, then they're not coming".'

'What did Dad say?'

'I couldn't hear properly because he was speaking quietly.'

Abigail was astonished. Who did this person think she was to start dictating about her girls' schooling and going on holiday with them, which was something else she hadn't been consulted on. She folded her arms and started tapping her foot on the floor.

Annabel was becoming a bit hysterical. 'I don't want to leave my school. I've got some nice friends now. And I don't even want a puppy any more. Even if I did, I wouldn't leave it behind, but I don't think the boarding school allows pets, so me and Dinky, because that's what I'll call my puppy, will run away together!'

Even Francesca, who would have usually rolled her eyes at such a statement, kept quiet because she recognised the seriousness of the situation, and she put a comforting arm around her younger sister.

'I think you'd better tell me just what's been going on. Difficult behaviour is not a description I'd ascribe to either of you, so something has caused this. Francesca, you'd better tell me. Annabel, calm down a bit.'

What transpired is that there had been a party on Saturday evening, and Brianna had decided to do away with the alcove and put a bar in its place. So, the settee and TV had gone. Understandably, the girls were upset because they felt their home was not theirs any more. First, their bedrooms and now their "den". This had resulted in a falling out between Brianna and the girls, especially when Francesca had accused Brianna of taking over. Abigail asked if that was all, or if there was more.

'She wanted us to wear bunny girl costumes.' Francesca looked wary when she said this.

'She did what!' Abigail asked in astonishment.

'She wanted us to wear bunny girl costumes and greet the guests when they arrived. I said no. Annabel wanted to, though, as she's always wanted a rabbit.'

'I did not! Mum! I didn't.' And she started crying again.

'Oh, now look what you've done, Francesca. Anyway, I don't quite understand. She wanted you both to dress up as bunny girls? Black swimming costume-type thing with a fluffy bobble on the back and rabbit ears?'

Both girls nodded. 'But I refused, and I told Annabel she should refuse. It didn't feel right. So I said to Brianna that we weren't going to wear them, so we were sent to our room for disobedient behaviour.'

'What did Dad say?'

'He didn't say anything.'

Abigail decided she would have a word with Andrew and get his side of the story. In the meantime, she reassured the girls that they were not going to boarding school and they spent the remainder of Sunday cuddled up on the settee, although none of them felt very happy.

CHAPTER THIRTY-ONE

In which Abigail gets a surprise visit

AFTER SUNDAY'S TROUBLING revelations, Abigail decided that Annabel and Francesca would not be going to Andrew's house for the time being until matters had been sorted out. She had been totally accommodating and had carefully created a drama-free arrangement. Yet, it wasn't being reciprocated at the other end and she couldn't accept, or tolerate, how this was unfairly affecting her daughters. So, she had texted Andrew and told him that he wouldn't be seeing the girls for the time being and, if he was going to make life difficult, she would have to take legal advice and set divorce proceedings in motion based on the fact that he had committed adultery. On the other end of the phone, she had received a cacophony of silence. *So be it; let battle commence*, she thought to herself and disconnected.

Abigail didn't have any clients on Thursday and so she took the day off. She was sat at her dining-cum-kitchen table, when the entry button for her apartment buzzed. She wasn't expecting anyone, but opened the door to let whoever it was in. Her apartment bell rang. Two women, who looked vaguely familiar, were standing outside. They looked like less glamorous versions of Juliana and Svetlana, when she realised that it was in fact them, except they were both make-up free and dressed in jeans, t-shirts and cardigans. They were also wearing glum expressions.

'Can we come in please, Abigail. We need to talk to you,' said Juliana, who then pushed past a surprised Abigail, followed by Svetlana.

'Of course, do come in! This is a surprise.'

Sitting down at the table, Juliana and Svetlana apologised for not having come to see her sooner, but they had only just found out from Francesca where they were now living.

Abigail was puzzled. 'When did you see Francesca?'

'At your house, or what used to be your house, if you know what I mean?' answered Svetlana.

'Ah, I see. But why were you at my house? Were you there as well, Juliana?'

Juliana nodded. 'Andrew and that woman had a party on Saturday. That's why we've come to see you. She's got to go!'

Abigail was astonished. 'I sense there's a story coming. Before I listen, would you like a tea or coffee?'

'Have you got anything stronger?' asked Juliana.

'It's only 11 o'clock. Bit early, isn't it?' was Abigail's response.

Juliana shrugged. 'S'pose you're right. Okay, tea for me please.'

'Coffee for me, Abigail,' said Svetlana, who was unusually quiet.

She made tea for Juliana, and a coffee for herself and Svetlana. 'Right, spill the beans because the girls came back much earlier than I expected, and they were very upset. So I realised something must have happened. What I don't understand is why you both want her gone because of my two.'

'We'll come on to that shortly. We want her gone because... well, you tell Abigail why you want her gone, Juliana. My story is a bit more... how do I put this? It's a bit more complicated.'

Before Juliana could speak, Abigail asked them if they knew the woman who was called Brianna Morgan. Juliana replied that she knew of her, but had never met her before. Svetlana replied that she knew her from her past, and her face reddened when she said this. Abigail knew she was going to hear something interesting, and sat back in her chair.

'Actually, Abigail, do you have any biscuits?' asked Svetlana.

Abigail said she did and got up and put some on a plate. Svetlana helped herself and ate it in two mouthfuls. 'Ooh, that's better. I was feeling queasy.' She took another one.

'Are you okay, Svetlana? Can I get you a glass of water?'

'No, these biscuits will be fine.' She patted her stomach and grinned.

Abigail looked closely at Svetlana and noticed that her cheeks had filled out slightly and her face looked fuller and softer. The penny dropped. 'Are you...?'

'Yes! I'm pregnant and I've got morning sickness.' She smiled happily and took another biscuit.

Abigail was shocked into silence. She looked at Juliana and shook her head in amazement.

'Don't look so shocked. It was your fault!' Svetlana laughed at the look on Abigail's face.

'How come?'

'Sven and I enjoyed looking after your two so much, and I saw how natural he was with them, that I sounded him out about having one of our own and he agreed. Also, and don't the pair of you think badly of me when I say this, but the baby is going to be my insurance. Sven's a good-looking man and he's wealthy, which makes him a sitting target for unscrupulous young women who will only be too obliging to pander to his needs and wants. I'm not getting any younger either, so I need to make sure my future is secure.' Svetlana patted her stomach. Abigail and Juliana must have made a face at what Svetlana had just said. 'Don't look so shocked you two! You're hardly an angel, Juliana. No offence.'

'No offence taken, I'm sure!' replied Juliana, looking offended.

'Anyway, I want that woman gone and I'll tell you why, and I don't want you judging me.'

Svetlana revealed that she hadn't made the grade in the modelling world; that although she had the figure and the looks, she just didn't have that special "something" that set her apart from the other models, of which there were many. 'I knew I was never going to be another Kate Moss, Cindy Crawford or Linda Evangelista.' She went on to add that, like many other aspiring and struggling young models, she still had expenses to pay and therefore supplemented any income she did earn if she was lucky enough to be picked for a shoot, by attending parties and functions frequented by influential people from the modelling, media and film world.

'We used to call her "the procuress",' explained Svetlana, 'because she used to procure young models for these events. This is Brianna I'm talking about.'

Svetlana then went on to explain that, although she never did anything to be ashamed of, it was all too easy to slide down the slippery slope to a world of drugs and being hired out for "private parties". 'So, I went to Brianna one day and told her I was getting out of modelling. She replied that she was in the process of setting up her own company, which she was calling Eve's Escorts, and wanted me on her books because she could see how popular I was amongst her clientele for the organisation she was currently working for. So, I worked for her for a while until I was headhunted…'

Juliana was just about to take a sip of her tea and snorted when she heard this.

'Excuse me, Juliana! I was headhunted!'

Juliana stifled a laugh and bent her head so as to hide the grin on her face.

'Anyway, as I was saying before I was so rudely interrupted, I was approached by Elite Escorts who were a well-known and long-established escort agency with "top drawer" clients, unlike Brianna's who were a bit on the dubious and dodgy side.'

Abigail noticed that the more Svetlana was talking, her accent was changing and she was becoming "Shirley of Croydon" again.

'Anyway, I joined Elite Escorts and was very successful, and I met Sven and the rest is history. You can imagine my shock, then, when I walked into the living room and saw the person I recognised from my past. She was also shocked. I could tell. As much as I didn't want to be reminded about that part of my past, neither did she, as she eventually got out of the escort business and I'd heard that she'd set up a company that organised events and dinners for the corporate world, which, to all intents and purposes, is respectable on the surface. Although I stopped attending functions with Sven, unless they were company dinners or the client was really important, I knew he used an events company. I didn't know it was her company, because I never ask Sven anything about what he gets up to outside the home. So, when we walked into your house, Sven said, "what's she doing here?" I said, "Who?" He said, "Brianna Morgan. She owns Eve's Garden, the events company we use", and that's when we saw each other. I can honestly say, Abigail, Andrew went down in our estimation when we saw who he was with.'

You still went to the party though, knowing Andrew was with another woman, thought Abigail, but stayed silent.

'I've prattled on a bit, haven't I? There's a little bit more. Sven and I decided to only stay for a short while. It didn't feel right for either of us. It was when we were leaving that we saw a light on in one of the bedrooms, and could hear voices. So we went up and saw Francesca and Annabel. They were in Francesca's room. They were watching TV and didn't look happy. I asked them what was wrong and they showed us the bunny girl costumes and that they'd been sent upstairs because they wouldn't wear them. I told them they did the right thing, gave them both a hug and then we left. That's why Sven and I don't want Brianna living next door. She's not a good role model and some of her friends are questionable.'

Abigail decided that it was now time for something stronger. She certainly needed some wine and asked Juliana if she'd like a glass too. 'I thought you'd never ask,' came the reply.

Svetlana asked for orange juice, and Abigail brought two glasses of white wine and an orange juice to the table. Turning to Juliana, she said, 'So, you've never met her but you know of her?'

'Yes, that's true. I was going through Rufus' pockets one morning after he'd got in very late after one of his "old boys' night's out" and I came across a card. It had the name of this woman called Brianna Morgan, CEO of Eve's Garden, which organised events. Of course, I didn't ask him about her because he would have known I'd been snooping.' Abigail reddened slightly and took a gulp of wine. Juliana was no fool. 'You too, eh?' Abigail nodded. 'Anyway, so I did a bit of research and found out as much as I could about the company. It all seemed above board and, as Svetlana said, respectable enough.

The thing is, there was always a problem when Rufus went on his Friday jaunts which she was obviously involved in to some extent, as she probably helped organise them. For example, one time he'd drunk so much that not only did he go to the wrong station to get the train home, but he got on a train that was going to York which is miles away and it was the last train of the day. The cleaner found him asleep in First Class the next morning. Honestly, I ask you. Luckily for Rufus, the cleaner put him on the early morning train to King's Cross and then I drove up to London and collected him. He was in a right state. Then, there was the time at your husband's... erm, I mean Andrew's...' Juliana had stopped talking as she felt awkward.

'It's okay, Juliana. He is still my husband for the time being.'

'Okay, so on the evening of Andrew's initiation ceremony, Rufus got very drunk and came home in a dreadful state yet again. Luckily, Sven and Andrew were on hand to make sure he got home safely. He went to bed fully-clothed. Drunk as a skunk, he was.' Juliana's accent was now revealing her Isle of Dogs origins. 'In the morning, he got undressed and left everything on the bedroom floor. Lipstick smudges everywhere, and I do mean everywhere. Disgusting! And he smelt of perfume. It was very strong and all around his... Oh, well, you don't need to know that but you probably get the drift. Anyway, I didn't know what she looked like because I couldn't find any photographs of her online, so when we walked into the party, Rufus went a funny colour. I thought he was having a heart attack. I said, "What's wrong, Rufus? You don't look well". And then Andrew came over, accompanied by Brianna, who kissed Rufus on both cheeks and winked at him. "Juliana," he said, "this is Brianna Morgan. She's the person who organises the boys' night's out". So I said to her, "So you're the one who encourages him to get in such a state and I'm the one who has to deal with it". Of course, that didn't go down well at all. Anyway, we only stayed a couple of hours and Rufus is now banned from going up to London on Fridays. So there you have it.'

'Right, so no wonder you both want her gone. I'm not sure, though, how I can help.'

'You don't need to help. Juliana and I have a plan and we wanted to make sure you're okay with this. It won't affect you or the girls, but it will probably have some impact on Andrew but not in a harmful way. If you are agreeable, there is one thing you could do for us,' said Svetlana.

Abigail was in a state of utter surprise. She just didn't know what to make of it all, but she was curious, nonetheless. 'What can I do for you?' she asked them both.

'Does Andrew wear boxers or Y-fronts?' asked Juliana.

'Boxers,' she replied.

'Can you get a pair of his boxers and send them to either myself or Svetlana?'

'That's going to be difficult because the girls aren't going there for the time being, but I can buy a duplicate of a pair he already has and send them. Is that okay?' Abigail was intrigued.

'Perfect! Send them to me,' said Svetlana. 'Oh, and I forgot. Tammy and Trixie send their love, and said they were sorry not to have seen you to say goodbye, and that you're missed at the care home.'

After Abigail had shown Juliana and Svetlana out, she sat down on the settee and tried, without success, to digest all that she had heard. It was beyond belief, and she was intrigued and curious as to just what those two were planning. She then realised that Andrew must have met Brianna Morgan for the first time at his initiation ceremony.

CHAPTER THIRTY-TWO

THE PLAN IS PUT INTO ACTION

ANDREW ARRIVED HOME and he was not in a good mood. Abigail had followed up her text to him with a phone call, and repeated that the girls would not be coming to the house in the immediate future until she was assured that the current unsatisfactory situation was resolved. He had tried to reason with her, and had failed. This was not the easy-going and compliant Abigail he had married; she had become a lot more assertive and self-assured. So he had hung his coat up on the coat stand and walked into the kitchen. Brianna was on the phone and, seeing the look on Andrew's face, she told the person on the other end that she would have to call them back later.

'What's up with you? You don't look at all happy.'

'I'm not,' he glumly replied. 'I've had a disagreement with Abigail over the girls and they won't be coming here for a while.'

Brianna clapped her hands. 'Thank the Lord for that!' she said, grinning. 'Perhaps now we can have some peace and quiet for a change, and no more drama.'

Andrew looked at her, an unreadable expression on his face. 'Anyway, what's for dinner? I'm famished.'

'I've been very busy today, Andrew. Two new projects have landed in my lap. I thought we could eat out.'

Andrew wasn't pleased. 'I've had a shit day, to be honest. The last thing I want to do is go out. All I want is a stiff g and t, dinner, and then an early night.'

Brianna folded her arms. 'Well, I've had a busy day too and I haven't had time to cook.'

'Well, you could have put something in the slow cooker. That's what Abigail used to do first thing in the morning, which freed her day up.' That was the wrong thing to say.

Brianna glared at him. 'Firstly, Andrew, I'm not Abigail and, secondly, do I look like a "slow cooker" type of woman?' She was dressed in a vibrantly coloured striped linen tunic, white palazzo pants and gold sandals.

Andrew looked her up and down and admitted that she looked as if she should be on a yacht somewhere drinking champagne, and not in a suburban kitchen dishing up a meal from a slow cooker. He sighed, realising he was beaten. 'Okay, you've got a point. Let me go and freshen up and we can go to The Royal Oak if that suits your ladyship.' He smiled wanly and was rewarded with a hug and a kiss.

Whilst Andrew was at the bar ordering the food and getting the drinks, Brianna surveyed him. She noticed that his tall, slim body, which was usually upright, was bending in a gesture of defeat and weariness. She also noticed that his hair was thinning, revealing the beginnings of a bald patch on the top of his head. She had a momentary flashback of the evening when she had first met him. She was introduced to him by Rufus, who had explained that Andrew and his wife had just moved into the area and this was his initiation ceremony. 'Let's make it a good one,' Rufus had said to her, with a wink.

She had been struck by how formal and polite Andrew was. In her opinion, a true British gentleman. He was smartly dressed, and she had liked his aftershave which was spicy. *I need to loosen this boy up*, she told herself. And loosened up he had. She had left them when they had gone for dinner and drinks at The Ivy in Covent

Garden, joining them later to facilitate their entry into a very exclusive, very private, *shibari* club situated discreetly down an alley. Brianna had arranged for the club's top Japanese hostess to attend to Rufus and Andrew. Sven, who had some Japanese clients flying in within the next two weeks, had gone to watch a *shibari* rope bondage show as he thought he might get Brianna to organise a visit for his clients. Meanwhile, Rufus and Andrew were drinking the club's most expensive whisky and Andrew was slowly unwinding. His tie had come off, with the help of Mitsuki, the hostess, and his shirt buttons were undone. He was totally relaxed with a smile on his face and Brianna noticed, when his demeanour had softened, how attractive he was.

As they left the *shibari* club, she had slipped the club's erotic-looking card into his jacket pocket. She had then accompanied them to the Pink Pussycat lap dancing club which, again, was discreet and very private. Here, Andrew had completely reverted to what must have been a younger version of himself before life's responsibilities took over. Her last image of him before she left was of him lying back while Savannah, one of the club's most supple and engaging lap dancers, entertained him. Before leaving, she popped one of the club's cards in his jacket pocket, along with one of her own business cards. She wanted to see him again, and thought there had been a spark between them. So, she would leave it for a couple of weeks and then contact him to see if she could offer her services. Now, here she was, sitting in a village pub drinking vodka and tonic, with Andrew who looked as if he had the weight of the whole world on his shoulders.

The following morning, Andrew got up, gave Brianna a quick kiss and then left for the office. She got up, showered, and put on leggings and a top to do her yoga exercises that she started the day with. The doorbell rang, as she always left the gates open if she wasn't going out. A good-looking, young man stood on the doorstep. He was carrying an Umbro sports bag, and was dressed in shorts, and a fitted white t-shirt which bore the logo, Ben's Fitness Services. He flashed Brianna a gleaming white smile. 'Good morning, Mrs Hetherington. Ben here, of Ben's Fitness Services. I'm here for your workout.'

Brianna liked what she saw, and was also disappointed. 'Oh! You've come to the wrong house. Mrs Hetherington's house is just up there on the left.'

'My apologies. Sorry, I didn't read the email properly. It said look for a large house with gates, and a gravel driveway. Oh well, that's a pity and a shame, seeing as you're already dressed in fitness gear. Look, I'll give you my card just in case you ever fancy a personal training session. I'd better ring Mrs Hetherington as well. She's a new client and I'm already a few minutes late.' He made out he was using his mobile phone. 'Yes, I'm on my way. I'll be a couple of minutes. Oh no! That's a shame. I hope you feel better soon.' He turned back to Brianna. 'Unfortunately, she's not feeling well and has had to cancel. Don't suppose you fancy...? Great! Let's get started then. Are you ready for a tough session?' He grinned as he went inside.

An hour later, Brianna waved Ben goodbye. She was exhausted as he had certainly put her through her paces, and she had enjoyed every minute. She liked challenges, whether they were physical or mental, and felt invigorated. She decided to cook a meal for a change. Fortunately, Andrew's wife had left a cookery book behind for the fancy oven and so she chose an easy recipe. She spent the rest of the day working, then about the time Andrew usually came home she opened a bottle of his favourite red wine to let it breathe. Changing into one of her long colourful kaftans, she put in gold and turquoise drop earrings and sprayed on Miss Dior perfume. Dimming the dining room lights, she put on some background music and hoped she had created the right ambience.

Over dinner, equilibrium between Andrew and Brianna was restored, and they both remembered why they had connected and were attracted to each other in the first place. They went to bed at 10pm and were just falling asleep when Brianna's mobile phone pinged to alert her to a text. She read it, smiled and turned out her light. Andrew was dying to ask who it was texting her at that time, but decided to play it cool.

The following morning, Andrew decided to go into the office late so he hung about and waited until Brianna got up to have a shower. When he heard the shower door close, he pressed the WhatsApp logo on her phone and, because she didn't use a password, he got directly into her messages. There was a text from someone called Ben who had written: *Enjoyed our session today* ☺ *Hope I didn't work u too hard! C u Monday at 10. Be sure to wear your Lycra again. Suits u* ☺ *Ben x*

Andrew closed down WhatsApp and put the mobile phone back exactly as he found it. Knowing that Brianna's character was of the flirtatious kind, he reasoned that the text was merely a bit of flirty bantering. He was aware, however, that he had fallen for her flirtatious and seductive manner, and so he decided to keep an open mind.

*

It was the following Monday and Andrew was getting ready for work. He was watching Brianna closely to see what clothes she would choose, knowing already that she had an appointment at 10 with Ben. She chose bright pink Lycra leggings, and a tight-fitting black tank top. She had put a bright pink hair band over abundant hair so as to prevent it falling over her face, then sprayed some perfume on her wrist. She was clearly in a happy mood because she was singing quietly to herself. Kissing her goodbye, Andrew said he would see her later and went downstairs. He shut the front door, retrieved a fold-away chair from the boot of his Aston Martin and walked out of the driveway. However, instead of going to the station, he walked up to the local garage, purchased a newspaper, a takeaway coffee and a BLT sandwich. He walked back towards Green Park Road, and then ducked into the driveway of the house that had been the temporary home of Cliff and Marnie Mitchelson. He went in through the side gate and into the garden where he took up a position behind the fence, which was obscured by a hedge, where he could see his house on the opposite side. He opened up the chair, took his binoculars out of his briefcase, and settled down to watch his house.

Just before 10am, a young sporty-looking and tanned male, carrying an Umbro sports bag, walked up the driveway and rang the doorbell. He saw the door open, and the young man went inside. An hour later, the door opened. The young man lingered chatting for a while, and Andrew could see a glimpse of bright pink leggings before the door closed, and the man left. He was smiling and whistling to himself. Then, 10 minutes later, a small van entered the driveway. The signage on the van was advertising *Dominic's Garden Services* in large red lettering. Beneath, in black lettering was *No Job Too Big or Too Small. Full gardening services offered from Bush and Garden Maintenance to Seed Planting.* A young man exited from the van and rang the doorbell. The door opened and Brianna came into view, still wearing her keep-fit clothes. The young man then disappeared into the house, leaving an hour later by the side gate. He was also smiling and whistling to himself as he got into his van and drove away. Again, Andrew had to keep an open mind, but the seeds of doubt and suspicion had been planted in his mind. With these thoughts uppermost, he folded away the chair and left it behind the fence to be collected later and made his way to the station to go into the office.

It was late in the evening. Brianna had gone to bed early because she was tired, which meant Andrew could go into his study and look up Dominic's Garden Services, and carry out a search for "Ben. Personal Training, Knighton and Cornham". Having satisfied himself that he now knew who Brianna was letting into the house, he too went to bed. Brianna's phone pinged twice. She was fast asleep. Andrew decided he would read the messages in the morning so as to keep one step ahead, but he had a good idea who they were from.

*

Over the past few weeks, just before the plan was put into action, and then once the plan was underway, a series of WhatsApp messages had been going back and forth between Juliana and Svetlana.

> *Svetlana to Juliana: Have spoken to Sven about our plan and he's in agreement. Have u spoken to Rufus?*

> *Juliana to Svetlana: Yes and he's up for it. But still grumpy because I've banned him from his Friday trips to London* 😁

Svetlana to Juliana: Have u spoken to Ben?

Juliana to Svetlana: Yes. He's going there on Tuesday. Will report back after visit.

Juliana to Svetlana: Everything going to plan. Ben now giving 'that woman' PT. 2nd session arranged. Also arranging for his gardening mate (Dom) to pay her a visit. He's messaging her at night time. Fingers x it at least makes A suspicious.

Ben to Brianna (both messages forwarded to Juliana and Svetlana): *Good work-out today Bri. Quite a sweaty session ☺ Dom says it was nice meeting u. He's lkg 4ward to seeing U next week. As I am x*

Svetlana to Juliana: Hope so. That's all we can hope for. Time to put the next part of the plan into action?

Juliana to Svetlana: Yes. Rufus is a sneaky sod! I knew he wouldn't like not going to London. However, he's come up with a gd idea. He suggests that he and Sven take Andrew out in London on Friday eve. He's under STRICT instructions that it's only dinner and drinks. NOTHING ELSE! So, because it's for a gd cause – I've agreed!! Can u ask Sven if he's up for it?

Svetlana to Juliana: He says yes. He suggested drinks at The Bar Below at Hide, followed by dinner at Hide. Restaurant is in Mayfair. He said he'll book. He's also under strict instructions not to take A on anywhere else cos it'll muck up the plan.

Juliana to Svetlana: Do u want me to do letterhead for PPC? I know where R keeps all his business cards and can base it on the club's card.

Svetlana to Juliana: Yes please. Btw have received boxers from Abigail. Guess what? They're pale pink! Don't think A would have chosen them. Prob a bd or Xmas present.

It was Friday. Andrew was looking very smart, and was in a good mood. He had read the texts and now knew that Brianna was having "PT" sessions, or perhaps that was just a euphemism for another kind of session, as he wouldn't put it past her. She was also employing the services of a young gardener, and he momentarily wondered what had happened to Unwin. So, forewarned is forearmed, and he gave no hint that he knew what she was getting up to when he wasn't there.

Brianna noticed how smart he was looking, and also that he smelt nice too. 'Mmm, you smell nice and you're wearing your best suit. What's the occasion?'

Andrew was feeling very smug and grinned. 'Rufus and Sven have invited me out for dinner and drinks tonight after work in London. I shouldn't be too late.'

Brianna frowned. 'It's Friday. The start of the weekend. I thought we could do something tonight, or even shoot off somewhere until Sunday. What am I going to do tonight?'

Andrew shrugged. 'Don't know, Bri. Watch TV. Facetime your friends. Anyway, I won't be late.' And with that, he kissed her quickly on the lips and went down the stairs whistling, leaving Brianna wondering what he was getting up to because he wasn't normally so jolly, and he never ever went out on a Friday evening without her, or left her alone.

CHAPTER THIRTY-THREE

ALL IS NOT WELL IN THE GARDEN OF EVE

ANDREW HAD COME back on Friday evening, slightly inebriated and in a rare amorous mood. Brianna wasn't amused. She had spent the evening alone. All her London friends were out or away, there was nothing on the television and she was bored. However, she felt that it wouldn't be fair to take her dissatisfaction out on Andrew who had obviously had a good evening. 'You had a good time then, I see,' she said good-naturedly.

'Indeed, I did. That Rufus and Sven are jolly good fellows. Right, I'm for bed. Are you joining me?' He wiggled his eyebrows at her suggestively.

'They didn't try to get you to go on somewhere, then? I wouldn't put it past them. I know what Rufus is like.'

'Nope. Those days are over. Just dinner and drinks in Mayfair.' He took her by the hand and they went upstairs.

On Monday, Andrew went off to work still in a chirpy mood. They had had a quiet weekend together and, although it was pleasant, Brianna was a social butterfly who thrived on entertaining and throwing a good party, and so she didn't want too many quiet weekends. The other thing was that she rarely went up to London now and was missing the energy and vibrancy of London. If she needed some human contact or a break from work, there were plenty of coffee shops she could visit or a park she could sit in, or shops to browse. Here, in Green Park Road, there was nothing within walking distance.

She found Cornham to be very parochial because, at heart, she was a City girl. Also, she hadn't made any friends. It was obvious Juliana didn't like her and she had no intentions of reconnecting with Shirley, as she knew her, and that feeling was clearly reciprocated. So, here she was, "Billy no-mates", which was completely alien to her, stuck in the middle of nowhere. Something had to change. She decided that she might, at some point, suggest to Andrew that they sell the house and move nearer to, or into, London where she could get her life back on track.

It was Tuesday evening, and it was getting dark outside. Two shadowy figures were just about visible in Green Park Road.

'What did you tell Rufus?'

'I told him I was just putting out the recycling bin. What did you tell Sven?'

'The same.'

'Have you got it?'

'Yes. The Jiffy bag is small enough to put in the post box.' Svetlana posted the bag into Andrew's post box.

Juliana then deposited the envelope. 'I'll text Abigail to tell her that everything, so far, is going to plan.'

'Okay, Juliana. Goodnight.'

'Goodnight, Svetlana.'

It was Wednesday. The postman usually came at about 10am and so Brianna went to the post box, as she was expecting some invitation samples to look at for one of her projects. She opened the post box and saw what she was expecting. There was also a white envelope edged in pale pink, addressed to Andrew, and marked "Private and Personal". The envelope smelled of roses. There was also a small brown Jiffy bag that had the same scent. Instantly, she became suspicious. Going back inside, she boiled the kettle and then steamed open the flap of the envelope. Inside was a sheet of A5 white paper, edged in pale pink. In the top left-hand corner was an image of a pale pink cat. She knew immediately that this was from the Pink Pussycat Club. There were a few handwritten words, which read:

The pussies have missed you! We were happy you came to see us again. Purrlease come visit again soon!

Ps: Snookie sends you lots of licks xx

Brianna was not amused. She put the sheet of paper back into the envelope and looked for a glue stick to seal the flap down again. Not finding any, she licked the flap and pressed down firmly. Next, she turned her attention to the Jiffy bag and looked inside. She could see pale pink fabric. On pulling the item out, it was revealed to be a pair of pale pink Jack Wills boxer shorts which were covered in red lipstick kisses. This time, she didn't reseal the bag and placed both the bag and the envelope on Andrew's desk in his study. She'd have words with him later.

Andrew came home, shouted a hello to Brianna and then went into his study. Almost immediately, he came out again and shouted to Brianna again. No answer. He went into the kitchen. She wasn't there, and neither was there a smell of anything cooking which probably meant no evening meal again. He went into the living room, where she was sipping a glass of champagne and casually turning the pages of a magazine. Andrew held up the boxer shorts and piece of paper. 'Brianna, what are these I found in my study?'

Brianna wrinkled her nose up at the smell, and then cooly gazed at him. 'Looks like a pair of boxer shorts and a letter, if I'm not mistaken. Both smelling of perfume.'

'Well, that's obviously what they are, isn't it? What I mean is why are they in my study?'

'I put them there. They're for you. They were in the post box this morning, addressed to you.'

'That brings me onto another matter. If they were addressed to me, then why was the Jiffy bag open? Also, it looks very much like the envelope has been opened as well. I think you need to do a bit of explaining.'

Brianna had the decency to redden a bit, but she wasn't one for backing down. 'What I'd like to know, Andrew, is why you lied to me. You said you only went out for dinner and drinks, but clearly that's not true! I think *you* have some explaining to do.'

Andrew looked perplexed. 'I did only go for dinner and drinks. Ask Rufus or Sven. I don't know anything about these things. Honestly, it's a mystery. Also, although I do have a pair of pale pink boxer shorts, I don't wear them anymore. They were a Christmas present. I don't even know where they are. Anyway, that still doesn't let you off the hook for opening my mail. Look, let's not argue. What's for dinner? I'm starving.'

'Nothing. Nothing is for dinner. I've been too busy with my projects and I've had this unpleasant surprise to deal with. I'm too tired and emotional now to cook.'

Andrew had heard enough. 'Well, if you didn't keep having these exhausting personal training sessions, then you wouldn't be so tired.'

Brianna looked at him through narrowed eyes. 'Have you been spying on me?'

'Most certainly not!' He, too, had the decency to blush. 'Then how did you—'

Andrew cut her off. 'Also, what's wrong with Unwin?'

'Who's Unwin?'

'The person who does the garden. Old bloke, thinning hair, red nose, always wears a check shirt.'

'Oh him! I was in the garden the other week and this strange man just walked in. Gave me quite a scare. I thought he was a trespasser and so I threatened to call the police.'

'Brianna! That's our gardener. What on earth—'

'Anyway, I've found a new one. He's very good.'

'Oh, I bet he is!'

'And what is that supposed to mean?' She narrowed her eyes at him again.

Andrew was on a roll now. 'Trimmed your bush lately, has he? Planted his seeds?'

Brianna threw back her head and laughed out loud. 'Andrew! What on earth are you going on about. You're not making any sense. Look, I'm sorry I haven't cooked. I really have been busy. Let's eat out. I'll buy. But not The Royal Oak. There's a new Thai restaurant opened up in Cornham, and I promise I'll cook the rest of the week.'

An uneasy truce was called. It wasn't to last.

*

Andrew was a very fastidious person. He abhorred clutter; everything had to be put away out of sight and he was obsessive about cleanliness. Abigail had just about managed to keep on top of things but, due to his pernickety nature, it meant that the living room was barely used and he spent much of the time in his study, whilst Abigail and the girls used the alcove in the kitchen. Of course, that was gone now because Brianna had turned it into a bar of sorts, with optics, and a counter with bar stools. There was another issue as well. Whilst she liked to have formal dinners in the dining room, as did Andrew, she also insisted that on occasion she be allowed to eat in the living room, especially when there was a favourite television programme on. The result was that the inevitable stains from food and drink were appearing on the carpet and the settee. Also, as she now worked from home as she couldn't be bothered to travel up to London, everything was spread out on the kitchen table and the butcher's block. And she was messy.

Andrew had come home from work, walked into the kitchen and saw nothing but mess. She hadn't even wiped up some spilt liquid. She was sat at the kitchen table. Laptop open. Sheets of paper spread out.

'Brianna, why do you work down here?' he had asked. 'Your stuff is everywhere. Why don't you use the small spare room upstairs as a study?'

'Exactly,' she had replied.

'What do you mean, "exactly"?'

'Exactly that. It's too small. I need a lot of space. Now, if we were to move Annabel into the spare room, or let her and Francesca share a room, then that's a possibility.'

'Out of the question. Not going to happen. Francesca and Annabel wouldn't like that at all.'

Brianna stood up and folded her arms. 'Well, it's not as if they visit anymore, do they?'

Andrew was irritated by the mess and ready for an argument. 'Whose fault is that then?'

'Not mine, that's for sure. Now, if you'll excuse me, I have a very important project to work on.' She turned her back on him and went to sit back down.

'No, I don't excuse you, actually. Don't you ever do any housework, or ironing? And why do my shirts have to go to the dry cleaners for washing and ironing?' Brianna turned back round when she realised that Andrew wasn't letting the matter drop. 'Abigail always washed and ironed my shirts. She also did the housework. Admittedly, it wasn't always done to my exacting standards, but at least the house was clean and reasonably tidy.'

Brianna wasn't one for backing down either. Hands on hips, and head tossed back, she responded with, 'For one thing, Abigail isn't the CEO of a very successful company. I am though. Also, she had plenty of time on her hands, unlike me. From what I gather, all she did was take the girls to school, do a bit of voluntary work, and then housework and the laundry, none of which takes a long time, I imagine.'

Andrew surprised himself when he replied with, 'This is a large house. She did it all, top and bottom, and without any help.' At that moment, he realised just how much Abigail had done for him and how she had devoted a lot of her time and energy to the house. Brianna made to leave the kitchen because she couldn't be bothered to argue further, but Andrew still had more to say. 'Also, she organised everything. I didn't have to worry about the garden, the windows being cleaned... on the matter of windows, have the window cleaners been?'

Brianna shrugged. 'Dunno. I haven't seen them, but then again, I'm not always here and I close the gates when I'm out.'

Andrew made a mental note to ring Barney Bright, and then lost his train of thought. However, he couldn't be bothered either to continue arguing and turned to go to his study. As he left the kitchen, it occurred to him that, yet again, there didn't seem to be anything in the way of food being cooked. That was something else Abigail always made sure of – there was always food on the table and a well-stocked fridge.

Brianna had never seen Andrew so annoyed, and he rarely if ever mentioned Abigail, so she decided that she needed to make amends. Knocking on his study door, she stood on the threshold. 'You're right, Andrew, and I'm sorry. The house is a mess. I'll try and be less messy, but I don't do housework. I loathe it. So, why don't we get a "Karlinka"? Caro says she's marvellous. Does everything!'

Andrew and Brianna had been invited by Caroline and Darius for dinner, and Brianna had noticed that they had a maid. Caroline had said she was called Karlinka and was indispensable. 'So, what do you think?' she asked Andrew.

Andrew had never known Brianna to back down from an argument and was surprised. 'It's true. Karlinka does do everything. She's their maid and probably costs them a small fortune. They're loaded. I'm not. However, I will agree to you looking for a cleaner and perhaps she'll do the laundry and ironing as well. What do you say?'

Brianna nodded and smiled. 'Good idea. I'll start looking tomorrow. Thank you, Andrew.'

'No problem, and I'm sorry I was so grumpy.'

Brianna closed the door, leaving Andrew with the question of what was for dinner still hanging in the air.

CHAPTER THIRTY-FOUR

THERE WAS ALWAYS A "TOP SECRET" PLAN

JULIANA AND SVETLANA had done all they could to make their plan work. However, there had been no sign or indication that Brianna and Andrew had split up. In fact, her sporty black Mazda had been spotted only a few days ago driving up Green Park Road. There was nothing more they could do, and they decided to pay Abigail a visit to update her.

It was a Saturday afternoon. Abigail, Francesca and Annabel, were sitting on the settee watching *The Adventures of Lemony Snicket*, which was a film they always enjoyed. The buzzer for the apartment entrance had been pressed. Seeing that it was Juliana and Svetlana, she let them in and stood waiting at her apartment door. Telling the girls to carry on watching the film, Abigail and her visitors sat at the table. Abigail offered them tea or coffee. Juliana asked for tea, and Svetlana also asked for tea because the smell and taste of coffee now made her feel nauseous. Abigail noticed that her pregnancy was well underway. 'Well, this is a nice surprise. You got the boxers okay, Svetlana?'

'Yes, thank you. This is why we've come to see you, though,' she replied. 'Juliana and I have done all that we can, but we don't think it's worked. She's still there.'

Abigail put her finger to her lip and gestured at her girls on the settee. 'Little flappy ears might be listening in.'

'Oh, right. Gotcha. We'll lower our voices,' said Juliana, leaning in towards Abigail. 'So, we don't think our plan worked but something has happened because Rufus invited Andrew out again and Andrew declined. Said he'd got into trouble last time for something he didn't do. Also, Ben told me that she's no longer having personal training sessions with him, although he thinks Dominic is still doing the garden.'

Abigail was confused and looked puzzled. 'Who's Ben and who's Dominic?'

Her visitors looked at each other. 'Of course, she won't know what we're on about, will she, because we've never told her what our plan was?' said Svetlana.

Juliana sighed. 'Sorry, Abigail. We've left you completely in the dark. We thought it was for the best so that you didn't get blamed for anything. We can't fill you in now.' She gestured towards the settee.

'We can tell her a bit,' said Svetlana. 'Ben is Juliana's personal trainer and she sent him round to see Brianna. Dominic is Ben's friend and he's a gardener, and he went to see Brianna. All you need to know is that these two are fit, good-looking, young men; ideal bait to lead cougars astray.' Svetlana winked at Juliana, who gave her a dirty look in response. 'We were hoping they would lead Brianna astray, but it hasn't worked.'

Abigail was finding it hard to take in, but something occurred to her. 'Why would Andrew need a new gardener when he has Unwin?'

'Who's Unwin?' asked Juliana.

'He does the garden.' Abigail still looked puzzled.

Somewhat impatiently, Svetlana said, 'We don't know anything about this Unwin person. Our aim was to get Brianna led astray by these two young men; one was a personal trainer and the other a gardener. Do you see?'

Abigail said she supposed so but was worrying now about Unwin who she had grown to like.

'Abigail, forget about Unwin for the moment.' Juliana's tone was kinder, which resulted in Svetlana apologising to Abigail for snapping, explaining she was feeling a bit queasy. Juliana then continued what she was saying. 'Also, Rufus told me that Sven had met up with Andrew for lunch very recently and he had seemed fed up. Evidently, he was grumbling about "the house going to pot". Those were his exact words; "the house going to pot", he had said. So, all we can hope for is that our plan has at least caused trouble between them and made Andrew realise he's made a mistake.'

With that, both women stood up, each giving Abigail a kiss on the cheek, and waved goodbye to the girls. Then, Svetlana remembered something. 'By the way, there's one of her parties on Saturday. Andrew told Sven. We haven't been invited. Not that we'd go anyway.'

Svetlana and Juliana left. On the settee, two pairs of ears were busy flapping away.

Later that night in bed, Abigail was still worrying about Unwin. She was also wondering just what they had needed the boxer shorts for. So many questions and thoughts were clogging up her mind, and she fell into a restless sleep.

In a bedroom just off the corridor, Francesca and Annabel were discussing what they had managed to overhear. 'Shall we do what we said we'd do?' Francesca asked Annabel.

'Yes. It doesn't sound as if Dad is very happy.'

'I'll ring him tomorrow, then.'

Annabel was chewing her lips. 'It's very bad what we're going to do, isn't it? We could get into a lot of trouble.'

Francesca patted Annabel's arm. 'It's for a good cause. Don't worry. It'll be fine. Now, I want to go to sleep. Off you go to your own bedroom. Night-night.'

As it was Sunday morning, Abigail was having a lie-in. Francesca and Annabel came into her room.

'Mum, we really miss Dad. Can we go and stay with him next weekend?' Francesca clasped her hands together in a praying gesture.

'Please, Mum. I miss Dad too,' added Annabel.

Abigail thought for a moment, and sighed. 'Okay, I suppose so. Don't get caught up in any dramas, though, which always seems to happen when you go there.'

'We won't,' replied Francesca. Can I call him now?'

'Yes, don't see why not.'

When Francesca and Annabel had been sitting on the settee, they had also been listening carefully to the conversation and had heard Svetlana say that there was a party on the following Saturday evening to which she and Sven hadn't been invited. This worked perfectly for the girls' plan. Francesca called Andrew. 'Hello, Daddy. How are you?'

'...'

'That's good. Me and Annabel really miss you, and Mummy said we can come next weekend. Is that okay?'

'...'

'Yes, we'll behave ourselves and we don't mind if there's a party. We can stay in my bedroom. See you next Saturday. Love you. Annabel sends her love too.' Francesca disconnected from her call and high-fived Annabel.

*

The week had sped by quickly. Andrew collected the girls on Saturday morning, and rushed off as he didn't want to get into any tricky discussions with Abigail. They arrived back at the house and the girls ran upstairs to their bedrooms to unpack. Brianna was out collecting the food and drink for the party, so Andrew was left alone with his daughters. He took the opportunity to catch up with their news and then, because the weather was mild, the three of them went and sat out in the garden.

Brianna came back. She was in a good mood, and looking forward to the party as the last couple of weekends had been just her and Andrew. She heard them in the garden and waved from the patio. 'Hello, girls,' she said brightly, 'long time no see.'

'Hello, Bri,' came the joint response, with a giggle from Annabel, resulting in a sharp look from Andrew.

'Well, I've got a lot to do,' she said and turned to go inside. 'Unless, that is, you'd like to help me? It would be great if you did.' She smiled and it was clear she was making a big effort.

Francesca and Annabel got up and said they'd help and went into the kitchen. Andrew let out a sigh of relief as he had been feeling very anxious. Perhaps the girls and Brianna were going to finally get on with each other. They were given the task of folding napkins and putting them on individual plates. Then piercing cocktail sticks through cubes of cheese, Chorizo and green olives. Andrew came into the kitchen and said that he'd leave them to it and went to his study.

Everything was going smoothly, until – in the lyrics of the Nancy Sinatra song (for those of you who remember the singer and the song), *and then you have to go and spoil it all by saying something stupid like...* 'Isn't this great, girls?' said Brianna, who was making sure all the glasses were clean. They nodded. 'See we can get along fine, can't we?' They nodded again. 'So, your dad and I were thinking that next summer we'd both take a break from work and do some travelling. We thought maybe

Australia, stopping off at Singapore on the way there, and Thailand on the way back. Would you like to come? It'd be fun. You'd be gone the whole summer. It would be both a holiday and an education for you.' Francesca and Annabel looked at each other. Brianna frowned. 'What's wrong? You don't look too keen. It would be a great opportunity for you both to see a bit of the world!'

'What about Mum?' asked Francesca. 'She'd be left on her own all summer.'

'Surely she's got friends. She could go on holiday too!' replied Brianna.

'All of Mum's friends are married. Anyway, we've never spent a long time apart from her,' replied Francesca.

'I'd miss Mum,' added Annabel.

Brianna didn't like it when she didn't get her own way and was exasperated. 'Honestly, you two. You need to become a bit more independent. You'll both be leaving home in a few years. I left home when I was 16. Couldn't wait to get away.'

Francesca had inherited Abigail's peace-making and compromising genes. 'I'm sorry if we seem ungrateful, Bri, but it just seems such a long way to go and to be away for so long from our mum. We could go away for two weeks with you and Dad.' This was said with a hopeful look.

'Nope. Not going to happen. There's something you're not taking into consideration either. If you don't come, then you won't get to see your dad for the whole summer. How do you think that will make *him* feel?' Brianna stressed the word "him".

Andrew had come into the kitchen and caught the tail end of the discussion. 'Make me feel what?'

'I asked Francesca how you would feel if you didn't see them all next summer because they don't want to come with us on our adventure to Australia, Singapore and Thailand.'

'Brianna, aren't you jumping the gun a bit? We haven't decided what we're doing yet. If you recall, we were just throwing ideas around. You said you wanted to go to the Far East and Australia. I said, if you remember, that I thought it was a nice idea in principle, but it meant I wouldn't see the girls all summer.'

'That's correct, Andrew. Which is why I suggested to the girls that they might like to join us. But they're obviously not keen.' She shrugged her shoulders and turned away.

'Brianna, in any event, I would need to speak to Abigail about this. Even if the girls did want to come, I would still need to discuss it with their mum.'

'Oh well, I suppose you're right.' She carried on with getting things ready for the party. 'I need some peace and space now, Andrew. I've a lot to do. Perhaps you'd like to take your girls out somewhere for a couple of hours.'

'Great. We'll give you some peace and space. What's it to be, girls? Trip into Cornham for some ice-cream?'

The guests were arriving, and Francesca and Annabel were holding a tray each of flutes of champagne for the guests to take as they came into the hallway. Andrew had pleaded with them to offer to do this because, he said, 'If you don't do this to get me back in her good books, my life won't be worth living.'

Annabel looked concerned. 'You're not going to die, Dad, are you?'

Andrew laughed. 'No, silly. It's just a saying. Nothing to worry about.'

So the girls had reluctantly agreed.

Once the party began to get noisier and the music louder, the girls went upstairs to watch television in

Francesca's bedroom. They both agreed that nothing had changed. Brianna was still trying to control things, and they realised they weren't really welcome in what used to be their home, and, in fact, it was beginning to feel more and more like not-home. Further, their presence was clearly causing problems between their dad and Brianna, and they agreed that their dad didn't seem that happy either. So, they decided to put their plan in motion.

Whilst the girls were upstairs, Andrew was downstairs and had gone out into the garden to get away from the noisy guests who, as usual, were drinking too much. Apart from Darius and Caroline Fortescue, who Brianna had invited because Darius was a client of hers and her and Andrew had recently gone to their house for dinner, he didn't know anyone else. She had invited some potential new clients, as well as some of her friends from London, and was in her element networking flitting from guest to guest. Andrew realised that he was virtually a stranger in his own home; that the house had, in reality, been taken over by Brianna. In the beginning, he had been impressed with her networking skills, and how she brought people together, and cultivated her friendships. There was a price to pay, however. Life with her wasn't peaceful or restful. She was on the go all the time, and she expected him to join in even when he didn't want to. He remembered when Abigail and the girls lived in the house. It would be full of girly chat and laughter. Furthermore, when he came home from work, even if he was late, which he realised he had been many a time, he was always greeted by Abigail asking how his day had been. Now, when he returned home, Brianna was either engrossed on her laptop, or chatting on the phone or Facetiming with her numerous friends and clients. He didn't get a look-in.

He realised he was miserable and bored, and decided to call it a night as he doubted he would be missed. He couldn't sleep and lay there. He knew when the party was coming to an end because he could hear the loud chatter in the hallway, then the front door opening, and the sound of tyres on the gravel driveway which would be the taxis coming to take the guests home. When all was quiet, he knew that everyone had left and closed his eyes. He heard the bedroom door open quietly. It would be Brianna. So he pretended to be asleep. Also, he knew that she wouldn't have tidied up or loaded the dishwasher; that would be done in the morning.

All was quiet. A door opened and two pairs of feet came out of a bedroom and went quietly down the stairs and into the kitchen. Out of the kitchen came two plates of half-eaten food, and a half bottle of red wine. Then the living room door was opened. A short while after, the two pairs of feet went up the stairs and two bedroom doors opened and closed.

It was morning. Andrew got up and went downstairs to get a cup of tea. He knew the kitchen would be in total disarray; it always was after one of Brianna's parties. What he wasn't prepared for was what he found in the living room. He couldn't believe what he was seeing. An empty bottle of red wine had been upended on the coffee table, the contents of which had spilled onto the cream carpet, which was now ruined. No amount of cleaning would restore it to its pristine condition. And then there was the food. Two upside-down plates of food – one on the cream leather settee, and the other on the carpet – had revealed smears of partially eaten food. Particularly bad was the chocolate cake which had been covered in chocolate sauce, and was now underneath the plate on the carpet. On the settee there was some sort of red sticky sauce. Andrew sniffed it and realised it was tomato ketchup which would probably leave a pink stain on the pale coloured leather.

He went to the bottom of the stairs and shouted for Brianna. There was no answer. He ran up the stairs and went into the bedroom and shook her awake. She was groggy and a bit hungover. 'What's up? What time is it?'

'Never mind what time it is. Just come and see what your friends have done to my living room. It's a total mess, and very disrespectful to do this in my home. I'm going to have to change the carpet and probably one of the settees.'

'What on earth are you going on about? You're not making any sense.'

Andrew was trying to keep his cool, but not managing it. 'Brianna, get up please and come and look. *Now!*'

'There's no need to shout. I've got a headache.' She sighed. 'Give me a minute. I'll be down shortly.'

She eventually came downstairs and went into the living room. She looked shocked. 'Who on earth has done this? What a mess!'

'Your friends, Brianna, have done this. Who else could it be? It wasn't me, and I don't think you would do something like this so, ergo, it must be your friends.'

'My friends wouldn't do this. Anyway, we were all in the kitchen or garden. They wouldn't have come in here.'

'How do you know they wouldn't?'

She shrugged. 'I just know. Have you asked your two?'

Andrew frowned. 'My two! Do you think Francesca and Annabel would do something like this? What a preposterous thing to suggest.'

Brianna stood her ground. 'Well, let's get them down here and ask them.' She went into the hallway and shouted upstairs for the girls to come down.

Francesca and Annabel sneakily smiled at each other and came down the stairs, and followed Brianna into the living room. Francesca and Annabel put their hands over their mouths and opened their eyes wide in shock. Removing her hand, Francesca asked who had done this.

'That's what we wanted to ask you two,' replied Brianna. 'Do you know anything about this?'

'No,' came the joint response. 'Why would we do something like this?' Francesca frowned. 'When we lived here, we never ate or drank in here because Dad used to get cross with us if we made a mess. That's true, Dad, isn't it?'

Andrew looked shamefaced and nodded. 'It's true. So, there's no way my girls would do something like this, which only leaves your friends. And for you to blame my two, well, it's the last straw for me. I'm going to take them back to Abigail and I'd like you to be gone by the time I get back. For me, this relationship ends here.' Andrew told the girls to go upstairs and get ready, and he went into his study, leaving Brianna standing in the living room wondering just what had happened.

Andrew drove the girls back to Abigail and came up with them. They were clearly in a good mood, but Andrew was looking glum.

'Did you have a nice time, you two?' she asked.

Francesca and Annabel grinned and nodded, which made Andrew look at them in surprise. Abigail turned her attention towards him. 'The girls are happy, but you don't seem happy. I'm sensing something has happened, so you'd better tell me exactly what it is.'

'I don't know why the girls are happy, particularly as Brianna has been her usual difficult self, but they won't be seeing her again because I ended the relationship with her this morning and asked her to leave. I've made a huge mistake, Abigail. I quite understand if you don't want me back, but will you at least consider trying again and moving back home?' Andrew looked really miserable.

Abigail was stunned into silence and wondered just what had happened. No doubt the girls would fill her in later. However, she felt sorry for Andrew and asked the girls what they thought. 'What do you think, girls? Shall we take Dad back and move back home?'

'Yes!' came the reply. They jumped up and joined hands with their parents and they all danced round in a circle. The girls began chanting, 'No more smelly cheese, no more smelly cheese!'

Andrew looked puzzled, making Abigail laugh. 'Don't even ask. It's best if you don't know.'

Andrew made to leave, promising to be back in the morning to help them load all their belongings into the car. He also suggested that they keep the apartment on for the time being, as they could all use it at the weekend because there was more to do in Knighton as a family. He also told Abigail that he would take the week off so that they could spend some time together, and that he would take the girls to school. He further surprised her by saying that he was selling the Aston Martin because, after all, it wasn't a family car.

In bed that night, Abigail fell asleep feeling that her world had come full circle and, in the process, righted itself. There were still some loose ends, though. She would never find out where Tommy and Toby had been on the evening of Andrew's initiation ceremony because the twins had put their houses up for sale, and had already vacated. Further, she reminded herself to ask Svetlana why they had needed a pair of Andrew's boxer shorts. Oh, and she needed to track down Unwin and ring Barney Bright.

THE END...

Well, almost...

CASSANDRA *poured herself a large glass of Merlot and rubbed her hands with glee. The girls had been accepted into the same boarding school as Apollonia, and now she could make her move. She would call Ingram tomorrow morning when he was in the office and give him the good news that she would soon be joining him in Singapore so that they didn't need to live apart anymore. She finished her wine and went to bed.*

*

INGRAM *sat back in his chair, hands behind his head and waited for his office door to open. At 11am precisely, his Japanese secretary, Yoko, entered with the tea trolley which contained everything needed for the daily tea-making ritual. He enjoyed watching her graceful and elegant movements, and the delicate way in which she first warmed the teapot, added just the correct amount of jasmine green tea leaves, then added the hot water. She then stirred the leaves and Ingram watched as she bent her head, pushing her jet-black long, silky hair behind one ear, to savour the delicate aroma of the leaves until she was sure it was the right strength for him. She then poured the tea through a strainer into a fine bone china cup and placed the cup and saucer on the table in front of him. Only then would he remove his hands from behind his head and place them on the table. 'Thank you, Yoko. Another perfectly made cup of tea, prepared with your usual* *care and attention. You remind me of my mother.' He smiled up at her.*

'Thank you, Ingram. I like to please you and make you happy.' She placed her small dainty hand on the desk, and Ingram intertwined his fingers with hers. They had been in a relationship for a while but acted with discretion as the company frowned upon relationships between the directorial staff and administrative staff. Yoko then wheeled the trolley out of the office, smiling a shy smile as she left.

*

INGRAM AND CASSANDRA. *It was 4:20am in England, and Cassandra was fast asleep. She was sitting atop an elephant and was gently swaying from side to side as the elephant made its way down the mountain path. The path was lined with people who had come out to see the visiting foreign princess and she repaid them by bestowing upon them her regal wave. The bell around the elephant's neck began to tinkle, getting louder and louder, until Cassandra came out of her dream and realised it was her mobile phone. It was Ingram. 'Do you know what time it is, Ingram?' she said groggily.*

'Yes, it's 11:20am.'

'No, the time here. Not your time!'

'Erm, 4:20am?'

'Yes, exactly. You woke me up from a glorious dream I was having. Anyway, I've got some good news. I was going to call you later, but I might as well tell you now. Oh, and why are you calling me? You never call me.'

'I want a divorce, Cassandra.' Ingram disconnected from the call, sat back in his chair and smiled.

THE END